MW00474685

# Rock Chick Regret

Discover other titles by Kristen Ashley at:
www.kristenashley.net

Copyright © 2013 Kristen Ashley
All rights reserved.

ISBN: 0-6158-2611-3
ISBN-13: 9780615826110

# Rock Chick Regret

Kristen Ashley

# Author's Note

A long time ago, at a scary time in my life, when I was alone, I tried to go it alone, and after having surgery to remove a benign lump from my breast, I attempted to redress my wound and shower by myself.

I nearly passed out. Crawling to the phone, I called my friend, Cris, who was a nurse. He dropped everything and came to my house. He helped me shower and redress my wound. I was mortified and told him so.

"I'm gay and a nurse. I wipe people's asses for a living. Do you think this fazes me?" he'd said to me. Then he lectured me on going it alone when I had friends.

I never did it again.

And this, my loyal readers, is exactly what the entire series of *Rock Chick* is about, as Sadie learns in the story you are about to read. You are never alone, not when you have friends. Learn from my stories and, through thick and thin, remember, if you have friends you are never alone.


Rock on.

# Prologue
# Loads of Practice

*Sadie*

The elevator pinged and I looked out into the plushly carpeted hall.

I took a deep breath.

As I let it out, I stepped one perfectly high, sling-back stiletto-shod foot soundlessly on the carpet. I turned right and walked the ten steps (I counted) to the door.

There was a brass plaque on the door. It said, "Nightingale Investigations."

Before I could chicken out, I turned the sleek knob and pushed the door open.

I knew there would be no balloons falling or streamers streaming, heralding my happily anticipated arrival but I didn't expect the intensity of the welcoming committee.

Or, one could say, *un*welcoming committee.

Shirleen Jackson was sitting behind the gleaming, polished, blond-wood reception desk. Standing in front of it was Stella Gunn and Kai Mason.

I knew Shirleen, and I knew she knew my father, and furthermore, I suspected she did a happy dance when he was handed a fifteen year sentence. Therefore, I expected her face to turn to stone when she saw me. And it did.

I knew Stella Gunn and Kai Mason because they were famous. Their romance had played out in the papers and on local news, and I'd watched it with avid fascination along with the rest of Denver.

All of them looked at me. None of them smiled.

I walked through the door. It fell closed behind me so I could see the rest of the room.

Luke Stark was leaning against the desk and his head came up from studying a manila folder. When he saw me, his face went blank and his eyes went cold.

I stopped myself from swallowing and, as per normal as I'd had *loads* of practice, I walked—back ramrod straight, chin up, one foot in front of the other, like I learned in deportment classes—to the desk.

"Hello, I'm Sadie Townsend. I have an appointment with Liam Nightingale," I said to Shirleen.

Shirleen looked me from top-to-toe, her tawny eyes frozen, and I knew her thoughts. I'd had twenty-nine years of people looking at me like Shirleen did and coming to one of three conclusions.

First, I was a spoiled rotten, rich daddy's girl and not worth the time.

Or second, I was the daughter of a dangerous drug lord, and by association, scum of the earth.

Or third, I was the daughter of a dangerous yet powerful and wealthy man and there might be some way to use me to get what they wanted.

I figured Shirleen was in the first category.

My eyes slid to Luke Stark, and I knew from his continued arctic stare that he was a mixture of both one and two.

I didn't even look at Stella Gunn and Kai Mason.

"Sit your fancy-ass down. Lee'll be with you in a minute," Shirleen said, and my eyes moved back to her.

I was a little surprised that she would be obviously rude, but I let it deflect off me like I was wearing armor. It hurt, like it always hurt, but I was damned if I'd let it show.

So I didn't.

I was good at this. I'd had loads of practice at this, too.

I turned on my heel, back still straight, chin still up, giving the impression that I was dismissing her and everyone in the room as beneath my notice.

This was another defense mechanism with which I had loads of practice.

I sat down on a leather couch and crossed my legs, relaying the appearance that I hadn't a care in the world. I magnified this by casually pulling my cream skirt up my knee and surveying my manicure like it was utterly fascinating.

I was wearing the palest of pale pink on my nails. The manicure was perfect, as it should be. It had only been finished two hours ago.

I was wearing designer from head-to-toe.

My hair was not dyed. It was naturally an ultra-light, golden-cream-strawberry blonde and also had this weird mix of natural soft ringlets combined liberally with waves. I wore it long and down my back. Today, I had the front pulled back in an expensive clip and it tumbled down to my shoulders and back. Although not dyed, the cut cost three hundred dollars.

I had on a cream, pencil-slim skirt that skimmed the knees and had a pleated kick pleat in the back. I also had on a little short-sleeved top, pale pink (to match my nails) with dozens upon dozens of pink pleats at the sleeves, capped with cream satin ribbon. The top had a square neckline and fit like it was made for me. My sling-backs were to-die-for with a slim, four-inch heel. They were uber-elegant.

I set my pale pink clutch on my knee and moved my eyes to a studied fascination of my shoe.

The door opened and I looked from my toe to the door.

Indy Nightingale and her sister-in-law, Ally Nightingale, walked in. I'd seen India Savage and Liam Nightingale's picture in the wedding column. She was a gorgeous redhead. He was an extremely handsome, dark-haired man. They were a beautiful couple, and if their photo was anything to go by, very happy.

I knew Ally from my not so happy run-in with Daisy a few months ago.

Daisy Sloan was friends with the Nightingale clan, and she had been my friend once.

Well, she'd almost been one.

The run-in hadn't been a run-in, exactly. I saw Daisy. Daisy's eyes turned to polar icecaps when she saw me. She whispered something in Ally's ear, Ally's eyes cut to me and they went hard.

That was it. Not a run-in, but not pleasant either.

Now Indy and Ally were laughing at something, but when their eyes moved in the direction of Shirleen they saw something in her expression. Theirs moved to me and their laughter died.

"Shit, I forgot. Is it Wednesday?" Indy asked Ally.

Ally's eyes went glacial as they rested on me.

"Yeah," she answered.

I didn't know exactly why Luke, Shirleen, Indy and Ally, and I guessed Kai and Stella (although I hadn't looked to be certain) hated me, but I suspected it was either because Daisy hated me or because they suspected I hated Hector Chavez. Rumor had it they were a close-knit group. The papers had talked about what had now become the semi-famous Rock Chicks of Fortnum's Bookstore and the Nightingale Men of Nightingale Investigations in their articles about

Stella and Kai. They were known to be crazy and fun and willing to lay their lives on the line for each other.

Even though a part of me was jealous as hell, I was glad Daisy had that. Daisy was a good person. She deserved it.

As for me, I'd never had a friend. Not a true, genuine friend in twenty-nine years. I used to feel sorry for myself about this. But then I realized it was just my life, and as with everything else, I learned to live with it. Either people didn't trust me, they didn't trust my dad, they didn't stick around, or they used me. I learned a long time ago to shut them down before they could rip out my heart, tear it to shreds, stamp on it, kick it around a bit and then spit on it.

When that happened, trust me, it was no fun. It hurt, *loads*, so I stopped it before it could start and didn't let anyone get close.

No one.

Ever.

That was until Daisy. But that didn't work out.

When Daisy hit the Denver social scene, I thought she was aces. She was not brittle and fake like everyone else of my father's, and thus my, acquaintance. She looked like Dolly Parton. She dressed like Dolly Parton. She had a voice with a country twang. She had a tremendously cool giggle that sounded like jingling Christmas bells.

She was real.

And she liked me, too.

But Nanette Hardy was ripping her to shreds at Monica Henrique's garden party a couple of years ago, really laying into Daisy like only vicious, catty Nanette could do. Monica was giggling and I was quiet and waiting for my chance to get in a good shot. My chosen topic was Nanette's husband getting rear-ended (literally) by the pool boy, which only Nanette didn't know about. Everyone else knew all about it and they were laughing behind her back.

Monica's face went pale and she was looking over my shoulder.

Nanette quit talking and I looked behind me.

Daisy was there.

I caught the pain in her eyes before she looked *at me* like I was slime.

Then she walked away.

I knew why. I'd been nice to her. I'd been hoping she'd be my friend. She thought I was talking behind her back, which was worse than what Nanette and Monica were doing. Everyone knew Nanette and Monica were bitches. It was expected.

I called Daisy half a dozen times and went over to her house twice. She wouldn't see me, or at least that was what her husband said when he turned me away from the door.

In the end, her husband Marcus had come to visit my father. My father had told me under no circumstances was I to try to communicate with Daisy Sloan again. He explained it was crucial, it was duty, it was business. Bottom line, Marcus was a powerful man, nearly as powerful as my father, and my father couldn't have Marcus as an enemy, so I needed to back off.

Ever the dutiful daughter, I didn't try to contact Daisy again.

I didn't blame her for thinking what she thought of me, though I would have liked to have the chance to explain. Even though I didn't blame her, it hurt all the same.

I never spoke to Nanette or Monica again. Well, that was, I never spoke to them again after the "incident" a couple weeks later when I outed Nanette's husband at a cocktail party at an art gallery. He took that opportunity to share he was gay. He divorced her and was now living in Miami with his boyfriend, Pedro. But how would I know all *that* would happen?

Nanette and Monica had been "friends" for years. I didn't miss them.

Daisy had been a semi-friend for a couple of months. I missed her.

"Is Hector here?" Ally asked Shirleen.

I just stopped myself from sucking in my lips. Instead, I stared at the plush carpet in the offices.

"Ally." It was a male's deep voice. I was guessing Luke Stark's as it was coming from his direction. His voice held a warning.

"I'm just asking," Ally said.

I gave the impression that this exchange bounced right off my armor too, but my stomach clenched.

God, I hoped Hector wasn't there. That would be awful.

I knew there was a chance I'd run into him as he worked for Nightingale now, but I was hoping he was busy doing private eye stuff, gallivanting around town bringing down perps, taking photos of cheating husbands in the act and whatever else private eyes did.

Even though Hector worked for them, I chose Nightingale Investigations because they were the best. Better than the best. My father said Lee could move his operation to New York or Los Angeles and corner the market on investigations, security and bounty hunting. He was that good.

One of the things my father taught me was always, but always, get the best.

"He's here all right." Shirleen answered Ally's question, and even though I felt my heart beating faster I allowed myself to lift my chin and look calmly and coolly at Shirleen.

She was pretty, middle-aged and hitting it well. She had beautiful mocha skin and the biggest afro I'd ever seen, but it suited her perfectly. She had magnificent eyes.

I knew she once was competition for my father in the drug scene, but she'd pulled out and gone straight. I admired her for that. That must have taken a ton of courage and it said a lot about her.

Still, it didn't stop me from staring her down. My cool blue eyes locked with her arctic tawny ones. We had a stare down and even though she was very scary, I won.

Then again, I always won. I was good at the stare down. I could hold a cool, calm, unaffected stare for hours. It was something else I had loads of practice with.

Once she looked away, I aimed my composed glance at Ally then at Indy. They had attitude, the good kind. I could see it *and* sense it. Regardless, they were also no match for me and both looked away before I did.

I knew I was not making friends and winning allegiances. That was the point.

These people would never want me to be their friend.

I looked down at my toe again and thought about Hector.

When I knew Hector, he'd been a man in my father's army. My father liked him a great deal. My father told me Hector reminded him of… well, *him*. Smart. Sharp. Good instincts. Loyal. Skilled. Hungry, but in a good way, an ambitious way.

My father had a high opinion of himself.

Hector was one of very few men my father trusted and respected, totally. It was a mistake.

What we didn't know was that Hector was also an undercover DEA agent. In fact, *the* undercover DEA agent that brought my father's empire down.

What neither Hector nor my father knew was that I helped him.

The Feds took everything: my father's house, his cars, his condo in Boca, his furniture. They froze his bank accounts. They even tried to get my trust fund but since it had been set up for me by my grandmother *before* my father was a Drug King, they couldn't touch it.

I was glad they took my father's stuff. It was tacky and ostentatious. My father had been a nothing, a nobody, and married a rich girl. He'd come up from nothing the hard way, the dirty way, the vile way, and he'd proven himself to my mother's family and the world by becoming rich, powerful and very, *very* frightening. He'd driven my mother to leaving us; that was how frightening he was. She left me behind. She left everything behind. Didn't even take a suitcase.

She just disappeared. *Poof.* Gone.

And she never looked back. Not once.

I'd been eleven.

I didn't dwell. I'd lost a lot by then. A lot of friends, a lot of servants I'd tried to make into friends (a mistake I learned early not to make again). My grandparents were all dead. Losing my mother was just another in a long string of loss. I was used to that, too, and it didn't faze me. Or, I should say, it did faze me. Truth be told, it destroyed me. I just never let it show.

Hector was something else.

I knew right away he wasn't what he wanted us to think he was.

I'm not a super-sleuth or anything. It was just that, you spend enough time around bad people; you know them when you see them.

You also know the good ones, too.

And there was something about him. Something about the way he held himself, the way he looked, the way he looked at me.

God, he was beautiful. Quite simply the most handsome man I'd ever clapped eyes on in my whole, entire life. This was saying something. My father surrounded himself with fit, athletic, good-looking men. His personal army was recruited specifically to reflect on him.

Hector had flatly refused the makeover my father usually demanded of the boys from the streets that he fashioned into gentlemen criminals.

My father respected that, too.

Hector was Mexican-American. He looked rough and was straight out tough. One look and you knew you did *not* mess with him. He had thick, black, wavy hair, black eyes, long legs, broad shoulders and a lean, amazing body. He knew who he was and what he wanted. And he had a confidence that was unreal.

It was hard to describe, but, put simply, he was magnetic.

He never gave a hint that he was who he was. Actually, I thought he was a cop, not a DEA agent. Still, I did what I could.

It wasn't much. I would just, say, leave my father's keys lying around when I knew he was going to be out of the house for a while but that Hector would be around. Then I'd notice the keys gone for an hour then back right where they were before. Then I'd get in my father's secret safe (he gave me the combo) and I'd take out files or books and I'd set them in locked file cabinet drawers, drawers to which Hector had the keys. I'd lay them right on top, a time saver. I'd wait, go back and put them where they were supposed to be.

Once, when I overheard something I thought would be useful, I even left a note in what I thought of as "Our Drawer". When I went back, it was gone and I knew my father didn't take it. He was playing golf.

The note was kind of stupid, not to mention playing with fire. My father could have found the note. He wouldn't have suspected me (I typed it out on my computer). He knew I would never, *never* do anything like that to him. But he would have gone through his workforce and someone would have gotten the blame.

I never did that again, by the way.

In the meantime, I tried to show Hector the cold shoulder. I really did, honestly. For months, I was what I knew all my father's men and all the society boys and all my father's colleagues called me. The "Ice Princess".

No, it was not original, but it was effective.

I was Pure Chill to Hector like I was to everyone else.

Then, one night, I melted.

I blamed lemon drops.

I'd gone out and had way too many lemon drops. They tasted like candy. I forgot they had so much vodka in them.

When I got home after a night with "the girls"—my semi-friends or, at least, the women my father wanted me to hang out with, which was to say the women who enhanced his reputation—what could I say, everyone around my father had a job, and that was one of mine—I'd been drunk.

I heard noise coming from my father's study. It was late and the house was dark, but this was not strange. My father worked odd hours, so I thought it was my father in the study.

I went to say goodnight like any good, dutiful daughter would do. Being a dutiful daughter was another one of my jobs and I did it both publically and privately. I didn't have the courage to get on my father's bad side, not even behind closed doors. I knew what he was capable of. My mother didn't leave for no good reason, trust me.

But it was Hector in my father's study. Looking back, he was probably in there for reasons my father would frown on, frown on so much he'd have ordered Hector's murder. No kidding. What did I say about my father's bad side? I was being very serious.

I was too drunk to think twice about what I was doing. Not to mention I fancied that I was half in love with Hector (in the very, very back of my mind, the only place I let my true thoughts free).

Seeing as I was three sheets to the wind, the very, very back of mind was at the forefront for one shining moment. This allowed me to do something I rarely did.

I acted on impulse.

I threw myself at him.

And Hector caught me.

He didn't even hesitate. I was all over him, he was all over me. We'd exchanged nothing but civilized pleasantries for months, and that night in my father's study, we went at each other like animals in heat.

I think it went like this:

Me, with tilty head and stupid smile, all the while unsteadily walking toward him: "Hi."

Hector, with cocked head and a small grin playing at his fantastic mouth as he watched me unsteadily walk toward him: "You okay?"

Me: "I will be when you kiss me."

Oh God, just thinking about it makes me cringe. But then again, it worked.

That was it. I had made it to him and was sliding my arms around his neck as I told him to kiss me. I pressed my body to his and he kissed me.

It was fantastic. It was so hot I couldn't believe I didn't melt on the spot. He was good with his hands, his tongue, his mouth, even his teeth.

Almost as good, he seemed to think I was good with those things, too.

After a while, he had me against the wall, my skirt up around my hips, his hand in my panties cupping my behind. His other arm was wrapped tight around my waist. Both were pulling me in deep, pressing me close to his hard hips. His mouth was at my neck. Mine was at his, both my hands in his t-shirt, running up the hot skin of his back.

I didn't think that it was tacky (my father would have thought it was tacky). I didn't think anything. I *couldn't* think anything. My entire mind was centered on Hector and what he was doing to me and how much I *liked* it.

Then Hector said, his voice a low, hoarse rumble against my neck, "I've been waitin' months for you to get in the mood to go slumming."

It was like someone had shoved me in a bath filled with ice.

He thought I was nothing but a society slut out for a quick, drunken fuck with the hired help.

I didn't know what I was expecting. But for some reason, some incredibly insane reason, I expected more from him. The fact he didn't give it to me cut through me like a blade.

I put my hands to his shoulders and pushed him away. I stared at him, eyes at Chill Factor Sub-Zero, as I calmly pulled my skirt down.

Then I put all my effort into walking away without falling on my drunken face. That would kill any chance at a brilliant exit, and at that moment I *really* needed to make a brilliant exit.

To my surprise, before I could make it three steps, I found strong fingers wrapped around my upper arm and I was jerked around to face Hector.

"Where you goin'?" he asked, his hair sexy and messy, because it was made that way by my hands, his black eyes glittering dangerously even as they were still hot on me.

I looked at his hand then back in his eyes. My heart was beating wildly but I ignored it. I had loads of practice at that, too.

"Get your hand off me." My voice was pure ice.

He let me go instantly.

I kept staring at him and I didn't know why.

No, if I was honest, I did know why. I wanted to say something. I wanted to explain. I wanted him to know that who he saw was not *me*. I wanted him to know that it was all show, all an act, all because I was scared of my own fucking father. All because I was scared of letting anyone close so they wouldn't get the chance to hurt me. That I was really someone else. I didn't know who, but I thought maybe she was nice. Maybe she could be funny if given a chance.

Maybe she could be interesting. Maybe she could laugh once in a while. Maybe, if someone helped her to be free, maybe she could be someone worth *something*.

I wanted above anyone I'd ever met, outside Daisy, to say this to Hector Chavez. I didn't know why, I just did.

While I was trying to find a way to explain, he spoke.

"Lotta things I thought you were. A fuckin' cock tease wasn't one of them."

The way he said it told me that the things he thought I was were just slightly better than being a cock tease.

I turned and walked away.

Six months later, I sat behind my father's defense table and watched Hector, cleaned up and wearing a suit (and looking *good,* by the way), as he testified against my father.

I didn't just watch Hector testify. I couldn't take my eyes off him.

Hector didn't even look at me.

He had no idea I was not there as the doting daughter providing moral support to her wayward father, which I pretended I was.

No, I was there to make certain sure my father went down.

I wanted to be certain sure so I could finally, *finally* be free.

I didn't take my life in my hands feeding Hector information on my father for *nothing*.

I had no idea I wouldn't be free. I had no idea that the shark-infested waters into which I'd been born, paddled in happily and unwittingly as a child and treaded water in warily as an adult, were far more dangerous without my father running interference.

I had no idea.

"Lee'll see you now," Shirleen said, and my head snapped up.

I was so stuck in my memory of Hector, I hadn't even noticed that the room had cleared. The only ones left were me and Shirleen. The phone had even rung. She was placing it back in the cradle and avoiding my eyes.

I stood and hesitated, waiting for her to come around the desk to show me to Nightingale. I had a fleeting thought that I might say something nice to her. Tell her she had pretty eyes, or... something. Make her see I wasn't the Ice Princess. Make her see *me.*

She started packing up, dumping fingernail polish, her cell phone and other flotsam and jetsam into her big, really cool (I thought, but would never have the courage to say) Louis Vuitton bag. Therefore she wasn't going to escort me to "Lee".

Without looking at me, she instructed, "Through the door, I'll buzz you in. His office is first on the right. Knock before goin' in."

There you go. I lost my chance to be nice.

So be it.

I walked across the room to the inner door. She buzzed as I took another deep breath, opened it and walked through.

⌁

"What can I do for you Ms. Townsend?" Liam Nightingale asked me.

I was trying not to hyperventilate.

I was supposed to be meeting with Nightingale. Just Liam Nightingale.

I walked into the room and Hector was there, sitting on the side of the desk, one leg up, cowboy-booted foot dangling, one leg straight, cowboy-booted foot on the floor.

One sight of him and I nearly swooned. I'm not kidding. Thank God loads of practice stopped me from doing *that*.

I walked into the office and tried to think of some lesson my father taught me about people's motivations. My only conclusion was that Nightingale was telling me where his loyalties lie. If I had some wild plan of vengeance against Hector to put into motion, Nightingale was having no part in it. There were going to be no secrets and nothing behind closed doors. Hector was going to be involved and would hear what I had to say, and I had no choice in the matter.

It took a good deal out of me, but I just looked at Hector and slightly lifted my chin. At this, his eyes grew dark, and if he could have curled his lip in disgust, I knew he would.

I had loads of practice at ignoring that kind of response, too.

I shook Nightingale's hand. He told me to call him Lee. I told him to call me Sadie. I sat in front of his desk and he sat behind it.

Then he'd asked what he could do for me, "Ms. Townsend", even though I'd told him to call me Sadie.

My father would read a lot into that and I did, too.

Lee was telling me this was a formal arrangement. Very formal.

I hated being called "Ms. Townsend" mainly because my father's real name was "Tuttle'. It wasn't a great name, but it was real and didn't sound like some stupid, made up name of a romance hero. But also because I never felt like "Ms. Townsend". People had been calling me that since I was six, mostly servants, lackeys and henchmen.

I felt like I was Sadie. I had no idea who Sadie was, but Sadie sounded to me like someone you'd want to know.

Ms. Townsend sounded like someone you wanted to avoid.

"I'd like to hire your agency," I told Lee, trying to blank out the fact that Hector was still sitting silent on the side of Lee's desk. He was looking at me. I saw him out of my peripheral vision, but I also *felt* his eyes on me. This might sound stupid but it was true.

"Why do you need the services of a detective agency?" Lee asked.

"I don't need the services of a detective agency. I need security. I need a bodyguard," I answered.

The air in the room changed. From the minute I walked in it had been even less welcoming than in the reception area, mainly because Hector was there. Now it went weirdly... electric.

"Why do you need a bodyguard?" Lee asked.

"I'm not safe," I responded.

"Why aren't you safe?" Lee persevered.

Oh damn.

If it had just been Lee, I still would have had trouble explaining this. There was no way I could explain it with Hector there too. How did I say it without sounding like I thought I was the end all be all of beauty, grace and all things feminine?

I couldn't exactly say, "Well, Lee, you know... when a crime lord goes down, unfortunately the crime doesn't go away. Instead, there's a war to see who will be the new king. For now, Ricky Balducci won that war. And Ricky Balducci is a lunatic. Now he and his three brothers are intent on acting out their version of a Shakespearean play by doing what they can to tear each other down in order to obtain the throne. Somehow, being the dead king's princess, I'm caught up in this mess because Ricky isn't the only Balducci brother who's a lunatic. They're *all* lunatics. And they've got it in their head that the one true king has me at his side. And they'll stop at nothing, *nothing*, to get me by their side. I have no family. I have no friends. I have no one but me to protect me against four insane brothers, and I'm absolutely, utterly, completely *terrified*."

Instead, I said, "I don't know how to explain it..." This was true. As you could see, it was hard to explain. "I just don't feel safe."

"You'll have to give me something more to go on, Ms. Townsend," Lee said to me.

My hands curled into fists in my lap. So tight, my nails dug into my palms rather painfully. This was the only reaction I showed to the possibility that this wasn't going very well. I knew Lee couldn't see my hands. What I didn't know was that Hector could.

"I'll double your fee."

As my father would say, if you meet with resistance, try throwing money at it first.

"Doubling my fee isn't going to lighten my caseload," Lee replied.

Oh my.

That was not good news.

Lee was opening a drawer. He sorted through it and took out a card.

"I'm not taking on any new clients right now. If this was an urgent situation, we'd consider it. Since it's just a feeling, I'm sorry but I'll have to refer you to Dick Anderson."

He stood and rounded the desk. I stared at him again, concentrating on not hyperventilating.

He couldn't say no. He was the best in the business. *Everyone* knew about him and the Nightingale Men. *They* could keep me safe.

I didn't know Dick Anderson. Dick Anderson sounded like the name of a TV private eye. I didn't want a wisecracking TV private eye who wore Hawaiian shirts or forgot to shave. I wanted scary-but-handsome Nightingale Men who'd put the fear of God into you by just cracking their knuckles.

I stood as Lee made it to my chair.

"Lee, please, reconsider," I implored, looking up at him, using his given name, trying to take the formality out of it, wondering how I could explain without sounding like a moron or a conceited daddy's little rich bitch.

He was super-tall. Then again, since I was five foot five, even in four inch heels, most men were taller than me.

"I'm sorry Ms. Townsend," Lee replied.

That was when I lost it. Lost control for the briefest moment because, truly, not kidding, the Balducci brothers were scaring me out of my mind. I knew something was going to happen. I knew it.

I leaned forward just a bit and couldn't stop myself from whispering, "Please."

Something flickered in Lee's eyes. He looked over my shoulder at Hector for an instant, then back to me.

"Call Dick," he said with finality, but his voice, which had been professional and cordial but slightly cold, had become a bit warmer and softer. However, a warmer and softer voice meant nothing to me in my current predicament. "He's a good man," Lee finished.

I looked at him for one second, then two. Then I nodded and turned.

I took two steps and stopped.

Hector was standing and staring down on me. He'd lost the disgusted look and his face was now just blank.

He looked good. Still rough but more handsome than ever.

I'd never have the chance again, and even though I didn't know what came over me—maybe it was the specter of The Real Sadie bursting out for a moment—I looked Hector in the eye and said with genuine feeling, "I hope you're well, Hector."

I looked away, squared my shoulders and left.

# Chapter 1

# Peace

I turned my black convertible Mercedes SLK into the parking garage under the Nightingale Investigations offices and swiped again at my eyes, thus swerving again and barely missing the wall before I righted the car.

I had no idea how I got there, maybe a mixture of luck and adrenalin.

I had no idea why I even *went* there, except it was close to my apartment. Not to mention I was together enough to know I couldn't go to the police. Also not to mention, it was in my mind since I'd been there that very afternoon.

But really, who cared? I was there. It was as good a place as any.

My car was a mess. I'd hit a couple of things on the way, I didn't know what. I felt the bumps, heard the crunching and scrapes but I just kept going.

I didn't park. I stopped on a screech of tires when I saw the door leading to the stairs. I couldn't wait for the elevator. Ricky could be right behind me. Not to mention I wasn't sure I could stand.

I threw open my car door, and just that took a lot out of me. So much that when I tried to get out, I fell forward on all fours (or all threes, as that was all the extremities I had working for me at that moment) to the concrete floor.

This took a lot out of me, too. So much that I threw up right there. I couldn't see much. The sweat and blood were stinging my swelling eyes, but I could see there was blood mixed with the bile on the pavement. I could also see my manicure was ruined, which pretty much stunk, but at that moment it was the least of my worries.

I pulled myself up using the car door and my one good hand. My other hand and arm were useless to me. Actually, my body was pretty useless considering that every inch of it screamed out in pain, but I tried to ignore that. I wasn't really certain that continuing to breathe was a good goal, but my body for some reason wasn't letting me give up.

I got to my feet and lurched forward.

I was in my nightgown, or what was left of it. I knew I had no underwear on. I had no idea if the remains of my nightgown were covering me, if I was decent.

I'd deal with that new humiliation later (if I got the chance).

I staggered to the door with the stenciled sign that read "STAIRS". It took me two tries, but I got it open and I pushed myself through.

※

# *Jack*

Jack Tatum stared at the screens in the Nightingale Investigations surveillance room.

Jack took night duty four or five times a week. The men thought he was crazy, but he liked it.

Since he was a kid, he had a weird sleeping pattern. It drove his mom nuts. He slept in the late afternoon and evening, was up all night and morning. His mom couldn't break him of it, the doctors couldn't, no one could.

Throughout his adulthood, to fit his life around it, he'd taken a number of night jobs (mostly security), but they sucked. This job was the perfect fit.

It was boring a lot of time, but when it wasn't boring, it was *really* not boring.

Jack liked the anticipation, he fed off it. Because when something happened, he had to be on his game.

Days, weeks, months of nothing happening could weaken most men's instincts.

But Jack was born to be sharp and alert at three o'clock in the morning. If something happened, he'd never let the team down.

That was why, when he saw on the monitors the Merc screeching to a halt in the garage, Jack was ready.

He reached out to the phone, hit the speaker button then number two and listened to it ring.

Luke and Hector had called in five minutes ago saying they'd be back in five. The car phone in their Ford Explorer was number two on speed dial.

Then Jack watched the woman fall out of the car. Her head fell down like she couldn't hold it up. One arm was dangling uselessly on the ground. She was wearing a silky, lacy nightgown, but it was ripped and torn.

He was rising out of his chair when he heard Luke's voice answer the phone.

"Stark."

"Fuck," Jack swore.

"Jack?"

"Get here, now. There's a woman—" Jack stopped as he watched her pull herself up using the car door.

For a second, he froze. She had clearly been beaten badly and was covered in blood.

"Jack. Status," Luke barked into the phone.

"Call an ambulance. I'm leaving the room," Jack responded.

"Jack—" Stark said, but Jack didn't reply. He didn't even disconnect.

He was gone.

⌖

## Sadie

I made it up three stairs then fell. My bloody hand slipped on the stair and I couldn't break my fall, so I banged my head.

It hurt.

Since I hurt, like, loads, like, *everywhere*, I thought that was a good time to give up.

So Ricky found me. So he finished what he started. I'd be unconscious during the rest of it, then I'd be dead.

Dead seemed a good option at that point. It meant no more pain and that was good. I was hoping for doves and angels and fluffy clouds, but I'd take there being no more pain.

I heard footsteps and panicked.

Ricky.

Maybe I wasn't ready for Ricky to find me just in case I didn't go unconscious, which didn't, unfortunately, seem to be happening for me.

3

I pulled myself up to try and escape, lost my footing and threw my arm out. Luckily, it caught on the handrail. My arm slid around it, holding on. My torso fell over because I couldn't hold it up. My head hung down because I couldn't hold that up either.

The rapid footsteps stopped and I felt hands on me.

"*No!*" I screamed and jerked away from the hands.

"It's okay. It's okay. You're okay."

The voice was a man's. Not Ricky's. I couldn't see him. I couldn't hold my head up, but he scared me all the same.

The hands came back.

"*No!*" I screamed again, leaned over and hanging on to the handrail like my life depended on it (which, in that instant, I had convinced myself it did) and pressing myself against the wall. "Don't touch me. Don't—"

"You're safe. An ambulance is coming," the man said, his hands gentle and trying to pull me away from the handrail.

"No. No ambulance. Nothing. Go away. Just leave me here."

I wasn't making any sense and I didn't care. I just wanted to be alone. I'd been alone my whole life, alone *and* lonely. It was a place I understood. It was a place I could be safe.

I heard a door open and I tensed.

"Fuck," another man's voice said as the strength in my arm at the handrail gave out. I let go and slid down, my knees banged against a concrete stair right before my face smashed into another one. My useless arm again didn't break my fall.

That hurt, too.

I didn't try to get up. I had nothing left in me.

"Pull the Explorer around." I heard a new voice say right before I was turned gently then lifted.

"Hector—" another voice said.

"*Do it!*" This was sharp and loud, but I didn't have the energy to wince.

I was being moved quickly, being held against something immensely warm.

"Sadie, you with me?" I heard a weirdly familiar voice say.

"I think so," I answered.

"Stay with me," the weirdly familiar voice ordered.

"I'll try," I replied, but felt myself slipping away.

Before the darkness could overwhelm me, I was jostled. The pain shot through me with renewed vigor. My eyes opened and I made a low, feral noise filled with agony that sounded scary, even to my own ears.

Then I could swear I saw Hector. He was contorting, going in and out of focus.

I was settled in his lap, but I felt his arm slide up my back and his hand positioned my head on his shoulder, my face in his neck. It was then I closed my eyes again.

"*Mamita*, staying with me means talking to me." Now I was thinking it was Hector who was the weirdly familiar voice.

Now, how bizarre was *that*?

We were still moving, but not like before. It was smoother and it hurt a whole lot less.

"I need to go to sleep," I told him.

"Hang on for a while, don't go to sleep."

"I think, if I go to sleep, it'll stop hurting. I need it to stop hurting."

After I said that, it felt like the knuckles of a hand came to my cheek. They rested there lightly for a second. Then it felt like fingers were sifting gently through the hair at the side of my head, pulling it way from my face.

Now that was even more bizarre because it felt nice. Nice and sweet and lovely, even though everywhere else there was pain.

"I know, *mamita*, but you need to stay awake."

"Why can't I sleep?" I asked.

"Because when you go to sleep, I want you to be somewhere with doctors so we can make sure you wake up," Hector told me.

I shook my head in his neck. "That's okay."

"What's okay?"

"It's okay if I don't wake up."

"Sadie, don't say that."

I snuggled closer to his heat and felt fuzzier. It wasn't a bad fuzzier but a good fuzzier.

There was an edging sense of peace sliding over me and I wanted it. Peace was good. Peace was *great*. I liked peace. Who didn't like peace?

"No, really," I whispered, letting the sweet, peaceful feeling steal over me. "It only matters if there's someone to care if you don't wake up. It's okay if

5

I don't wake up because there's no one to care." After I said that, with tremendous gratitude, I welcomed the peace.

⌥

## *Lee*

Lee held the phone to his ear, listening to it ring, but kept his eyes on Hector and Luke.

"Yeah?" he heard Eddie say in his ear.

Eddie Chavez was Lee Nightingale's best friend. He was Hector's brother. Lastly, he was a cop.

"I'm at Denver Health. Hector and Luke just brought in Sadie Townsend," Lee told Eddie.

"Fuck. What happened?" Eddie asked, and Lee could tell by his voice that Eddie was up and on the move.

"Don't know. Jack called me in. She drove into the parking garage under the offices. Jack showed me her tape. He recorded her driving into the garage and getting out of her car. Maybe five minutes he got before he left the surveillance room to get to her so he didn't switch to the camera on the stairs. She was in bad shape, covered in blood."

"Luke and Hector brought her in?"

"Luke says Hector wouldn't wait for an ambulance."

They both knew what that meant. They also both knew what Sadie meant. They'd been through this a number of times before.

So far they'd been lucky, but luck had a way of running out. It had, in the past, gotten pretty fucking ugly.

But never this ugly.

"I'll be there in ten," Eddie said.

Lee moved several steps away from Luke and Hector.

"Something else," he said to Eddie.

Silence then, "Shit."

"Jack says she was in her nightgown and wasn't wearing any underwear. She was bleeding between her legs."

More silence then some cursing in Spanish then, "You called the boys?"

"Jack's on it."

"You better call Shirleen. There's the chance Vance, Mace and Luke'll lose it too."

Lee thought there was a chance, if this woman meant what Lee thought she meant to Hector, that Eddie might lose it, too.

"Jack's on it," was all Lee said.

"You got any idea who did it to her?"

Lee closed his eyes and clenched his jaw. It took an effort but he got control.

"She came in this afternoon, asking for protection. There's rumors she's having troubles with the Balduccis, but she didn't confirm and she didn't explain. I sent her to Dick Anderson."

"Anderson is in Alaska, visiting his son."

"*Fuck!*" Lee exploded, and Luke and Hector's eyes sliced to him.

Hector didn't look good. Hector looked about ready to blow.

Lee watched as Luke closed in on Hector, not enough to be predatory but enough to offer containment, then Lee turned his back and walked several more feet away.

Lee did not have a good feeling about this, and Lee's feelings were normally right on target.

"Eddie, it had to take everything she had to come to us with Hector there."

"You're blaming yourself, *amigo*. You didn't beat her up and rape her."

"She asked me for protection. I sent her away. Told her we had a full caseload."

"Do you have a full caseload?"

"Yeah. But my caseload lightens when a five foot five, one hundred pound woman needs protection from someone who'd beat her close to death and rape her."

"Lee, you need to keep your shit together. This is Sadie Townsend. We know—"

"We know," Lee interrupted.

"Then you gotta keep cool because Hector is gonna lose it."

Lee glanced at Hector. He was surprised Hector hadn't thrown a chair through the window by now. Hector was a very edgy guy.

Lee pulled in a breath. "Hector's gonna lose it."

"I'll be there in ten."

### *Eddie*

Eddie turned to Jet.

His fiancée was already out of bed and getting dressed.

"Lee needs Indy," he said.

Jet nodded then pulled a t-shirt over her head.

"Sadie's gonna need—"

Jet yanked the t-shirt down and walked to Eddie. She leaned in, put her hand on his stomach, got up on her tiptoes and kissed him lightly on the mouth.

"I'll take care of it. Get to Hector," she said.

When she moved away, Eddie grabbed her by the neck and pulled her to him.

His kiss wasn't light.

Then he was gone.

### *Lee*

By the time the doctor came to the waiting room, Luke, Hector and Lee had been joined by Eddie, Lee's brother Hank (also a cop) and four men that worked for Lee: Vance, Darius, Mace and Bobby.

Lee had pulled in the boys because if Hector (or Luke, for that matter) went gonzo at whatever news they were going to get, they were going to need manpower to lock them down.

Lee had recruited men who, it turned out, had a strong ethic about women and how to treat them, and an even stronger ethic about how they felt about men who didn't treat them right. This wasn't on the job application, but bottom line, it was the only kind of man Lee would have in his employ.

So this was a situation that could blow his men apart. It had happened before and they knew the drill, but it had never been this bad.

What he wasn't prepared to see was Jet walking in with Indy, Roxie, Ava and Stella. He wasn't prepared for it, but when Jet smiled at Eddie and he realized Eddie had arranged it, he was glad for it. Nothing soothed the savage beast like a woman's touch. His wife Indy's crew (known as the Rock Chicks) would likely be busy that night.

Indy walked straight to him, put her arms around his waist and kissed the underside of his jaw. Usually this worked like magic, but Lee didn't feel soothed.

She tipped her head back to look up at him and whispered. "It'll be okay."

"Yeah," he said, but he didn't agree. She hadn't seen the tape. Fuck, but he'd never forget what he saw on that tape.

"It's always okay," she said, breaking into his thoughts.

"You don't know who this is," Lee replied.

"Yes I do, but Lee…" She hesitated because she didn't want to say what she was going to say next. Then she continued, "You have to know, Daisy doesn't think much of—"

Lee looked down at Indy. "Hector does."

Indy's head jerked at the shortness in Lee's tone.

Then she got closer. "Is there something I don't know?"

"There's something no one knows. No one knows why he pulled out of the DEA after that job. At least no one knew until today, until she walked into my office."

"Do you think he had a thing with her?" Indy whispered.

Lee turned to her. "Did you see her?"

Indy scrunched her nose, looking uncomfortable. "I saw her in the reception area. She's gorgeous, but she was cold as ice. Do you know they call her the Ice Princess?"

Lee shook his head and ignored her last comment. "I saw her too. I also saw Hector watching her the entire time I spoke to her."

"Was it intense?"

Was it intense?

Hector never gave anything away, anything that was personal.

He gave it away that afternoon. He couldn't take his eyes off Sadie.

"It was intense. Tonight when he got to her, Hector wouldn't wait for an ambulance. He picked her up and made Luke drive them here."

Indy's eyes grew wide. "Was that smart?"

"No."

"Holy crap," she whispered as her eyes slid to Hector.

"Doctor." They heard Stella say, and everyone turned as the doctor walked in wearing scrubs, a white lab coat and an unhappy expression.

"Anyone here for Sadie Townsend?"

Everyone looked at everyone else, except Hector who said a sharp, "Yes."

The doctor looked at Hector as Stella moved close to him. "Are you her partner?"

"Yes," Hector lied, bold, bald-faced and without hesitation.

The doctor's face changed and it wasn't a good change. "We need to go somewhere and talk."

"Say it," Hector snapped.

The doctor's face scanned the crowd, then his eyes went back to Hector and said, "Sir, I think—"

"*Fuckin' say it!*" Hector barked, his body rigid, his face filled with fury, and the doctor took a step back as Stella took another step in, getting close, putting her hand on Hector's arm and keeping it there.

"I don't think you under—" the doctor began.

Lee got close to Hector. So did Eddie and Darius. Hank, Vance, Mace and Bobby closed ranks. Luke was already close. The doctor took this in and his body relaxed.

"Just say it," Shirleen appeared by the doctor, and she was speaking quietly. Lee hadn't even noticed she arrived. This was unusual for Lee Nightingale. There wasn't a lot he didn't notice, but that night his mind was on other things.

"You're amongst Sadie's friends," Shirleen went on, also bald-faced lying and also without hesitation.

The doctor looked at Shirleen. She smiled encouragingly, but he said, "We have a policy—"

"Ain't no policy when there's friends," Shirleen interrupted. "We all gotta know. We'll all eventually know. Just tell it like it is."

The doctor sighed, pulled his hand through his hair and looked at Hector. "She's been beaten badly."

"I guessed that." Hector voice was sharp and impatient.

The doctor nodded and went on, "Five broken ribs, a broken wrist, dislocated shoulder, severe concussion and multiple cuts and contusions. She's had to have a deep cut on her cheek stitched. She's been admitted."

The doctor stopped. His back went straight and everyone held their breath.

"I really think—" the doctor hesitated, eyes on Hector.

"She's been raped," Hector said for him.

The doctor did another group scan, then nodded and took a step toward Hector. "I'm sorry but yes, Sadie's been raped."

"Fucking hell," Hank muttered from behind Eddie, and the atmosphere in the room changed to a strange, uneasy hopelessness. It wasn't a feeling they were used to and it didn't sit well with a single one of them.

"We've done a rape kit and called the police. She's sleeping now. Sir, if you can—"

"Take me to her," Hector cut in.

"You have to understand what you'll—" the doctor started.

"I found her, I brought her in, I know what I'll see," Hector bit out. "Fucking... take... me... to... her."

The doctor nodded. "Follow me."

Eddie's eyes cut to Lee, then to Darius. Then Eddie followed Hector as Hector and the doctor walked away. Darius followed Eddie.

Luke turned on his boot and without a word left the room.

Lee turned to Bobby and said simply, "Follow him. He has an alibi everywhere he goes."

Bobby nodded and followed Luke.

Lee's eyes stopped on Ava. Ava was Luke's woman. She was watching the door Luke just walked out of, and her face was pale.

Finally Lee turned to Indy. "Phone Daisy."

"But—" Indy began.

"Do it, gorgeous. Now."

Indy dug in her purse for her cell.

⋈

## *Marcus*

The phone rang and Marcus Sloan slid away from Daisy's body, rolled and grabbed it from its cradle.

With his eyes on the clock, he said, his voice curt, "It's barely five o'clock in the morning."

"Marcus? I'm sorry, it's Indy. Is Daisy there?"

Marcus felt an unaccustomed chill slide up his spine as Daisy moved, rolled, and he felt her eyes on him in the dark.

"Is everything okay?" he asked Indy, as always wanting to make any fall his wife was going to take a softer one. She'd already had more than her fair share of the hard ones. These days she only experienced some bumpy rides with the Rock Chicks, though some were bumpier than others.

So far, they'd been lucky.

"No. Everything isn't okay. Lee wanted me to call her. I'm not sure why, but…" She hesitated, and he could tell she was seeking privacy before she started talking again. Daisy was up on an elbow now and he could feel her body getting tense. "The thing is, Sadie Townsend was beaten up really badly tonight."

Marcus felt it like a punch in the stomach.

Ricky fucking Balducci. Or one of his fucking brothers.

"Fuck," he whispered.

"What?" Daisy was sitting up and Marcus sat up, too.

Marcus turned and snapped on the light. Twisting back to his wife, he shook his head.

"Is she going to be all right?" Marcus asked.

"I… there's more," Indy replied.

Marcus waited and Daisy slid closer.

"What is it?" Marcus prompted.

"She was raped."

Marcus threw the covers back on the bed and knifed out.

"Where is she?" he snapped.

"Denver Health," Indy answered.

"We'll be there in thirty minutes."

He didn't say good-bye. He put down the phone then walked to the closet.

"Marcus, honey bunch, you're scarin' me," Daisy said from the bed.

"Get up, darling. Get dressed. Sadie Townsend is at Denver Health. She's been beaten up and raped."

Daisy's gasp was sharp and Marcus heard rather than saw her jump from the bed.

That was his wife. She still thought Sadie had shoved a knife in her back and yet she was out of the bed like a shot.

He didn't look forward to telling her what he was going to have to tell her.

He got dressed. Daisy got dressed and he stood over her while she pulled on her boots.

"I have to tell you something," he said to her bent head, and it snapped up so she was looking at him.

"Tell me later. We have to—"

Marcus shook his head then crouched in front of her. Daisy took a breath at his unusual actions and he knew she was preparing.

"First, you must know I did what I did because Seth Townsend was a dangerous man. I didn't want you anywhere near him. Not even if near him meant being around Sadie."

Daisy's eyes narrowed. "What did you do?"

"It's what I didn't do."

She stood and put her hands on her hips.

Marcus knew this was a very dangerous pose for Daisy to assume.

"Okay then, what *didn't* you do?" she asked, looking down her nose at him.

Marcus stood, too, then pulled his fingers through his hair. "I didn't tell you about Sadie."

Daisy jutted out a hip. This was an even more dangerous pose.

"What didn't you tell me about Sadie?"

He ignored her and continued, "And, I didn't tell you about Nanette and Monica."

"Marcus, honey bunches of love—" Daisy started warningly, losing patience when Marcus hesitated.

Marcus went on, "I didn't tell you that I've known Sadie for ten years and I've known what kind of woman she was since I first saw her. I didn't tell you that she would no more talk about you behind your back than I would."

Marcus watched his wife's face grow pale.

He continued, "I also didn't tell you that after you thought she did, she called the house and came by and tried to explain, and I didn't let her."

That was when Marcus watched his wife's face go red.

He carried on, "Then I forced her father to warn her off." When Daisy's face looked in danger of turning purple, Marcus kept explaining (quickly). "I did it to protect you."

Daisy's brows were drawn and her eyes were narrowed when she asked, "Is that it?"

"No."

"Well then, finish it."

Marcus blew out a sigh. "Lastly, I didn't tell you that she was the reason Nanette's husband left her for the pool boy. Which, if I read Sadie's actions right—considering she outed Charles Hardy in front of a room full of people and he was so relieved, he didn't give a damn but Nanette was so humiliated, she hasn't shown her face in society since—was Sadie's retribution for Nanette being mean to you."

Daisy glared at him.

Marcus waited.

Then Daisy spoke. "Let's get to the goddamned hospital."

# Chapter 2

# Stretch My Legs A Bit

*Sadie*

I knew I was in the hospital before I opened my eyes.

Hospitals had a certain feel and a certain smell, and before I opened my eyes, I experienced both.

The first thing I saw was the ceiling. Then I decided if they had a suggestion box, before I left, I'd suggest they should get a ceiling cleaner. Sick people were on their backs a lot and the ceiling looked filthy. Major gross. Sick people didn't need to see *that*.

Then I realized I had to go to the bathroom, like, bad.

This kind of stunk, considering, when I looked down at my arm, there were tubes and stuff sticking in it. Not easy to get to the bathroom with tubes stuck in you.

I also saw my wrist was in a cast, but I blanked that out as quickly as I saw it.

I was kind of hoping some of those things sticking in my arm were what was taking the pain away.

I remembered the pain. I would never forget the pain. But I had the strength of mind borne of *loads* of practice to set the pain, and what caused it, aside.

For now.

As I looked down at my arm, on the floor I saw something weird.

It looked for all the world like a pair of cowboy boots. Not just cowboy boots, but jeans and cowboy boots. Not just jeans and cowboy boots but legs in jeans and feet in cowboy boots. The legs were crossed at the ankle and stretched straight out.

I followed the legs up, up, up until I saw Hector "Oh my God" Chavez sleeping in a chair by my hospital bed.

Maybe I wasn't awake. Maybe I was dreaming.

I stared at him. His hair was a mess, his clothes were wrinkled (or more wrinkled than normal) and he needed a shave.

What was *he* doing there?

Oh my.

I remembered.

Oh no.

I remembered.

He'd been there. Last night, he'd *been* there.

He'd carried me from the stairs to the car then I passed out.

I woke up again when there was a commotion. A commotion caused when Luke Stark and a security guard were trying to pull Hector out of my emergency bay. Hector didn't want to go, as in, *really* didn't want to go.

How bizarre was *that?*

Maybe I dreamed that, too.

I closed my eyes. Then I remembered I had to go to the bathroom.

Well, I knew one thing. I sure as certain wasn't going to call the nurse, just in case Hector wasn't a dream. I didn't want him around when I explained what I needed.

Therefore I knew what I had to do. There was really only one choice.

It took some effort, but I managed to twist and look at the bottom of my IV stand thingie. In the TV shows, they had wheels.

I sighed in relief. My IV stand thingie had wheels. I reached out, grabbed it and rolled it a bit down the bed and then stopped.

Hector's legs in jeans and feet in cowboy boots were in the way.

Darn. What to do now?

"What are you doing?"

My head jerked up and I saw Hector was no longer asleep. He still had his head against the high back of the chair. His forearms were still resting on the arms, hands dangling, and his long legs were still stretched out in front of him, crossed at the ankles.

But his black eyes were open and they were on me.

"What are you doing?" he repeated his question, then got up and approached the bed, coming to a stop at the side, towering over me.

My eyes followed him, my head tilting back as he got up and closer. I didn't answer.

"Sadie, talk to me. What are you doing?"

I didn't even try to be Ice Princess. In the circumstances I forgot all about being Ice Princess. I forgot that "Ms. Townsend, Ice Princess" even existed.

"I thought I'd take a walk," I answered.

His eyebrows went up. "You thought you'd take a walk?"

He sounded like this was more bizarre than the fact that he was even there, which *I* thought was mega-bizarre in the extreme.

"Yes, I thought I'd stretch my legs a bit," I told him.

"You thought you'd stretch your legs a bit," he repeated, still sounding like he thought I was a touch crazy.

"Are you going to repeat everything I say?" I asked.

"Are you going to start making sense?" he returned.

I let go of the IV stand thingie and leaned back. "What's wrong with taking a walk?"

He stared at me hard for a second then looked away and lifted his arm. He tore his fingers through his hair, dropped his arm and looked back at me.

"We'll call the nurse; see if you can take a walk."

"I'm sure I can walk."

"We'll call the nurse."

"I don't want to call the nurse."

"Why not?"

That was a good question.

I didn't have a good answer (or, at least, one I would tell him), so I said, "Because."

Then my eyes searched my room, fell on the bathroom (just checking, for when my time came) and they went back to him.

But when they went back to Hector, he was looking over his shoulder at the bathroom.

Before I knew what was happening, he moved my IV stand thingie. He threw back the covers, put an arm behind my knees and one at my waist and lifted me up, one hand shoving the IV stand thingie in front of us as he carried me to the bathroom.

At first, I was frozen in horror.

Then I said, or more like whispered (also in horror), "What are you doing?"

He didn't answer. He walked to the bathroom and gently set me on my feet inside it. He turned on his boot, walked out and closed the door behind him.

Someone, please tell me that did *not* just happen.

All right. All right.

Taking just enough time to set that aside, too (for now), I went about my business. This was unpleasant. It hurt.

I set that aside, too.

When I was done, I stood in the bathroom, looked down and surveyed myself.

I was in a hospital gown, luckily not one of those that had the back open all the way down. Just a big opening at the upper back tied shut. I had a cast on my wrist, two bags dripping into my arm from the IVs, and a completely ruined manicure.

I saw bruises and cuts on my arms, more bruises around my good wrist, and, pulling up the gown, I saw some on my legs, loads of bruising on my knees.

My midriff hurt, like loads. In fact, I hurt all over and I had a dull headache. Other, more specific parts of me ached, too, but I was setting that aside.

I went to the mirror and looked at myself. Then I reached out and grabbed the sink with my good hand at what I saw.

I dropped my head forward, closed my eyes and leaned into my hand.

My own visage was burned into the backs of my eyelids. Two black eyes, very swollen; not shut, but not pretty either. My nose was also seriously swollen, but didn't look broken (but what did I know?). And a huge white bandage was taped to my cheekbone and I knew what that hid. I'd felt the skin opening there. And I'd felt the blood.

Monstrous.

The door opened behind me and I heard the sound of boots. Then I felt heat at my back. Just that: no touch, just his heat.

"Sadie," Hector said softly.

"Go away," I replied, even more softly.

He didn't go away. He picked me up again and did the whole carrying-me-pushing-my-IV-stand back into the room thing, laid me on the bed and threw the covers back on me.

I laid back and pulled the covers high up with my good hand, which, luckily, as I was right-handed, was my right one. I held on to the covers, closed my eyes and turned my face in the opposite direction of Hector.

"*Mamita*, look at me." His voice was still soft.

"Go away," I repeated, my voice was still soft, too.

"We need to talk."

"Go away."

"Sadie," he murmured gently.

That was when I found her. She wasn't very far. She slid into my skin easily because normally, she lived there.

I opened my eyes, turned my head and looked at Hector. Regardless of what had happened to me last night, what he had seen, what he'd done last night and just now and the way I looked, I was calm, assured and ice cold.

"Go... away," I enunciated it very clearly so there was plenty of time for the icicles to form on both words.

It was then, to my shock (because no one penetrated the ice fortress; no one, not even my father), Hector leaned forward so close he was barely a couple of inches away. He put one hand on my pillow and the other one hit the bed low, by my waist.

I drew in breath.

Still with a soft voice he said, "She's in there. Now I've seen her twice. Three times, if you count when you lost it in Lee's office and nearly ripped open your palms with your own fuckin' fingernails."

Oh my.

He didn't give me a chance to respond. He kept talking. "I know she's in there and I'm warnin' you, Sadie, I'm gonna pull her out."

The Ice Princess, as ever, stayed calm.

"Do I have to call security?" I asked like it was all the same to me.

He didn't answer. I started to stare him down and I waited for him to look away.

He didn't look away.

Instead he said, "I know about you."

"You don't know a thing about me," I retorted acidly.

He just smiled, and I'd never really seen him smile, not full-on. I'd seen him grin. I'd heard him chuckle at something my father said. But not a smile.

It was lazy, it was slow and it was glamorous.

Then he said, "I'll give you time. You've been through hell, but when the time is right, I'm gonna pull her out."

At his words, The Ice Princess (who never let go), started slipping. I held on to her by my mental fingernails and pulled her back.

"Maybe you need to get some sleep," I suggested.

Hector didn't respond. He stared at me and I stared at him.

Again, I waited for him to back down, to look away.

He didn't.

So for the first time since I could remember, I did.

My eyes slid to the side and then something even weirder happened. While I was looking away, he leaned in deeper. I felt his hand cup the back of my head. He lifted it gently and he kissed the top of my head.

I froze.

No one but no one but *no one* had touched me like that. No one, not since my mom left. No one.

Did I say *no one?*

He left his hand there with his lips pressed against my head. Not for a second, but for a long time.

It felt like eternity. It felt like a sweet, wonderful, lovely eternity.

Now, seriously, no kidding, how bizarre was *that?*

Before I could get myself together and jerk my head away, the door opened and I heard said in a country twang, "Oh, damn! Sorry."

It was then I jerked my head away. I got up on my elbows, looked across the room and saw Daisy and Marcus Sloan standing inside the door.

⚞⚟

"Ralphie, it's me, Sadie," I said into the phone.

"Sadie? Where are you?" Ralphie asked, sounding concerned as he would do. I was never late for work, much less a no-show.

I sat in the bed with the phone to my ear, my eyes on the door, and I didn't know what to say.

⚞⚟

I'd had a small stroke of luck.

The minute Marcus and Daisy appeared was only a moment before the doctor appeared. For privacy, Marcus and Daisy quietly left, but weirdly, Hector did not.

Hector grabbed the control thingamabob on the side of my bed and did the whole lifting-the-back-of-the-hospital-bed-thing for me. I sat up, and as Hector stood beside my bed (for all the world like he was my loving boyfriend or something), the doctor told me (or, more accurately, *us*, acting for all the world like Hector was my loving boyfriend or something) what was wrong with me (like I didn't know), and said I would be released that afternoon. But, even so, someone needed to be around to keep an eye on me.

Then he turned to Hector and asked for, "A word?"

Hector nodded to the doctor then (no kidding), leaned down and kissed the top of my head (again!) and they both walked out.

I stared at the door, trying to figure out what was going on.

Then I realized I might only have moments, so I twisted, grabbed the phone and put it on the bed.

I dialed Ralphie.

⌖⌖

Ralphie was the closest thing I had to a friend.

He probably wouldn't describe me as a friend; more an employer which was what I was.

Three years ago, I opened an art gallery. The Feds didn't get that either, as I'd opened it with my trust fund and my father didn't launder money through it, though they looked and looked to find some nefarious purpose for my gallery so they could seize it, like they did everything else. But they didn't find anything because there was nothing to find. I made certain sure of that.

I opened it because I needed more to do with my time than just be Daddy's Little Princess—which was getting old—and I had an art degree from Denver University. So why not?

It turned out I was good at it. I had an eye for art and I could put on a really good opening. I'd had years of practice at being a good hostess, always standing next to my father's side. So you could imagine how pleased it made me that something he taught me eventually came in handy.

I hired Ralphie, and in my gallery (which I named "Art", because I really don't have much of an imagination and it kind of said it all) Ralphie and I had fun. He knew he was my employee and everything, but he was good to be around. He was a bit crazy in a nice way and we'd have a laugh.

Ralphie was a tall, slim, blond-haired, blue-eyed, ultra-elegant, unbelievably beautiful gay man. Swear to God, he could be a male model. Not kidding.

We didn't socialize outside of work.

Of course, every year, I did take him and his partner, Buddy, out for a fancy dinner at Christmas, during which I gave Ralphie his Christmas bonus. I also took him and Buddy out for a fancy dinner for Ralphie's birthday, during which I gave him his birthday present. A beautiful, pink Armani dress shirt with matching pink and maroon tie (year one), a Royal Doulton figurine (year two) and the glass paperweight he had his eye on for ages at Art but couldn't afford (year three). I also took them both out for drinks to celebrate after we made that sale of the beautiful, bronze sculpture of the female torso. We'd had that sculpture for months. It cost a fortune and it was our biggest sale ever.

Oh, and Ralphie and I would always do his performance evaluations over French martinis at the Oxford Hotel Cruise Room. The evaluations lasted ten minutes so Buddy always joined us because, well, why not?

Buddy was yin to Ralphie's yang.

Buddy was black, bald (shaved), had a thick goatee and a well-maintained, very muscular body. He was Butch with a capital "B" and he dressed like Freddie Mercury (white wife beater tank top, super-tight jeans, black motorcycle boots and studded black belts) when he wasn't dressed in scrubs (he was a nurse on the Neurosciences Ward at Swedish Medical Center) or dressed to go out with us to fancy dinners at the Cruise Room (Buddy looked good in his Queen Front Man getup, but you didn't wear a wife beater to the Cruise Room, no way).

Buddy was funny, too, and really sweet. Kind of a gentle, butch, Freddie-Mercury-on-steroids-look-alike except black and, well… bald.

Although Ralphie wasn't my friend, technically, nor Buddy, for that matter, he was all I had.

And I needed someone.

⋙⋘

"I'm at Denver Health," I answered Ralphie.

"*What?*" Ralphie screeched, and in my mind I could see his blond eyebrows hitting his hairline.

"It's okay. I just had a little accident," I lied.

"An accident that puts you in the hospital? Oh my *God*."

"It's nothing," I assured him. "Just observation. They're letting me go today."

Ralphie instantly responded, "I'll be right over."

"No!" My voice was sharp and my eyes were glued to the door. Hector or Daisy and Marcus could walk back in at any moment.

I had enough to deal with. I didn't need Ralphie showing up. Ralphie could be a bit... dramatic.

"What do you mean, no?" Ralphie asked.

"I mean, actually, I'm calling because I need you to do me a favor. I'm sorry to ask but—"

Ralphie interrupted by saying, "Anything."

I blinked in my tense surveillance of the door at Ralphie's quick offer of assistance. What could I say? I hadn't had a load of times in my life where anyone offered me assistance. Heck, I hadn't had a load of times in my life where anyone offered me anything.

I shook off my surprise and said, "There are spare keys to my apartment in the drawer at the gallery."

"I know where they are."

"Could you go to my place, get me some clothes, shoes... um, under-wear, and bring them to the hospital?"

"I'll do it right now."

For some reason, his words made tears sting my eyes.

"I'm going to be in testing," I lied again. Also blinking again, this time for a different reason. "So, could you just leave them at the nurse's station?"

"Sure, but I can—"

"No, no, I don't want to waste any more of your time."

"Sadie, it isn't—"

I interrupted again. "No really, it's okay. The testing could go on for a while."

Ralphie was quiet then he asked, "Are you okay?"

"Yes, fine, just a small accident. Banged my head a little. I might be out of work for a couple of days though."

Or weeks, but I'd come up with other excuses later.

"Okay," Ralphie agreed, but he didn't sound like he bought it.

I drew in a silent breath, then on the exhale I thought of something else.

"Just so you know, my place is a bit of a mess—"

"Now, Sadie, *that* I don't believe. You are Queen Clean."

That sounded more like the Ralphie I knew.

"No, it's just that—" I started but Ralphie cut in.

"Don't get your panties in a bunch because I'll see a speck of dust. I promise, I won't report you to the Tidy Patrol if you left a bowl in the sink."

"Ralphie—"

"I'll be there soon."

"Ralphie—"

"Toodles."

Disconnect.

Oh my.

Oh well, I'd figure out some excuse for why my apartment looked like...

I stopped thinking about what my apartment looked like—and more importantly, why—and set it aside. I'd deal with that later, too.

I put the phone back, pulled the cover up and laid back, thinking of what to do next so I wouldn't think of all the things I was trying not to think about.

The door opened. I immediately closed my eyes. I heard footfalls, footfalls that stopped by my bed.

"Sadie, sugar, you asleep?" Daisy's country twang whispered.

I pretended to be asleep.

Now, Hector being there was bizarre beyond bizarre, but Daisy and Marcus being there was bizarre *on top* of bizarre.

They hated me. Why were they there?

"I think she's asleep." Daisy was still whispering.

"Sleep is good." I heard Marcus's deep voice say.

Silence.

I waited for them to leave. Then I heard a feminine crying hiccough which was followed by a masculine, "Sh."

It took all the Powers of the Ice Princess not to open my eyes and tell Daisy I was okay, which I was not, but some lies were good. I'd learned that from loads of practice, too.

I listened to Daisy cry and Marcus soothe her for a while, then he said, "You've been here all night. Let's get you home."

Thank God. Finally.

"No," Daisy's voice was clogged with tears, I could tell even on that one word. She kept talking. "I'll just go down to the gift shop, get a magazine and stay with her. Hector said he won't be back for a while."

At least *that* was something.

"You sure, darling?" Marcus asked.

Daisy didn't answer, but I heard footfalls again. The door opened and closed.

I opened my eyes. I was alone. That was until whenever Daisy got back with her magazine.

I thought about how much energy it would take for me to understand what on earth was going on.

Then I realized, just before I fell asleep (for real this time) that I didn't have enough energy to figure it out.

⌘

I opened my eyes and saw Daisy sitting in the chair where Hector slept.

She was wearing shoulder-to-toe dark denim, fawn-colored fringe falling from the shoulder pads of her blazer. More fringe down the sides of her skintight jeans. She had on fawn-colored, spike-heeled, platform, round-toed boots, her jeans tucked into the boots. There was more than a hint of rhinestones and rivets sprinkling her outfit *everywhere*.

She looked like she was going to get up and start singing, "Jolene". Instead, she sat, legs crossed and read *National Enquirer*.

Darn. Now what?

I couldn't feign sleep and avoid her forever. Or could I?

"Sadie?"

My eyes moved to Daisy's and she was looking at me.

There was the answer. I couldn't feign sleep and avoid her forever.

I didn't respond. Instead, I sat up and lifted my good hand to pull my hair away from my face. When I dropped my hand, my hair tumbled back in my face again.

I sighed.

"Let me get that," Daisy said softly, and I looked at her again.

Her *Enquirer* was on the chair. She was up and digging through her purse. She yanked something out and dumped her purse on the night table.

She showed me a big, pale pink clip.

"Voila!" she said as if she'd pulled a rabbit from a hat, not a hair clip from a handbag.

"Turn your back to me," she ordered, and even I wasn't Ice Princess enough to tell her to go jump in a lake.

I turned my back. Her hands went through my hair, her long fingernails gently scraping my scalp.

It felt nice. It reminded me of when I was little and my mom used to brush my hair at night before I went to bed. Sometimes when my mom would brush my hair, she would tell me stories. Sometimes they were funny stories, sometimes romantic, sometimes adventurous. I used to love when my mom brushed my hair and told me stories.

Daisy carefully pulled and scraped my hair for longer than was needed then she twisted it and I felt the clip go in.

Her hands went to my shoulders and she gently turned me around to face her. When I did, her eyes were on my hair. Then her gaze dropped to mine.

"All better," she said.

"Not even close," I replied.

There she was, bitchy Ms. Townsend rearing her ugly head.

Daisy's teeth bit her lip and her eyes sparkled with tears.

"Sadie, sugar—" she started, but before she could say more, the door opened and Hector walked in.

Really, no more. I got it. I was the daughter of a Drug King, a bad man who probably destroyed many lives. But seriously, how much penance could a daughter do for her father's sins? I mean, *I* didn't sell heroin to school kids for goodness sakes!

I'd had enough.

I picked up the call button thingamabob and stared at it, found the button for the nurse and pressed it.

Then I saw Hector's belt buckle and abs by the bed.

Darn.

"Sadie," Hector called.

I kept my head down and hit the nurse call button again.

"Sadie," Hector repeated.

My head came up and I looked at him.

"Why are you here?" I snapped.

He opened his mouth to speak, but before he could I turned my head and looked at Daisy.

"And why are *you* here?" I asked her.

"I thought I'd—" Daisy started.

"No, actually, I don't want to know," I interrupted. I reached out and grabbed my IV stand thingie. Then I threw back the covers and scooted to the side of the bed, rolling my IV with me. It hurt but I did it anyway, and I didn't even wince.

"Sadie, get back in bed," Hector ordered, but I had my legs over the side and I stood up.

I walked two steps, wheeling my IV stand thingie with me (the IV stand thingie kind of bit into my bid for Queen Ice, but I'd just have to work it).

I turned to them, hand on my IV stand and stood my ground.

"Both of you, leave," I demanded.

Daisy's eyes slid to the opposite side of the bed where Hector was standing. My eyes went there too. He didn't look happy.

"I'll ask you again, *mamita*, get back in bed," he said.

"That isn't asking, that's telling," I retorted.

"Then I'll *tell* you again, back in bed," he shot back.

"No," I replied.

He started walking around the bed... toward me.

I wondered, in the nanosecond before I started retreating, why he seemed completely unaffected by my Chill Factor. Everyone else went into deep freeze.

Not Hector.

I had, of course, noticed that his body was preternaturally hot. Maybe that was it.

"Hector," Daisy said softly as Hector advanced.

Something in her tone must have reached him because all of a sudden he stopped. So I stopped too.

Hector and I squared off and went into stare down mode. While we were doing this, Daisy came forward cautiously, but didn't get too close to Hector or to me.

"Sadie, we're here——" Daisy started.

Again I didn't let her finish. My eyes broke from Hector's dark ones and cut to her.

"I know why you're here." I motioned to Hector. "And I know why he's here. You wanted to get a good look at how the mighty have fallen."

Daisy's body jerked like I hit her at the same time I saw her flinch.

Hector didn't flinch. His eyes narrowed, his face went dark, and let me just say, it was scary.

Nevertheless, I was on a roll. I was beyond Ice Princess. I was Sorceress of the Antarctic, and a bitchy one at that.

It hurt me to do it. It hurt more than my body hurt. But I had to.

I didn't know why they were there and I didn't care. It started like this, people being nice, doing nice things, maybe trying to be kind.

It never ended like that. Never.

I went on, "Well, you had your look. Now you can go."

Totally ignoring my order to go, Hector took a step forward. I took a step back.

He stopped. So did I.

We went into stare down again.

Finally he said, "The police are here."

That surprised me, but I covered before it could show.

"Why?" I asked.

Then Hector answered, "So you can swear out a warrant so they can go after—"

At his words, Sorceress of the Antarctic disintegrated, melted in an instant, and I lost it.

Utterly.

"*No!*" I shrieked so loud and shrill I was surprised the TV screen didn't burst.

He couldn't say it. Not out loud. Not to *me*.

I retreated again.

"Oh, sugar." I heard Daisy say, her voice trembling, but Hector was coming at me and I kept my eyes on him.

His face wasn't dark anymore. There was something else there, something I didn't want to see.

I closed my eyes to block it out, lifted my hand to ward him off, all the while wheeling my IV stand thingie and walking backwards. My back hit the wall.

"*Mamita,*" Hector murmured gently when I stopped. He didn't touch me, but he was close enough I could feel his heat.

With nowhere else to go, I turned my head away.

"Sadie?" another voice called.

I opened my eyes and peered around Hector's body. I could see both Ralphie and Buddy standing just inside the door.

Hector stepped to the side and I saw them fully.

Ralphie was carrying an overnight bag. Buddy was carrying a huge vase of exquisite white calla lilies, my favorites.

They were staring at me and they looked pale (yes, even Buddy; I didn't know black people could go pale, but he did).

"Sweetie?" Ralphie said hesitantly.

Even though he called me "sweetie" (and he'd never called me "sweetie"), Ice Princess clicked into place.

"I'm okay," I said immediately.

One second Ralphie was across the room. The next second I was in his arms.

"Oh Sadie, sweet 'ums. You didn't have an accident, did you?" he asked, his voice whisper-soft, one arm around my waist, the other hand stroking my back.

"Ralphie, I'm fine." I held my body rigid and spoke to his throat.

He leaned back and looked down at me. "Sweetie, you are *not* fine. I can see, can't I? I didn't go blind in the night like a bad Jodie Foster movie. And I just got back from your apartment. It's a disaster. What on earth happened? Who did this to you?"

This was not working well for me. It was all coming at me. Everyone was *talking* about it. How could I set it aside to deal with it later when people were *talking* about it?

"I'm gonna break his fuckin' neck." Buddy was now at our side.

I turned my head and looked up at Buddy. He got a close look at my face and I saw his teeth clench.

Then he repeated between his teeth, "I'm gonna break his *fuckin'* neck. Who did it?"

"I'm fine," I said again.

"You have a cast on your wrist," Ralphie pointed out, and I looked back at Ralphie.

"I'm fine," I repeated.

"You have a bandage on your face," Ralphie went on.

I could take no more and really, could you blame me?

So I screamed, "*I'm fine!*"

Ralphie had never seen me lose my cool, never. Therefore at my scream he winced. Then for some reason, *he* ignored my Chill Factor. His arms got tight and he pulled me close.

And no one had held me like that for as long as I could remember.

And I couldn't bear it anymore.

I shoved my face in his ultra-elegant shirt and clenched his uber-stylish suit jacket in my good hand and I cried.

I didn't care who saw me. Not even Hector.

Fuck it. I could take no more.

It was not wracking, sobbing, loud crying. It was silent, body-jerking, soul-wrenching crying.

Through it all, and it seemed to last a long time, Ralphie held on.

"Get it out, sweet 'ums, give it to Ralphie," he muttered finally.

"I have to go home," I said into his shirt.

"You can't go home," Ralphie replied.

"I have to go home. I have to get out of here," I said back, but I didn't take my face from Ralphie's shirt.

"You'll go home," Buddy said from close to our side, and I felt another hand slide around my waist as Buddy got closer and affected a group hug.

"Thank you," I whispered, not looking up, not looking at Ralphie or Buddy, and definitely not Hector or Daisy.

"You'll go home, Sadie," Buddy said. "You'll go home with us."

# Chapter 3

# I Waited

### *Hector*

Hector sat, leaned forward, elbows on his knees, his left hand dangling, his right hand holding a Jack and Coke.

Actually, he'd started out the night adding Coke but he hadn't bothered with it for the last two drinks.

"*Hermano*, you gotta talk," Eddie said to him.

Hector looked at his older brother. Eddie was sitting across from him in Hector's living room.

The living room was a pit. He'd been working steadily on the house now for months, but there was a lot of work to do. He'd barely scratched the surface. The living room was a jumble of unpacked boxes and furniture, most of it covered in heavy, plastic sheets. Hector was refinishing the floors in the study and dining room. He should have started with the living room.

Hector looked back to the floor and said, "I fucked up. I know it and I'll fix it."

Then at the thought of "fixing" Sadie, unwanted and disconnected memories flashed through his brain.

Her standing at the sink in the bathroom at the hospital.

Her crying silently into her friend's chest.

Her saying she wanted to take a walk instead of admitting she had to use the bathroom.

Her bloody face, bloody legs and the limp body he held as she told him there was no one to care if she woke up.

He lifted his glass to his mouth and threw back the Jack, draining it dry. He leaned forward and tagged the mostly empty bottle which was on the floor by his boot. He poured another heavy measure and set the bourbon back down.

He was drunk. He knew he was drunk and he didn't give a fuck.

"Tell me how you fucked up," Eddie prompted.

Without hesitation, Hector replied, "I waited."

That was it. He'd waited. He'd waited for Sadie to come to him.

After that night in her father's office, he should have taken what he knew was his.

And he shouldn't have fucking waited.

⋈

At first, when Hector Chavez started to get close to Seth Townsend, he thought Townsend's daughter was a useless rich bitch; a beautiful one, but still useless.

Then, because it was his job, he watched her and her father. And he saw that Townsend didn't hide anything from Sadie. He wasn't concealing how he was able to give her a very good life. She knew all about it. She seemed to have no problems with that, which made Hector wonder if she was somehow involved in the operation.

Hector looked into it and found she wasn't involved.

She was clean. Squeaky clean.

In Hector's experience, no one was squeaky clean. This made Hector suspicious. So he watched her closer.

And watching her and her father (but mostly her) made him uneasy.

Being from a big, loud, loving and in-your-business Mexican-American family, he'd never seen anything like it.

There was no affection, no teasing, no loving displays.

There was also no visible abuse.

There was nothing.

Mostly that nothing came from Sadie. She was like a robot. Not just around her father, but all the time.

She did everything right, everything exact, everything perfect. The way she dressed, ran her father's home, organized his parties, everything.

She seemed to be able to do it with minimal effort. She never got stressed, frustrated, on edge. She was never anything but completely together and in control.

Further, she didn't invite closeness or affection, not only from her father but from anyone. She didn't laugh or joke or lose her temper or display the barest hint of a personality.

She just did her job. All the time. 24/7.

All that nothing made Hector want to make her feel something, but she didn't invite that either. She was ice cold.

This had the perverse effect of *really* making Hector want to make her feel something.

Then she started helping him, feeding him information.

He couldn't fucking believe it. Not just because she was doing it, but because she was really not good at it.

He'd even walked up to her father's office door and seen her place a file in the drawer where she put information for him. The house had been empty before he entered it. He knew, and undoubtedly she knew, that Seth was away, but it was still risky as hell, especially leaving the fucking door open.

He'd stepped to the side so she couldn't see him, guarding the door in case someone showed, and disappeared when he heard her preparing to leave the room.

Anyone could have walked up and seen her do that. If anyone else but him had seen it, she'd have been dead.

Like her mother.

In the end, he had to spend his time trailing her in order to protect her so she wouldn't do something immensely stupid and get caught helping him, thus blowing his cover and getting him, and more than likely herself, killed.

And she was taking the risk for nothing. Most of it wasn't even good information. Drug lords didn't tend to keep sensitive shit in the safe in their home. However, he couldn't tell her that.

She never let on to anyone, not even a hint, that she knew who he was or that she was trying to help destroy her father.

She was always the Dutiful Stepford Daughter.

When she'd walked in that night, smiling a sweet but highly inebriated smile and telling him to kiss her, he didn't hesitate. He had already made up his mind that when it was over, when he'd brought Townsend down, Sadie would be his. He couldn't move in on her early. It could have fucked up the case and he'd been working it for over a year.

But when she'd put her hands on him, pressed her body into his and he could smell her expensive perfume close up for the first time instead of the hints he caught when she drifted by him, he lost control and couldn't stop himself from accepting her invitation.

This did not make sense. She was not his type.

He liked his women to have long legs, pronounced curves and lots of attitude. She had the curves but she was petite, and what personality she displayed was frigid, nowhere near the hot-headed, in-your-face attitude he liked in his women.

He didn't give a fuck about this. Bottom line, he wanted her. When she gave him his shot, he took it.

He'd been furious when, close to the point of no return, she'd walked away, leaving him hard and aching for more of her.

At the time, he thought she was playing games. When he had time to think about it, he decided, in her drunkenness, she'd lost control too. But she'd found hers, and in the end, the games she was playing were games she needed to play so she could end up alive and breathing after he took down her father.

That was much better than dead, like her mother was assumed to be.

Eighteen years ago, Elizabeth Townsend approached Indy's father, Tom Savage, a cop and the widower of Elizabeth's close friend, Katherine.

Elizabeth Townsend had wanted to be free of her husband, her life, and wanted it for her daughter, too. She didn't want Sadie to grow up the daughter of a drug dealer. Therefore, she started to inform on Seth, who had yet to make the big time, giving Tom information.

Until one day, she just disappeared.

⌘

Although Hector had been furious when Sadie had walked away from him, he'd waited and not approached her, even though he wanted to. He knew he was close to closing the operation.

It was just over a week later when the DEA moved in.

He kept firmly detached from the process after. He demanded that other agents interrogate her, and he didn't get involved when they investigated her assets. He wasn't surprised when she'd walked away and didn't look back when the Agency froze the accounts and seized all property.

She'd done her job and she was moving on.

When they told him they were going to transfer him to DC, he quit. He'd had enough. Although he got off on the hunt, he'd never been big on rules and policy.

Furthermore, Sadie couldn't get to him in DC.

He bought a house, went to work for Lee, who also was not big on rules and policy, and waited for her to come to him.

He didn't think it'd take long. He'd never had a sweet piece go that hot for him that quickly, nor had he ever lost that much control. He had no doubt that when their lives were no longer on the line she'd make her approach. She was a trust fund princess who walked away leaving him aching; it was going to have to be her that made the next move.

Sadie and he had unfinished business. He knew it, and he knew she knew it, and Hector intended to finish it.

However, by the time she made an appointment with Lee, he was losing patience.

⧊

He'd heard about Ricky Balducci and his brothers. Word on the street was Sadie was marked. The Balducci Boys had an unspoken deal: win Sadie, win the throne.

It was insanity and it was talk. The Balducci brothers were known for being both insane and entirely full of bullshit.

He was surprised that Sadie had come to Lee, and he knew when she asked for protection that she'd been getting pressure from the Balduccis. Why she didn't share this information with Lee he didn't know, but he didn't care either.

He didn't want Lee involved. He could take care of it on his own. When Sadie left he told Lee he'd look into it. By this he meant deal with the Balduccis and deal with Sadie.

Her time was up. He was done waiting.

That night, he followed her from her gallery to her apartment and waited outside in case she went out.

She stayed in.

He left her, thinking she'd be safe in a high rise with security. He had an assignment with Luke that night and he decided he'd come back in the morning. He'd planned to return, make sure she got to work, then he'd take Luke, Mace, Darius or Vance and go have a word with the Balducci Boys.

After that, he'd go to Sadie.

He didn't have that chance.

~~✦~~

"You waited?" Eddie asked.

Hector sat back, took another drink and leveled his eyes on his brother.

"She handed me her father."

He heard and saw Eddie suck in breath.

Hector nodded. "Fed me info. Not good info, but she fed it to me all the same. You remember that situation out in Stapleton, I gave you the heads up?" Hector asked.

Eddie's eyes flared and Hector knew he remembered. It had been a big bust and the Denver Police Department had been fully informed ahead of time who would be there, when, and what they would find. It was the only piece of decent intel that Sadie had passed him.

"Sadie?" Eddie asked.

"She wrote me a fuckin' note," Hector told him.

"Jesus Christ," Eddie muttered. "She wrote you a note?"

This time Hector shook his head. Not to Eddie's question, but in disbelief at the memory.

"She's the worst fuckin' informant I ever saw. Broad daylight, door open, she's rifling through the safe. Christ, you wouldn't believe it. Spent half my time building the case against Townsend, the other half keeping an eye on her."

At this Eddie started laughing, and although Hector wouldn't have thought it possible, he smiled.

Eddie quit laughing and said, "Word was, she stood beside her father through the trial."

Hector replied on a dying smile, "She played her part. She was good at it. She'd been doing it a long time. It was her final show. I pulled in a favor, checked the logs. She hasn't visited him once."

Eddie let this sink in then he started, "You know her mother—"

"I know," Hector cut him off.

They stared at each other. They both knew the risks Sadie took and they both knew the guts she displayed by taking them, even if she didn't do it well.

"Does she know about her mother?" Eddie asked.

"Doubtful."

Eddie stared at Hector a beat and then said on a sigh, "Townsend's a piece of shit."

Hector took another shot of Jack and didn't reply. There was nothing to be said. Seth Townsend was definitely a piece of shit.

The silence stretched.

Then Hector said quietly, "Heard about Zano's visit to Balducci."

The air in the room went on alert.

"What'd you hear?" Eddie asked, but he knew the answer. He'd heard about it, too.

"I heard that Marcus called in a favor. Ren Zano went for a visit. Balducci tried to avoid him. Zano was persistent. Zano reported to Marcus that Ricky had a black eye, a broken nose and what looked like fingernail scratches from his brow down his cheek," Hector answered.

Eddie waited.

Hector didn't make him wait long. "Balducci told Zano he got in a bar fight."

Eddie leaned forward. "Hector, you have to stay cool."

Hector drained the glass again, bent forward and tagged the bottle for a refill. He emptied the bottle in his glass and returned it to the floor. He leaned back and trained his eyes on his brother.

"This is not a situation where you stay cool," he said it calmly, belying his words, but there was no hidden meaning to what he'd said, and it was clear just how much he meant it.

"What's this woman to you?" Eddie asked.

"She's mine," Hector replied.

Eddie leaned back and tore his fingers through his hair, then dropped his arm.

He knew what that meant. He'd felt it too, about five minutes after he decided he'd stop at nothing to get Jet in his bed. Now he and Jet were getting married.

Eddie went on, "When you were there, did she give you more than information on her father?"

"Yes and no. She let the mask slip once. She let it slip again today, so now I know who's hidin' behind it."

"And this means?"

"This means she's mine. No one touches what's mine. And they sure as fuck don't beat her, rape her and leave her broken. Did you see her fuckin' house?"

Eddie shook his head, but he knew what Hector meant. "Lee did the walkthrough with Matt. They took pictures. He told me about it."

"I went there this afternoon. It looked like—" Hector started.

Eddie interrupted, "It looked like she fought him, used everything she had. They've got the rape kit. They've got Jack, Luke and your testimony. The doctors and nurses at the hospital. Zano'll testify, he told Marcus he would. And they've got the photos of the apartment looking like a war zone. She walks into a courtroom and the jury gets a look at her and Balducci, they'll make up their mind before the evidence is presented. According to Indy, she looks like a fuckin' fairy princess. Ricky Balducci resembles an ape. She presses charges, he's fucked."

"She refuses to talk to the police. Didn't see them at the hospital and then she was discharged and went to stay with friends. The cops followed. They were turned away at the door."

"She has to press charges."

"You don't know Sadie."

It was then Eddie asked the six million dollar question, "Do *you* know Sadie?"

"I know that whatever she has in her mind is gonna stay there. That woman has a will of steel. She had to, livin' with Townsend. When she woke up this morning, she asked to take a fuckin' walk." Hector leaned forward and shared, "You should have seen her Eddie. Covered in blood, couldn't hold herself up, arm hangin' useless, wearin' nothin' but a torn up nightgown. She wakes up from that and she asks to take a walk, says she wants to stretch her legs a bit. *Dios mio.*" Hector sat back again and muttered. "Will of fuckin' steel."

Eddie let this sink in too, but he looked pleased about it.

Finally he said, "Then we take Balducci down another way."

Hector responded immediately, "I know what way Balducci is gonna go down."

Eddie shook his head. "Lee's on it."

"There's only one way a man pays for doin' that to a woman."

Eddie leaned forward at the tone of his brother's voice. "Hector, listen to me. Lee's going to dismantle his operation. He's already workin' on it. Marcus is on board. Zano knows Sadie and he's pissed. He's going to his Uncle Vito to bring the Zanos on board. Doesn't matter. Lee and Marcus have already made it their fuckin' mission."

Hector knocked back the rest of the Jack, kept his eyes on his brother, but didn't reply.

Eddie kept trying, "Sadie's covered. The car was towed for repairs. Vance has already been in it, planted a tracking device. Tonight he's wirin' her store. When she settles, he'll do the same to wherever she stays. She'll be protected."

Hector stayed silent.

"*Mi hermano* you gotta be smart," Eddie advised.

"How smart would you be if you came home to your house a disaster, finding out Jet fought for her life before having her wrist broken, her shoulder dislocated, her ribs broken, her cheek ripped open, her eyes blackened, her nose bloodied and she'd been violated?"

Eddie pressed his lips together.

"That's what I thought," Hector finished.

Eddie didn't give up.

"Let Lee do his work. Concentrate on Sadie."

"Sadie's lost to me for now. She needs time."

Eddie's brows went up. "You're backin' off?"

"Yeah, I am. I waited before, I'll wait again. This time she has a deadline. I'm givin' her a month."

At that, Eddie smiled.

Then he said, "Okay, then. Promise me you'll work with Lee."

"I'm not working with Lee, but I'll talk to him. He's not heading this operation, I am. Lee, Marcus and Zano want in, I'm good with that. But when Ricky Balducci goes down, I want him to know I brought him down. I want him to know why. And I want to make the fuck sure he *stays* down."

Eddie sat back and nodded.

Then he said, "You know I'll do—"

Hector broke in with a warning. "I don't intend to play clean."

Eddie's black eyes turned glittery. "Like I was sayin', you know I'll do what you need me to do."

It was Hector's turn to smile.

# Chapter 4

# Hash Marks

*Sadie*

*One month later...*

"Ralphie, get away from the window," Buddy ordered.

I lifted my head to see Ralphie holding the curtain wide and standing, bold as you please, staring out the window.

"It's Hispanic Hottie this time," Ralphie informed us, and then Buddy and I watched him wave.

Oh my.

"Hispanic Hottie" meant Hector was sitting outside in a brown, old model Ford Bronco, probably drinking coffee. I could visualize Hector lifting his chin at Ralphie's wave. I could visualize it because I'd seen it before, several times.

Sometimes Ralphie would even make a pot of coffee and walk out to Hector's Bronco to give him a warm up, carrying milk and sugar. Ralphie informed me Hector took a splash of milk and one sugar, like this was information which I could impart on Saint Peter and he would lead me straight through the Pearly Gates to the right hand of God. I'd only watched Ralphie's "Alice the Waitress" impersonation once, doing it while peeking through the curtains. I saw Hector get out of the Bronco, close the door and lean against it while Ralphie poured him coffee and chattered away.

I also saw Hector's amused yet glamorous smile (yes, I could see it, clear as day, from all the way across the road; it was hard to miss).

I'd never looked again.

My eyes moved to the blackboard that was on the wall by the window. Ralphie put it there weeks ago. On it was a list of names and next to the names there were hash marks. Once I started getting visitors on a regular basis, visitors that came in the evenings when I was home, stayed from thirty minutes to over a couple of hours and never came to the door, Ralphie decided it would be fun to keep track.

The list included "Hawaiian Hottie" (that was Kai Mason), "Just Plain Old Hot Hottie" (that was Luke Stark), "Alaskan Hottie" (that was some big blond guy, named thus because Ralphie said he looked like he could fell a tree by blowing on it and only men from Alaska could do that kind of thing), "Surfer Dude Hottie" (that was a smaller guy with real sun-streaked hair), "African-American Hottie" (that was a black man with twists in his hair) and "Native American Hottie" (that was, well, a native American hottie; or another one of Lee's men whose romance had been reported in the papers, Vance Crowe).

By far and away, Hector had the most hash marks.

I twisted my head to look up at Buddy. He looked down at me and grinned. I shook my head.

Then I gave up on Ralphie and settled back in. I was snuggled up to Buddy on the couch, lying curled in a fetal position, my head on his thigh.

It was Saturday evening and we were in the throes of a *Veronica Mars* marathon (season two DVD). I decided that when I left "Ms. Townsend, Ice Princess" behind, the New Sadie was going to be like Veronica Mars. She was plucky, cute as a button and she had a smart mouth.

I figured, given some practice, I could be plucky and cute and have a smart mouth.

In life, I learned, given enough practice, I could do anything.

⚜

It had been one month and two days since I'd been raped by Ricky Balducci.

Never in my life had so much happened in one month and two days.

Never in my life had most of it been so good.

First of all, Ralphie and Buddy installed me in the guest bedroom of their brownstone.

When I got there, Buddy made me do three days of complete bed rest. They brought me food and fawned over me like I was a true life princess. Buddy even helped me shower, and when I got embarrassed he said, "I'm gay and a nurse, I wipe people's asses for a living. Do you think this fazes me?"

I got over being embarrassed after he said that.

I didn't go back to work for two and a half weeks. By the time I did, the bruises and swelling had gone and most of the cuts were disappearing.

In that time Buddy and Ralphie went to my apartment. They cleaned it up and packed me up. Everything I could want or need was brought to the brownstone and moved in, making the guestroom less of a guestroom and more *my* room. They also arranged some of my stuff around the house, making the house less Ralphie and Buddy's house and more *our* house.

Everything else I owned was put in storage.

Then Buddy called a real estate agent friend of his and put my place on the market. Without asking me and without me telling them what happened, they decided the memories there were too bad for me to go back. I would get a new place in what they referred to as an indefinite, "Later, when you're ready," and I would stay with them in the meantime.

I didn't quibble.

For starters, I didn't particularly want to go back to my apartment. But also, it felt nice having someone take care of me. No one had taken care of me since I was eleven years old and I liked it. I liked it enough just to let it happen.

So I did.

⚑

About a week after I moved in with them, the doorbell rang. Buddy answered it and came back with a short, heavyset lady with spiky, salt and pepper hair and clear blue eyes.

Buddy introduced her as his lesbian friend, Bex. After I shook her hand, Buddy informed me Bex was a counselor at a rape crisis center.

Then Buddy and Ralphie left me with Bex, going, they said, to get Chinese takeout.

At first I was angry. Then I was scared. But Bex talked to me about my gallery, about Buddy and Ralphie, about my shoes, about season tickets for the Colorado Shakespeare Festival in Boulder, about loads of things. But not about me getting raped.

An hour slid by before Buddy and Ralphie returned, and I realized, only at the end right before she left when she handed me her card and told me to call her anytime, that I liked her.

It took me another week to call her. She's come to visit me twice. She's lovely.

By the time Bex came around, we'd already had the parade of hotties sitting outside the brownstone guarding the door, keeping me safe, and Ralphie had put up the blackboard.

I was ignoring the parade of hotties and what that might mean.

Ralphie and Buddy didn't ignore it. They thought it was *very* interesting and would talk about it all the time.

I didn't participate in their discussions. That would defeat my efforts at ignoring it, which, come hell or high water, was exactly what I was going to do.

Eventually, they'd go away.

Right?

<hr>

By the time I went back to work, Ralphie and Buddy had showed me how to check the Ice Princess at the door.

I'd never been in a house filled with love.

In the beginning it made me uncomfortable because I felt like I was weird. They were so at ease with each other; affectionate, relaxed, calling each other nicknames, doing things that showed they cared.

It was bizarre.

They also did it with me.

There was no personal space in Buddy and Ralphie's house. You cuddled on the couch. You kissed cheeks when you walked in the door from work. You left notes when you were going out, making sure you gave details about when you'd be home.

Ralphie brought up my coffee in the morning. He pushed me aside in bed, sat in it with long legs stretched out, back to the headboard and gabbed about everything while I sipped my coffee and slowly came awake.

While I watched TV, Buddy forced me to sit on the floor between his spread legs and gave me head massages (he said he loved my hair).

They bickered about who was going to make dinner (why, I didn't know, considering Buddy did all the cooking) and they nagged about whose turn it was to take out the garbage. I'd always thought "bickering" and "nagging" were ugly words, but the way Ralphie and Buddy did them, they were sweet.

I tried to give the cold shoulder, indicate I needed my personal space (especially then), but they wore me down.

It took about five days.

              ⌖

My second day back at work, the door opened and the Rock Chicks came in.

All of them except Daisy, but including Shirleen Jackson.

I stared in horror.

With no sign of an arctic glare, Ally smiled, waved and said, "Hey, Sadie."

Like I was actually A Sadie, not A Ms. Townsend.

I tell you, it was bizarre.

They all introduced themselves to me and Ralphie while Ralphie stared at them like they were from another planet. He did this mainly because they were all gorgeous and they were so damned friendly it was unreal.

There was Indy, Ally and Stella, but also ladies named Jet, Roxie, Ava, Annette and, of course, Shirleen.

After a while, Ralphie started staring at *me* like I was from another planet because I went Queen Ice.

I didn't know what was going on, but I didn't like it and I didn't want any part of it. But there was no way I could ignore it when it was in my own fucking gallery.

Therefore, the Ice Princess clicked into place.

The Rock Chicks were oblivious to my wintry demeanor, chatting away with Ralphie and me like we did it every day.

Eventually Shirleen broke off and wandered the gallery shouting out, "Oowee," this and "Oowee," that, and finally stopped in front of a painting Ralphie and I'd had hanging for three months without a single nibble of interest.

"I gotta have me *that!*" Shirleen called across the gallery. She turned to Jet who was closest to her. "Wouldn't that look good in my rec room?"

I looked at the painting. It was a canvass painted entirely in purple. Just purple. Most people thought it was just canvass painted purple, therefore no nibbles. It was a beautiful purple though, and I loved it.

I wasn't certain sure it was "rec room" material, however.

"It's perfect," Jet agreed.

Shirleen looked in my direction. "I'll take it."

Ralphie swooped down on Shirleen in an instant and snatched her credit card out of her hand before she'd cleared it from her purse.

"I'll get my boys, Roam and Sniff, to come and get it," she told us, leaning against my counter.

"We have a delivery service," Ralphie informed her while I was wondering who in their right mind would name their children Roam and Sniff.

"No, Roam's drivin' now. He needs practice negotiating downtown. I'll give him the Navigator. He'll do just about anything to drive the Navigator," Shirleen replied.

"They're street names," Indy muttered to me under her breath.

I turned my eyes to her. "Sorry?"

"Roam and Sniff. They're street names. Shirleen is their foster carer. They were runaways," Indy explained.

Something about this hit me somewhere deep. I tried to entertain the idea of my father seeing the error of his ways, giving up the drug world, going to work for a private investigator and taking in runaways like Shirleen.

It almost made me want to laugh. I did not, of course, laugh.

Instead, my eyes went glacial like she'd imparted information on me which I found highly uninteresting and I said, "Oh." Then I turned to Ralphie and announced, "I'm going to The Market, getting us coffees."

Ralphie's eyes were startled when he looked at me, and I could tell he was shocked at how rude I was being.

He glanced around the girls and then said hesitantly, "Okay, sweet 'ums."

Without a backward glance, I left.

When I returned with the coffees, the Rock Chicks were gone and Ralphie gave me the third degree. I deflected the third degree until that evening, when Ralphie enlisted Buddy and they ganged up on me. They did this with the addition of lemon drops, which we drank sitting on stools around their kitchen island (they had a fabulous kitchen, all chrome and gleaming black cabinets and granite countertops; it was Buddy's domain, he cooked like a dream).

I held out, for a while.

But lemon drops always did me in, eventually.

After around lemon drop three, I told them about my dad. A few sips into lemon drop four, I told them about my mom. Sucking back lemon drop five, I told them about Hector and added on what I knew about the Rock Chicks, the Nightingale Men, and the cherry on top was my history with

Daisy. During lemon drop six, I shared what happened when Ricky Balducci broke into my apartment. We were all crying by this time, me uncontrollably, so it was uncertain how much they understood because I didn't figure I was making much sense.

Ralphie slept with me in my bed that night, holding me close all the night through, and the next three days he didn't leave my side.

It was somewhere at the end of day three when I was sitting in between them on the couch and Ralphie had pulled up my feet and was massaging them, and Buddy had pulled my head onto his shoulder, and I was super comfy that I realized I had my first, genuine friends.

They liked me. *Me*, Sadie—whoever she was. But whoever they thought she was, they liked her.

They didn't take. They just gave and expected nothing back.

That night they'd introduced me to plucky, cute, smart-mouthed Veronica Mars.

Veronica was in the middle of some elaborate scheme involving a wunderkind schoolmate who knew everything about computers, and they were going to blow the lid off some big mystery involving mostly high school students when I whispered, "Thank you guys."

Neither Buddy nor Ralphie responded, but Ralphie gave my feet a long squeeze and Buddy sighed.

The next day, Indy, Ally and Roxie came back without the rest of the Rock Chicks, and they brought coffee. They told me the coffees at The Market were nothing compared to what Indy's barista, the guy who worked the espresso machine at her bookstore (they referred to him as "Tex"), could make. They told me Ralphie and I could come to the bookstore anytime and Tex would make us the special on the house.

This time they didn't chat or buy three hundred dollar purple paintings. They just left the coffees for me and Ralphie, smiled and left.

"I think—" Ralphie started, eyes still on the door after they left.

"Don't start," I interrupted him.

Ralphie snapped his mouth shut. He looked peeved, took a sip of his coffee and then his eyes bugged out.

"My *God*. This is fab-you-*las*," he exclaimed, staring at his white paper cup.

I took a sip of mine and my eyes bugged out, too.

He was absolutely right.

⌖

Several days later, Marcus Sloan walked into Art.

Ralphie was installing a painting at someone's house, so I was, for the first time since The Ricky Incident, alone.

This stunk. I didn't want to be alone, and Ralphie *really* didn't want me to be alone, but I had to get on with my life eventually, so I encouraged him to go.

I was doing okay until Marcus came in.

Being alone was one thing but I didn't want to be alone with Marcus Sloan.

⌖

I knew that I couldn't lean on Buddy and Ralphie forever. Eventually I had to pick up the threads of my life, find my own place and learn to take care of myself again.

I'd heard nothing from Ricky or any of his crazy brothers. I didn't press charges because I was my father's daughter. When you were down and you found an advantage, you didn't squander it. You waited and used it when the time was right.

Rape was a felony. If found guilty Ricky would go to prison. I knew I could press charges and I knew I'd win. And I had time. There was a statute of limitations, but by then I was hoping the Balduccis would have moved on to new prey. In the meantime, they knew I could go to the police anytime and cause Ricky, and all the Balduccis, a world of hurt.

I had one card to play and I wasn't going to play it too soon. If I brought down Ricky, I had three more brothers who could come after me. Right now he was Top Dog. I didn't need another Balducci dog after me, putting in his bid to make me his prize.

If I kept my card, they all had to sit back and wait for me to play it. In the meantime, they could concentrate on tearing each other apart.

At least, this was what I told myself.

However, telling Ralphie and Buddy about it and talking with Bex was one thing. Facing Ricky Balducci again was another. I wasn't ready for that.

I knew it made me look like a wimp, but I could live with that. I was holding it together. Seeing Ricky might make it come flying apart.

I'd put it together once, with the help of Ralphie and Buddy, but I knew I couldn't do it again.

※

Marcus walked up to me at the counter and smiled.

"Sadie," he greeted me softly.

I just stopped myself from putting my hand to the bandage that, at that point, Buddy still put on my face in the mornings to hide the healing cut.

I didn't need the bandage anymore, but I wasn't ready to go out in public with my scar on display. That would take another few days and another night of lemon drops for Buddy and Ralphie to get me to give up what they called "The Bandage Crutch".

"Sweetheart, you're gorgeous. You'll always *be* gorgeous. Trust me," Buddy had said.

It took a while, but I trusted him. People looked but they didn't say anything, and I knew I'd get used to it with enough practice.

Instead, I looked coolly at Marcus Sloan, who I'd always thought was handsome. Daisy chose well. Marcus was a colleague of my father's and I knew he wasn't clean, but I also knew he was nowhere near as dirty as my father.

"Marcus," I replied.

"You're..." he hesitated, "well?"

"Never better," I informed him and I saw his eyes flash in response.

He didn't hide it and he didn't let my flippant answer put him off.

"How's business?" he asked.

"Excellent," I replied in a tone that didn't invite further discourse.

Marcus watched me for several seconds, his eyes giving me the impression that he missed nothing, and furthermore, I wasn't fooling him. Then he nodded and started to wander the gallery as if he had all day to peruse my wares.

I watched him.

"Are you here alone?" Marcus asked from across the gallery, his eyes on a display of exquisite glass paperweights.

"Yes," I answered and kept my eyes on him.

He picked up a paperweight. "Is that wise?" Marcus asked quietly, study-ing the paperweight.

The reminder that he knew about what happened to me and the indica-tion that he cared that I might not be safe made my heart lurch.

I ignored it.

"Ralphie will be back in ten minutes," I told him. I didn't know why I was forthcoming with that information but I was.

"Good," Marcus responded. He put the paperweight down and continued to wander the store.

He didn't speak again until he went back to the paperweight. He picked it up and brought it to the counter.

"Can you gift wrap that for Daisy?" he requested.

"Certainly," I replied and then busied myself with the invoice, his credit card and the gift wrap.

He was silent until I started to put the finishing touches on the bow. My gift wrap was a matte pistachio green, ultra-thick paper. The inside was a sump-tuous, opalescent cream. And the bow was powder blue organdie. It was Art's signature wrap and I thought it was lush.

"You should know, I never told Daisy you came to see her or called her after Nanette's party," Marcus said.

My head came up and I almost (but still managed it) couldn't hide my surprise.

His eyes locked with mine. "She knows now," he went on.

"Is that so?" I asked with sham fascination, but my heart was beating in my chest.

"She's not happy I kept it from her," Marcus explained.

I just stared at him.

"She had a tough time in that social circle. You were the only one she liked. When you were gone, she missed you."

My stomach clutched. Painfully.

I didn't let it show. Instead, I put his wrapped box in a powder blue bag with the word "Art" in fancy pistachio script on the side, the handles made of pistachio satin ribbon, and I handed it to him.

The door opened and Ralphie walked in. Marcus looked at Ralphie, nod-ded then took the bag.

His eyes came back to mine. "She still misses you," he finished.

Then he was gone.

It wasn't until a few days later I realized that even though I knew, after watching hundreds of customers make hundreds of decisions about hundreds of purchases, Marcus had decided what he wanted the minute he picked up the paperweight, but he still stayed until Ralphie returned.

Now, how bizarre was *that?*

꿈

"What are you doing?" Buddy asked Ralphie as I watched Veronica Mars mouth off to her father (but in a plucky, cute as a button kind of way).

I lifted my head again and looked at Ralphie, who was still at the window.

"Nothing," Ralphie replied.

I put my head back on Buddy's thigh as Buddy muttered under his breath, "Jesus."

My mind was occupied with Veronica's episode-to-episode dilemma.

See, Veronica was torn between Duncan, the high school class president good boy, and Logan, the high school ne'er-do-well bad boy. Personally, I was kind of rooting for the bad boy because he was great at delivering a one-liner. However, the good boy was so sweet. The wildcard was Weevil, the leader of a high school, car-stealing, Hispanic, biker gang. I thought Veronica had good chemistry with Weevil, and Weevil had great eyelashes and fantastic tattoos.

Therefore, my mind on Duncan, Logan and especially Weevil, I didn't have time for Ralphie's antics.

I heard, but didn't pay much attention to, Ralphie leaving the room.

I heard, but didn't pay much attention to, Ralphie opening the front door.

Lastly, I heard, but didn't pay much attention to the murmur of male voices. Ralphie and Buddy had a big gay posse, and this gay posse showed up loads. Usually this degenerated into copious French martinis or lemon drops or cosmos and impromptu viewings of *Auntie Mame* (the Rosalind Russell version, *not* the Lucille Ball version) or *Steel Magnolias*.

Alternately, this could degenerate into a round of arm wrestling.

It was anything goes at Ralphie and Buddy's house.

"Look who finally came in from the cold," Ralphie announced, and my head came up when Buddy muttered, a lot louder this time, "Jesus."

I stared, mouth open and everything, at Hector "Oh my God" Chavez, standing in Buddy and Ralphie's living room.

He was wearing jeans, black boots, a flannel shirt (untucked), and you could see his white t-shirt at the open collar. His thick, black hair needed cutting and he needed a shave.

He'd never looked better.

I kept staring as Buddy gently pulled me up to a seated position, then stood up slowly as Ralphie started the introductions.

"I'm Ralphie, and this is my lover, Buddy, and I think you know Sadie," Ralphie said as I reluctantly got to my feet.

Hector had a small grin playing at his mouth. He shook a smiling Ralphie's hand. Then he shook a frowning Buddy's hand. Then his eyes cut to me.

I'd checked the Ice Princess at the door. She wasn't allowed in, not to Buddy and Ralphie's house.

What did I do now?

I didn't have a chance to figure it out.

Hector moved, came right to me, right in my space. One of his arms slid around my waist. He pulled me to his warm body, gave me a gentle squeeze and he kissed my temple.

That's right. *He kissed my temple.*

"Sadie," he said against my temple.

I tilted my head back and stared at him.

I couldn't speak. At least my mouth was no longer hanging open; for that I could be grateful.

While Hector looked down at me and I stared up at him silent, Ralphie decided to speak.

"Sadie, what's the matter with you? Hispanic Hottie has been out with his posse of cute boys, warning off the bad guys for *weeks,* and now he's in here and you have your chance to say thank you and you're silent as a ghost," Ralphie snapped.

"Ralphie—" Buddy said warningly.

Hector moved to my side, close to my side, and he looked down at me.

"Hispanic Hottie?" he asked, brows raised and lips still struggling to hold back a grin.

Oh my God. I wanted to die. Go live with the doves and the angels and leave this world forever.

Instead, my eyes sliced to Ralphie and they narrowed. Ralphie ignored my narrowed eyes.

"I know!" Ralphie exclaimed. "We'll have a drink and all watch Veronica Mars. I think in the next episode she gets roughed up in a pool hall. Anyone would need a drink while watching *that*."

I didn't want to have a drink while watching Veronica Mars with Hector "Oh my God" Chavez. I wanted Hector to disappear in a puff of smoke, and then I wanted to give Ralphie what for.

Hector didn't disappear in a puff of smoke. Instead, he said, "That'd be good."

My heart sank. Ralphie clapped in delight and grabbed Buddy, who was still frowning, and dragged him from the room.

"What should we do? Martinis? Margaritas? I know! Beer!" I heard Ralphie say as he and Buddy disappeared into the kitchen.

I stood frozen to the spot, staring in the direction of the kitchen and wondering what the heck to do.

Hector's flannel shirt filled my eyesight and I began to panic.

I wasn't me. I was kind of Sadie-in-the-making when I was in Buddy and Ralphie's house. Therefore, I didn't have my armor.

I wasn't wearing head-to-toe designer. I was wearing faded jeans and one of Buddy's hooded sweatshirts and it was huge on me. I didn't have on my Manolos or Jimmy Choos, giving me four inch heels and a little height. I was barefoot, French pedicured toes on full display. My hair wasn't arranged perfectly. It was pulled up in a messy knot at the crown of my head.

At least I still had on my makeup from working at the gallery all day, thank God.

"Sadie," Hector called, breaking into my frenzied thoughts about my appearance, and further, what *he'd* think about my appearance.

My eyes traveled up his shirt, the column of his brown throat, past his strong chin and his full lips to his black eyes. My heart skipped when I saw what was in his dark eyes.

Oh darn.

"How you doin'?" he asked softly.

"I'm fine," I answered immediately.

His eyes flared with annoyance, and without hesitation he got in my space.

And *then* (no kidding) his hand came to my jaw, and his thumb trailed across the cut on my cheek (it was fading, very, very slowly, but it was still there and would be there until I made an appointment with the plastic surgeon).

I held my breath while he watched his thumb trace the scar, then his palm moved along my cheek. His fingers slid into the hair at the side of my head and his hand cupped me behind my ear.

His eyes came back to mine.

"*Mamita*, I asked, how are you doing?" Hector repeated, his voice was calm, but he was enunciating his words clearly, indicating he cared about my response. And further, I better not try to blow him off again because he wasn't going to like it.

I hesitated then, do not ask me why, I whispered, "Better."

It was then, close up, I saw his eyes get warm, and my stomach pitched at the sight.

Right after that, still standing frozen, Hector close, totally in my space, hand still in my hair, I watched his head start to tilt down.

"I've got *the best* idea!" Ralphie shouted from the door. Then he said, "Oh no. Sorry."

Hector's eyes closed with what appeared to be frustration (I swear to *God*). He dropped his hand and stepped to my side again.

"Do you, um… want me to come back?" Ralphie asked.

"No!" I cried instantly, sharply, and maybe a little loudly.

Ralphie looked at me, eyes narrowed. After a second though, they cleared and he smiled like he was really happy about something.

"Well, Buddy's in the kitchen, grating cheese like a grating fool. We've decided to do nachos." Ralphie's gaze moved to Hector and he informed him, "It's the food of your people."

I closed my eyes.

Someone, please tell me that Ralphie did *not* just tell Hector that nachos were the food of his people.

While I was devising the lecture on cultural awareness I was going to deliver to Ralphie the minute Hector left, I heard Hector's soft laughter.

My eyes opened again and I saw Ralphie forge into the room.

"I have to go get sour cream. You," Ralphie pointed to me, "need to go smush up avocado for the guacamole. And you," Ralphie's pointed finger moved to Hector, "need to get yourself a beer. It's stressful doing stakeouts. I should know. I've stalked my fair share of lying, cheating, no-good boyfriends. The bastards."

Then, after sharing this morsel, Ralphie hurried out in search of sour cream.

We heard the door slam behind Ralphie and I stood there, unsure of what to do, and wondering how rude it would seem if I ran upstairs, locked my bedroom door and barricaded myself in the closet.

"Sadie——" Hector started.

"Am I going to get help with this guac or what?" Buddy shouted from the kitchen.

I took a deep breath and looked up at Hector. "I need to go smush avocado," I told him, feeling like an idiot.

At my words he smiled at me, slow, amused and glamorous and I didn't feel like an idiot anymore.

⋈

It happened after nachos and beer. After Veronica got roughed up by the evil Fitzpatrick clan at the pool hall. After I took the nacho platter and plates back to the kitchen and came back with more beer for everyone. After, when I came back, I saw that Ralphie had affected a seating jumble which meant Buddy was in the armchair where I'd been sitting and the only place for me to settle was between Ralphie and Hector on the couch. After Buddy gave me an "I'm sorry but life will be hell if Ralphie doesn't get his way" look.

It was in the middle of Veronica instigating an ingenious plan to foil new baddies when Ralphie leaned forward, shoved his arm under my knees and yanked up my calves, pulling my feet into my lap.

This meant my body twisted and my shoulder collided with Hector's side. Hector had, for the sake of comfort on the smallish couch (this was what I told myself for my peace of mind) put his arm along the back of the couch (an arm I felt there like it was a snake coiled to strike).

I put my still casted wrist into the cushion by Hector's hip and turned to glare at Ralphie.

"What are you doing?" I snapped.

"Foot massage," Ralphie replied, eyes on the TV screen, his hands on my feet starting to massage.

I pulled my feet away. "I don't want a foot massage."

Ralphie grabbed my ankles in a firm hold and tugged them back into his lap, a move that made me collide with Hector's side again.

I leaned away from Hector as Ralphie said, "Everyone wants a foot massage."

"Well, I don't," I returned.

"You do," Ralphie shot back.

"I don't," I snapped.

Ralphie's eyes swung from Veronica to me. "You *do*."

Ralphie and I went into a stare down, a stare down I was going to win if it killed me.

I could snuggle up to Buddy on one side of the couch while Ralphie massaged my feet on the other side. I was never, no way, going to lean into Hector (which was my only choice) while Ralphie massaged my feet.

Never.

The stare down lasted until (seriously, no kidding), Hector's arm circled my shoulders. He put pressure there, my elbow buckled and he pulled me into his side.

I tilted my head back. "Now, what are *you* doing?" I asked.

Hector looked down at me and said, "Relax."

"I'm uncomfortable," I replied.

He smiled at me. I stared at him. Not a stare down stare, but a fascinated one.

I thought about it for a nanosecond and then I gave in. I'd look like a fool if I kept fighting.

I could deal with this. I'd dealt with worse, *loads* worse. After Hector left, I'd give Ralphie a piece of my mind so he understood *exactly* where I stood on the issue of Hector.

I glanced over at Buddy to see if I might have some support, but Buddy was watching Hector. Finally his eyes slid to me. He gave me a wink then he went back to Veronica.

No support from Buddy then.

I sat there, Ralphie massaging my feet, and I glared at the TV screen, willing Veronica to take me away.

After a while, Hector's fingers started to make lazy circles on my shoulder.

That felt nice, sweet and lovely.

Darn it all to hell.

Fine. I could deal with that, too.

I focused on Veronica. Veronica and me, we could make it through. We always got away unscathed or, well… if not unscathed, at least still breathing.

I settled into Hector and Ralphie kept massaging my feet.

Veronica Mars, plucky, high school girl detective only had three seasons. It might last a while, but eventually, it would be over.

❧

I opened my eyes and saw nothing but flannel shirt.

My senses came to and I realized that I didn't hear Veronica's smart mouth. I heard a sports commentator talking about a game. I didn't feel my feet in Ralphie's lap. I didn't feel Ralphie at all. Someone had switched off all the lights in the room except one, which meant that only a soft glow came from a beautiful Restoration Hardware floor lamp across the room.

I was no longer curled into Hector's side and Hector was no longer sitting on the couch.

Instead, my torso was mostly pressed into Hector. My head was resting on his chest, my arm was wrapped around his middle and Hector was reclined back on a diagonal, his feet up on the coffee table.

Oh my.

I tilted my head to look at the armchair. Buddy was gone.

I slid my cheek against Hector's soft shirt and looked up at him.

He was lounging, asleep, head resting on the back of the couch, arm around me curled at my waist, hand resting gently on my hip.

My sleepy mind whirled and I realized I knew how it happened.

No one could get a foot massage from Ralphie (he gave good foot massages) while leaning into Hector's immense, comforting heat and not fall asleep. Even when Veronica Mars was solving the mystery of the lost proceeds for the Senior Trip that were stolen from the school's Winter Carnival.

No one.

Now, how did I get out of *this* predicament?

I decided I would scoot away and leave him there. He looked comfortable enough. I'd escape upstairs and sleep in the next morning, sleep in until I knew for certain sure Hector was gone.

Though, before I left, I'd put a blanket over him, just in case he got cold.

I took my eyes from him and cautiously edged away, lifting myself up and pulling my arm from around his abs.

His hand went from relaxed and resting, to tight and firm on my hip.

I angled my head to look at him and found, in my movements, I'd brought my face closer to his.

I noticed immediately he wasn't asleep anymore. His eyes were open and he was looking at me.

Darn.

Before I could think (and thus stop myself from speaking), I whispered, "I didn't mean to wake you."

Then I watched close up as his face warmed. It warmed in a way I'd seen it warm before. The way it warmed that night in my father's study when I was sliding my hands up his chest and around his neck right before I asked him to kiss me.

I stopped breathing.

He kept looking at me, and I felt a weird sensation that I knew was complete and utter fear, mingled bizarrely with the barest hint of anticipation.

His gaze dropped to my mouth.

My mouth went dry.

The anticipation fled, the fear took hold and I started to panic.

I was about to push away, run away, get out of there as fast as my French pedicure toe-nailed feet would take me when his fingers at my hip flexed, and I fought through the fear and focused on him again.

"I need to get home," he said softly.

At his words, the panic disappeared and relief filled me.

I nodded. He did an ab curl, pulling up, taking me with him until he was on his feet and he planted me on mine, right in front of him.

Then, before I could move away, he grabbed my hand and I had no choice but to walk him to the door.

He stopped there, hand still in mine, body so close I could feel his heat, and he looked down at me.

"I go out, I wait until I hear you lock the door," he informed me.

I nodded again.

Then he went on, "Tomorrow night, I'll be back. Seven o'clock. I'm taking you to dinner."

The panic came back and my mouth dropped open. Hector "Oh my God" Chavez wanted to take me out to dinner?

How bizarre was *that?*

My mind scrambled for an excuse and, thankfully, I had one.

"I can't. Buddy and Ralphie and I have plans," I told him and it wasn't a lie. We were going out to dinner and they were taking me to a drag show afterwards. They'd decided, after all that was my life, it was high time for me to start having fun.

"Then Monday. I'll be here at seven," Hector replied immediately, and I opened my mouth to speak but he lifted the other hand, the one not holding mine (still!) and put his finger to my upper lip.

I stopped breathing again.

He took his finger away. "It'll be casual. There'll be no reason to put on your designer armor."

Oh my God!

He knew about my armor! He even said it, straight out!

How did he know?

Oh... my... *God!*

Before I could figure it out or ask or get over my panic attack, he murmured, "Monday. Seven."

Then he squeezed my hand and he was gone.

I stared at the door for what seemed like forever and, finally, from outside I heard Hector's voice say sharply, "Lock."

I jumped to the door and threw the lock.

I put my ear to it and heard his boots on the steps outside, and I stayed there even when I could hear them no more. After a while, I turned toward the stairs and came to a jarring halt when I saw Ralphie sitting on one of them looking at me.

"How long have you been sitting there?" I breathed.

"Was up on the landing, listening to him ask you out. Came down after he left," Ralphie replied.

"Ralphie, we need to talk about—"

"If you think we need to talk about how you don't want anything to do with Hispanic Hottie, then you need to think again, sweet 'ums."

"Ralphie—"

"I don't want to hear it."

"Ralphie!"

He stood and looked down at me. "You deserve your little slice of happiness. You've waited long enough for it and worked hard enough to earn it and I'm gonna see you get it."

Before I could protest, he turned and walked up the stairs.

I closed my eyes and took a deep breath.

Darn.

# Chapter 5

# Screaming Orgasm

---

### *Sadie*

"We are not watching YoYo," Buddy snapped at Ralphie as he opened the door to the gay bar on Colfax and stepped back to let me precede him.

"We are so watching YoYo," Ralphie snapped back, getting up close to me, putting his hands to my waist and crowding in behind me, shoving me through the door.

"No YoYo," Buddy returned.

"Oh so YoYo," Ralphie shot back.

I started giggling.

They were arguing about watching Bex's black pug, YoYo. She was going on vacation and needed someone to look after her dog. Bex had brought her around that day so we could meet her.

Buddy didn't like dogs, but on sight, Ralphie and I fell in love with the snorting, wheezing, teeny-tiny, squirming, adorable pug.

"We watch YoYo, you're gonna start in on me about getting a damn dog again and I've made myself clear on this subject about a million times," Buddy replied.

"Excuse me, but *I* can't wear the cute doggie sweaters I bought online. We *have* to get a dog so I can dress her up in those sweaters," Ralphie threw in.

"I told you not to buy those sweaters. Why would anyone buy doggie sweaters when they don't have a dog?" Buddy was losing patience.

"I *love* dogs. I'm always telling you a house isn't a home without a pet. And anyway, I'm Queen Accoutrement, Expert at All Things Accessory. I *need* a dog. Dogs are the end all, be all, new, hip accessory." Ralphie didn't care that Buddy was losing patience (he never did).

They were now both behind me, propelling me forward, and I was laughing straight out.

That was until my eyes adjusted to the dark light of the bar and I saw front and center, at a bunch of tables pushed together, all the Rock Chicks. Every one of them. Including a black-haired lady I hadn't met.

And also including Daisy.

I stopped dead and the smile disappeared from my face.

Ralphie ran into me and said, "Sadie, sweets, get a move on, I need a cocktail."

I didn't get a move on. I stood rooted to the spot, staring at the Rock Chicks.

Then it hit me. They hadn't seen me yet so I still had a chance to escape!

I was about to whirl when my eyes caught on something all the way across the bar.

Lounging, shoulders against the wall, was Lee Nightingale. Next to him, at first horrified glance, I thought was Hector. Staring in shock, I realized it wasn't. It was someone who looked like Hector, but was just a shade less rough around the edges. By the look of him he had to be related to Hector, however. There was no way they weren't blood.

The Rock Chicks hadn't seen me, but Lee and his companion most definitely did. Both of their eyes were locked on me, and after a second Lee started to push away from the wall.

I decided it was time to go.

I whirled. "We have to go," I said to Buddy and Ralphie.

They were both stopped just inside the door, looking down at me, and I saw the surprise hit their faces.

"Go? Why? We just got here," Ralphie said.

I put my hand to his chest and leaned in. "We have to go. Now. Just go."

Ralphie resisted the lean, his eyes scanning the bar as Buddy asked me, "Are you okay?"

No, I wasn't okay. But I wasn't going to explain it, not now. Maybe I'd do it later, like tomorrow or, say, when I *could* explain it (which might be never).

I knew the moment Ralphie saw the Rock Chicks. His face registered recognition, he smiled over my shoulder and waved.

I grabbed his wrist and pulled his hand down. "Don't do that! Turn around and go!"

"What's goin' on?" Buddy asked.

"We are *not* going," Ralphie said to me, his voice telling me he was digging deep into his battle trenches. And when Ralphie dug in, Ms. Townsend, Ice Princess or even Sorceress of the Antarctic would never win the battle.

"What's goin' on?" Buddy repeated.

I didn't give up. No, actually, I couldn't give up. Too much was at stake.

"We're going," I said to Ralphie.

"Are not," Ralphie returned.

"Are so."

"Are not."

"We're going!" I yelled.

"What's goin' on!" Buddy shouted.

"Sadie," Lee Nightingale said.

I looked to my left, then up, and saw Lee standing there.

Someone, please tell me Lee was not standing there.

Someone else, please tell me that Had-to-Be-Hector's-Relative was not standing beside him.

This *stunk*.

I dropped Ralphie's wrist and turned to Lee.

Luckily, I wasn't casual, barefoot and in a huge sweatshirt. I had on my armor. A bone-colored, pencil skirt, a matching, fitted, silk-knit turtleneck and a pair of lush, beige, spike-heeled Jimmy Choo boots. My hair was pulled severely away from my face, but burst in a riot of waves and curls from the clip at my neck. I had a thick, heavy, pure gold bangle at my wrist and long, wide, gold hoops at my ears.

Barring the cast on my wrist it was *the* Ice Princess Outfit to end *all* Ice Princess Outfits.

Therefore, as I was unsuccessful at avoiding it, when the time arrived, I was ready.

"Lee," I said, assuming Chill Factor Sub-Zero.

Lee ignored the Chill Factor Sub-Zero. Something, by the way, which was happening all the time these days, and it was beginning to get on my nerves.

"How are you?" Lee asked, his voice not professional or cordial, but warm and genuine.

"I'd be a lot better if people would stop asking me how I was," I replied immediately and icily. "I got raped. Unfortunately, it happens every day."

"Sadie!" Ralphie hissed angrily from beside me as I watched Lee flinch.

He actually flinched, like I'd slapped him across the face. Which, verbally, I had.

I was *such* a bitch.

My stomach clutched and if I didn't get away I was going to start crying. And *that* could *not* happen.

I turned to Ralphie and announced, "I need a drink."

Ralphie was having none of it.

He switched on the attitude, complete with hand on hip and clipped, "What you need to do is apologize to Mr. Hot Guy here."

I glared ice daggers at Ralphie, but he didn't back down.

"Fine," I declared, giving up in order to get away. "I'll get my own fucking drink."

Then, without looking at Lee or Hector-Relative-Guy, with back straight and head held high, I walked to the bar.

I stopped at the bar telling myself I could do this. This was a walk in the park for me. I'd survive this and whatever next torture life had to offer me. I could survive it all.

The bartender asked me what I wanted and I told him, "Three lemon drops. No wait! Four."

I was going to double up. I'd need serious vodka flowing through my veins to get through this night. And get through the night I would.

Fuck them. Fuck them all. Fuck the world!

"What was *that* all about?" Buddy asked from beside me, and I looked at him, then over my shoulder toward the door.

Ralphie was talking to Lee and Hector-Relative-Guy, and now Indy and Daisy were with them.

Darn.

I turned back to the bar.

"That was Lee Nightingale," I informed Buddy.

"I know. After you played the screaming-bitch-from-hell and flounced away, he introduced himself," Buddy replied.

I looked at Buddy. "*The* Lee Nightingale. The one I asked to help me before I got attacked."

Buddy's face went gentle and he said, "I know who Lee Nightingale is. I remember your story, every word of it, sweetheart."

I nodded once, and, holding close to the bitch in me, I said, "Well, there you go then."

Buddy stayed silent for a second then he told me, "The man with him is Eddie Chavez, Hector's brother."

Oh, well, that was *just great*. He couldn't be a far removed cousin, *noooo*. He had to be Hector's fucking brother.

"And?" I clipped, looking back to the bartender as he started putting glasses in front of me.

"Sadie, it's Buddy you're talking to. Set the bitch aside."

At his words I swallowed. Then I took a deep breath and turned back to him.

"I'm sorry," I mumbled.

"You want to go, we'll go," Buddy offered.

I picked up a lemon drop and took a sip. Then I sighed.

"We'll stay for a drink." *Or two,* I thought. "Then we'll go."

"Whatever you want, but Sadie?" I looked back to him and he started talking again. "He regrets not helping you. It's written all over him. You let him think he deserves to feel that regret, then you aren't who I thought you were."

He was right. I knew he was. Furthermore, if I let Lee think he was some-how to blame for what happened to me, I wasn't only not who Buddy thought I was, I wasn't who I *wanted* to be.

I couldn't meet Buddy's eyes. Then, because I had to, because this was Buddy, I whispered, "I can't help myself sometimes. You know, being a bitch. It's a defense mechanism. I needed her. Since my mom went away, I needed her, the Ice Princess, to get through—"

Buddy's hand slid along my shoulders and he got in close before he inter-rupted, "I know."

I leaned into him while the bartender finished our lemon drops then I paid for the drinks. When I was done, Buddy turned us to face the room.

I chanced a glance at the Rock Chick table and I knew they knew I was there. Only Shirleen's eyes were on me, but my presence was no longer under the radar.

My eyes moved to Ralphie and he, Lee, Eddie, Indy and Daisy were standing further in from the door and they had been joined by a man I hadn't noticed before. He was huge. No, enormous, with wild, blond hair and a thick, russet beard. His eyes were on me as the others around him were talking. And, I could swear, as they all talked, I could see in the dim light of the bar, his face was getting red.

Then it got redder. Then it got even redder.

Then abruptly he detached from the group and stomped over to me. There were people in his way but they scattered upon seeing his big bulk heading their way, and he cut a swath through the crowd straight to me. He stopped in front of me and looked down at my face.

"You look like a fairy princess," he boomed. Yes, *boomed*. His voice was so loud it filled the noisy bar.

People turned our way. I stared up at him, not knowing what to say to that strange opening remark and way too shocked to even consider pulling out the Ice Princess.

I decided "thank you" would be appropriate, so that's what I said.

"I'm Tex," he announced.

I guessed (and was surprised by the fact) that this was Indy's barista.

"I'm Sadie," I told him.

"I know who the fuck you are. I also know, given the chance, I'm gonna snap that motherfucker's neck," Tex returned.

This time I guessed he was talking about Ricky. If someone told me that I would be having this conversation, I would have expected that, at his comment, I would be embarrassed. Somehow with Tex, I wasn't embarrassed.

Now, how bizarre was *that?*

For some reason, I smiled. And then I tried on New Sadie just to see how she fit.

"You make good coffee," I told him.

I held my breath and waited for his response.

"Anyone can make coffee," Tex replied.

I pushed New Sadie, though from his reply I wasn't sure she was working for me. "Not like you. You're a master."

"Well, darlin', you think I make good coffee, why the fuck haven't I seen you at the store?" he asked.

"I—"

"Bullshit," he interrupted me before I even got started.

Before I could think, my eyes narrowed. "What do you mean 'bullshit'? You didn't even hear what I had to say."

"Whatever it was, it was gonna be bullshit," Tex shot back.

It was then I heard Buddy laughing from beside me, and I decided to stay silent. Really, what else could I do? This guy was crazy.

Tex turned to Buddy. "Who're you?" he demanded to know.

"I'm Buddy, Sadie's friend." Buddy put out his hand.

Tex took it. They shook, then Tex's blue eyes turned to me. He leaned in then down, grabbed my hand and started dragging me across the bar.

Yes, *dragging me across the bar.*

"Excuse me!" I said to his back, trying to pull my hand from his and not succeeding.

He looked back at me but kept walking as people jumped out of his way. "Tonight, you sit by me."

"But—"

"No lip!" he boomed as he led us to the Rock Chick table.

Oh blooming *heck.*

❦

There were some good things about the evening.

One, Tex positioned me in a chair at the end of the tables by him that was slightly away from the table (for better viewing of the stage) and thus not easily reached by the Rock Chicks.

Two, Ralphie was having a blast. It was clear he was becoming one with the Rock Chicks, and I liked it that he was having a good time.

Three, although they all smiled at me when given the chance, none of the Rock Chicks engaged me in conversation. They couldn't, I was too far away. Not to mention within five minutes of sitting and after Buddy and Eddie delivered the lemon drops, the show started.

Four, Daisy was at the opposite end of the table from me, and even though I caught her watching me once, she looked away the minute I saw her (this wasn't good, exactly; it made my heart hurt a little, but it was safe).

Five, drag shows were *great.* I *loved* them. All the glitz, glamour, makeup, fancy dresses with feathers and beads, accessories and big hair. It was fantastic. The minute the first Drag Queen came out (her name was Burgundy Rose and she was also the hilarious, sharp-tongued MC) and lip-synced Celine Dion's "My Heart Will Go On" with more diva gravitas than even Queen Diva Dion could, I was transfixed.

❦

But there were also some bad things about the evening, too.

First, Tex leaned into me when the second song began and boomed into my ear, "If there's a shootout or somethin', you stick with me."

After he said this, I blinked at him, not certain sure whether I should laugh, and then I realized he wasn't kidding. I didn't laugh, but I did surreptitiously scoot my chair closer to his.

Second, Hector showed up during the third Drag Queen, who was singing "I Will Survive'.

Like a sixth sense, I looked to the door and caught him walking in.

He looked good, wearing a close-fitting, burgundy, long-sleeved t-shirt, jeans and boots. He still needed a haircut, but somewhere along the line he had shaved and, if possible, he looked better than ever.

I looked away before he saw me, but with quick glances I watched him go to the bar, get a beer and then station himself next to Lee and Eddie at the wall.

"Work it, woman!" Tex boomed at the Drag Queen, and I jumped. I looked away from Hector, luckily before he caught me watching him. And, I couldn't help myself, I smiled at Tex. His big head was bouncing to Gloria Gaynor, and, well, this big, crazy guy getting into a Drag Queen lip syncing to Gloria Gaynor was just plain old funny.

I suspected Eddie had called his brother, but I could deal with that, too. I'd watch the show, drink my lemon drops, and when it was over get Buddy and Ralphie to get me *the heck* out of there.

Simple.

⌖

At lemon drop number five, I realized it was high time I bought a round.

The Sadie-I-Wanted-to-Be would buy a round. Wouldn't she?

I leaned into Tex. "I'm going to go get a round," I told him to gauge his reaction to my friendly gesture.

"Budweiser," he boomed in response without taking his eyes off the stage and the Queen who was singing Natalie Cole's "This Will Be (An Everlasting Love)".

My eyes scanned the table and there were different-sized glasses with different-colored liquid scattered around. How was I to know what everyone wanted unless I asked them?

Impossible!

Then I had an idea and I leaned back into Tex. "What about everyone else?"

He tore his eyes from the stage, spared a glance at the table, looked back at the stage and boomed, "Shots."

I looked at the Rock Chicks. They were all singing out loud (and it was a *very loud* out loud) and dancing in their chairs with their arms over their heads (except Ally and Ava, who were both standing by the stage, singing, dancing and waving dollar bills at the Queen).

Obviously, they didn't mind anymore what they drank. Shots it was.

I got up and went to the bar and when the bartender asked for my order, I turned to the table and counted then back to the bartender and said, "Eleven shots and a bottle of Budweiser."

"What kind of shots?" the bartender asked.

Oh no.

What kind of shots? I didn't know what kind of shots. I'd never been out with girls who drank shots. What kinds were there?

"Shots of liquor," I answered.

The bartender blinked at me then said impatiently, "I didn't think you wanted shots of orange juice."

Well, he didn't have to be mean about it.

This New Sadie thing was hard. The Ice Princess would have had him in cryo-freeze by now.

I shook off my desire to zap him with The Ice.

"What are my choices?" I asked.

He blinked again then started listing them off fast, "Tequila, Sambuca, Kahlua, Jägermeister, anything like that. Then there are the mixed shots, B-52, fuzzy navel, sex on the beach, blowjob, screaming orgasm, quick fuck—"

"Stop!" I yelled, putting a hand up to emphasize my need for him to stop talking just in case he missed it from my yell. Then I pointed to our table. "It's for them."

The bartender's eyes went beyond me to the Rock Chicks and he said, "Eleven screaming orgasms, comin' right up."

Phew.

All right, fine. That wasn't so hard.

I could do this. I could buy shots for the girls. Maybe, when I got back to the table, I might talk to one of them. Even introduce myself to the black-haired lady.

It was then another bartender came up to me and handed me a piece of paper.

"This came from that lady down at the end of the bar." He pointed to the end of the bar. I looked in that direction but I didn't see any lady. There were just a bunch of gay guys hanging around.

When I looked back, the new bartender was gone and my old one, Impatient Snappy Bartender, put Tex's Budweiser in front of me and started to line up empty shot glasses.

I opened the paper and nearly fainted at what I read.

*Sadie,*

*I've been looking all over for you, baby, then once I found you, waited to get close.*

*It's your mother.*

*Don't make a scene. Go to the back like you're heading toward the bathroom and then leave out the backdoor.*

*It isn't safe for me to approach you. It isn't safe for anyone to see me.*

*But I can't wait to hold you.*

*Come alone and make sure you aren't followed. -Mama*

After I finished reading the note, my heart beating a mile a minute, I scanned the bar, looking for anyone that might be my mom.

*My mom!*

In a gay bar!

I didn't care where I saw her. I just wanted to see her.

There were women here and there, but most of them were sitting at the Rock Chick table.

Then, I thought, why on earth was I hanging around?

I dropped the note, and without delay, I headed toward the bathroom. But I didn't even bother acting like I was going to use the facilities. I walked straight to the end of the hall, pushed open the back exit door and I was outside.

The door closed behind me and I looked around. There was a muted streetlamp that illuminated the dank back alley. There were several dumpsters, some stacked boxes, some old kegs, but no Mom.

I stepped out further away from the door. "Mom?" I called.

Then I felt movement behind me. I started to turn but he had me.

I began to scream, but a hand went over my mouth and I was yanked into his body, hand at my mouth, other arm rough around my waist.

"Sweet, sweet Sadie." I heard crooned in my ear, and at his words, I started to tremble.

I knew that voice. It wasn't Ricky Balducci. It was his brother, Harvey.

He was walking forward, taking me with him, talking in his Crazy Balducci Croon the whole time. "Sweet Sadie, bein' stupid, bein' very stupid."

I tried to pull free, twist my head away, and I made noises under his hand as loud as I could.

"Got herself protection, got herself some boys who think they can fuck with the Balduccis. Didn't Ricky teach you nothin'?" Harvey said in my ear, still walking, pushing me forward.

My heart was beating so hard it hurt. I was twisting my head sharply, at the same time struggling against his other arm.

I was no match. He had six inches and at least a hundred pounds on me.

Someone, please tell me this was not happening. Not again.

"I won't make the same mistake as Ricky. When I'm through with you, you're still alive, you'll call off the boys and you'll keep your fuckin' mouth shut about Ricky."

No, it seemed like it was going to happen again. Unless I could stop it.

I opened my mouth and bit into the flesh of his hand so hard I felt his blood fill my mouth. At the same time I lifted a Jimmy Choo boot and slammed the spiked heel down on his foot and immediately made a mammoth effort to twist free.

Harvey yelled out in pain and released me. I took off, spitting his blood out to the side as I did.

"You fuckin' *bitch!*" he screamed in rage, and in a flash he caught up with me, arm around my waist. He swung me up and around and then planted me on my feet all the while I tore at his arm with my fingernails.

I no sooner was set on the ground when something strong wrapped around my wrist.

Before I could lift my head, I was pulled free from Harvey with such force I went sailing, and only stopped when I collided with something else.

I looked up to see what I collided with, ready to flee, and saw Eddie.

I didn't flee mainly because it was Eddie, but also because his arm went around my waist—not in a Harvey way but in a hold-her-before-she-falls way—and he pulled me back a few steps then stopped. When he stopped, his other arm came around me and he pulled me close to his body.

I kept looking at him, partially still panicked, partially so relieved I could cry that this episode with a Balducci had a different ending than the last one. Then I saw Eddie's face was scary stony and his eyes were locked on something beyond us.

I looked at that something.

Hector had Harvey Balducci pinned against the brick wall with nothing but his hand at Harvey's throat. Lee was standing two feet behind and beside him. Harvey was gagging and trying to tear at Hector's hand, kicking out uselessly with his feet. It was not just gagging. It was eyes-bugging-out, face-getting-purple, life-flashing-before-your-eyes gagging.

I stood, my heart thundering, and tried to get my thoughts in order.

Then my thoughts came into order and I realized that Hector was strangling Harvey. Not only that, but Eddie and Lee weren't doing a thing to stop him.

Visions of Hector wearing prison blues filled my head, and he didn't look half as good in prison blues as he did in those jeans and that skintight t-shirt.

The visions spurred me into action and I pulled against Eddie's arms, but they went solid.

"Stop!" I shouted.

Neither Hector nor Lee looked at me. I struggled against Eddie's hold, but he held on tight.

"Stop! Stop it! *Stop!*" I screeched.

Then I heard more people arrive; female exclamations and gasps then running feet.

"Lee, do something!" Indy was beside me and she was shouting at Lee.

Lee didn't move. He just watched Hector like it was some kind of weird, new-fangled, in-the-alley-behind-a-gay-bar outdoor play.

I tell you, *bizarre.*

Then I saw a whirl of motion and Daisy was there. She charged Hector full-on, head down, moving with such velocity she knocked him to the side.

Thank God. Little Daisy to the rescue, and no prison blues for Hector.

I sagged against Eddie.

The relieved sag lasted two seconds. Then I straightened and went tense because Daisy wasn't trying to save Hector from a murder charge. She was trying to get to Harvey.

And got to him she did.

I watched frozen as she went at him, nails scratching, boots kicking and fists punching.

Harvey was bent over, sucking in air at the same time trying to ward Daisy off.

He failed.

No one tried to stop Daisy, either. No one.

Somehow she got him on his back and jumped him, beating him about the face and chest, completely out-of-control. So out-of-control, I could hear her grunting and crying hysterically, all at the same time.

"You…" Punch. "Let…" Another punch. "Sadie…" Claw to the face. "Alone." Then she leaned in to his face and she finished on a high-pitched screech, "*You let her alone!*"

Finally I yanked free of Eddie and ran to Daisy, grabbing her from behind by her raised wrist, my other arm going around her waist. She fought me and we struggled as I pulled her up.

"Daisy, it's me," I whispered in her ear, holding on tight. "Sadie. I'm fine. I'm okay."

Daisy whirled on me, breaking from my hold as I noticed Eddie move around us, and I felt movement behind us as Hector, Lee and Eddie, soon to be joined by an advancing Tex and Buddy, started to deal with Harvey.

"You *ain't* fine!" Daisy screamed in my face. "And you *ain't* okay!"

"Daisy—" I started.

"You can't do this alone!" She was still screaming, tears streaming down her face. "I know it, I *know* it. You can't do this alone." She put her hands over her face and cried behind them, mumbling a repeated, "You can't do it alone."

Cautiously, I got close and then, feeling strange, I slid my arms around Daisy like Buddy or Ralphie would slide their arms around me.

"I'm not alone," I whispered to her bent head.

She raised wet eyes to me. They were bright and they were flashing. "Damn straight," she snapped.

I couldn't help it. Her snapping a full of attitude "damn straight" with tears streaming down her face for some reason struck me as funny.

"You need a screaming orgasm," I told her authoritatively, like I even knew what one was.

She blinked. "What?" she asked.

"The shots I was buying everyone before I came out here. They should be done by now."

She stared at me like I might just be touched then nodded slowly. "Well, sugar, I gotta admit, you're right. I could use a screaming orgasm about now."

"Let's get you inside," I said, moving my arm to around her shoulders and leading her toward the backdoor.

I looked and saw all the Rock Chicks and Ralphie standing by the door and all of them were watching me.

Maybe one day I could deal with them all at once, but right then I'd been attacked (again!) by a Balducci and Daisy was in no shape for anything but whatever a screaming orgasm was.

So I looked away from them and kept going in a beeline toward the backdoor while I went on, "Maybe we'll order one of those sex on the beaches too."

⚞⚟

We all (that was, every last one of the Rock Chicks, Ralphie and me) had our screaming orgasms. Then we had our sex on the beaches. We then tried fuzzy navels.

Hector, Lee and Eddie didn't join us for our Festival of Shots, but Buddy and Tex came back, faces tight and set, and they looked like they were standing guard.

No kidding, standing guard.

I looked around, tried to find the bartender who gave me the note, but he was nowhere to be seen.

Indy disappeared, then for some reason Diva Drag Queen of the Evening, Burgundy Rose, came out (Indy at her side), walked right up to me and pulled me into a deep hug.

I stood there rigid with shock at this new unexpected turn of events, but she didn't seem to mind. In fact, after she was done hugging me, she gave me a huge, loud kiss on the cheek, then leaned back and started swiping at the lipstick with her thumb.

"I'm Tod," she said in a male voice, still swiping my cheek with her thumb.

"Hi, Tod," I said without anything else to say like "What in *the heck* are you doing?" or an Ice Princess "How *dare* you touch me?"

"I'm a Rock Chick by default," Burgundy Rose/Tod said.

"Oh," I replied, sounding stupid. Well, that explained it.

"I'm Indy's neighbor," he went on, and stopped swiping my cheek. Thankfully, it was my good cheek, but still.

"Okay." I still didn't know what to say.

"What size shoe are you?" he asked, apropos of nothing.

I stared at him then thought it best to answer. "Six and a half."

"Damn," he muttered, "I could *work* those boots." I kept staring and he kept explaining, giving a flick of his hand to the Rock Chicks. "All the girls share shoes. We're all the same size."

"Oh," I repeated, a little stunned that he might want to borrow my boots. Not that I minded, of course. Just that I'd never had a girlfriend (or a gay boyfriend, for that matter) who wanted to borrow my boots.

For some reason, the idea of him wanting to borrow my boots made the weird cold I'd felt since Harvey got hold of me melt clean away.

"Oh well, I can admire them from afar. Not like I haven't had tons of experience with *that*," Tod shared, then his head snapped around toward the stage and he muttered, "Shit, gotta go, song's about over." He gave me another cheek kiss, another thumb swipe at the lipstick he planted there, and then he was off.

I stared at his beaded-gowned back.

Now, seriously, how bizarre was *that*?

I was still staring when Hector and Lee appeared.

I hadn't yet recovered from my encounter with the Drag Queen when Hector took my hand in his, firmly in his, and without a word to me or anyone, he walked me out the front door, through the parking lot, straight to his Bronco.

I didn't struggle. My night was way too weird to struggle. I didn't have it in me. I was just going to let the rest of my night ride out to its conclusion. I figured that was best.

Veronica Mars would have a wisecrack to deliver, but I hadn't yet made it to the Wisecracking Sadie version of my new self. I couldn't even order shots competently. I was in no position to offer a smart-mouthed remark.

He stopped me at the side of his Bronco with a tug on my hand and then got close. I did a quick scan of the parking lot, but there was no sign of Eddie or Harvey.

"Where's Harvey?" I asked, looking anywhere but at Hector.

"*Mamita*, look at me."

I kept avoiding his eyes and started to say, "I should probably—"

When he spoke again, his voice was edging away from gentle. "Sadie, goddamn it, look at me."

I looked at him. He lifted the hand he still held, got closer and pressed our clasped hands against the heat of his hard chest, mine on the inside.

Oh my.

"You want your friends with you, okay, but right now, we're goin' to the Station and you're gonna press charges against Ricky and Harvey Balducci."

Oh no I was *not*.

I tried to step back, but Hector's hand tightened. It didn't hurt but it sent a message, a message I read and listened to for reasons completely unknown, or maybe reasons I didn't want to know.

"Marty and Donny Balducci won't get near you. You have my word on that," Hector went on.

Without a way to retreat, I just shook my head. Hector's other arm slid along my waist and he brought me closer to his body. So close our bodies were grazing from hips to waist to belly.

My entire mind focused on the body grazing.

"Sadie, I'm askin' you to be smart."

"I *am* being smart," I replied, still thinking about nothing but his body and my body and his body grazing my body.

"Tell me what's in your head," he encouraged softly.

What was in my head was that I was *still* thinking about his body touching my body, how I liked it and I feared it. Both of those feelings swirled and agitated and were making me a crazy mixture of scared, confused and excited.

"I need you to let me go," I whispered, mind getting muddled with panic, my eyes on his throat.

"Sorry?" he asked.

I tilted my head back to look at him. "Please," I said so softly even I could barely hear it. "Let me go."

Without hesitation his hand released mine. His arm went from around my waist and I took a step back, but he wasn't ready to let me go completely.

His hand came to the side of my neck to stop further retreat, but his body wasn't close anymore and my fuzzy brain became sharper.

I looked up at him and said in all honesty, "I can't deal with this now."

Hector stared at me a second and I had no idea what he saw, but thankfully whatever it was made him nod. His hand squeezed me affectionately at my neck.

Yes, that's right, *affectionately.*

"We'll get the other's statements," he told me. "Eddie called a squad car. They took Harvey in. You can come in and press charges in the morning."

I nodded, even though I wasn't going to press charges; not in the morning or any time.

Clearly, the Balducci brothers weren't going to leave me alone while they waited for me to play my card, but I couldn't think about what that meant right now. I'd think about it later when Hector's hand wasn't at my neck, I hadn't survived the latest Balducci Brother Attack and I didn't have five lemon drops and three shots coursing through my system.

I felt his hand loosening like he was going to let go, and quickly, before I lost the courage, I asked, "Are you going to get into trouble?" I paused then went on, "For choking him?"

Hector's head jerked ever so slightly at my question like it surprised him, and his eyes narrowed.

He stared at me again for what seemed like a long time, then his face cleared, and I could swear, he was fighting back a grin.

"So that's what's in your head," he murmured as if he was talking to himself, and as if whatever he thought was in my head pleased him a great deal. I wasn't going to think about a pleased Hector until later either.

"Well?" I prompted less quickly and a bit more annoyed this time.

I watched him continue to fight the grin as he replied, "I think I might get away with getting physical when I caught Harvey Balducci in the middle of a kidnap attempt."

I sighed quietly but with relief.

Well, at least *that* was good news.

Then I asked, "Will Daisy get into trouble for attacking him?"

He shook his head. "As far as any of the witnesses were concerned, Daisy Sloan was simply in on the rescue, and maybe her nails slipped a bit."

My eyes got round as I repeated, disbelief dripping from my words at his stunning prevarication, "Daisy was in on the rescue and her nails... *slipped a bit?*"

It was at that Hector stopped fighting back the grin and let it happen.

I stared. His grin was nearly as good as his smile. Who thought that could even be possible?

Then, before I could answer my own question, his head dipped.

Then, seriously, no kidding, his lips touched mine in a barely-there kiss.

After that, while I was blinking rapidly and trying to remember how to breathe, his head came up and he said, "Time for you to go home."

All I could think was; he was so right. It *was* time for me to go home.

Tomorrow I'd think about all of this. Tonight, I was done. *So* done.

"Time for me to go home," I agreed.

His grin turned into a blinding, white smile. He leaned in again, but only to kiss the top of my head this time.

He took my hand in his and he walked me back into the bar.

# Chapter 6

# It's My Lip Gloss

*Sadie*

"He's here, he's here. *Oh my God*, he's here… and he looks *good!*" Ralphie chanted, dancing around by the window.

Oh my God.

Hector was here. It was seven o'clock and Hector was here.

I looked at the display on the DVD player. No, it was seven-oh-two.

But Hector was still here.

To take me out to dinner.

And he looked *good!*

And we were going to "talk". I knew we were going to "talk" because Hector called Art in the early afternoon and told me so.

I didn't want to talk. I didn't even want to go to dinner!

How did this happen?

Oh… my… *God.*

~~*~~

That afternoon at Art, I unwittingly answered the phone (as you do when, say, you run a business), and without even a hello Hector said in my ear, "I'm standin' in the Station, Eddie's with me and he says you haven't come in yet."

Oh my.

"Well——" I started.

He interrupted me, "You don't come in, they gotta let Harvey go."

I tried again, "I just——"

"They let Harvey go and you don't tell them what Ricky did to you, I still got four Balducci brothers to deal with rather than bein' down to two."

My body went tight and I stared unseeing at the counter, unable to process his words.

"What?" I asked.

"I think you heard me," he answered.

I heard him all right.

"I heard you. I just don't know what you mean."

"I mean," he explained, but I could tell he was losing patience, "if Ricky and Harvey are out of commission, I just gotta go after Marty and Donny."

I kept staring at the counter. "Why are you after the Balducci Brothers?"

Silence then a soft, "*Mamita*, are you shittin' me?"

Quietly I answered, "No."

More silence then, still soft, "Tonight, after dinner, we're gonna talk."

He gave me an opening. My back went straight and I took it.

"Hector, about dinner—"

"Seven o'clock. You aren't there, I'll find you."

Disconnect.

I kept staring at the counter and tried to decide if Hector could find me.

Then I decided Hector could very likely find me.

Then I spent the next six hours alternately having panic attacks and letting Ralphie talk me into things. Things like closing down the shop. Things like going to Cherry Creek Mall. Things like buying a new outfit for my dinner with Hector. Things like buying that new Coach handbag I *did not need*. Things like agreeing it was a good idea that Ralphie bought the cute doggie food and water bowls, even though I knew Buddy would lose his mind. Things like trying on everything Ralphie threw at me in thirteen different stores without losing my patience or calling on the Ice Princess (not even *once*).

"Ralphie, calm down," Buddy said to the still-dancing Ralphie.

Ralphie was in no mood to calm down. He rushed to me and grabbed my arms.

"Sweet 'ums, your outfit is *perfection*. He's wearing jeans, a shirt and a leather jacket. Thank *God* we didn't go OTT with that slutty top from Bebe."

There was no way on earth I was ever going to buy that slutty top in Bebe that Ralphie forced me to try on. Of course, I didn't tell him that in Bebe, or now.

The doorbell rang. Thoughts of slutty tops flew out of my head and all the breath went out of lungs in a whoosh.

Then, without looking at Ralphie or Buddy, I turned on my stiletto heel, rushed to the powder room and slammed the door.

I looked at myself in the mirror.

Ralphie talked me into keeping my hair loose and giving it what he called "just a wee bit more volume", so there was tons of it falling in waves and ringlets around my face, on my shoulders and down my back.

I went light on the makeup, mainly because heavy looked, well, heavy. The scar on my cheek was still too angry to hide without looking like I was trying to hide something. Anyway, my hair did the work a heavy makeup job would do (as I mentioned, there was *loads* of it) and I also had my signature MAC lip gloss on: a soft pink with a gentle shine.

I loved that lip gloss.

I had on a silvery-purple blouse with a mandarin collar; rows of soft, generous ruffles floating down in a V at the bodice and little ruffles making up the short sleeves. I paired this with my new Lucky jeans, a thin silver belt and silver strappy sandals. Finally, I was wearing my diamonds-in-platinum tennis bracelet and my diamond stud earrings.

I stared in the mirror thinking maybe I was still OTT.

Did one wear diamonds and platinum when one went out with the ex-DEA agent that put one's father in prison?

Did one wear a silver belt *and* silver strappy sandals *ever?*

Was one absolutely *mad* that one was not climbing out the window right now?

A sharp knock came at the door and I jumped.

"Sadie! Hector's here," Ralphie called unnecessarily as I *knew* Hector was there. Just two seconds ago, Ralphie was chanting it.

"Coming!" I shouted back, and then realized Hector would know I was in the powder room. If I stayed in there very long, Hector would wonder what I was doing. I didn't want to go out there to have dinner with Hector, but I also didn't want Hector to wonder why I needed a long bathroom break.

"Blooming heck," I said into the mirror. Then I pulled in a deep breath and whispered, "You can do this Sadie. It's just dinner, a talk. You can talk to Hector. You've had boyfriends, you've had lovers. Okay. They didn't stick around very long because your father warned them off, but you aren't a frightened little

81

Kristen Ashley

virgin. You're a grown woman. An experienced, grown woman. An experienced grown woman who can take care of herself. You can talk to him, tell him you aren't interested. Get him to understand and back off. You can do it. Right?" I leaned in closer and repeated, "Right?"

Another sharp rap at the door.

"Sadie!" Ralphie snapped.

"Coming!" I shouted and whirled, yanked open the door in full snit and stomped out, glaring at Ralphie. "For goodness sake, Ralphie, can a girl fix her lip gloss without her crazy, gay roommate banging down the door?"

"No," Ralphie shot back. "Not when Hispanic Hottie is waiting to take her out to dinner."

"Stop calling him Hispanic Hottie, his name is Hector," I returned.

"I call 'em as I see 'em. He's Hispanic..." Ralphie lifted one hand and then continued. "And he's hot." He lifted the other hand then he shoved them together like he was squeezing an accordion. "Hence, Hispanic Hottie."

"You could argue about this all night," Buddy called from down the hall. Our heads swung in that direction and we could see both Buddy and Hector "Oh my God, now for a different reason" Chavez standing there, by the door, both of them watching The Ralphie and Sadie Show. "But Hector's waiting and Ralphie, we've got a reservation," Buddy finished.

I didn't hear the last part of what Buddy said. I was staring at Hector, who was looking like he was trying not to laugh and not succeeding very well. It was a full-on, light up the room, beyond amused, glamorous smile.

Couple that with him being clean-shaven, his hair still an unruly mess, but now a slightly-less unruly still sexy-as-ever mess, wearing a black, tailored shirt, a pair of jeans, a black leather jacket, black cowboy boots and a fantastic, wide, black belt with a heavy, matte silver square buckle... well, I not only could no longer hear, I couldn't speak or move.

I could only see.

Oh my.

The answer was yes. One could wear diamonds and platinum with the ex-DEA agent that put one's father in prison.

I wasn't OTT. I needed a lot more sparkle and glitter to go out with a man that was just plain beautiful.

"You ready?" Hector asked, and I jolted out of my stupefaction.

No. I was definitely not ready.

"Yes," I lied and walked toward him.

He watched me walk, and the way he did it made me acutely aware of everything about me. Every tiny movement. Every last hair on my head.

"Okay kids," Ralphie said, trailing me. "Don't be too late. Don't do any drugs, drive smart, and even if *all* the other kids are doing it, think twice. If you're going to be over your curfew then make sure you call your daddies or we'll get worried."

I stopped in front of Hector but turned to Ralphie.

I leaned up to kiss his cheek and whispered, "Shut up."

He grinned at me.

I turned to Buddy. He helped me on with my to-the-hip, black trench coat, handed me my deep-green, patent leather Lanvin bag with the chain link strap and then I kissed his cheek, too.

"Seriously, Sadie, you're gonna be late, you phone," Buddy said to me, but his eyes were on Hector.

"I'll phone," I promised.

With that, Hector took my hand and we were out the door.

Darn.

Here we go.

Hector walked me to the Bronco so fast I nearly had to run to keep up. Once there, he opened the passenger door, helped me in, then slammed it when I settled. He rounded the front and got in the driver's side, but instead of turning on the truck, he twisted toward me.

"Give me your cell," he demanded.

I blinked because everything was happening really fast.

"Excuse me?" I asked.

"Your cell," he repeated.

Confused at this strange start to a date, I pulled out my cell phone and handed it to him. He took it, flipped it open, punched numbers into it and then hit the green button.

In a second, I heard his cell phone ringing. He pulled it out of the inside pocket of his jacket and flipped my phone shut. Then, with me still silent and watching him, he hit buttons on his phone, *loads* of buttons. My phone rang. He flipped his shut, mine open and returned his to his jacket pocket. Then he started to hit buttons on my phone, *loads* of those too, even more than what he did on his phone.

"Do you," I tried to be polite after he kept on hitting buttons, "mind telling me what you're doing?"

He flipped my phone shut and handed it to me, his eyes coming to mine.

"You're programmed into my phone, I'm programmed into yours," he told me. "You got my cell, my house, the office and the control room at the office. The control room is set as the top choice in your phonebook. You ever have a situation, *any* situation, you call there. Someone is there 24/7, and they'll take care of you. Got that?"

Slowly, not certain sure how to react to Hector giving me his cell phone and home phone and office phone and offering me 24/7 access to someone who would "take care of me", I nodded.

"Now," he went on, his voice softer, he was leaning closer and I wasn't keeping up. "I'm gonna kiss you, because, *mamita*, the way you look right now, I gotta fuckin' kiss you."

Oh *my*.

I guessed Ralphie was right. My outfit *was* perfection.

He got way closer, his fingers slid into my hair at the side and they cupped my head.

"You all right with that?" he asked quietly, eyes looking into mine.

Again, slowly, I nodded, though I also wasn't certain sure I was "all right with that".

"Thank Christ," he muttered.

Then he kissed me.

It started soft, sweet, and then I put my hand to his shoulder and felt the heat there. I liked it and moved in closer so I could feel the heat from his body.

His arm slid around my waist, bringing me even closer right before his tongue touched my lips. I opened my mouth at the touch and that was it. It was rewind to my father's study.

I curled my arms around his neck, pressed my body to his and the kiss went from soft and sweet to hot and wild.

Within minutes, he pulled me out of my seat, twisting me so I landed in his lap and both his arms went around me, one locked at my waist, the other one sliding up my neck and into my hair.

I kissed him back like I couldn't exist without my lips on his, his tongue in my mouth. I was out-of-control and didn't even care.

Then he tore his mouth from mine and buried his face in my neck. For a second, we both just sat there, breathing heavily.

"You taste better than I remembered," he said into my neck and his voice sounded deeper than normal.

I swallowed and closed my eyes tight. My heart was beating wildly. I felt safe and snug in his lap with his arms around me. I was excited in a good way. And his heat was seeping into me everywhere and I liked it.

I liked all of it.

His head came out of my neck and he looked at me. "And the way I remembered it, you tasted fuckin' great."

My rapidly beating heart tripped.

"It's my lip gloss," I said stupidly.

A slow smile spread on his face. "*Mamita*, trust me. It isn't your lip gloss."

I didn't answer, mainly because I was in his lap, I had just made out with him (again) and he was smiling at me close up.

Where was my Ice Princess now, I ask you? There *were* moments I could still use her. What was she? On vacation?

"Time to feed you," he told me.

Thank God.

Relief from full-on Hector, his mouth, tongue and heat. I could use that quite desperately. I needed to get my head together. This was not going well, mainly because it *was* going well.

It wasn't supposed to go well. It was supposed to be a disaster.

"Okay," I agreed, but didn't move.

He kept smiling as he leaned in and gave me a brief kiss, then twisted me back in my seat. He started the Bronco. I put on my seatbelt, he put on his and we took off.

Considering how the first ten minutes of our date went, I was a little worried about the rest of the night.

⚡

Hector parked on a residential street in the Highlands.

I looked around, thinking maybe there was a corner restaurant or something. He got out. I threw open my door, but he was there before I could alight. He took my hand, helped me out and kept hold of my hand.

Kristen Ashley

"Where are we going?" I asked as he walked me up to what looked like a house.

"Dinner," Hector replied.

I stared at the house. It was a nice house; small, neat yard, cozy.

Then, because it was a house, I began to panic.

"Is this your house?" I breathed as we made it to the front door.

Hector pulled open the heavy security door, stepped in, turned the knob to the front door and looked down at me.

"No. *Es mi mamá's.*"

Blooming heck!

*His mother's?*

Someone, please tell me Hector didn't live with his mother.

He pulled me to him, put his hand to the small of my back and guided me into the house. Once in, he shut the door, took my hand and we walked into the living room.

I came to a dead halt at what I saw.

Eddie was there with Jet. Indy was there with Lee. Big crazy guy Tex was there with some pretty, older, blonde lady. Lastly, a short, round, Mexican-American woman was laughing with the pretty, older, blonde lady.

They all turned to me. I prepared to turn and run.

Hector felt it. He dropped my hand, his arm went around my shoulders and he pulled me tight to his side.

Now would someone please tell me that, on our very first date, Hector didn't bring me to a dinner party at his mother's house?

"This is Sadie," Hector told the room.

Yes, Hector brought me to a dinner party at his mother's house.

Then the night, already bizarre in the extreme, got more bizarre.

The short, round, Mexican-American woman (who I was assuming was Hector's mother), walked up to me. She stopped right in front of me, her eyes sharp on my face. I felt the Ice Princess arrive back from vacation and start to slide in place, but something made me push her out and send her packing again.

"Hello," I said softly.

Then, no kidding, I watched in fascination as tears filled the woman's eyes.

Yes, actual tears.

Her hand came up and started toward my scarred cheek. I pulled in my breath. The hand halted then dropped.

She sucked in her lips and I saw her biting them, tears still shining in her eyes. She reached out and wrapped her little hand around my casted arm. She held it in front of her, her head tilted down. I couldn't see, but I could tell she was looking at my wrist.

I leaned a bit forward and asked softly, "Excuse me, but are you all right?"

Her head came up and she dropped my arm. "You look like a fairy princess," she whispered in a croaky voice.

I'd heard that before and I still didn't know what to say.

I didn't get the chance to say anything.

"Who would hurt a fairy princess?" she asked me as one tear slid down her cheek.

My body jerked then went solid, and, belatedly cluing in after being made fuzzy by the beginning of my crazy date with Hector, I realized she knew I'd been raped.

Instead of this making me panicked or embarrassed or angry at Hector (or Lee or Indy or Tex or Jet or whoever) for telling her, I leaned even closer to her.

"Mrs. Chavez," I said gently, but she wasn't looking at me anymore. Her eyes sliced to Hector and she started yelling at him in rapid-fire Spanish.

Yes, yelling. And, yes, in Spanish.

I tried to take a step back because, well, she kind of scared me, but Hector still had a tight hold on me.

Then she started waving her arms around and she spun, stalked up to Eddie, got in his face and started yelling at *him,* still in Spanish.

Then she turned to Lee, wagging her finger at him and then she yelled at *him* (in Spanish).

"*Mamá,*" Hector said low, cutting into her tirade.

She spun around from wagging her finger at Lee and glared at Hector.

"*Cómo?*" she snapped.

"Sadie's hungry," Hector told his mother, throwing *me* right under the bus.

"No!" I cried instantly. "No, really, carry on, um… yelling at people. It's your house. Do whatever you want. I'm good. I'm not hungry at all."

She pointed at me and I could tell just by looking at her I was in trouble.

"You! Too skinny!" she declared, jabbing her finger at me. "We eat. *Mi hijo* likes curves. Any real man likes curves. We gotta work on your curves!" Then she stomped out of the room, and within moments we heard pans crashing and other various extremely loud kitchen noises.

I scanned the room and everyone was smiling at me; Indy and Jet were both even giggling a little. I didn't think there was anything to giggle about.

I looked up at Hector and glared. He was looking down at me and grinning.

He dipped his face close to mine and whispered, "She likes you."

Blooming *heck*.

⚑

I got through the dinner at Hector's mother's house (her name, by the way, was Blanca, and the pretty, older, blonde lady was Nancy, Tex's girlfriend and Jet's Mom) with only a few uncomfortable incidents.

⚑

First, after we all sat down and passed around Blanca's delicious food and everyone had started eating, Blanca threw her napkin down, stomped to me and snatched my plate right out from under my raised fork. She then stormed around the table, stopping at each platter full of food and mounding more and more on my plate. Then she stalked back to me and dropped my plate in front of me with a curt, "Too skinny!"

I looked down in horror at the virtual mountain of food on my plate.

Blanca went back to her seat at the foot of the table (Eddie was at the head, Jet to one side of him, me on the other side) and she started gabbing happily like she hadn't just made a huge Food Scene.

When I thought it was safe, I turned to Hector and whispered, "I can't eat this much food."

His eyes cut to me and they were dancing. "Relax, *mi cielo*, I'll take care of you."

Then, if you could believe it, he *did* take care of me. Throughout dinner he alternately ate off his plate *and* (when Blanca wasn't looking) my plate until both were empty.

How bizarre was *that?*

⚑

I did okay through dinner, though it made me feel weird, like I felt when I first moved in with Buddy and Ralphie.

See, these people were friends. In fact, it was clear they'd known each other for years, so they were beyond friends. It was hard to describe, but since (except for Hector, Eddie and Blanca and, of course, Jet and Nancy) there were no blood ties to bind them, and yet they still chose to spend their lives together, it was more like a close-knit, happy, relaxed family-of-their-own-devising. They laughed, talked, gossiped, smiled and teased each other with fond affection.

Outside of Ralphie and Buddy's friends, I'd never been around anything like it and I didn't know how to act, what to say. I only knew that the Ice Princess was *really* not welcome here. I couldn't click her into place to help me cope even if I wanted to.

I also knew that New Sadie was not ready for this experience, not even close.

So I stayed quiet, smiling a little when someone looked at me or there was a joke that I should have laughed at, but was too stressed out to relax and be real, like them.

I felt like an outsider looking in, removed, not unwelcome just that, well...

I didn't belong.

⚔

The second incident happened while everyone was chatting and the stragglers were finishing up their meals.

Hector had pushed his chair a bit away from the table, and to my shock he pulled my casted wrist onto his thigh. Then the tips of his fingers touched the tips of my fingers that were exposed by the cast.

His touch made me go warm.

I turned to him and he was looking down at our hands.

"When do you get this removed?" he asked quietly.

"Wednesday," I replied, wanting to pull my hand away if only for sanity's sake, but thinking it might not be a good move at Blanca's table. I knew one thing: there was no way on earth I was going to survive another scene and I also knew I'd do just about anything to avoid it, including letting Hector touch my hand.

"Good," he murmured.

I swallowed.

His black eyes came to mine and there was something burning there so strong, I felt my heart start to beat faster.

"She's pulling away," he whispered.

"Excuse me?"

He didn't explain himself, instead he said, "Sadie, you're safe here. You can be the girl I've seen the last few days."

Oh my.

My body tensed and Ice Princess slid into my skin before I could stop her.

"I don't know what you mean," I replied coldly, even though I knew *exactly* what he meant.

He lifted my casted hand to his mouth and (no kidding, right in front of everyone!) kissed the exposed fingers there.

Ice Princess melted in a steaming, hot puddle.

Then he murmured, "You know what I mean."

Darn.

My eyes flitted to the table. Indy was watching me, and when my eyes hit hers, hers slid quickly away, but I could still see her smile. I saw Tex was also watching me, but he didn't look away. He was grinning at me broadly, so it was my eyes that slid away. Unfortunately, they caught Blanca's and hers were shining with tears (again!).

Blooming heck.

I looked back at Hector. "Please let me go," I whispered.

He let me go and I took in a relieved breath, but it stuck in my throat when his hand went to the seat of my chair. He gave a firm tug which pulled my chair right next to his chair so our thighs were pressed together. Then he sat back and draped his arm around the back of my chair.

There was no way I could scoot away or put him in deep freeze (which would have been my premier choice), so I just sat there, tense, while everyone tried to pretend they weren't grinning at each other because of Hector and me.

So I tried to pretend they weren't trying to pretend and told myself I could get through the night.

How much worse could it get?

The next incident happened when Blanca started to clear the table.

Jet and Indy got up to help her.

I threw my chair back and took that golden opportunity to get away from Hector. I decided I should help clear the table, too. Even though I'd always lived in a house with help who cooked for us and cleared our table, I *had* helped Ralphie and Buddy at their house.

I could do this.

Problem was, I had a cast on my arm. Not so easy to stack plates and carry platters still heavy with food, even though everyone had finished eating (one thing was certain sure, Blanca was generous with her hospitality).

Still, it was either help or sit close to Hector's side, everyone thinking we were something we were *not*, or we were not going to be after Hector and I had our talk.

I decided plates were my best bet so, balancing some plates and cutlery precariously, I followed Jet and Indy to the kitchen.

Disaster nearly struck when I hit Blanca's kitchen. The plates teetered and some forks and knives fell to the floor.

Before it could get worse and I had to buy Blanca a new set of stoneware, Indy turned from depositing her load on the counter and deftly grabbed the plates in my hands as Blanca bent down and picked up the cutlery.

"I'm sorry, Mrs. Chavez," I said to her, feeling like an idiot.

She straightened and ordered, "Blanca, *mi hija*. You call me Blanca." Then she put the cutlery in the sink and swept out.

But Jet was at the sink, rinsing dishes, and for some bizarre reason she was giggling.

I didn't want to know but I *did* want to know, and not having the will-power to stop myself I asked, "What's funny?"

She threw me a dazzling smile (Jet was Eddie's fiancée; she was blonde, green-eyed and very pretty, but when she smiled, she was a heart-stopper).

"Do you speak Spanish?" she asked.

I shook my head.

"*Mi hija* means, 'my daughter'."

Oh my.

Blanca just called me her daughter. *Her daughter.*

That could not be good.

I moved closer to Jet. "Seriously?"

"Seriously."

Indy giggled a little as Jet handed her a rinsed plate to put in the dishwasher.

I started to organize the plates and cutlery on the counter so Jet could more easily rinse them.

"Do, um, Mexican-American women call people that for——?" I started.

"Nope," Jet interrupted me. "I didn't get an *hija* until…" She looked to the ceiling then finished, "I think it was the third time I saw her."

"You win!" Indy cried and then burst out laughing. Without hesitation Jet laughed with her.

And at that moment, I couldn't help it. They were so engaging (even though it seriously weirded me out, *all* of it), I laughed with them.

Blanca came in, depositing more stuff and then started banging around the kitchen again, preparing to serve dessert.

"Can I do something?" I asked her.

"*Sí*, you can make the coffee," Blanca answered, and I was relieved. I could definitely make coffee *and* do it one-handed. I'd had loads of practice at that at Buddy and Ralphie's place.

She showed me where to find the coffee stuff then swept out again, carrying dessert plates.

Immediately, when Blanca left, on a whisper I asked Jet, "Do *you* speak Spanish?"

"A little," Jet replied, squirting dishwashing liquid into a dirty pot and then turning the tap into it.

"What does *mamita* mean?"

She looked at me, eyes knowing, and grinned big. "It means 'little mama'. It's an endearment, like a guy calling his girl 'babe'."

Oh my.

Hector called me "babe".

Blooming heck.

I kept going. "What about *mi cielo*?"

Jet blinked. "Hector called you *mi cielo*?"

I nodded.

Her big grin went even bigger. "It means, literally, 'my sky' but it's also an endearment, a little, um…" She looked for a word. "Stronger than *mamita*," she finished.

I didn't know what to make of that, but I wasn't sure it was good. I mean, it was good if I was a normal, Veronica Mars-type person, but it wasn't good as I wasn't a normal, Veronica Mars-type person (which I wasn't).

"He calls you *mi amor*, you're really in trouble," Jet went on before I could run screaming from the house.

"Why?"

"That means 'my love', and that means he's serious," Jet replied then went on with a big smile. "Or, I should say, *more* serious."

I couldn't stop myself from leaning into her and whispering, "I think I'm in trouble."

"Sister, you are *definitely* in trouble," Indy said, and she was smiling at me too, like this was a good thing.

I didn't think this was a good thing. In fact, I was more than a little worried it was a very, *very* bad thing.

I shook off my feelings of foreboding, and lastly, because I had to know, I asked Jet, "What was Blanca saying in the living room when Hector and I arrived?"

Jet shook her head. "She was talking too fast and I'm not fluent or anything, but I think the gist of it was that if Hector, Eddie and Lee didn't wreak vengeance on, um..." she stopped.

"It's okay, I get it," I said softly because I saw she was uncomfortable. She gave me a different smile, this one less dazzling but far more sweet.

Somehow Blanca (who didn't know me from Eve), having a tizzy on my behalf made me feel strange, but it wasn't a bad strange. It was a weird, happy strange.

It wasn't *that* strange. I used to feel that way around my mom.

But it *was* a strange I hadn't felt in a very long time.

Jet's eyes slid to Indy, but I had exhausted New Sadie's reserves so I turned away and finished up the coffee.

Surprisingly, and thankfully, they didn't push it.

░▓░

The last incident happened after dinner was over.

We were all heading back to the living room for more coffee and Blanca had claimed Hector. They walked in front of me, her arm around his waist, his arm around her shoulders, head tilted low as she talked to him in Spanish.

Everyone but Indy and Lee were in front of them. I walked behind them, Indy and Lee behind me.

A few steps from the living room door I decided it was time. I had my opportunity so I stopped and turned to Lee.

"Can I talk to you a second?" I asked.

Lee and Indy stopped. Lee's eyes came to me and he nodded.

Indy said, "I'll just—"

My gaze swung to her and I interrupted, "No, it's okay. You can stay. This won't take long."

Indy nodded, but she took Lee's hand and it looked like she was bracing. Lee just kept watching me.

Throughout dessert, I practiced what I was going to say so I was ready.

I took a deep breath, squared my shoulders, looked at Lee and said, "I've spent my life around bad people. Bad people that did things to hurt other people and they had no regrets."

"Sadie—" Lee started.

"Please, hear me out."

Lee stopped talking.

"It was hard, living in that world," I told him.

He was silent. Indy was silent. I went on.

"It would be harder living in a world where a good person blamed himself for what a bad person did." I paused then delivered my grand finale, what *I* thought was rather decisively (if I did say so myself), "You share no responsibility for what happened to me."

Immediately Lee said, "I appreciate that, but it doesn't change the fact that I—"

I interrupted, "You hold on to this regret, it's going to..."

Now what did I say?

I didn't expect Lee to do anything but feel off the hook. He was messing up my grand finale! I didn't think to practice different responses to his possible responses! Why couldn't he just agree and let it go so we could go have coffee?

This being nice to people was *hard*.

Oh well, I just had to make it up. "It's going to be..." I searched for a word. "Very um..." come on Sadie! "*Upsetting*," I finished.

Both Indy and Lee were staring at me.

I was spent. I had no more, but I didn't feel it was appropriate to walk away.

Finally Lee grinned and said, "I wouldn't want to upset you."

His tone was bizarre. Then it hit me that he was teasing me.

Yes, *teasing me.*

The Ice Princess reared her head. "Well. Yes. See that it doesn't happen."

For some reason what I said made Lee burst out laughing. It made Indy do the same.

They laughed right in the face of the Ice Princess!

How bizarre was *that?*

Lee moved in (shattering my Ice Fortress, by the way), threw his arm around my shoulders and walked me into the living room, Indy following.

"I'll see it doesn't happen again," he said, still sounding like he was teasing. Then he said, "I promise."

Startled at the change in tone, I looked up at him. He was no longer teasing. He was very serious.

Before I could react, he deposited me at Hector's side. Hector lifted his brows at me.

I pulled my lips between my teeth. Hector saw I wasn't going to share and he sighed.

Thirty minutes later, we left.

It was finally over.

And I survived.

*Thank goodness.*

# Chapter 7
# Okay

After Blanca's dinner, when Hector and I arrived back at the brownstone, my mind was on other things. *Loads* of other things.

Therefore, I didn't protest when he walked me up to the door, took the keys from my hands, unlocked and opened the door for me, and, with his hand on the small of my back again, guided me inside.

Automatically, I turned to the alarm panel and hit the code, flipped the hall light switch then turned back to Hector.

For some bizarre reason, he was looking up the stairs.

Then he looked at me. "Stay here, by the door, until I come back."

I only had time to blink at him before he was gone, taking the stairs two at a time.

What on earth was he doing?

I did what I was told, standing by the door, feeling like an idiot, and he came back.

I opened my mouth to speak, but before I uttered a noise, he walked right by me, through the hall, his hand raised, index finger pointed skyward and muttered, "One more minute."

I stared at his departing back then heard as he walked around downstairs. A light came on in the living room and Hector reappeared. He walked to the end of the hall, opened the door to the powder room. I saw the light go on then off then he came out, closed the door and came back to me.

"Okay," he said. He reached around me, locked the front door then grabbed my hand and pulled me in the living room.

"What was that?" I asked his back.

He stopped and turned to me. Shrugging off his jacket, he threw it on an armchair. "Walkthrough. Making sure no one was here."

My head did a surprised little shake as I threw my bag on the chair, took off my trench and tossed it on the chair with my bag.

"But," I reminded him, "the alarm was on."

He got in close, lifted a hand, and while he shifted my hair off my shoulder, he explained, "Can't be too careful."

"Oh," I said because there was nothing else to say, and anyway, I was recovering from the shifting-the-hair-off-my-shoulder move.

Hector kept looking at me.

What now? What did nice girls do after dinner with their date's mother and select close friends?

I wracked my brain. Finally, ever the good hostess, it came to me.

"Do you want a drink?" I offered.

"How much time do we have before your friends get back?" he asked in return.

I, personally, thought this was a weird question, but I didn't tell Hector that.

Instead I shrugged. "I don't know. Since I moved here, they've never gone out without me."

Then I realized Ralphie and Buddy never *had* gone out and left me home alone. Not for over a month. I was probably putting a major crimp in their social life.

And I didn't even notice.

Now what kind of genuine friend wouldn't even notice she was putting a crimp in her friends' social life?

Oh my, it was high time to call the real estate agent lady and get out of their hair. If I didn't, they might not like me anymore. And I couldn't lose them this soon.

Hector broke into my thoughts about real estate and Buddy and Ralphie's social life and said, "Then, no, I don't want a drink."

His answer confused me. I didn't understand why the timing of Ralphie and Buddy's return had anything to do with anything, but I didn't have a chance to ask.

Hector's hands came to my hips and slowly he pulled me close. His arms slid around me loosely and his chin tipped down so he could look at me.

"We have to talk."

Oh my.

With all that happened, I forgot about our talk.

All right, that was okay. I could do this. I could do anything. I survived dinner at his mother's house, didn't I?

"Okay," I said, mentally girding for our talk.

He didn't speak. Instead, his head bent and he touched my lips with his. My heart stuttered and I instantly ungirded.

All right, maybe I couldn't do this. I couldn't even stay mentally girded for a whole second!

"You just kissed me," I accused him.

His mouth moved like he was fighting a grin (again).

"Yeah," he answered.

"Kissing isn't talking," I informed him helpfully, like he didn't already know this fact.

More fighting the grin. "No," he agreed.

He pulled me closer so my body was lightly pressed to his.

"Well, are we going to talk?" I asked.

He was watching me closely and for some reason there was no grin fighting anymore.

Then he answered, "Yeah."

I waited.

He pulled me closer so my body was not so lightly pressed to his. In fact, I was so close I had to lift my hands and put them on his chest, right below his shoulders.

"Do you want me to start?" I asked, again trying to be helpful as I thought nice people would want to be.

"You have something to say?" he asked.

I thought about it.

I suppose I had a million things to say. I hadn't practiced any of them yet because I was too busy practicing what I was going to say to Lee. Talking to Lee took precedence, but I sure as certain wished I'd practiced *something* to say to Hector.

"Give a fuckin' mint to know what's goin' on in that head of yours," Hector muttered, breaking into my thoughts.

I ignored him and said, "Right now, I don't have anything to say. I reserve the right to say something later though."

At this, Hector started laughing. It was silent but I could feel his body moving with it. This confused me even more.

"What's funny?" I asked.

"You," he answered.

Me? *I* was funny? I'd never been funny.

Ever.

I tried to think of the last time I was funny.

No, there was no last time.

I was just not funny.

"What's funny about me?" I asked with curiosity.

He shook his head and brought me even closer so my body was deep in his. His arms were around me tight and my hands had to slide up to his shoulders.

"It'd take too long to explain and we got more important shit to talk about."

"Oh," I said, disappointed because I still kind of wanted to know what was funny about me. "Okay."

All of a sudden, he switched the subject. "What made you go out the back last night?"

I shrugged again. "Some bartender came up to me, handed me a note. It said it was from my mom, she'd been looking for me, finally found me and she was out back and I should meet her. I figure Harvey paid someone to give it to me."

Instantly and inexplicably, the air in the room changed. A current ran through it, strong and dangerous, and Hector's arms tightened further.

My body tensed.

"Are you *fucking* shitting me?" he asked, enunciating every word clearly from between his teeth.

"No," I whispered, because the change in him was kind of scaring me.

All of a sudden, he let go. I felt the loss of his heat like a blow and watched him walk away, tearing his hand through his hair. He stopped at the window, yanked the curtain back and looked at the street.

I stared at him, unsure what to do. One second he seemed to be kind of mellow but amused. The next he seemed anything but mellow and amused and his body language was saying to stay well away. Because of that, my head was telling me to run away.

Instead I called hesitantly, "Hector?"

"Give me a minute, Sadie," he said to the window.

I felt it prudent to give him a minute seeing as, for some bizarre reason, he seemed a tad bit upset (which was an understatement). Then after what felt like about a hundred minutes, he spoke.

"I'm losin' patience with this."

"With what?" I asked.

He kept looking out the window. "Usin' your fuckin' mother to get at you. How fuckin' low. *Fuck!*" he exploded.

Again, I was confused. In my experience people could do things a lot lower than that.

"This is Harvey Balducci we're talking about," I told Hector as if that explained everything which, to me, it did.

Hector's eyes turned to me.

"I mean, he's a jerk," I went on. "And he's crazy. And, well... he's a jerk."

"People don't do that shit," Hector told me.

That was when I laughed. I mean, seriously, people did that "shit" all the time.

"Oh, yes they do," I replied sagely.

Hector dropped the curtain, turned fully to me, his face hard and he said, "Sadie, no. They don't."

Instantly, my laughter died. "You know they do, Hector. You lived amongst us. My kind of people sell drugs and guns and kill people and kidnap them and rape them—" I stopped because Hector started toward me.

I lifted my hand to stop him, finally realizing what I had to say. It all came to me in a flash. I was going to tell him we were different, this would never work. I didn't belong in his world.

Simple as that.

But it was like Hector didn't see my hand. He kept coming at me until he was right there.

My hand hit his chest. He pulled me into his arms again and said, "Those aren't your kind of people."

"Yes, they are. Don't you remember—?"

"I remember you feeding me information on your father."

My body went rigid and I gasped (*not*, I belatedly realized, the kind of response to have when I was trying to keep my clandestine informant status a secret).

I tried to cover. "I don't know what you're talking about."

"Sadie, I saw you do it."

I blinked at him.

Oh my God.

Did he see me do it? How could he see me do it? That was just crazy. It was also impossible.

I kept lying. "You must have been mistaken."

He shook his head. "*Mamita*, I walked right up to the door and watched you do your thing, and for some crazy reason you did it while you kept your father's office door wide open."

"That was so I could hear if someone was coming!"

Oh no!

How stupid could I be? I'd given it away.

Blooming heck!

He pulled me closer. The dangerous current slid out of the room and he looked like he was fighting a grin again.

I stared at him. I mean, really, it was hard to keep up with his mood swings.

"Your plan didn't work. You didn't hear *me* coming."

Oh darn.

I watched his face and realized, indeed, he *did* see me do it.

Now what did I do?

I put my other hand to his shoulder, this time to try to push away. It didn't work.

I gave up and my eyes slid to the side. "Oh well, then, you knew." I tried to act like it was nothing.

"Helluva risk you took," he said.

I shrugged.

"Anyone could have seen you do it. You were lucky it was me."

He certainly wasn't wrong about *that*.

He went on, "You could have got yourself killed."

I bit my lip because he wasn't wrong about that either.

"Why *did* you do it?" he asked softly.

I pulled in both my lips, bit them, let them go and answered simply, "He was not a nice man."

"No," Hector agreed, and my heart lurched.

I ignored the lurch and looked at him.

With his easy agreement, he'd given me my opening. My father always said you should never waste an opportunity. So I didn't.

"There you go. That's why this, you and me and everyone else and your mom and all of it, everything, isn't going to work," I told him.

His chin jerked back after I finished talking, then his face went dark in another mercurial mood swing. "You wanna explain how you came to that conclusion?"

"Yes," I told him truthfully, my back going straight. "I'm not like you and your people. I'm Sadie Townsend. My father is Seth Townsend. I don't belong with your people. I never will."

His arms got tight again. The scary current came back into the room and his face got close. "*Mamita*, I think you're a little crazy."

I shook my head. "Not crazy. I just know who I am, what I am and where I belong. All your family and friends are very sweet and nice and everything, but you know, they know as well as I know, I don't belong. I think it's best for all concerned if this just ended here."

There. I did it. It was hard, but I kept my cool. I made sense. I didn't get emotional.

I wanted to get emotional. Actually, truth be told, I wanted him to kiss me again. I wanted him to hold me in his lap and feel snug and secure and feel his heat hit me. I wanted to have dinner at his mother's house again. I wanted to do the dishes and laugh in the kitchen with Jet and Indy again. I wanted Lee to tease me again.

But I knew I couldn't have those things.

I could accept genuine friendship from Buddy and Ralphie because, well... I didn't know why. Maybe because, when something happened (and it would) and I lost them, I would just lose two people and I'd lost more than that in my life. I'd come to love them enough and feel strong enough to ride that wave... until it ended.

If I accepted whatever it was that Hector was offering me, there was a whole gaggle of people I would lose.

Really, there was only so much a girl could take.

And my father always told me to play to your strengths, but more importantly, know your limitations. And I knew my limitations.

"Is that what you reserved the right to say?" Hector asked, breaking into my thoughts.

I nodded and pulled away.

However, it must be noted, I didn't actually *get* away. He leaned into me and one of his arms wrapped around my waist, the other hand slid up my back, along my neck and went into my hair.

I was getting the distinct impression that I should start girding again.

"All right, now I'll say what I gotta say," Hector announced.

Oh my.

I should have girded.

Again, I didn't expect him to have a response. I thought he'd just agree, leave and then, well… that would be that.

He didn't agree. And before I could stop him, he started talking. And what he said robbed me of the ability to do anything but stand pressed against him and stare.

"You got cameras in your gallery, the front and back entrances, your back office and the store. You got more cameras on this brownstone, front and back entrances. Your car has a tracking device. So does your purse. Your alarm has been rewired to send a simultaneous alert to the control room if someone breaches the system. All that shit is monitored in the control room at Nightingale Investigations offices."

See what I mean? Nothing to do but stare.

Hector kept talking.

"I know you know we've been watching the house. We meant to be visible and didn't try to hide. Point of that was to show the Balduccis this was not a safe place for them to get at you, and to show them, straight out, you're protected. The minute Ralphie took off and left you alone in your gallery, Monty, who manages surveillance, saw you alone and put the call out. No one was close enough to get to you quickly, but Lee knew Marcus was. Lee called Marcus. Marcus dropped everything, walked out of a meeting, went to the gallery and stayed until Ralphie came back."

Oh… my… *God.*

I knew there was something weird about Marcus being there!

"Ally planted the tracking device in your purse when they visited your gallery. Lee heard that the girls had planned to go there to meet you and see if you were okay. He took Ally aside, gave her the device, told her what to do. Shirleen's assignment was to divert your attention. While you were watching Shirleen, Ally grabbed one of your lipsticks and planted the device in the cap."

I could not believe this. Mainly because it was unbelievable.

And Ally sounded like she was a little bit like Veronica Mars!

"We've been tracking you, watching you and protecting you since you left the fuckin' hospital," Hector said. "As for me, obviously you haven't cottoned on to the situation, but bottom line, I'm gonna do whatever it is I gotta do to make you safe. Which means something has to give with the Balduccis. They don't get to pick how it's gonna give, I've already decided. They fuck up along the way, like Harvey did last night, then I'll take advantage. We're working with Marcus and the Zanos—"

"The Zanos?" I breathed, interrupting him for the first time, too shocked by this news to stay silent.

Vito Zano was a friend of my father's. I didn't know if he was dirty or not, but he was funny and I liked him. Ren Zano, his nephew, was very good-looking and very nice (and I didn't know if he was dirty or not either). I always had a bit of a crush on Ren, but, per usual, I didn't let it show.

That was, of course, I had a bit of a crush on Ren until Hector came along.

"The Zanos," Hector affirmed then went on, "You press charges against Ricky and Harvey, after what Ricky did to you, he goes away a long time. This would be strike three for Harvey since he isn't the smartest of the bunch and has been caught before. He goes in again, no one would see him for a while. Marty and Donny aren't so dumb as Harvey. They're just crazy. Ricky goes down, my guess, Marty assumes the throne, but Donny'll give him trouble. The Ricky-Marty-Donny rivalry is lore and you're caught up in that, so they have to go down, too. I'm workin' on it. So are Lee, Marcus, Vito and Ren. It'd help if Ricky and Harvey were out of commission, which means—"

Finally I stopped him. "It means I'd have to see Ricky again."

He kept silent. I closed my eyes. Then I clenched my teeth.

Then I opened my eyes and, do not ask me why, I shared.

"I can't, Hector." It came out as a whisper. "I want to press charges but I can't."

He let me go. His heat left me and a burst of cold hit me, shaking me out of the stupor induced by all he'd said, all he'd done, all that *everyone* had done.

But he didn't go to the window again. He took my hand and walked me to the couch.

Then (no kidding) before I knew what he was up to, he sat down. His hands went to my waist. he pulled me into his lap and his arms went around me.

105

Then he said softly, "You can do it Sadie, I know you can."

He was wrong.

I shook my head. "I can't."

"You fed me information on your father."

"I know."

"You risked your life to help that investigation."

"I know."

"How can you do that and not do this?"

I shook my head again. "I don't know." And I didn't.

Hector stared at me and I looked at him.

Then I had to say something just so he wouldn't think I was an utter coward.

"I'm not a total wimp," I assured him, trying to shake the uneasy feelings beginning to crawl along my skin that I was talking about this with *Hector* of all people. "I have a plan. See, if I don't press charges—"

Hector broke in, didn't even try to listen to my plan. "You can't play with these guys."

"But—"

"Sadie, *mi cielo*, you know it far better than I do. You play with these guys, you'll lose."

I felt the telltale lump hit my throat. I swallowed. It didn't work.

I swallowed again. It still didn't work.

Then before I could stop it, to my horror, I started crying.

Really! Where was my Ice Princess? Why did she come along when she wasn't wanted and disappeared when I needed her? She was beginning to *really* annoy me.

When the Ice Princess didn't show, with no other choice so he wouldn't see me cry, I shoved my face in his neck.

He dropped to the side on his back, taking me with him. He rolled us and then we were lying on the couch, me snug between the heat of him and the soft back of the couch.

One of his arms held me close at the waist. The other hand cupped the back of my head and held my face to his throat.

"Let me take care of you," he whispered through my sobs.

"Okay," I whispered through my sobs too, too tired to fight it anymore.

"I'll come get you tomorrow, take you to the Station."

I took a ragged breath.

Then, even though it scared me, I agreed.

"Okay," I repeated.

"Eddie'll be there. You want Ralphie there or anyone else—"

"Bex," I said immediately.

"Bex?"

"She's B... Buddy's f...f...friend. He introduced me to her," I said, but it took a long time because my voice kept hitching. "She works at a rape c...c... crisis center."

Hector's arms went tighter. "Okay, we'll call Bex."

"And Daisy," I went on.

His arms tightened further and I snuggled in closer.

"And Shirleen," I said, though I had no idea why.

"Shirleen?"

"She seems like a nice lady," I explained to him, but also to myself.

"She is," Hector said quietly.

We laid there and Hector held me. This went on for a long time.

I knew I should put a stop to it. All of it.

But I didn't.

How bizarre was *that?*

Finally, once the tears were subsiding, I called, "Hector?"

"Yeah?"

"Why?"

"Why what?"

"Why do you want to take care of me?"

His body went still for a few seconds, then he kissed the top of my head. "We'll save that for another talk."

I didn't think I wanted to have another talk with Hector. This one didn't go so well for me.

I found out he knew I was his informant (which was kind of embarrassing). I found out he'd been tracking me and doing more to protect me than he and his buddies sitting in cars outside the house. He *totally* didn't listen when I explained why we wouldn't work. And he got me to agree to press charges against two of the Balducci Boys, blowing my plan out of the water and playing my ace in the hole way faster than I intended.

No, this talk didn't go well for me.

Still, I was getting kind of sleepy. Tears always exhausted me, and a big old crying fit like that did me in.

Furthermore, I was full of Blanca's food.

Lastly, but most importantly, Hector's heat and closeness made me feel warm, snug and safe and I hadn't felt warm, snug and safe in *forever*.

So, instead of protesting the very idea of another talk that also could go very badly for me, I said, "Okay."

Then I snuggled even closer, not even caring what I was doing, and doing it because I liked to feel Hector's arms go tighter and tighter until he was holding me super close.

And once I was super close, snug, warm and safe in his arms, I fell asleep.

# Chapter 8
# Man of the Month

*Sadie*

I opened my eyes and the first thing I saw was the muscular column of a man's throat.

As this didn't happen to me every day, I thought it best to take stock of my surroundings.

I was in the living room on the couch and I was wrapped up in what appeared to be Hector. Although I kept my eyes trained on his throat, it couldn't really be anyone else.

By wrapped up, I meant that his arm was draped around my waist, my arm was draped around his waist, my top leg was thrown over his thigh, his leg was cocked between my legs. My other hand was flattened against his chest and the rest of me was pressed up close to the rest of him.

Oh my.

Somewhere along the line someone had thrown a blanket over us. His body was warm; the blanket was keeping in his warmth and I felt ultra cozy.

Memories of the night before flooded my brain and my coziness exited my body like a shot.

I needed to get the heck out of there, pronto. I tilted my head back to assess his consciousness. The minute I did, his chin dipped down and he looked at me.

Well, that answered that question. He was awake.

"Hi," I said for lack of another opening.

His face warmed and it dawned on my somnolent brain that he looked good when he woke up, especially his warm, sleepy, black eyes.

Oh my again.

Before I could think of anything else to say or do, his face started coming toward me and, all of a sudden, he was kissing me.

Yes, *kissing me*.

In the morning. On the couch. Tangled up with me.

For a nanosecond, I thought I'd pull away, but then I realized how much I liked his lips on my lips. Then the kiss deepened and I realized that I *seriously* liked his lips on my lips, but I liked his tongue in my mouth even better.

So I kissed him back.

This time it wasn't filled with urgency and fire. This time he was taking it slow, making it sweet, building the burn.

I liked it.

I liked it so much, I pressed closer to him and his hands started moving on me.

They weren't urgent either, not invading, not demanding. His touch was light, soft, and it felt really, super *good*.

That made me press closer. My hand dipped under his shirt and I felt his skin at his back. His heat was immense, his skin was smooth and I felt the hard muscle under it.

I liked that, too. I liked it so much I wanted more of it. I liked it so much I would give my entire trust fund to get more of it.

"Mornin' kids," we heard Ralphie say.

My body froze. Hector's mouth broke from mine and he looked in my eyes.

"Who's for coffee?" Ralphie went on and didn't stop. "Buddy's hangin'. Tied one on last night, so you'll have to make do with Breakfast a la Ralphie."

I lifted my head to look over Hector's shoulder and saw Ralphie disappear toward the kitchen, wearing his robe and scratching his behind.

I settled down and stared at Hector, torn between laughing, crying and panicking.

"We just got caught making out on the couch," I informed him on a whisper, as if he hadn't been present at the event.

"Yeah," Hector agreed, his lips doing that fighting-a-grin thing again.

Then it happened. I kind of exhaled sharply through my nose, and, unable to control it, I pressed my face in his throat and started to giggle. Within seconds, I was beyond giggling straight to laughter, my body shaking with it.

Hector rolled to his back, taking me with him so I was on top. The whole time, I kept laughing.

Later, when I was kind of laugh-hiccoughing, I lifted up, my forearm on his chest, my other hand coming up to wipe my eyes.

"That was funny," I told him, eyes rolled to the ceiling, swiping underneath my right one.

"I can see," Hector said.

I looked at him. He was grinning, but I realized belatedly he hadn't been laughing.

"Didn't you think it was funny?"

"*Mamita*, it was funny, but I've never seen you laugh like that before. No way in hell I was missin' the chance to watch that."

My stomach pitched at what he said and I was left speechless, the smile dying on my face.

"And there it goes," he mumbled, watching my mouth.

"Do you laugh a lot?" I asked, but for some reason I didn't expect him to answer. Maybe because it was kind of a personal question.

His arms were around my waist and he gave me a small, affectionate squeeze.

Then to my surprise, he answered, "On a scale of one to ten, with one being Sadie and ten being Indy, I'd say I'm at about a five."

"Does Indy laugh a lot?"

"All the time."

My body, which had gone tense, relaxed, and I smiled at him.

"That's good. I like her," I told him. "She's nice. She deserves a life of laughter."

Mr. Mood Swing's face grew dark and his voice sounded angry when he asked, "And you don't?"

"I didn't say that."

"It was implied."

I thought about what I said, then my eyes narrowed in confusion. "I didn't imply that either."

"Wasn't it you who stood in this room last night tellin' me you didn't belong with 'my people', sayin' you were Seth Townsend's daughter and that's the reason you didn't belong?"

"Well, I am Seth Townsend's daughter." And I was!

"*Tu padre* was a drug dealer, *you* were a drug dealer's daughter. You can't pick your father. No one blames you for the choices he made. You did the best you could with the hand you were dealt."

I tried to rewind our morning from kiss to now to see where we went awry, but Hector gave me another squeeze and the rewind hit pause. This squeeze was affectionate, but it was an *annoyed* affectionate.

"Your lot in life is not payin' for what your father did. You got a different lot in life. You chose your path the minute you started feedin' information to me through that drawer."

"What does that mean?"

"That means a lot of girls livin' your life wouldn't make that decision if it meant they couldn't live in big houses, wear designer clothes and drive expensive cars."

I blinked at him. "Hector, I don't know if you know this, but I *do* have a trust fund."

"You got three million dollars in a trust fund. That is not gonna give you the kind of life you lived with your father."

He was right, of course. Three million dollars was a lot of money, but my father was worth loads more (before the Feds seized it, of course).

This was all making me a bit uncomfortable, so before I could think better of it, I blurted, "Can we go back to the jovial, fun-loving portion of the morning?"

He stared at me, still angry for a minute, then his face cleared and he blew out a sigh.

"Wish you'd picked the tongue in my mouth, hand up my shirt portion of the morning."

I kind of wished I picked that, too.

He gave me another squeeze. I caught his grin and I realized that now *he* was teasing me.

My stomach did another pitch.

"Sweet 'ums, I know you're going for the world record for longest date in the history of man, but we have paintings to sell so we can pay on our Z Gallerie credit card," Ralphie said from the door to the kitchen.

Hector and I turned our heads and looked at Ralphie.

"I don't have a Z Gallerie credit card," I told Ralphie.

"Yes, but *I* do. Come on you two, up and at 'em." Ralphie clapped his hands. "Chop chop."

This time, *I* blew out a sigh.

Hector did an ab curl. I came up with him and ended up on his lap. He stood and set me on my feet. I realized then I was shoeless and Hector was bootless.

"How did my shoes get taken off?" I asked, staring at my feet.

"Buddy and I woke up Hispanic Hottie when we got home," Ralphie said. "Well, Buddy did. He was being really loud. Anyway, I got Hector a blanket, he took off your shoes and that's all I saw. I had a hunk a burnin' love to get to bed before he hurled on the hall carpet."

I looked at Hector. "I slept through that?"

Even though I asked Hector, Ralphie answered, "Like a baby."

I was a light sleeper. I'd wake up at a kitten's mew. How could I sleep through *that?*

"Come on, I made coffee and I'm thinking toasted brioche with marmalade. Yum-a-*licious!*" Ralphie went on.

"Thanks, but I have to go," Hector said, and Ralphie's eyebrows went up.

"Have you *had* brioche?" Ralphie asked.

"No," Hector answered.

"You don't want to miss brioche," Ralphie advised him.

Hector threw Ralphie a smile and then turned to me. His arm went around my waist and he pulled me gently to him so our sides and parts of our fronts were touching.

His head bent to mine, he gave me a quick kiss and he looked into my eyes.

"I'll go home, shower, change. I'll call Eddie and Shirleen. Shirleen'll call Daisy. You call your friend Bex. I'll come back and take you to the Station. Tell Bex to meet you there in two hours," Hector told me.

Oh no.

In all the goings-on, I forgot I promised him I'd go to the Station.

I opened my mouth to say something but Ralphie got there before me.

"The Station?" he asked.

Hector's eyes swung to Ralphie. "Sadie and I talked last night and she's agreed to press charges against Ricky and Harvey Balducci this morning."

I watched as Ralphie's face went pale and his hand came up to hold onto the doorjamb. His reaction alarmed me and my body went tight in preparation to go to him.

Before I could move, Ralphie breathed, "He's going to pay?"

I felt the tears hit the backs of my eyes just as I saw them shimmering in Ralphie's and heard the tremor of feeling in his voice.

"He's gonna pay," Hector said.

Ralphie blinked, got himself together and took his hand from the door-jamb.

"You... are... a... miracle worker!" he announced to Hector. "You are officially Ralphie's Man of the Week. No! Man of the Month! I'm making you a certificate!"

I felt Hector's body start to shake with laughter as Ralphie charged into the room.

"Go! Do your business. We'll get Sadie ready," Ralphie said, grabbing my hand, yanking me out of Hector's arm and pulling me toward the hall.

I looked behind me as Ralphie pulled me away and saw Hector leaning down to pick up his boots.

When he straightened, his eyes came to me, and still grinning, he said, "I'll be back in an hour."

My heart was beating and I was scared out of my mind. In the cold light of day, I was *not* sure about this pressing charges business.

But the only thing I could get in before Ralphie dragged me into the hall was, "Okay."

⚞⚟

Hector, Buddy and I walked into the Station.

Ralphie had gone to Art to open up.

After Hector left, Ralphie woke up Buddy and shared the news that I was going to the Station. Buddy (according to Ralphie) jumped out of bed "lickity split".

Buddy spent the morning gulping down copious amounts of ibuprofen mixed with acetaminophen with the addition of caffeine in his coffee. Still, he looked like hell, but Buddy didn't have a shift that day (thus, him allowing himself to tie one on last night) and Ralphie informed me there was no way "on God's green earth" I was going to the Station without one of them with me.

While I showered, drank coffee, ate toasted brioche with orange marma-lade and did my hair and makeup, Ralphie picked out my outfit. It was as Queen Ice as you could get.

Winter white, plain front, light wool trousers with wide legs and a cuffed hem. This was paired with a winter white, silk, tailored blouse. For contrast, Ralphie added a slim, ice-blue belt and ice-blue, 50's-style, ultra-pointed-toed, pencil-heeled, sling-backed pumps. My ensemble was completed with a winter white, Italian leather, tailored blazer, my diamond studs and diamonds-in-platinum tennis bracelet.

Pure ice.

Hector held my hand as we walked into the Station, Buddy (still looking peaked), on my other side.

In the lobby were Daisy, Shirleen, Luke Stark and a big man with light brown hair and a muscle-bound frame. In fact, one look at him and I was certain sure that God had seen fit to give this man *twice* as many muscles as other men were granted.

Daisy rushed to me the moment she saw me. "You okay?" she asked.

"I'm scared to death," I answered.

Hector squeezed my hand.

Daisy grabbed my casted wrist and held on. "Ain't no one gonna hurt you, not here, not again. Comprende?"

I nodded.

"We're gonna be right here. You won't be alone," she went on.

I nodded again.

We advanced to where Luke, Shirleen and the other man were standing.

When I got within a few feet of her, Shirleen crowded in, pulled me away from Hector and Daisy and gave me a fierce hug.

"Child," she said softly into my hair.

Then she let me go.

That was it. But that was all there needed to be. Shirleen Jackson gave good hugs.

"Sadie, this is Luke Stark and Jack Tatum," Hector said when Shirleen moved away. "They work for Lee and they're here to give their statements. They were there the night you drove into the garage."

At that, my body froze solid.

Bex told me a lot of people blocked out what happened to them. Not me. No, I remembered every last second. Including scrambling in the stairwell in nothing but a nightgown.

I instantly decided I couldn't do this.

Right before I could turn on my heel and run, Jack spoke. "I'm just gonna say, I like Hector's plan for takin' Ricky down a lot better than this shit. I don't like the idea of him gettin' a cushy jail cell for the next fifteen years. No man makes a woman end her night slippin' in her own blood on some stairs—"

"Jack," Luke growled (yes, he *growled*).

I felt, rather than saw, Hector's body grow tight, and that dangerous current was snapping all around the lobby.

"Thank you," I said quickly in an effort to fight back the current.

Jack stared at me. Then he said, "What?"

I pushed back the panic, tamped down the fear and sallied forth so Hector didn't come to blows with his colleague because he'd been an *eensy* bit too honest at an inappropriate moment.

I explained, "You got to me first. You were nice. Thank you."

Jack stared at me again. Then he muttered, "Jesus."

I decided to take that as a muscle-bound man's way of saying "you're welcome".

I took a deep breath, straightened my spine, looked up to Hector and asked quietly, "Can we go and do this now?"

His arm slid along my shoulders, he pulled me into his side and looked down at me.

"Yeah, *mamita*, we can go do this now."

⚔

We walked into a big room that was full of people, phones ringing and lots of desks.

It didn't go silent when we walked in, but the noise definitely muted.

My eyes caught Eddie, who was standing at a desk in the middle of the room. Beside him was a middle-aged man, shorter than Eddie by several inches, definitely rounder, and he had dark, thinning hair.

Their eyes came to us immediately upon entering the room. I saw Eddie look at his brother before his eyes moved to me. Then he smiled.

His smile was nearly as nice as Hector's.

"Willie, Brian, Tony, Jorge, she's here. Round 'em up," the man beside Eddie said, pointing to some uniformed officers that were standing several feet away, and then he twirled his finger and pointed to the door.

The officers didn't waste time. They took off.

Eddie and the man walked to us.

The man stopped, Eddie didn't. His arm went around my waist and he leaned in and kissed the side of my head. While I was recovering from that, he stepped back.

"This is Detective Jimmy Marker. He's gonna take care of you. Bex Cusack called and said she'd be here in twenty minutes. We'll start after she arrives," Eddie told me.

I nodded.

"They weren't jokin', you do look like a fairy princess," Detective Marker remarked.

I nodded again, now completely unfazed by this remark, then I sighed. "I get that a lot."

Detective Marker stared at me for a second, then he spoke again. "Willie, Brian, Jorge and Tony just went out to pick up Ricky and Harvey. We already called the hospital and made appointments to get statements from the staff who took care of you. Got officers jumpin' at the chance to nail those two jack-asses, so Luke, Jack, you're up now. Luke, you're with Melvin. Jack, you're with Danny. Hector, I wanna talk to you."

Without delay, Luke and Jack moved into the room, separated and went to different desks.

I didn't even have a chance to take this in before Detective Marker kept talking. "Lee sent the photos of your apartment over this morning. I woulda liked to have had a chance to send the lab boys over after the incident, but if someone will let us in now, we'll comb the place, see if we can find anything that places Ricky there."

"I can let you in," Buddy volunteered.

Detective Marker looked over his shoulder and called, "Adam, we got access to Sadie's apartment. Call the boys."

A man across the room immediately picked up a phone.

I blinked.

Boy, these guys didn't mess around.

Detective Marker's eyes were on me again and he caught the blink. "We're police. We don't like crime," he informed me.

"I don't like it either," I assured him, just in case he was wondering.

"I wasn't finished," Detective Marker said.

"Oh," I murmured.

"I got a wife, three daughters. Rape's on the top of the list of crimes I don't like," Detective Marker declared.

I swallowed then moved closer to Hector. When my hand found his and his strong fingers closed around mine, I nodded.

"I know who you are," Detective Marker said and I held my breath. "So I suppose, the way you grew up, you don't get this so I'll explain it to you now. You're standin' there holdin' Hector Chavez's hand. Hector's Eddie's brother, Eddie's one of us. We don't like crime, but we *really* don't like crime when it happens to one of us. You're one of us now. Ricky Balducci is goin' down. I don't care how it happens, but me and every man in this room is gonna do whatever the fuck we gotta do to make it happen. You with me?"

"I'm with you," I whispered.

"All right then," he nodded. Then he smiled (which made him a lot less scary) and he reached out and squeezed my arm. "Badass Cop Speech is over, let's get this done."

Without anything else to say, I said, "Okay."

❦

"V... I... fuckin'... P!" Tex boomed the minute Shirleen, Daisy, Hector and I walked into Fortnum's Used Bookstore (Buddy was at my apartment with the "lab boys").

We stopped several feet in front of the door and I took in the scene.

There was a large open space at the front of the store, a counter in front of rows of bookshelves, an espresso counter against the back side wall. Tons of comfortable-looking chairs, couches, armchairs and tables littered the middle. It smelled musty, dusty, but looked really cool in a lived-in, sit-back, stay-awhile kind of way.

Even though it was well beyond coffee hour, there were people every-where. Most of the seats were taken. There were three customers waiting in line to order, two standing at the end of the espresso counter waiting for their coffees.

Indy and a big, gray-bearded, long-gray-hair-in-a-ponytailed man wear-ing a black T-shirt that demanded you "Ride the Range" and a black leather vest with a rolled red bandana on his forehead were standing behind the counter.

Tex and Jet were behind the espresso counter. Ally was clearing coffee mugs from the seating area.

"You!" Tex boomed, pointing at the people innocently sitting on the couch in front of the big, glass window at the front of the store. "That's VIP seating. Up! *Move!*"

Without a word, as if this had happened before and they had loads of practice, the people grabbed their mugs and laptops and scurried to the corner table.

"You!" Tex pointed to me. "Sit!"

"You better sit," Shirleen whispered sideways to me. "Indy's face is gettin' red. She hates it when Tex bosses around the customers. She looks like she's gonna blow."

I didn't want Indy to blow so I nodded to Shirleen and hurried to the couch.

"I'm makin' you a special," Tex shouted to me.

"Okay, Tex," I thought it best to shout back. Then I sat down.

"You're gonna hafta wait. That's Sadie. She's a VIP," Tex informed the next person in line, like they didn't already know this fact really, *really* well.

Daisy sat down on one side of me, Shirleen on the other side. They sat close, like sentries.

I looked helplessly up at Hector. He was doing that fighting-a-grin thing again.

I narrowed my eyes at him. The grin grew into a glamorous, white smile.

My eyes un-narrowed and I stared at him. He shook his head and went to the counter where Indy was.

Ally bustled up, precariously balancing used coffee mugs.

"You okay?" she asked.

I nodded. "It wasn't that bad. Detective Marker is nice," I told her.

She smiled and her eyes danced in a mischievous Veronica Mars type of way. "I wasn't talking about that. I was talking about Hector taking you to Blanca's for dinner last night. What *is* it with the Chavez men taking their women home to meet their Mama? They know better. Blanca's a nut. First time Eddie took Jet home, Blanca had the whole family over, plus half the neighborhood."

I gasped, sorry for Jet, but also thankful that I didn't have to deal with half the neighborhood last night. What I had was enough!

All of a sudden, Jet was there. "It's true," she told me. "I got snockered on margaritas."

"And Eddie threw your cell across the yard and shattered a margarita pitcher," a newly arrived Indy shared.

"I still wish I hadn't missed that," Daisy muttered.

"Boy's got good aim," Shirleen put in. "Damn waste of margaritas though."

"Why'd he throw your cell phone?" I asked Jet.

"Well, I kind of had some bad men after me. One called me. Eddie took the phone away from me and heard what he had to say. It made him a little..." She hesitated. "Miffed."

"Miffed! Eddie Chavez *miffed!* I love it," Ally hooted.

"He wasn't miffed, the man was *pissed!*" Indy put in, a huge smile on her face.

Boy, he would have to be beyond miffed to throw a cell phone.

I looked at Hector, who was talking to the guy with the bandana.

"I just bought a new cell phone. I like it," I told them.

"Keep it away from Hector," Ally advised, then burst out laughing.

So did everyone else. I looked around at them, not sure what was funny.

I mean, I *did* like my cell phone. It was fancy and you could even get e-mail on it.

Tex shouldered in and handed me a big mug. "Butterscotch sandie latte. That's butterscotch and pecan syrup. If that don't trip your trigger, woman, nothin' will," he announced. Then he shouldered back through and returned to the espresso counter.

I turned to Daisy. "I don't mean to be mean or anything but, isn't he a bit... *odd?*"

Daisy started giggling and it sounded like Christmas bells. I couldn't help but giggle with her.

She put her arm around me and gave me a squeeze. "Sugar, that ain't the *half* of it."

I took a sip of my latte. My eyes bugged out.

Trigger tripped.

Hector and I spent about an hour at Fortnum's. Hector spent most of his time talking on his phone. I spent my time talking to the girls, Duke (the guy with the bandana, who had a very deep, gravelly voice and was somewhat intense in a scary, but not overly-scary, way) and Tex.

Tex made me go behind the counter so he could teach me how to make espresso. Since I had an espresso maker and so did Ralphie and Buddy, I showed him my stuff.

He was impressed.

Then I told Hector I had to get back to the gallery. We had an opening next week and Ralphie was having to do all the work. Even if I was pressing charges against one brother for rape and another brother for assault and attempted kidnapping which, for normal people, would mean they could probably take the day off, I couldn't sit back and let Ralphie do all the work.

I said good-bye to the girls, Tex and Duke. Hector walked me out to his Bronco, helped me in and we took off.

⬚

Hector double-parked in LoDo (what they call lower downtown in Denver) right outside Art.

Like this was perfectly legal and he had all the right in the world to double-park, he casually flipped on his hazards and walked me into the store.

We walked in, Ralphie looked up and called, "Hey Double H, Buddy called. Said he's making his famous seared tuna in citrus and flash-fried noodles tonight. You missed the brioche. You *cannot* miss the tuna. That would be a crime against gastronomy."

I stared at Ralphie.

Someone please tell me that Ralphie didn't just invite Hector over to dinner.

Someone else please tell me that Ralphie hadn't given Hector the nickname "Double H".

"What time?" Hector asked.

"Six-ish," Ralphie replied.

"I'll be there," Hector said.

Yes, Ralphie just invited Hector over to dinner. *And* Hector accepted.

I took stock of my life and asked myself if it was in my control.

Kristen Ashley

In a nanosecond, I came to the conclusion it wasn't in my control.

Before I could speak to either of them to tell them I needed to get my head together, to deal with the day, to cope with my decisions, to understand my feelings, to figure out what I was going to do next, Hector's arm came around my shoulders and he curled me into his heat.

All thoughts of mind-organization and future-planning swept out of my brain and I looked up at him.

"See you at six," he said.

I nodded.

His other hand came up and his fingers sifted into the hair at the side of my head.

"You did good today," he said quietly.

"Thank you," I replied.

"I'll call if I hear they picked up Ricky or Harvey before I come over tonight."

"That would be nice."

"Sadie?"

"What?"

"You with me?"

I blinked in confusion and said, "Yes." And I was, wasn't I? I was standing in his arms for goodness sake.

"This is Sadie?" Hector went on.

I blinked again. "Yes."

"My Sadie?" he kept at it.

This time I blinked for a different reason.

*His* Sadie? Was there a Hector's Sadie? Was *I* Hector's Sadie? Did Hector think I was his Sadie?

Oh… my… *God.*

Before I could process what he said or get close to processing what that meant, I watched him smile, then he bent his head and kissed my lips.

"Yeah," he said, his face an inch away. "It's my Sadie."

"What are you talking about?" I breathed.

"I thought she slipped away. You were acting like Stepford Sadie."

"Stepford Sadie?"

He kept smiling. "Yeah."

My back went straight and my confused stare turned into an *annoyed* stare.

I mean, really! Stepford Sadie?

"I'm not Stepford Sadie. I'm Ice Princess Sadie," I informed him because, well, he should get it right!

"Whatever. Just as long as she's gone," he muttered. He touched his mouth to mine again, then *he* was gone.

I stared at the door as it swished closed behind him.

In a flash, Ralphie was by my side. "He... is... *lush,*" Ralphie breathed. "I wanna take a bite outta him. Dee-*licious.*"

I decided immediately I didn't want to talk about Hector being lush and I *definitely* didn't want to talk about taking a bite out of him.

"My life is out-of-control," I told the door.

Without hesitation, Ralphie did the same move Hector had that morning, except different, less possessive and protective, just as sweet. His arm went around my shoulders and he pulled me into his side and partially to his front.

"Sweets? My advice?" he asked.

I put my head to his shoulder, my arms around his waist and I nodded.

"What I can see with that man, the safety bar is locked tight. Put your hands straight up and enjoy the ride."

Oh my.

# Chapter 9
# You Sleep Here Don't You?

*Sadie*

"Aaahhooow," Ralphie yawned with an exaggerated stretch. "I'm tuckered out. Time for beddie bye. Buddy, baby, you comin' with me?"

I looked from Hector's shoulder (where my head was resting) to the end of the couch (where Ralphie was stretching) to the armchair (where Buddy was sitting).

Then I rolled my eyes and went back to staring at the credits rolling on the TV.

Seriously, how obvious could you be?

⚞⚟

Dinner went okay if you didn't count one minor incident.

⚞⚟

Buddy hadn't just made his famous tuna and noodles. He'd set the dining room table and even lit candles. He also served his spinach salad with pumpkin oil balsamic vinaigrette before the tuna, and chocolate almond torte with vanilla-essence whipped cream for dessert.

I changed out of my Queen Ice outfit, and in the two seconds between our arrival home at six-oh-five and Hector's arrival at the house at six-oh-five-and-two-seconds, I stared at the contents of my closet, trying to find a casual-dinner-at-home-with-Hector-and-my-two-gay-roommates outfit.

Impossible!

In a dither, I opted for a pair of jeans and a black camisole over which I wore a gray cardigan (well, it wasn't just a gray cardigan, it was a gray cardigan from Anthropologie; it had a hood and wide sleeves with tiny black lace ruffles at the sleeves and around the hem). I decided, since the cardigan said more than "casual-dinner-at-home-with-Hector", I'd go barefoot.

Barefoot was as casual as you could get.

I put my hair in a big ponytail and headed down.

Since Ralphie talked a mile a minute and Buddy wanted the lowdown on The Search for Harvey and Ricky (the lowdown was that Harvey had been snagged; Ricky was still "at large", and I kind of wished it was the other way around), I didn't have to say much.

This continued at dinner, mostly Ralphie talking enough for everyone, and, when he could get a word in edgewise, Buddy demanding details from Hector on how things would go once Ricky and Harvey were both caught.

This took a turn when, somehow, we got on the subject of dog sitting YoYo, and Ralphie shoved me, kicking and screaming, right in middle.

"Sadie wants to watch YoYo," Ralphie told Buddy when it was becoming clear he was losing the fight.

My head snapped up, and I saw from across the table Hector's eyes come to mine and one side of his mouth twitched.

"Sadie, is that true?" Buddy asked.

I widened my eyes at Hector in a non-verbal, *Help me!*

Hector remained silent but his mouth kept twitching.

"Sadie, tell him. You loved YoYo, didn't you?" Ralphie prompted.

I decided to be Hector and remain silent.

"Sadie?" Now it was Buddy's turn to prompt.

I made the new decision to extricate myself pronto. "I don't get a say. It isn't my house."

This was a bad decision.

"What do you *mean* it isn't your house?" Ralphie snapped.

I looked at Ralphie. Ralphie looked angry.

"Well, what I mean is——" I started.

"You sleep here, don't you?" Ralphie asked.

"Yes, but——" I tried again.

"Your clothes are here," Ralphie pushed.

"Yes, but, what I mean——" I kept trying.

"You shower here, put your makeup on here, watch Veronica Mars here, come home after work to, um... I don't know? *Here!* Don't you?" Ralphie pressed.

"Yes, I guess so, but——"

"You *guess* so?" Ralphie's eyes had narrowed.

"Ralphie, you wanna let her talk?" Buddy cut in.

Ralphie sat back, crossed his arms on his chest and glared at me.

"All I'm saying is that I'm a guest, and as a guest I don't have any say in these kinds of decisions," I explained.

Ralphie looked at Buddy and snapped, "She thinks she's a guest."

"Sadie—" Buddy started.

Ralphie interrupted, "What? Are you moving out?"

My gaze slid to Hector, who was now smiling at the remains of his chocolate almond torte. I wanted to throw my plate at him.

I, of course, did not.

Because, even though he deserved it, that would be rude.

I answered Ralphie, "Well, yes."

Hector's head came up and his smile vanished.

"What? When?" Buddy asked sharply.

I looked at Buddy. "I realized last night that you guys have been looking out for me for a while now so it's probably time to get out of your hair."

"Buddy doesn't have hair," Ralphie clipped.

"You know what I mean," I said quietly to Ralphie.

"No, Ms. Sadie Marie Townsend, I do not know what you mean." Ralphie didn't take a hint from my quiet tone.

"Maybe we should talk about this later." Buddy was eyeing the now completely unamused Hector.

"That would be good," I said with relief.

"You better believe we'll talk about it later," Ralphie threatened. He swung his glare toward Buddy. "So what's the verdict on the fucking dog?" he demanded.

I held my breath wondering what Hector might think of all these shenanigans. I bet Blanca didn't say "fucking" at *her* table.

Buddy's eyes came to me.

Then he sighed.

"We'll watch YoYo."

⇤⇥

After dinner we settled into the living room and watched *Walking Tall* (The Rock version, which Buddy declared was the only version that was worth a shit due to The Rock being a whole lot easier on the eyes than Joe Don Baker).

This was not normal Ralphie and Buddy viewing fodder, but I figured they were being good hosts to macho man Hector. I didn't really see Hector sitting though *Auntie Mame* or *Steel Magnolias*.

Of course, they finagled me into the middle of the couch position, but Ralphie didn't have to try the massaging my feet move. Hector pulled me into his side right away.

I'd had a rough day and decided not to fight it.

Anyway, he was comfy and warm.

⌫⌦

Now the movie was over and Buddy and Ralphie were off to bed.

"'Night, sweets," Ralphie said, kissing my cheek.

"Goodnight," I replied.

Buddy leaned in after Ralphie. "See you in the morning, Sadie." Then he kissed my cheek too.

I smiled at him. "See you."

"Hector, later." Buddy lifted his chin to Hector.

"Double H, you the man," was Ralphie's bizarre goodnight.

Then they were gone.

Now what did I do?

I twisted to look at Hector. "You want to watch another movie?" I asked.

He shook his head.

"An episode of Veronica Mars?" I tried.

More head shaking.

"A game?"

Still more head shaking.

Oh no.

I was out of options.

Hector wasn't.

His arm around my waist curled and his other hand came to my hip. He turned me and pulled me into his lap.

His eyes warm on my face, his arms around me loosely, he asked, "You doin' okay?"

"Yes," I answered.

He gave me a mini-squeeze. "Tough day for you," he said softly.

Something about that question hit me somewhere deep.

It wasn't fun, reliving what Ricky did to me in front of a camera in an interrogation room, even if Bex was with me, Detective Marker was really nice and I knew Daisy and Shirleen were out in the hall. It also wasn't fun reliving what Harvey did to me.

The fact that Hector would realize this would take its toll—even if I was trying to set it aside and not make a big deal of it—meant a lot.

I pulled in my lips and bit them.

I could have gone all Ice Princess on him, but when he was being nice and I had nothing to keep myself shielded from that would just mean I was a bitch.

So I whispered, "I'll be okay."

At my whisper, he grinned. "I knew you could do it."

The warmth in his tone and the approval in his eyes made my stomach pitch.

It was then I decided I needed my Ice Shields up.

"Nobody likes a know-it-all," I said coldly.

His grin got bigger. He shook his head and I got the impression he thought my Ice Shields were lame and scrawny.

He got to his feet, taking me with him then setting me on mine.

With his head tilted down to look at me, his hand slid around to the back of my neck and up into my hair. I just barely controlled a delicious shiver (but I did it).

"I gotta get home. Get some sleep," he told me.

I felt a wave of disappointment hit me. I'd spent all but about five hours in the last twenty-seven with him (yes, I'd counted). It would be weird for him just to go.

I didn't tell him that. Instead, I nodded.

He dropped his hand but caught mine and took me with him as he walked to the door.

Once there, he stopped, turned to me, his fingers wrapped around my cast and he looked down at it.

"Who's takin' you to get this removed?"

"Bex."

His gaze lifted to mine. "She can't do it, you call me."

It wasn't really a request, but I still said, "Okay."

He dropped my cast and tugged on my other hand. I leaned forward. His head came down and he kissed me, slow and sweet.

He lifted his head an inch and murmured, "I wanna hear the locks."

I wasn't breathing really well so I decided not to try to talk and simply just nodded again.

He left. I went to the door, turned the locks and put my ear to it so I could hear his boots walking away.

When I couldn't hear them anymore, I said to the door, "Blooming heck."

I walked up the stairs, into my room and went to my nightwear drawer.

I used to wear nothing but silky, lacy nighties to bed. On Day Nine at Ralphie and Buddy's house, after they moved my stuff in, I took every last one of them and threw them in the kitchen garbage.

I don't know why. I just did.

From that point, I wore t-shirts and yoga pants to bed.

On about Day Seventeen at Ralphie and Buddy's, Ralphie and I came home from the gallery and there were two big pink and white-striped Victoria's Secret bags on my bed. In them were two pairs of silky, lacy pajama bottoms with matching camisoles, two pairs of soft cotton and lacy pajama bottoms and matching camisoles, two pairs of soft knit pajama bottoms and matching camisoles and two pairs of silk, tailored women's pajamas.

Buddy'd had the day off and he'd obviously gone shopping.

They must have seen my nighties in the garbage.

I didn't say anything. Neither did they. But I mentally added a percent to Ralphie's merit increase at his next performance evaluation.

I pulled off my clothes, pulled on my jade green pajama bottoms and matching camisole with smoky gray lace at the bodice and hem of the camisole and pajama pants (they were very pretty; Buddy had good taste in women's nightwear), went to the bathroom off my bedroom, brushed my teeth and washed my face.

Then I went to bed.

I tried to settle in but I couldn't.

I tossed and turned, thinking of Harvey in jail and Ricky still "at large". Thinking Ricky was likely pretty angry at me while he was still "at large".

Thinking that Hector had taken me to his Mom's house on our first date and how weird and scary that was. Thinking that Daisy was again my friend, Ally intrigued me, Indy and Jet were sweet and Shirleen gave good hugs.

I tried to clear my mind and tossed and turned some more. But I couldn't settle.

It was all going to get worse. I knew it. If either Harvey or Ricky fought it, I'd have to testify. I'd have to tell a room full of people what happened to me and I'd have to see both of them again, and I didn't want to do that.

Not ever again.

And I didn't know what was happening with Hector. I was getting in deep and it seemed I couldn't stop myself. Not that he was giving me the chance.

If I was honest with myself I liked to be around him. He made me feel things, things I hadn't felt since Mom left. It was more than safe. It was comfy, snug and content, like I didn't have to be looking over my shoulder all the time, wondering what his true intentions were, guarding myself from the sharks circling. He was real. He wasn't hiding anything. He wasn't out for anything.

He was just Hector.

And in the very, very back of my mind where I let my true feelings lie, I had to admit that it was more than just liking being with him. I liked him kissing me, touching me. I liked it loads. So much, when it was happening it didn't even occur to me to push him away.

I should be pushing him away.

I couldn't get used to this, I knew. I knew better than to let anyone in.

I was going to have to get rid of him and to do it I was going to have to bring back the Ice Princess.

It was on that thought, my cell rang.

I threw my covers back, jumped out of bed and ran to the fluffy, chintz armchair in my bedroom, snatching my cell off the top of my purse before it woke Ralphie and Buddy.

Before I could think twice, I flipped it open and put it to my ear.

"Hello?"

"Sadie, you stupid cunt!"

My back went straight at the c-word, but the vicious voice kept talking in my ear.

"You shoulda let me deal with Ricky and Harvey. Shit, you stupid cunt."

He said it again!

"Who is this?" I asked.

"You dumb bitch. Settin' Chavez and Nightingale on us. What the fuck?"

I knew this voice. I wasn't sure which but it was either Donny or Marty Balducci.

Blooming heck.

Those crazy Balducci Brothers!

Why?

Why, why, why, why, *why?*

Someone please tell me, what did *I* do?

He kept talking. "You're gonna pay, you bitch, you're gonna fuckin' pay."

Disconnect.

I stood there in the dark, cell to my ear, and I could feel my heart beating in my throat.

Then I flipped my phone shut and ran out of my room, across the hall and right to Ralphie and Buddy's closed door.

I lifted my hand to knock and stopped.

It had to be after midnight. I couldn't wake them. They both had to work the next day. They had jobs, lives. They'd already seen me through a rape and an attempted kidnapping. What kind of friend would lay a middle-of-the-night threatening phone call on their door, even if the call did include the c-word (twice!)?

If I kept dragging them into my mess, I was going to use them up. I couldn't use them up.

I already owed them...

I closed my eyes and shook my head.

I owed them too much to ever repay. I couldn't use more.

I stepped away from the door and kept backing up until I hit the opposite wall. I slid down, my knees coming up until my bottom hit the floor. Then I wrapped my arms around my legs, pressed my cheek against my knees and took in deep breaths.

I could do this. I could get through this all by myself. I'd just calm down and go to sleep. I'd be okay. I was always okay.

Well, if not okay-okay than at least okay...*ish*.

My phone rang in my hand. I jerked back and my phone went sailing in the air.

I scrambled to catch it but it dropped to my side. My hands went to the floor and searched blindly in the dark until my fingers hit the phone.

I snatched it up, flipped it open and put it to my ear. "Leave me alone!" I hissed.

"Sadie."

It was Hector.

I closed my eyes tight and swallowed my heart, which was lodged in my throat.

"Hang tight, *mamita*," he told me. "I'll be there in ten."

I blinked into the darkness. "What?"

But he'd already disconnected.

I stared at my illuminated phone for what could have been seconds or hours. Then I flipped it shut.

My eyes moved to Buddy and Ralphie's door and I willed it to stay closed.

Then I thought about how my life was such a *fucking* mess and it was all down to my *fucking* father and the *fucking* Balduccis.

Then I wondered why Hector was coming over. I mean, I get a nasty phone call in the middle of the night and five minutes later he calls and says he's coming over?

How bizarre was *that?*

All of this must have taken ten minutes because I heard a knock at the door.

I ran down the stairs, and with my ear to the door, I called, "Who is it?"

"Me," Hector said.

I unlocked and opened the door.

He put a hand to my belly, shoved me back, stepped in, closed the door behind him, twisted and locked it. After locking it, he turned to me, my mouth opened to say something and he pulled me roughly into his arms and held me tight.

The panic crawling through my system slid away instantly and I sagged into him.

I took a shaky breath then tilted my head back to look at him. "What are you doing here?"

"Brody, our computer guy, patched into your cell. We monitor your calls and we can listen to them. Jack heard Marty Balducci. He called me. I came."

Oh my.

Simple as that. *He called me. I came.*

I dropped my head and rested my forehead against his chest. Hector's tight arms got tighter.

"He's not gonna hurt you."

I wanted to laugh. I did not.

"They've already hurt me. One of them raped me. Another one attacked me in an alley and tried to kidnap me in order that he could rape me!" I whispered on a hiss directly to his chest.

"*Mamita*, look at me." His tone was gentle.

I shook my head.

"Sadie, look at me." This time, his tone was firm.

I sighed and looked at him.

"He's not gonna hurt you."

I shook my head again.

"I'm tellin' you, *mi corazón*, he's not gonna hurt you."

Instead of fighting him, I shoved my face in his chest. I did this mainly because I figured I wouldn't win.

I also knew what "*mi corazón*" meant. It meant, "my heart", and I didn't even have to ask Jet if that was a step up in endearments.

I realized that my arms were around him and I brought my cold hands up to the heat of his chest. I was still carrying my cell phone and now *I* wanted to throw it into a margarita pitcher. He stroked my back for a while until I couldn't fight it (it felt too nice), and I started to relax into him.

He must have felt the tension leave me, but he held my relaxed body for even longer until it seemed kind of weird that we were standing there, not talking, just him holding me.

Finally, he said, "If you're gonna be all right, I'll go home."

Instantly the panic started crawling again, and before I could think, my head snapped back and I cried, "No!"

Blooming heck.

Someone, please tell me I didn't just do that.

To cover, I jerked out of his arms, all the while shaking my head with the hand holding my cell phone up in the air.

"No, no. Go home. It's okay. Don't listen to me. I'm just——" I started but he reached out, pulled the cell out of my hand then his fingers wrapped around my wrist.

He tugged me into the living room, straight to the decorative chest that held the extra toss pillows and blankets (Z Gallerie, of course). He opened it, pulled out a blanket, handed it to me and walked us to the couch. I watched in stunned silence as he threw my cell on the coffee table. He sat, yanked off his boots then reached out and pulled the blanket from my arms. He tossed it to the end of the couch. His hands came to my hips, and with a gentle tug he brought me off my feet. His hands went tight on my hips as he leaned back and I fell with him, Hector controlling my fall and me landing right on top of him (yes, right on top of him!). He rolled me to the side so I was stuck between him and the couch. Then he did an ab curl, nabbed the blanket, shook it out and placed it over us.

When he settled on his back, his arm around me, me tucked to his side, my cheek on his shoulder, I belatedly found my voice and asked, "What are you doing?"

"Go to sleep, Sadie."

"I—"

"Sadie, go to sleep."

"But—"

"Please, *mamita*, I'm wiped."

I snapped my mouth shut.

Well, so much for siccing the Ice Princess on him to get rid of him.

That was my last thought before I gave up the struggle, and within minutes, I fell asleep.

# Chapter 10

# Powder Room

*Sadie*

"Wakey wakey, kids. Time for coffee," Ralphie said, and I opened my eyes.

I could see the coffee table and Ralphie's legs in his robe walking across the living room. Again, since this wasn't my normal upon-waking vantage point, I assessed my situation.

I was on the couch, my legs bent. Something heavy was resting on my waist and there was immense heat coming at me all down the back of my body.

It would seem Hector and I were spooning on the couch. Sometime during the night, I'd moved from having my back, pressed to the couch and my front tucked into Hector's side, to being in front of Hector at the front of the couch.

How I slept through that I had no idea.

The arm around my waist curled around more, slanting across my midriff, and I was pulled up to sitting. Then two hands came to my waist and I was pushed to a standing position in front of Hector. Hands to my shoulders, he turned me to face him, and before I could say "boo", his head descended. He brushed my mouth with his, giving me a soft, sweet, morning kiss. His head lifted, he turned and left the room.

Frozen to the spot, breathing nowhere near normal, I heard the powder room door open and close.

My body jerked out of its stupor and I ran upstairs to my bathroom.

I forced my mind to still as unbidden thoughts of last night rushed into it. Thoughts of crazy Marty, incarcerated Harvey and still-at-large Ricky. And also thoughts of Hector coming to my rescue.

Instead, I forced myself to think about my most recent predicament, and I decided to take it one step at a time. Each step taken would get me through, for now.

I'd think of all the rest of it... later.

First, brush teeth then floss teeth and then wash face. After that make sure I didn't look like a fright. Then put on something so I was wearing more than just silky, lacy pajama bottoms and a camisole. But not something that would make me look like I was embarrassed or a prude because that would show weakness and my father told me (time and again), even if you had a weakness, you should never, *never* expose it.

Finally find my Ice Princess, click her into place and… proceed.

I took a deep breath, forced all other thoughts out of my head and went through my mental morning to-do list.

By the time I walked into the kitchen I was fresh-faced and fresh-breathed. I'd put on my full-length, cream, cotton, waffle-weave robe (but I didn't close the front because that might show I lacked confidence) and I was certain sure I could handle whatever came at me.

Hector was sitting on a stool at the island, so was Buddy. Both of them had a steaming mug of coffee resting in front of them. In the air I could smell the brioche toasting and Ralphie was at the counter manning the toaster.

"Hey there, sweets. Coffee?" Ralphie asked me, twirling a knife in the air.

"I'll get it," I replied and moved into the room not looking at Hector.

Hector, by the way, was one of those things I was going to think about later.

I made my coffee (dash of milk, one sugar, just like Hector).

"Double H is staying for brioche this morning," Ralphie informed me happily, like this was akin to William Shakespeare rising from the dead for the sole purpose of eating brioche with us while reciting a couple of his sonnets.

"That's nice," I said, but it didn't sound like I meant it. It sounded cold and uninterested.

Ralphie's head snapped around so he could look at me closely.

I gave him a look that said, *What?*

He gave me a look that said, *You know what!*

"A few things we need to go over," Hector said into Ralphie and my non-verbal exchange, apparently oblivious to my cold shoulder.

Unable to do anything else, I turned Ice Princess eyes to Hector.

He wasn't looking at me. He was looking at Ralphie. "From here on in, Sadie goes to and from work with you. She isn't alone at the store and she doesn't go anywhere unless she's with one of you or one of the men. She needs to go somewhere and she doesn't have someone with her, you call me and I'll take her or arrange an escort."

Well, maybe it should be said at this juncture that I *wasn't* certain sure I could handle whatever came at me.

I stared at Hector.

What was he on about?

"Why?" Buddy asked, also wondering what Hector was on about.

"Sadie got a threatening phone call last night from Marty Balducci," Hector replied.

"*What?*" Ralphie screeched.

Buddy stood up, body tense, eyes swinging to me.

My Ice Princess took a hike and now I was staring *in horror* at Hector.

What was he doing? I wasn't going to tell them about the call! Telling them about the call would take me one step closer to using them up.

I didn't want them worried. Or, *more* worried.

If he told them this, he would use them up. He couldn't use them up!

"She got a—" Hector started to repeat, but I came to and frantically acted to put a stop to his words.

"No!" I shouted, interrupting him and quickly advanced across the kitchen.

Hector black eyes came to me and he stood as I approached.

"I need to talk to you a second," I told him.

"Sadie, they need to know—" Hector started, but I'd made it to him.

I reached up, put my healthy hand over his mouth and put my casted hand into his chest. Then I pushed him toward the door, Hector walking backward, me moving forward, my hand still over his mouth.

He wrapped his fingers around my wrist, pulled it from his mouth and halted at the door, making it clear he wasn't going anywhere.

I changed tactics, immediately twisted my hand so it was holding his and I walked around him, tugging him behind me and praying he'd change his mind and come with me instead of resisting. I didn't want to engage in a kitchen tussle with Hector in front of Buddy and Ralphie. Firstly because it would be embarrassing. Secondly because I'd lose.

He came with me (thank goodness!) and I pulled him into the living room. My step stuttered and I had to make a quick decision.

I knew Ralphie and Buddy could hear if we stopped there. So I dragged Hector through the living room, down the hall and into the powder room. I flipped on the light and closed the door.

Hector looked around us with obvious surprise that we were in a powder room, and who could blame him. A powder room wasn't exactly the primo choice for this particular tête-à-tête (or *any* tête-à-tête) but it was the only option open to me. I wasn't going to take him to my room. The very thought of Hector in my bedroom made my toes curl.

When his eyes came to me, the surprise was gone and he was smiling his close-to-laughter, white, glamorous smile.

"Don't you smile at me, Hector Chavez," I snapped, not sounding like myself. Not sounding like Any Sadie That Ever Existed. Sounding weirdly like Attitude Sadie and, if you asked me if I could even be Attitude Sadie, I would have told you, "heck no".

"We're in the bathroom," Hector told me, still smiling.

"We are. I don't want Ralphie and Buddy listening in," I told him.

"Why not?"

"Because I don't want them to hear what I have to say."

He started laughing softly (yes, laughing!) and said, "I got that, *mamita*. But why not?"

"I didn't want them to know about the phone call. You've got to go out there, say something that'll make them not so worried and then… I don't know…" I stopped because I *didn't* know. My mind was racing and I couldn't catch a thought.

Hector was still laughing softly. "Say something to make them not so worried about one of the Balducci brothers threatening you over the phone in the middle of the night? Tell me how I'm gonna manage that?"

"I don't know!" I cried, losing it in my panic. "Make something up. You're a private investigator. Veronica Mars is a private investigator-type person, too, and she lies all the time!"

"Veronica Mars is a character on a TV show," Hector informed me.

"So?"

Hector's stared at me a beat, read my panic, his smile faded and his face got serious. "Sadie, I'm not gonna lie."

"But—"

He came in close (or *closer*; we couldn't *not* be close as we were in a powder room).

"What I wanna know is why do you want me to lie?"

Oh darn.

This was a sharing situation, as in, me sharing my private thoughts. I couldn't do that. I couldn't tell Hector that I'd never had any friends and I'd grown to love Ralphie and Buddy and I was terrified of losing them.

People were, well... people. In my experience they had only so much to give before they expected something in return.

I didn't have much to give in return. Heck, I didn't have *anything* to give in return.

But I couldn't tell Hector that. He'd think I was pathetic.

When I didn't answer, I watched in alarm as Hector's face got *more* serious and he closed the minute gap that was still between us. He put a hand to the side of my neck, sliding it up so his fingers went into my hair, his thumb resting along my hairline. His other arm curled around my waist and he pulled me into the heat of him.

"I don't wanna say this, *mamita*, but I have no choice. It's understandable, you not thinkin' clearly with all that's goin' down. But I have to remind you what's at stake here," Hector said.

"I'm thinking clearly," I informed him, and I certainly knew what was at stake.

He shook his head. "You aren't."

"I am!" And I thought I *was*.

His face dipped closer and I watched his eyes go a weird mixture of warm and intense. I'd never seen anything like that before and I had a feeling it did not bode well for me.

I was right.

"Sadie, a month ago, I got back to the office after finishing a job with Luke and walked into a stairwell to see you, literally, fall on your face because you didn't have the strength to hold yourself up."

I pulled in my breath so sharply, my lungs started to burn.

He kept talking. "You were wearin' nothin' but a torn nightgown and you were covered in blood. I carried you to the Explorer and you couldn't even hold your head up. You passed out in my lap after you told me there was no one to care if you woke up. I live to be a hundred, *mamita*, I'll never forget it. Not one fuckin' second of it."

I closed my eyes and tried to turn my face away, hateful, humiliating memories charging through my brain and making my blood run cold. I didn't want these memories. But more, it was unthinkable that Hector shared them with me.

His hand at the side of my head put gentle pressure there to keep me facing him, foiling my mini-escape-Hector plan. I opened my eyes again and he was still looking at me with that warm intensity.

"The next day, the two men in your kitchen walked into your hospital room. They took one look at the state of you and it rocked their world."

The burning in my lungs intensified.

"Stop talking," I whispered.

He didn't stop talking. "Then they did everything in their power to take care of you and help you heal. And, from what I can see, they did a damn fine job of it."

"Please stop talking." I was still whispering.

Hector still didn't stop talking. "A few nights ago, I watched you walk away from a bartender who hadn't finished your order. You went down the hall, past the bathroom and then you disappeared out the backdoor. I followed you only to find you'd walked right into the hands of Harvey Balducci. He had you clean off the ground. You were fightin' him and you were losin'. Daisy didn't stop me, I would have squeezed the life out of him. And you didn't stop Daisy, she would have kept on beatin' him."

"Hector—"

He shook his head to stop my interruption and kept talking. "You don't have a lot of experience with this kind of thing, so I'll explain it to you. Sadie, these are the actions of people who care about you. What happens to you happens to you, but in a way, it also happens to the people around you that care about you."

I felt tears start to sting my eyes and I clenched my teeth to stop them.

Hector saw it and his face dipped even closer. "If you're in danger, they got a right to know. You keep it from them, somethin' happens to you and you end up—"

"Enough!" I snapped.

My finely honed defense mechanism clicked into place and Sorceress of the Antarctic made an appearance precisely when I needed her.

Finally!

My back straightened, my chin lifted and, even though I couldn't see them, I knew my eyes weren't warm, and they were no longer filled with tears. They were shards of ice.

"Fine," I clipped, my voice cold.

Hector's eyes went even more intense as they scanned my face.

Then he murmured as if to himself, "Fuckin' hell, I lost her."

I ignored his words because there was no point in responding. He had, indeed, lost *her*.

New Sadie was a memory. She had to be. This was no place for her.

"I'll talk to Buddy and Ralphie. You do," I hesitated, "whatever you have to do."

"Sadie——" he started, giving me a gentle squeeze.

"No," I interrupted him and pulled away. Yanking out of his arm and jerking my head from his hand, I took a step back. "It's fine. You're right, perfectly right. Thank you for the lesson in kindness and morality. You're right about that, too. I don't know much about that either."

His eyes flashed and he clipped out a, "Goddamn it," but I was already out the door.

I marched back to the kitchen so fast my robe flew out behind me.

I halted inside the kitchen and looked at Buddy and Ralphie who were both sitting close together at the island. Buddy's arm was around Ralphie's shoulders. When their faces turned to me, I noticed they looked worried.

Blooming heck!

I felt Hector enter the kitchen but I ignored him. I prepared to make an Ice Princess Speech. Something I'd never really had to do before, but I figured I could pull it off.

It was time to be mistress of my own destiny or I'd lose everything. I was sick of losing and I was going to put a stop to it, right *fucking* now.

I took a deep breath and charged in. "Last night, a couple of hours after Hector left, Marty Balducci called me. He was angry about me pressing charges against his brothers. He said he was going to take care of Harvey and Ricky and I'd been a stupid bitch," I announced.

Buddy's arm dropped from around Ralphie's shoulders. They both straightened and I kept talking.

"He told me I was going to pay."

Ralphie's eyes closed slowly. Buddy's face went tight.

I went right on talking. "He called me the c-word."

Ralphie's eyes flew open and he gasped.

"Twice," I went on.

"The c-word?" Ralphie breathed, his face getting red.

"Yes," I clipped, then continued, "Hector's people are monitoring my cell calls. One of them heard it, told Hector and he came back around."

"Why didn't you come to us last night? We're just across the hall," Buddy asked me.

"I didn't want to wake you," I answered.

"You..." Buddy's eyes were wide, then he shook his head in disbelief. "You didn't want to *wake* us?"

"That's right," I told him, my voice pure ice. But I watched with a sinking heart as Buddy started to look mad, and I knew he was mad at me.

I hated it that he was mad at me, but I kept going. This time my glacial gaze slid across the whole room, including in its frosty path Hector, who was now standing by the island, leaned against it, taking in my performance with a blank face and his arms crossed on his chest.

"Now, what you all don't understand, but I'll explain to you, is that this isn't unusual for me. Dealing with these kinds of people, this kind of behavior, it doesn't faze me. It's been my life for twenty-nine years. I will admit that I've never been the target. But I also know how these people work. These are my people, this is my world and you have my sincere apologies for dragging you all into it with me."

"Sadie, sweetie—" Ralphie was getting up, but I lifted my hand and shook my head. He took one look at my face, blinked slowly and settled, wordlessly (a miracle!), back on his stool.

"I don't know what to do, but I'll figure something out and I'll inform you of my plans when I've come to some conclusions. In the meantime, I know that the situation is grave and I appreciate all your help in keeping me safe." I was barreling toward my grand finale. I swept across the room, snatched my coffee cup from the counter and started toward the door. "Now, I'm getting ready for work." My eyes went to Hector. "Enjoy the brioche and have a nice day," I finished.

Then on that, I made the best exit I could on bare feet with no makeup, my heart in my throat, my stomach in a knot and wearing silky, lacy pajamas and a robe that, I realized belatedly, I should have tied closed.

I got to the foot of the stairs, thinking I'd made a clean getaway and no one would hear me if I cried in the shower, when an arm sliced around my waist, laying waste to any hope of a successful exit.

In a smooth move that had to be in contention for the Smoothest Move in the History of Man, Hector curled me around to face him. He took my coffee cup out of my hand, leaned to the side, placed it on a stair (without spilling a drop!), came back to me and locked his other arm around me, both of them going tight.

When he was done with this, my heart was hammering. I looked up at his blank face, Sorceress of the Antarctic thankfully still firmly in place.

"Let me go," I demanded.

"Not a chance," Hector returned instantly, the blank look disappearing as his eyes flashed with annoyance. Then he said what I personally thought was bizarrely, "Spent a year hopin' you'd give me the opportunity to try this. Now that you have, I'm gonna take it and we'll see how it plays out."

Before I could ask what he was talking about or demand him to let me go again or, better still, tear out of his arms and make a run for it, one of his hands slid up my back into my hair. His head lowered, I opened my mouth to protest, and his mouth was on mine.

I put my hands to his shoulders to push him away at the same I pulled my head back. But his head came with mine, his tongue slid inside my mouth and (damn and blast!) my Sorceress of the Antarctic disintegrated right on the spot.

His heat hit me (and another kind of heat hit me in other places) and my hands stopped pushing at his shoulders. I went up on tiptoe, my casted hand curled around his neck, the fingers of my other hand slid into his thick hair.

Apparently unable to control myself, I pressed into him and kissed him back.

This was one of his urgent, fiery kisses. The ones that tore through me, taking all reason and rational thought with it, and leaving me with nothing but the heat and the desire to lose myself completely in the kiss and in *him*.

Right when it was getting good, and later, when I thought about it, when I knew that he knew that he had me right where he wanted me, his mouth broke from mine. He lifted his head barely an inch, but he kept me locked to him.

His eyes were as fiery as the kiss and back to intense. They scanned my face quickly before he said, "Now that *my* Sadie is back, I'll tell *her* that I'll be at the gallery to pick her up and take her to the hospital to have the cast removed.

I don't give a fuck if Bex is there, *mamita*, you aren't fuckin' goin' without me, and I won't be pleased if you make me look for you. I'll also tell you that tonight, we're goin' out to dinner, just the two of us. We're gonna enjoy the goddamned meal, and after, we're gonna have another talk. If I'm not at the gallery to pick you up at closing then I'll be here at the house at seven."

I was breathing heavily and trying to sort out my thoughts when he continued.

"You do somethin' stupid, Sadie, Buddy, Ralphie and I'll have a conversation. We might have to rethink your situation and you may not like what we come up with. But I'm tellin' you this: I'm keepin' you safe, and you agreed to let me take care of you. And that's what I'm fuckin' gonna do, whether you like it or not."

Without another word, he let me go.

I teetered a bit without his arms around me and his body to lean into. Before I got myself sorted, he'd walked around me without looking back.

When I turned and stared into the living room doorway, he was nowhere to be seen.

After a couple of seconds, I heard Ralphie ask from the kitchen, "Is she okay?"

"She will be," was Hector's very firm and also very annoyed answer.

I closed my eyes.

This was not going well for me.

Not at all.

⚜

I stared at my exposed wrist and felt a weird sense of calmness settle in me.

My wrist looked kind of strange but the cast was *gone*.

I only thought about the cut on my face when I saw myself in a mirror or noticed someone's gaze on it. I could forget it, sometimes lately for hours.

But for the last five weeks, the cast was a second-by-second reminder of what Ricky Balducci did to me.

And now it was gone.

I pulled in a deep breath as I let the calm settle. One more step toward healing. One more step toward the time when I might go whole days or even weeks without remembering.

"Sadie, girl," Bex called, and I looked up at her.

I couldn't help it. I smiled.

Bex and I were alone in an exam room. They'd taken the cast off then a physical therapist had shown me some exercises to strengthen my wrist. He gave me a squeezy ball and some leaflets filled with instructions and diagrams. He left and the nurse had gone off to get the paperwork for me to sign. Then we could go.

Hector was there but outside the room talking on his cell.

As Hector told me, he showed up at Art at ten to two (double-parking again) just in time to take me to the hospital. In preparation (because I figured Hector would do as he said, and I was not wrong), I called Bex and asked her to meet us there.

On the way over, I'd given Hector a blast of The Ice. But he acted like I was "His Sadie" (whoever the heck *that* was) and not a wintry cold bitch, thus he totally ignored The Ice.

This, I had to admit, both irritated me and kind of scared me. But I'd started practicing The Ice Treatment when I was eleven. Eighteen years and I'd perfected the art of The Ice Treatment. I knew if I stuck with it, I could and would deep freeze Hector.

Eventually.

I mentally shook my thoughts clear and said to Bex, "Yes?"

Her eyes moved to the door and back to me. "What's going on with Hector?" she asked. "You two seeing each other?"

Even though I wanted to explain it to her, I didn't.

Firstly, she might not get it. Secondly, she might feel like giving me a lecture, and I could *not* deal with another lecture right now. Hector had delivered the powder room *and* hallway lectures. And after I came down from getting ready, both Buddy *and* Ralphie had lectured me in a gay roommate tag-team talking to. I had to say I was up to *there* with well meaning lectures. Lastly, I was feeling a calm I hadn't felt in a long time and I didn't want anything to shatter that.

So I responded, "Kind of."

"You been intimate?" she asked.

By the way, Bex was a pretty straightforward woman. She could be softly-softly, but most of the time she cut-to-the-chase.

I pulled my lips in, feeling the calm slip away, and then replied, "Just making out a couple of times."

It was her turn to smile. "That's good."

She didn't know the half of it.

She watched my face and her smile got bigger.

"It's not going anywhere," I said quickly before she got the wrong idea.

At my words, her smile disappeared.

"Why not?" she asked.

I shrugged and my eyes slid away.

She pulled her chair closer, but she didn't touch me. Still, her getting closer made my gaze come back to her.

Her face was gentle. "Sadie, you know, what Ricky Balducci did to you was not an act of intimacy. It was an act of violence."

I inhaled sharply through my nose, but nodded fervently in the hopes she'd think I understood and she'd move off this particular subject.

My hopes were quickly dashed.

"What you do with someone who cares about you is an entirely different thing. It's a good thing, giving and, hopefully, getting." She gave me a small grin.

I nodded again and squirmed a little bit. I did not want to be talking about this. Ever.

My mom had disappeared way before it was time to have The Sex Talk and my father never bothered. I'd had a couple of lovers; one in college, one after. Both of whom I liked as much as I would allow myself to like anyone. Also, both of whom my father frowned upon and sent packing.

I knew what sex was. I'd even had good sex.

I knew what Ricky did to me wasn't *that*.

Bex, unfortunately, did not have clairvoyant powers so she couldn't read my mind, and therefore she kept talking.

"It's going to be difficult. You can get it confused, but try to remember that letting someone close to you like that, letting them show you why it's good, having that togetherness, it's part of healing."

"Okay," I responded immediately.

She scooted even closer and I got the impression she wasn't buying into what Tex would call my "bullshit".

She kept at it. "I'm not saying you should go faster than you're ready. I'm just saying your mind can shut down to that part of life and it's important not to shut it off, twist it so you're convinced it's wrong or dirty. It's important to remember it's right, it's natural and it can be very, very good."

I blinked and my gaze slid away. Then I sighed and set aside the bullshit.

"Okay," I whispered.

Bex wasn't quite done.

"If you've got worries, talk to him. I think Hector's the kind of guy who'll listen and wait until the time is right for you. But keep him in the loop and let him know where your head is at."

There was no way I was going to keep Hector in *that* loop (or *any* loop, for that matter).

I didn't tell Bex that.

Instead, I said again, "Okay."

"You need to talk to me, you know where to find me," she finished.

I nodded then looked at her, and in an effort to change the subject, I informed her, "We're going to watch YoYo for you."

She gave me a gentle smile that I understood, with a gratitude so strong I felt like hugging her (however, I did not), meant she was finally letting me off the hook.

"I know," she said.

Luckily the door opened, the nurse walked in, and the latest trauma in a life full of traumas was thankfully over.

And I'd survived, yet again.

⌐☈☞

After I signed the paperwork, Bex went back to the rape crisis center and Hector took me to Art.

During the ride I didn't speak. Hector didn't either. I found this uncomfortable. Hector acted like this was perfectly normal. This made me want to throw my squeezy ball at him.

Of course, I did not.

Hector parallel parked in a very unusual prime spot a door down from Art.

Before he had the Bronco's ignition shut down, my door was open and I was out, around the front of the Bronco and hoofing it on my Manolos down the sidewalk toward the gallery.

I was feet away from the door when an arm tagged me around my shoulders. I came to a rocking halt and he turned me into him.

My body went rigid and I lifted my chin to grant him with a patented Chill Factor Sub-Zero glare.

"I have to get to work," I informed him.

"You're welcome," he said in return, looking down at me, unaffected by Chill Factor Sub-Zero, his fantastic mouth fighting a grin.

Seriously a squeezy-ball-throwing-moment if there ever was one. However, I was not at a distance which would allow for it, and further, an action such as that would not befit The Ice Princess.

"For what?" I asked instead of throwing my squeezy ball at him.

"For the ride," he replied.

Chill Factor Sub-Zero descended sharply to Chill Factor Dry Ice. "I suppose I shouldn't have to remind you that I didn't *ask* for a ride."

He lost the fight and grinned casually in the face of Chill Factor Dry Ice.

"True enough," he said calmly.

I waited for more, but apparently that was it.

"Are we through here?" I asked, cocking my head and deciding to shift into saccharin-sweetness.

His face dipped to mine. "Not even close," he whispered, and his black eyes went warm and started dancing like he was enjoying this (enjoying this!).

Blooming heck!

I was using all my good stuff on him! And none of it was working!

All right, fine. He was going to challenge the Ice Princess then that was *just fine*.

Beware Hector Chavez! The next Ice Age cometh, as Ralphie would say, *a la Sadie*.

I zapped him with a mental ice ray and pulled out of his arm. I turned, opened the door and walked into Art.

I was confronted with Ralphie entertaining a full bevy of Rock Chicks *sans* Shirleen, but with a new person I'd never met before. He was a middle-aged man, tall, built solid (but with a teensy beer belly), dark hair with some gray in it and Indy Nightingale's blue eyes.

Everyone was drinking coffee.

"What's going on?" I asked, walking toward the counter.

"Tex sent over coffees to celebrate your cast being removed," Daisy told me on a grin. "Yours is probably cold though. We been here awhile."

"I'll nuke it," Ralphie said, snatching a white cup off the counter.

"I'll do it," Ava offered.

Ralphie handed her the cup with a grateful smile. She took it and headed to the back of the gallery where our little kitchenette was.

I saw Ralphie's eyes come back to me and I didn't like the look in them.

I looked around the room. Then I *felt* the room.

Something was not right.

My eyes went to the man I didn't know.

"What's going on?" I asked again to everyone, but my eyes didn't leave the man.

I realized, belatedly, his eyes had been on me since I walked in.

An unhappy, "oh no what now?" chill slid across my skin and I braced.

Hector materialized close to my side (furthering my sense of foreboding) and I heard him say, "Tom."

I looked to Hector then back to the man. The man got closer and lifted his chin to Hector, showing me they knew each other. His gaze slid back to me.

Indy came with him. She was looking at me too. Looking at me funny. Looking at me in a way that made me a little scared.

All of a sudden I had the insane urge to reach out for Hector's hand like I would have done yesterday or the day before (or, probably, the day before), but I wouldn't allow myself to do it now.

Those days were over.

Whatever life had to dish out to me next, I was going to handle it on my own. No more leaning on anyone else. It was time for a new New Sadie. A Take Charge Sadie.

"I'm Sadie Townsend," I told him.

"I know who you are," he said gently.

I watched with alarm as his gaze moved to the scar on my cheek. It grew soft and then (no kidding), it grew moist.

"This is my dad, Tom Savage," Indy introduced, and my eyes went wide.

Oh no.

Were we going to have another Blanca Type Incident?

I mentally prepared for another demonstration of why these people were so darn nice, but my preparation wasn't enough.

Nowhere near.

"You look just like your mother," Tom Savage said.

His six words hit me like six sharp blows and my body jerked with the power of them.

I swallowed, wondering if I heard him right, then whispered, "I'm sorry?"

The Rock Chicks and Ralphie were closing in and I felt Hector's heat hit me as he drew nearer. But I only had eyes for Tom Savage.

"You know my mother?" I asked when he didn't repeat himself.

"Knew her, yes," he answered.

I put my newly exposed hand to the counter and held on. It wouldn't do to collapse in a dead faint. That wouldn't exactly say Take Charge Sadie.

"It seems, when we were little, we knew each other, too," Indy put in and my eyes moved to her.

She was fishing in the back pocket of her jeans and she pulled out a picture, stepped toward me and handed it to me.

I took it and looked down.

In the picture was a little redheaded, blue-eyed girl—maybe two years old—and a baby. The little girl was sitting on a couch with the swaddled baby in her arms. You could tell she was giggling into the camera, pleased as punch to be holding her living doll.

The baby's head had a shock of ultra-light, golden-cream-strawberry blonde hair.

The little girl was obviously Indy. The baby... me.

"Oh my God," I breathed, not taking my eyes from the picture. I took one step back, then two, and ran into something solid. Hector's hands settled on my shoulders as I stopped retreating and stared at the picture.

Finally, I looked up at Tom. "How...?"

Tom took a step toward me. His eyes moved to Hector and he stopped.

He looked back at me. "Lizzie, your mother, was a friend of my wife, Katherine."

I blinked, unable to process this because, frankly, it was un-processable.

My mom and Indy's mom were friends? How could that be?

"She was?" I asked.

Tom nodded. "Katherine and Kitty Sue, Lee's mom, were thick as thieves all their lives. They met Lizzie in high school and she became part of their tribe. They were both bridesmaids at your mom's wedding."

Instantly I felt saliva fill my mouth and I swallowed it down.

This couldn't be true. It simply couldn't be true.

Could it?

I didn't know anything about my mother. I had nothing of her but memories. My father had removed all traces of her after she left us. No photos, no trinkets, no letters, not a stitch of her clothing. Nothing. We never spoke of her after she left. Not once.

"Mom and Dad are on vacation in Hawaii. They're coming home on Sunday," Ally piped in.

I came out of my thoughts and I looked at her. She was staring at me too, and she didn't look like feisty Veronica Mars at all. Her look was both gentle and concerned.

It was too much to take in so, confused, I asked, "What?"

"My mom, Kitty Sue, your mom's friend, she's in Hawaii. We've called her and she told us to tell you she's looking forward to seeing you again when she gets back."

I was shaking my head, still not understanding, but Ally kept on.

"I guess me, Lee and Hank, my other brother, knew you, too."

"No," I whispered.

"Yes," Ally replied, and she gave me a hesitant not-at-all-the-Ally-I-kind-of-knew grin.

I pulled in my lips, and before I could pull together my thoughts, Tom came closer and put his hand on my arm.

"Sadie, you were a part of our lives for a while. Then we lost Katherine—" Tom said and my gaze snapped to him.

"You lost Katherine?" I repeated.

"She died. Cancer. When Indy was five. A few years after that picture was taken," Tom replied, and at that, my eyes sliced to Indy, and all of a sudden my body started trembling.

Indy's mom died. Tom's wife died. My mom's friend died.

I shook my head, wanting to escape, wanting to run, to hide, to get *the heck* out of there, but I didn't.

Instead, I looked back to Tom. "I'm sorry," I said softly.

His fingers squeezed my arm. "It was a long time ago," he responded, but I could tell by the look in his eyes that time hadn't healed this particular wound.

"I'm still sorry," I told him.

"Thank you," he replied and dropped his hand. "What I was saying was, once Katherine died, things with your dad…" He stopped then went on, "See,

I'm a cop. So is Malcolm, Ally's father. It wasn't... your mom... with your father bein'... she didn't feel..." He stopped again. I could tell this was difficult for him because I saw his teeth clench. Then he kept going. "Once Katherine was gone, she didn't bring you around anymore."

That was when it finally hit me. All of it.

Sometime, a long time ago, my mom had friends. Good friends. People that probably loved her, *loads*. Made her laugh. Made her giggle. Made her feel special. Made her feel safe.

Which meant...

Sometime, a long time ago, I'd been one of them.

Sometime, a long time ago, I'd been the baby of The Nightingale/Savage/Townsend Clan.

Sometime, a long time ago, my mom lost her friends and I lost my chance to be a good, normal, nice person surrounded by genuine friends. People that truly cared about me.

I lost all that had been their life. All that made them laugh with each other, tease each other, take care of each other.

Heck, Indy had just gotten married! I could have been one of her bridesmaids!

I tried to hold on, but I couldn't help it. I could feel the tears welling in my eyes.

I thought I was used to the loss, but apparently, I wasn't.

And that *stunk*.

"I hate my father," I told Tom Savage quietly. Before I could stop it, my breath hitched (repeatedly) and I hissed, "*I hate him!*"

Hector's hands disappeared from my shoulders. His arms slid around my chest, his body got closer and I felt his jaw against the side of my head.

Still I tried to gain control (this, by the way, didn't work, and I felt the tears slide down my cheeks).

"Sadie, sugar—" Daisy whispered gently, and at her words the Rock Chicks and Ralphie pulled in ever closer.

"I want you to come over for dinner tomorrow," Tom invited. "Indy and Ally'll be there. So will Lee, Hank and Roxie. Hector, too. The whole family."

The whole family. He said, "The whole family." I'd never had a "whole family". Not their kind of family.

Well, I guess I did, once. But I lost it before I knew I even had it.

I pulled in my lips. Hector's jaw left my head and his arms gave me a squeeze.

There was no way I was going to dinner at Tom Savage's house with all my babyhood friends reunited. There was no way I was going to set myself up for that kind of loss. There was no way I was going to let *any* of this go on any longer than it had to.

The only thing I knew was that I had to devise a plan to get myself safe. Safe from the Crazy Balducci Brothers *and* safe from any further emotional turmoil.

Tom must have read my intent on my face because he added, "I have pictures. Of your mother. You could—"

I immediately changed my mind. "I'll be there."

Hector gave me another squeeze.

Tom gave me a smile.

Indy threw her hands up and yelled, "Party!"

Ally laughed with obvious relief on the word, "Righteous."

I relaxed into Hector's warmth, looked down at the photo and made my decision.

I'd let myself have this one small gift. A gift, I told myself, that was from my mom.

Then, as soon as I could finagle it, just like my mom, I was going to disappear.

# Chapter 11

# Hector's Rose

*Sadie*

"Sadie, maybe you should come in and talk. I'm not sure this is—" my dead grandmother's financial manager, Aaron Lockhart, said in my ear.

"Please Aaron, just do it," I interrupted him.

It was after work. I was in my bedroom on the landline, not delaying a minute in putting my newly formed plans in place.

One thing my mom left me was Aaron Lockhart. He was old as the hills, stooped, had wispy white hairs across his liver-spotted scalp and he still worked full-time because, he told me, when he tried retirement his wife nearly drove him to murder.

Since he liked his work, and his freedom, he got in his car every morning at 8:30 and his driver drove him to his office in the Denver Technical Center (known as DTC). He left work at 5:30, which gave his wife plenty of time to have a couple of martinis and mellow out a bit before he got home (he told me this, too).

Aaron and I had never been close. My father didn't like him and wouldn't allow it. But in an ironclad agreement devised by my dead (but clearly, while she was alive, shrewd) grandmother when she set up my trust, he was appointed to manage my trust fund, which had not been touchable until I was twenty-one. He also managed the income derived from the flat in London I inherited, which had been rented out since around the time of the Blitz to an old lady named Mrs. Burnsley. He further managed a small villa on Crete, which was hired out to tourists. I'd never been to either of these properties. My father also wouldn't allow that. But I'd seen pictures. The flat was close to Covent Garden. The villa was in a small fishing village by the sea.

When I opened Art, I asked Aaron to help me to keep it clean, away from my father and entirely law-abiding. And he did.

Aaron was one of the few people I knew who, regardless of his age, was not frightened of going head-to-head with my father. I admired him, totally trusted him and I'd always liked him. But, as ever, I'd never let it show.

I'd just asked him to find out Mrs. Burnsley's plans for her future in my flat as well as the schedule of occupancy on the villa in Crete. One or the other of them might well be my next destination or a future one, as the case may be.

As I didn't want to put old lady Burnsley out of her home or devastate excited tourists who were looking forward to their time in the sun on a Greek Island, I'd also charged Aaron to find other properties. I didn't care where just as long as they were manageable on a fixed income, and there was at least an ocean between me and the Crazy Balducci Brothers. I also asked him to set up an auction of my belongings that were in storage.

Finally, I asked him to find a way to sign over Art to Ralphie and Buddy without a dime needing to change hands. It would be my thank you for taking care of me. It wasn't much, but it was the only good thing I had to give.

I wanted no memory of my old life. I was going to pack up my suitcases, board a plane and set up a new life far away where no one had heard of Seth Townsend. Where no one knew who I was, what I was or what had happened to me. And where I could find some peace to decide who was the new me, get used to her, and if I was lucky and I could forget Ralphie, Buddy, Daisy, Hector and all that came with them, maybe, I could be content.

I heard the doorbell ring and pulled in my breath. Hector was there to take me out to dinner.

"I'd prefer to have a chat about this," Aaron said to me as I listened to far away, muted male voices.

"My mind's made up," I told Aaron.

"Please, Sadie, as a friend of your family, a particular friend of your grandmother's, afford me this one courtesy," Aaron pushed it.

"Sadie!" Buddy called up the stairs. "Hector's here."

Darn it!

I had to get off the phone before someone came up to get me and I had no idea how I was going to get away alone to talk to Aaron. In my current circumstances with Hector's edict being followed to the letter by Ralphie and Buddy (and, by the way he was acting, Ralphie had appointed himself my personal, very well-dressed, completely unskilled, gay bodyguard), it was impossible.

Why did everything have to be so *difficult?* It was my money and my property, for goodness sake!

"Sadie!" Buddy called.

I put my hand over the mouthpiece and yelled, "Coming!"

"Sadie?" Aaron said in my ear.

I took my hand off the mouthpiece. "Either you do it or I hire someone else to do it," the Ice Princess told Aaron. "Your choice, but I want it done and I want it done as fast as possible."

I heard Aaron sigh. I knew he was going to give in and I felt a quick charge of relief.

"I'll see to it," he assured me.

Thank God. One thing checked off the to-do list.

"Thank you. I'd be grateful for that."

"Sadie!" Now it was Ralphie yelling from closer to the door and I knew he was climbing the stairs. "Double H is here."

I covered the mouthpiece again and shouted, "I know! I'll be right down!"

"Seems you're busy. I'll let you go," Aaron said. "Stay well."

"Thank you," I replied.

Then I heard the disconnect.

I had the phone in the receiver and I was snatching up my purse when Ralphie burst in.

"Ralphie!" I whirled to the door. "I said I was coming."

"I thought you were climbing out the window," Ralphie retorted.

I wished I'd thought of that and made a mental note to remember it in case I needed it in the future.

"Get a move on, sweet 'ums. I think I already taught you this all important lesson, but I'll repeat as necessary. We don't keep hot guys waiting at the door. Skanky guys, yes. Slimy guys, definitely. Hot guys, um... no."

I gave Ralphie a glare. My glare deflected off Ralphie's grin and pinged around the room until it disintegrated.

I squared my shoulders, found My Ice and headed out my bedroom door.

⛓

It was debatable whether one could call Hector and my "just the two of us" date "enjoyable".

Firstly, I dressed in my armor, head-to-foot (but not toe) silvery-gray.

I had on a shimmery, boat-necked, long-sleeved, tight-fitting, knit shirt with a small, delicate pendant of diamonds shaped in the form of a flower hanging from a platinum chain at my neck and matching drop earrings. This was paired with a slim-fitting, just-above-the-knee, somewhat-shimmery, silvery-gray skirt with four, precise kick pleats, one at the front and back of each of my knees. Elegant, gray, patent leather pumps with a spike heel and black toe. A couple of scent-refreshing sprays of my signature perfume. A quick shake of my fingers coated in my favorite pomade (to define and separate the curls and waves) through my otherwise unencumbered hair. My black trench coat completed my ensemble.

When I walked downstairs and Hector, wearing jeans, boots, a skintight white, long-sleeved t-shirt and black leather jacket (what a pair we were!), saw I changed out of my nice but somewhat casual day wear into Ice Princess Gear, he gave me a little, amused grin and shake of his head.

I ignored him, bestowed goodnight kisses to my roommates and swept, head held high, out the door.

Secondly, Hector informed me in the Bronco that Buddy had given the police the keys to my storage facility. The "lab boys" found nothing to place Ricky at my apartment such was the immaculate cleaning job Ralphie and Buddy did. However, they did find traces of blood and hairs on my couch and mattress. Some of it, he explained, they figured was mine. Some of it, they hoped, would belong to Ricky.

I hoped so too, but I didn't share.

However, I did wonder how this was going to affect the auction of my "estate".

I didn't share that either.

Lastly, Hector took me to a Mexican restaurant off Broadway, down south in Englewood. It was called El Tejado and it was *not* the kind of place where you wore a shimmery, silvery-gray outfit and little diamonds shaped as flowers.

I ignored my discomfort, walked into the casual, worn-in restaurant like I went there every day and sat down in the booth. I planted my behind dead center so Hector would get *no* ideas that he was sharing my seat with me.

He slid in opposite me, still grinning, and I got the impression my act didn't convince him. Further, he found it highly amusing.

I ignored this, too.

Dinner, luckily, didn't last long. They didn't mess around with taking and serving your order and I figured that had something to do with the line at the door. A line, incidentally, that we circumvented by Hector smiling at the lady behind the cash register, her face lighting up in recognition, the two of them exchanging rapid-fire Spanish and her elbowing her way through the crowd and seating us at a booth that was getting its finishing wipe down by a busboy. This, I noted with a glance at the door, was not greeted with delight by the waiting customers. But I ignored that, too.

There was barely any conversation due to my avid fascination of, at first, my menu, then the restaurant's décor, then every person in line waiting to get in, then my fellow patrons and, finally, my newfound wonder at watching a no-sound Mexican soap opera on the television above the bar.

No matter how tasty the food was (and it was tasty), I hardly ate a bite (thank goodness Blanca wasn't there or she would have had a conniption). Hector paid. We slid out of the booth. He walked me to the Bronco with his hand on my elbow. Then it was over.

Dinner down, I just had to survive "the talk".

If in one day I could survive three lectures, a sex talk, a reunion with the husband of my long, lost mother's best friend, the revealing of the knowledge that Indy, Ally and Lee were babydom playmates and a "just the two of us" dinner with Hector then I could survive "the talk".

No problem.

I stared out the window of the Bronco wondering if I might be in Crete next week or next month. Then I wondered if I would like Crete. Then I wondered if they spoke any English on Crete. I was mentally planning on downloading English to Greek lessons on my iPod when Hector parked on a street.

I came out of my thoughts, looked around and immediately realized my mistake at letting my mind wander.

We weren't outside Capitol Hill where the brownstone was located. We were somewhere else. A clean, tidy, well-established, family neighborhood with clean, tidy, well-kept houses with clean, tidy, well-kept lawns and moderately-priced vehicles lining the street.

"Where are...?" I started, my head turning toward Hector, but he was out of the Bronco and rounding the hood.

Blooming *heck!*

He opened my door.

"Where are we?" I asked the minute he did.

He grabbed my hand, and with a firm tug he pulled me out of the car. He dropped my hand and I fell into his waiting ones. He swung my around, set me on my feet on the sidewalk and twisted to slam my door. Then he took my hand again and charged up the sidewalk.

I walked double-time to keep up with him, all the while pulling at his hold. "Hector, where are we?"

He didn't look back when he answered, "My place."

Blooming, *blooming*, heck!

"Why are we at your place?" I asked when he stopped at the front door.

"Privacy," he replied. He unlocked the door, shoving it open, and before I could make a run for it, he had a hand in the small of my back and was pushing me in.

I entered and stopped.

I was standing on a two step-up, dark wood platform. Half walls to either side, made of the same wood and columns at the end of each. Straight ahead, down the two steps and about five feet away was a wall. Along its side, a set of dark wood stairs and matching banister.

On the left side of us was a room that held a jumble of furniture and boxes, but also a beautiful, tiled fireplace that looked like it had been scrubbed, the wood of the mantel sanded and refinished to a warm sheen. The walls looked freshly painted in a dusky gray-blue and the floors were obviously refinished. There were closed French doors I couldn't see through at the other end of that room, well down from the wall that separated the room from the stairs.

On the right side of us was another room filled with paint cans, brushes and tools (hand tools as well as big, heavy power tools with lots of cords). The fireplace in that room looked grimy and as yet untouched, but refinished, it'd be gorgeous. Beyond that room was an open doorway which led to a kitchen.

Hector's hand at my back guided me down the steps and we stopped. He headed left. I heard the rustle of plastic and I turned to watch him.

He was uncovering a big, overstuffed armchair covered in midnight blue twill. Once uncovered, he dragged it into the empty but renovation implements room and positioned it in the center.

On the way back, he shrugged off his jacket and threw it on the banister. Then he came to me, walked around me and pulled off my trench. He tagged my purse, threw my coat on his and hooked my purse straps around the newel post.

After doing all of this, he grabbed my hand. We strode to the chair and sat. Then he tugged my hand again sharply until I went off-balance. His hands went to my waist and he guided my body until I was seated in his lap.

I didn't protest any of this, not because I didn't want to. But because I was coming to terms with the fact that, obviously, Hector was fixing up his own house.

This affected me deeply, for two reasons.

First, for as long as I could remember, my father had a personal groomer who came to the house every two weeks. She trimmed my father's hair, gave him a clean shave and finished off with a manicure. My father's fingernails were perfectly clipped and shone so brightly it was almost like he was wearing a coat of clear polish. As far as I knew, he never picked up anything but a fork, a pen, a book or a golf club in his life. Never a hammer or a paint brush. *Never*. He'd also never operated anything with a cord except, perhaps, his razor (though, I must admit, I'd not familiarized myself with his personal hygiene).

In fact, most every man of my acquaintance was much the same.

Second, because of the above, when I was seventeen or eighteen I had this stupid, silly, girlish, in the very, very back of my mind daydream that one day I'd find a *real* man. A man so unlike my father as to be his antithesis. A man who was strong enough to take me away from my horrible life, living in my beautiful but cold ivory tower with bad people swarming around me like killer bees. We'd fall in love and he'd whisk me away. We'd buy some junker bungalow that we'd fix up, intermingling our renovation efforts with having and raising a plethora of children who we would spoil rotten and love to distraction. Often we'd cease our duties, laughing at each other, paint dabs on our cheeks and dust in our hair, while our children frolicked amongst our jumble of restoration paraphernalia.

A jumble that looked an awful lot in my head like the house I was sitting in at that very moment.

That dream died ages ago. In fact until just then, I'd forgotten I'd even had it.

"Sadie?" Hector called.

I gave my head a little shake and looked at him.

"What?"

"You looked miles away."

I wasn't miles away. I was right there.

In fact, my whole life, I never felt as *right there* as I did at that exact moment.

"Are you fixing up your house?" I couldn't help but ask.

He looked around at the abundance of evidence of this very fact obviously scattered around us. His mouth twitched and his eyes came back to me.

"Yeah," he answered.

"Oh," I said softly, not knowing what else to say, but for some reason I could feel my heart beating in my throat.

One of his hands slid slowly up my back. The other arm came to rest across my lap.

"You okay?" he asked, his eyes doing a scan of my face.

No. No, I was *not* okay. It hit me that I didn't even know what "okay" felt like. I'd never actually felt "okay".

At that precise moment, however, what I felt like was asking Hector if I could paint his living room. And that, I figured, was probably seriously *not* okay.

"Yes," I answered.

"Sadie," he said softly.

I focused on him, noticed he was watching me closely and I wondered what he saw.

"What did you think of me when you first met me?" I asked before I could think better of it.

His fingers were warm on my neck and he gave me a gentle squeeze.

He didn't hesitate with his answer. "I thought you were beautiful and I thought you were cold."

This didn't offend me. A lot of people thought that way because I wanted them to think that way. So I nodded.

"Do you want to know what I think of you now?" he asked.

I really didn't. I wasn't sure I could take it, but for some bizarre reason I nodded again anyway.

"I think you're even more beautiful and I think you're totally lost."

My brows went up. "And you think you can help me find my way?"

He shook his head. His eyes went warm and I got another neck squeeze coupled with a tightening of his arm around my waist.

"*Mamita*, only you can find your way. I just wanna be along for the ride."

My belly went warm and I decided in that instant, in that house with Hector, after he said those words, that before I left this life behind forever, I'd give myself one more gift.

And on that decision, I leaned forward and kissed him.

It wasn't a peck on the lips. It was *a kiss,* and just like the first time I threw myself at him, he caught me. Instantly.

He leaned in, pulling my body across his lap as he took over the kiss. It went from Sadie Hot to Hector *White* Hot. I wrapped my arms around him, feeling myself melt with the fire he shot through me from his body, our locked lips and his talented tongue.

His mouth trailed to my ear. My hands yanked at his shirt until I had it out of his jeans and I could get my fingers under it, inside it and up the smooth skin and hard muscle of his back.

I turned my head and whispered in his ear, "I like the way you kiss."

His tongue touched my neck. I shivered, felt his lips smile there, and then his mouth came back to mine.

Our mouths touching, his eyes looking deep into mine, he muttered, "Good."

Then his head slanted and he kissed me again. This time hotter, deeper, longer, making me feel things I hadn't felt in a long time. Good things. Delicious things. Tingles along my skin, wetness between my legs and a belly tied up in glorious knots.

It felt so good I squirmed in his lap and gently scored a path down his back with my fingernails, showing him (I hoped) that I wanted more.

He groaned into my mouth. That felt good, too.

His arm moved from my waist to behind my knees and he stood up. Taking me with him, carrying me while kissing me to the stairs, up the stairs, down a hall and into his bedroom.

I guessed that meant he knew I wanted more.

He set me on my feet by the bed and leaned over. He turned on the bedside lamp, sat on the bed and tugged off his boots.

I watched him. Coming out of my desire-fuelled stupor, my senses coming back to me and my mind asking me what in *the heck* did I think I was doing.

Then he leaned forward and down. He grabbed my ankle, lifted my foot between his legs, slid off my shoe and threw it to the side. His head came up, eyes on mine as one hand held my ankle firmly. His other hand trailed up the back of my calf, moving only to his fingertips as they swept behind my knee then kept going partially up the back of my thigh before his touch fell away.

Oh... *my.*

He put my foot down and repeated this move with my other leg.

Before I could do a thing (like, say, tear off my clothes and throw myself at him), he stood in front of me so close our bodies brushed. The tingles had started to spread again, this time far more frantic, as he pulled off his t-shirt. At our proximity, this maneuver meant his t-shirt caught under my breasts and slid over them. I sucked in breath and reached out quickly to grab his waist and hold on because I was pretty certain sure my legs were about to give out.

He tossed his t-shirt toward my shoes and my hands tensed at his waist when I saw his chest. It was smooth, well-defined and he had a small, broken heart inked in blood red, outlined in barbed-wire black, tattooed on his inside, left pectoral.

Like someone else (an even *newer* New Sadie) had taken over my body, I leaned forward and put my mouth to his incredibly cool tattoo. Then I put my tongue there, too.

I liked the taste of his skin. I liked it so much I slid my tongue to his nipple, and that was that.

His hands went to my shirt. He whipped it over my head, dislodging my mouth from his chest, and tossed the shirt aside. His arms locked around me. My head went back, his head bent and he kissed me.

This kiss, I could feel right away, was not under his control. It was even hotter, deeper and so urgent I felt it stirring in me. My body responding wildly, I shoved my hands under his arms and wrapped them around him as tight as I could.

Still kissing me, his hands slid down my bottom, pressing me deeper into him so I could feel his hardness against my belly. At the feel of it, a thrill raced through my entire system.

When his hands moved back up, his fingers found the skirt's zipper and tugged it down. Then he shoved my skirt over my hips until it fell to my feet.

His arms went around me and he fell back to the bed, me on top of him. He rolled me to the side so I was on my back, his mouth on me everywhere. My neck, behind my ears, down my throat, across my chest. It felt good. No, it felt *tremendous*. I thought there was nothing better in the whole world until his lips closed over the dove-gray satin of my bra right where my nipple was.

I felt his tongue through the satin then he sucked deep.

Waves of pure goodness shot from my nipple to between my legs and my hands slid in his hair.

"Oh my God," I breathed. "Do that again."

He did as I asked. It felt even better than before and I arched into him, wanting more. His hand slid down my belly, into my panties, between my legs. I felt his fingers on me, sliding through the wetness...

And I froze.

Unbidden, unwanted ice water filled my veins. I clamped my legs shut and my fingers fisted in his hair.

The desire knotting in my belly vanished. It was panic in my belly now, sheer and mad, and my only crazed thought was *escape*.

His hand froze, his body stilled and his head came up, but I didn't look at him.

I let him go and rolled, dislodging him and his hand, and put a knee to the bed to launch myself away. I got about a foot before he tagged me and dragged me backward into the heat of his body.

"*Let go!*" I screamed in a voice so shrill, so full of terror, it hurt my own ears.

"Sadie, calm down," he whispered into the back of my neck as his arms wrapped tight around me, one at my stomach, one at my chest, pulling me into his hard body. "You're safe. We'll stop."

"I have to go," I demanded.

I felt his gentle, "Sh," at my neck and I saw his hand reach out, nab a blanket at the end of the bed and pull it over my body.

I was trembling head-to-foot regardless of his heat and the blanket. Trembling so violently I could swear I felt the bed shaking with it.

The humiliation was excruciating, crippling, and I felt tears clog my throat.

"I have to go," I repeated, my voice sounding funny.

"Quiet, *mi corazón*," he said gently.

I stayed quiet but I went on trembling, staring unseeing across his bed to his wall. He went on holding me tightly, his face in my hair, his warm breath on my neck. After long moments, his heat penetrated the cold in my veins and the tremors stopped.

It was then I realized I did it to him again. I came on to him and took him somewhere I didn't intend to go. I didn't know I didn't intend to go there, but that was the way it ended all the same.

"I'm sorry," I whispered.

He gave me a squeeze. "Why?" he asked.

"I did it to you again," I told him honestly. It cost me, but he deserved honesty and not the cold bitch I treated him to the last time I walked away from him.

He rolled me to face him, arranged the blanket so it was covering me again and slid his hand through the side of my hair, pulling it away from my face. His hand went down my back until his arm was locked around me again.

I looked into his eyes. They were warm and gentle, not hard and angry.

Well, thank God for *that*.

Finally, he said, "Don't worry about it."

"I didn't intend—"

"I know you didn't."

"I feel like an idiot."

"Don't," he said firmly.

I pulled in my lips, nodded (even though I still felt like an idiot; I mean, this *was* embarrassing) then dropped my gaze to his throat.

"Put your arms around me, *mamita*," he ordered.

I didn't want to, but I did, and for some reason, this made me feel better.

"Can I ask a favor?"

I nodded again.

"Stay here tonight."

My body went tight.

"No, Sadie." His fingers came to my chin and lifted my face to look at him. When my eyes were on his, he leaned in and touched his mouth to mine. He pulled away a couple of inches and said, "I just want you beside me. That's it."

"Buddy and Ralphie—" I began, using my one and only easy (but good) excuse.

"I'll call Buddy and Ralphie."

Darn.

If Hector called Ralphie and Buddy and Ralphie answered he'd probably leap for joy. I figured Buddy's reaction would be far less dramatic but along the same vein.

I chewed my lip. Oh heck, what could I say?

First off, I'd already slept with him twice. It was on a couch, but still. Secondly, I could hardly say no after this latest episode. Lastly, I wanted to stay with him. He made me feel snug, warm and safe.

Boy, my plans never really worked out, did they?

"Okay," I agreed.

He didn't grin, look amused or glory in his triumph. He pushed up, kissed the top of my head, then slid away.

I sat up, holding the blanket to my front and watched as he walked across to a dresser, pulled open a drawer and yanked something out.

I stared in fascination at his brown-skinned, muscled back. It had a tattoo, too. This one on his right shoulder blade, bigger than the other one. It was a skull, wearing an elaborate crown, its grinning teeth clenching a beautiful rose. The skull and crown were all in black, the petals and stem of the rose, though, were in full, striking color. Although I was no tattoo expert, I had an art degree so I felt safe in saying the rose was exquisite. You could see the artist had taken their time and they were skilled at their craft. It was, quite simply, stunning.

It was *way* cooler than the broken heart.

He slammed the drawer, turned and walked back to me. He gave me a white t-shirt then wrapped his hand around the back of my head, leaned in and kissed the top again. Then he walked away and went to another drawer. He got something else and headed to the door.

He stopped, put his hand to the knob and looked at me. "Get changed, *mamita*. I'll call the boys and I'll be back."

I nodded again. He closed the door and I heard the floorboards creak as he walked away.

I stared at the doors and rewound the evening, wondering how I got myself in this latest predicament. Without lemon drops to blame (I had diet with my spicy beef burrito), I could only blame the power tools.

Now what normal girl got turned on by power tools? I was so weird!

Then I realized he could be back any second. It didn't take a year to call Ralphie and Buddy.

I threw the blanket back, tugged on the t-shirt (which was huge on me, by the way), undid my bra underneath it and squirmed and contorted until I pulled it off. I snatched up my clothes, folding them, my bra between my shirt and skirt. I put them on the dresser and dashed back to the bed which, I noticed belatedly, was unmade. I rearranged the pillows that were slightly scattered but partially stacked so that they were evenly placed. I sat cross-legged in the middle of the bed and pulled the covers up around my waist. I tucked them tightly around me and stared at the door.

When it didn't open immediately, I looked around the room.

I noticed a dresser, a closet (one door open, one Hispanic Hottie that clearly hadn't been taught how to properly hang clothes), boots and running shoes scattered against one wall and a laundry hamper overflowing in a corner.

Incongruous to the room, an expensive flat screen TV sat on a handsome, dark wood, heavy, masculine TV stand that rested at the wall opposite the bed. It had electronic equipment and stacks of DVDs on display on shelves underneath it.

Boy, gay or straight, rich or poor, men really liked their TVs.

The room hadn't been refinished. The once utilitarian cream of the walls was grubby. The white skirting boards chipped. The wood floors notched and needing sanding and refinishing.

Did a man bring a woman to such a room? Such a *house?*

If that man was Hector, a *real* man who didn't give a damn what anyone thought of him, the answer was yes.

My stomach pitched and it hit me for the first time just how profound it was what Ricky took from me.

Because a normal, free New Sadie, fresh from a life under her father's thumb, should have had a different end to a "just the two of us" date with Hector.

On that dismal thought, the door opened and Hector was there.

He was carrying his clothes and boots and wearing a pair of pajama pants, a thick, navy elastic band at the waist, plaid flannel legs. The thing was, he'd cut them off at mid-thigh (and, to be honest, had not done a great job) so the hems were ragged. They looked like they'd been worn about five million times and the waist hung low so I could see his defined abs and hip bones.

Oh my blooming *my.*

His head came up. He saw me sitting in his bed and his body jolted to a halt like he'd hit a wall and he froze.

I blinked.

Now, really, how bizarre was *that?*

I stared at him. He stared at me.

The way he was looking at me made me feel funny, really funny, *seriously* funny (but in a good way), so I blurted, "Is everything okay with Ralphie and Buddy?"

His chin jerked back and he came unstuck.

He walked to the laundry hamper and answered my question with a, "Yeah."

I watched him move. He moved well.

I tried to stop thinking about how well he moved.

"Um…" I muttered. "Isn't it kind of early to go to bed?"

And it was early, at the latest nine.

"Yeah," he said and dumped some clothes on the hamper. They immediately tumbled off the top and fell on the floor. He apparently didn't notice this. He twisted and tossed his boots into the pile by the wall. I watched them sail and land with a thump.

Then my eyes went back to him. I caught the crowned skull again before he turned and came to the side of the bed.

"Should we watch TV or something?" I suggested.

He was carrying his jeans. His eyes came to me as he dropped his cell on the bedside table and then emptied his pockets.

There was something immensely weird but very lovely, snugly, comfy, warm about sitting in his bed and watching Hector empty the pockets of his jeans. Before I could plumb the depths of this weird, lovely, snugly, comfy, warm feeling, Hector spoke.

"Yeah," he said again, his eyes lazy on me, and that made me feel weird, lovely, comfy warm too!

"Do you have to move furniture around?" I asked him. "Because, if you do, I can help."

A glamorous smile hit his mouth and my breath caught. "Move furniture around?"

"You know, downstairs."

He laughed softly, shook his head and jutted his chin to the wall. My eyes moved to where he was indicating.

Oh boy. We were going to watch TV in Hector's bed.

This was not good. In fact, how was I here at all? Why did I agree to this?

I rewound the night frantically even though I'd done the same thing only moments before. It came back to me in a humiliating rush and I swallowed.

I was there for a reason and there I had agreed to stay.

Blooming heck.

"What if we want popcorn? We can't eat popcorn in your bed," I told him, sounding maybe an *eensy* bit desperate.

He twisted. I got a look at the King of Skulls on his back shoulder again, and he tossed his jeans in the general direction of the hamper (they hit the target but also rolled off and fell to the floor, and he didn't care about that, either). Then before I knew what he was about, he'd turned around, doubled at the waist and put his fists into the bed, close to my thighs.

This meant his face was close to mine.

"First of all, *mamita*, I don't have any popcorn. Second, you barely touched your dinner. Now you wanna eat?"

I thought fast (this, by the way, was *not* easy).

"My mind was occupied at dinner. Now, I'm feeling peckish," I lied. I would probably throw up if I ate anything, I was so nervous.

He shook his head, laughing low again, then lifted up, pulled back the covers and slid in.

My heart stopped.

He arranged the pillows behind his back (I will note, he completely devastated my efforts at equal pillow disbursement of not ten minutes before). His arm curled around my waist and he pulled me backwards so my back hit his side, my legs uncrossed and my shoulder and head were pillowed on his chest.

Oh, I *got* it. I didn't *need* pillows. I was using his chest as a pillow. So *that* was why he could hog them all.

I felt him move, saw his hand holding the remote in my peripheral vision and the TV snapped on. A ballgame appeared and the hand disappeared.

As if he hadn't just settled us comfortably in his bed like we'd be sharing our golden wedding anniversary the next evening and not doing this for the *very first time ever*, he continued the conversation.

"Your mind at dinner was occupied with an attempted freeze out, which, *mi cielo*, is cute, I gotta admit. But it's only fair to let you know, it's not gonna work."

My body went still. He thought the Ice Princess was cute? *Cute?*

The Ice Princess was *not* cute! I knew grown men that feared her!

Well, maybe not feared. Perhaps they just disliked her and gave her a wide berth.

It was good I was moving to Crete because if he thought my Ice Princess was *cute* then I was in a mess of trouble.

"We'll order a pizza if you're hungry," he told me.

I crossed my arms on my chest, stared at the TV and contradicted my earlier lie, "I'm not hungry."

His arm came around me. His forearm resting on my chest, his fingers curled around my opposite shoulder.

"You want something, let me know," he said and he sounded distracted.

Obviously the game had called his attention.

So I thought it might be safe to ask an eensy, teensy, tiny, little personal question just because I was dying to know, and since I didn't get the gift I intended to give myself that evening, I was going to go for something different.

"What's the tattoo on your chest mean?" I asked casually, like whatever answer to a brokenhearted tattoo question would mean nothing at all whatsoever to me.

"Belinda," he replied, still sounding distracted.

I was not distracted. My body went still again.

"Belinda?" I asked.

"My ex," he answered.

Oh... my... *God*.

He had a tattoo of a broken heart on his chest. No, he had a tattoo of a broken heart over his heart on his chest! A tattoo he got for Belinda!

"Was it a bad break?" I was still going for casual, but my voice sounded breathy.

Now, why did I ask that? Why? What was wrong with me? Now I was punishing *myself* and getting *myself* into stupid, terrifying situations.

"You could say that, since she broke it off three months before the wedding."

Before I could think better of it (or, say, think *at all*), I shot up to a seated position and twisted to look at him, my mouth open.

Then I snapped it closed.

Then I spoke. "She broke up with you three months before your wedding?"

*Oh my God!*

Hector had been engaged. He'd nearly been married!

Oh my *GOD!*

He didn't move. His body still reclined on the pillows, the sheets to his waist, his chest displayed. Only his eyes came to me.

"Yeah," he answered.

"Why?" I asked.

"She wanted a nine-to-five guy who mowed the lawn on the weekends. I'm not a nine-to-five guy who mows the lawn on the weekend. She couldn't handle me being on assignment, away for days or weeks or even months, not being able to contact her. She tried to talk me into a desk job. I told her the man who put the ring on her finger was a field agent for the DEA and that's who she'd have to marry. She saw I was serious, pawned the ring, got her mom to call the church, hall and guests and took a vacation at an all-inclusive in Acapulco."

My eyes narrowed.

"She *pawned* your *ring?*" I spat, sounding frighteningly like Ralphie.

But seriously. Who would pawn Hector "Oh my God" Chavez's ring? Who would try to make Hector something he was not? Who would go to Acapulco alone when they could go to Acapulco *with Hector?* On their honeymoon even!

Was she nuts?

I realized belatedly that Hector was smiling a huge, blinding white smile at me.

Oh no.

What had I given away?

He did an ab crunch. His hands came to my shoulders, twisted me so my back was to him, his arm went around my chest and he pulled me into my earlier position. But this time his arm was wrapped tighter.

"Calm down, *mamita.* My sister Gloria went to her house and roughed her up when she got back from Mexico. It was a couple of years ago. You can stand down."

There was the answer. I'd given it *all* away.

Darn it!

I decided to move attention off me "standing down". "Your sister Gloria roughed her up?"

"Catfight. Not pretty. Word is, Gloria won."

I wanted to laugh and clap my hands for an absent sister I would probably never meet.

Of course, I did not.

"She broke your heart," I said to the TV.

His fingers did a squeeze on my shoulder. "I'm over it."

"It hurt enough for you to tattoo it on your chest," I pointed out.

"I didn't get the tat because she marked me. I got the tat to remind myself of the lesson I learned. She was beautiful. Great body, fantastic in bed and she could be sweet when she wanted, but most of the time she was a nagging bitch. Every time I see the tat, it reminds me not to be led around by my dick."

All right then, more proof that Hector was as real as you could get.

It was clear, at this juncture, it was time for me to steer us into safer waters.

"So, what's the skull with the crown and the rose mean?"

Hector's body tensed and the air in the room immediately felt heavy. My body tensed at his reaction and the feel of the air.

Eyes on the TV, I didn't even try to be casual when I whispered, "Hector?"

He sighed. His body relaxed, but his arm around me got tighter.

"I got it to celebrate nailing your father."

Of course.

He got it to celebrate, forever and ever, putting King Drug Man, Mr. Death to many (probably), better known as my *fucking* father, in prison. That was *just great*.

Well, if I didn't already have my proof that we were ill-suited, it was tattooed on Hector's *fucking* back.

"And the rose clamped in his teeth?" I asked. Wanting to know what that meant. Perversely looking for more reasons to buy my tickets to Crete and fill my luggage with beach towels, even as I was wearing Hector's t-shirt and lying in his bed with his arm around me.

"The rose is you."

Plans of buying beach towels flew out of my head. My stomach dropped, my heart seized and I could feel a tremor shiver through my body.

"Me?" I whispered.

He did another ab crunch. His arm moved to around my waist. He twisted me so I was facing him and reclined, me pressed mostly to his front with my face close to his.

I put my hand on his chest and pressed up, but his arm went solid at my waist and I stilled.

"You," he said firmly, his eyes back to that warm intensity. "In time, this arm..." He squeezed me with his right arm but lifted his left. "Right here..." His right arm left me and he pointed to the inside of his forearm. My eyes moved there then back to his as his arm came around me again. "Is gonna have the same rose. Because you belong on my arm. Do you understand what I'm sayin' to you?"

I understood what he was saying. I understood what he meant when he said "My Sadie" now, too.

The tremor shivered through my body again.

"Sadie, do you understand what I'm sayin' to you?" he asked again, his tone no less firm, but it had grown slightly soft.

I was staring at him, but I forced myself to nod. I couldn't trust myself to speak.

His arm went tight around me, sliding partly up my back, hand catching under my shoulder blade, bringing me to him. He kissed me, slow, sweet, mouths open, tongues tangling, toes (or at least *my* toes) curling.

His mouth broke from mine and he murmured, "Now, we've had our talk. You know where I stand. Can we watch the game?"

I nodded again. His arm loosened. I turned, rested against him and stared, unfocused, on the game.

Blooming heck.

I wasn't in a mess of trouble. I was beyond trouble. I was in so deep, I was over my head. And the water felt so warm, snugly, comfy, lovely that I was beginning to wonder if I minded drowning.

# Chapter 12

# I Think I Made Hector Mad

*Sadie*

My sleeping body jerked awake when I heard the loud noise from somewhere too close for comfort.

Then it froze when I heard the crash.

I had nearly a nanosecond to assess my position tucked tight against Hector's warm body, his arm around my waist, my cheek on his left pectoral, my hand resting dead center on his chest. But before that nanosecond was over, his heat vanished and a blast of cold hit me.

I lifted up on an arm, my heart racing, pulling back my hair with my other hand and seeing Hector's shadowy body moving beside the bed.

He had the bedside drawer open. I heard a soft thump as he put whatever it was on the nightstand and then his hand immediately came out, his fingers closing around my wrist. He lifted up my arm and I felt him press something in my hand.

"Stay here. You feel a bad vibe, hear something you don't like, you dial 911," he whispered. Then he tagged whatever was on the bedside table and disappeared from the room.

I stared at the door and heard noise, voices, and visions of Marty or Ricky blowing Hector's beautiful head off danced sickeningly through my head.

I threw back the covers in a flurry and tiptoed across the room to the side of the door. If someone was going to come and get me, I wasn't going to be sitting in bed waiting for them.

I pressed my shoulder against the wall by the door and assessed my options.

I had Hector's cell phone in my hand. This was lame.

I could get one of his boots. I could seriously clobber someone with one of Hector's boots.

Or I could get one of my spiked heels. I could poke someone in the eye with the spiked heel. That would sting.

On that thought, I heard raised voices. Hector's and a female's. They were yelling at each other in Spanish. Although this was yelling, it was not bad vibe yelling. It was irritated yelling.

I took a deep breath and crept out the door, down the hall, and the yelling kept going, mostly the female.

I made it to the top of the stairs and looked down.

There was a light on and Hector was standing at the foot of the stairs, his back to me, the King Skull on display, a gun held loosely in his hand.

In front of him were three Hispanic women. One of them (the one yelling, who was also gesticulating wildly with her arms) was short and gorgeous. She looked like a younger, less round but no less fiery version of Blanca.

A relative.

I let out a breath and put my hand holding the cell phone to my chest.

The minute I did her eyes lifted to the stairs. She stopped yelling and her mouth dropped open.

I wanted to turn and run back to the bed, pull the covers over my head and wait until Hector got back.

Instead, New Sadie clicked into place, took her hand from her chest, waved the cell phone at the woman and called, "Hi."

Hector twisted and looked up at me. I watched him bite his bottom lip, and as I'd never seen him do that before, I didn't know whether he was biting back a smile or annoyance.

I took in a deep breath and walked down the stairs.

All three women watched me descend. All of them had their mouths hanging open.

I thought this was bizarre. Hector was Hispanic Hottie. He'd nearly been married to *Belinda*. It wasn't like he'd never had a woman at his house.

Hector stepped to the side when I got to the bottom and I stopped next to him.

"Sadie, this is my sister Gloria. Gloria, Sadie," Hector introduced us when I came to a halt.

So this was Catfight- Rough-Up-*Belinda* Gloria.

I couldn't help it. I smiled at her.

Her eyes bugged out.

Now, this was bizarre, too.

Hector rapped out something in terse Spanish and Gloria blinked.

Then she said to me, "It's just like *Mamá* said, you *do* look like a fairy princess."

Oh. That again.

I shrugged.

Eyes still on me, she breathed, "*Dios mio*, please tell me it's just a little hard to be that beautiful."

I stared at her, not knowing how to react.

On the one hand, what she said was really sweet and that made me feel nice.

On the other hand, it was more than "just a little hard" to look like me because looking like me made me a Balducci Brothers Target of Terror.

On this thought, of their own accord, my fingers started toward the scar on my cheek. For some reason when I did this, Hector's body gave off his angry electric current and it began snapping around the room.

His arm slid around my shoulders and he tucked my front into his side. His other hand came up, his fingers wrapped around my raised wrist and he pulled my hand to his chest. While he did this, he barked low, angry Spanish words at his sister.

She shook her head then nodded, and her face going a bit pale, she said, "I'm sorry, Sadie. I didn't think."

So, Gloria knew what happened to me, too.

This time, I mentally shrugged. It was way harder than the fairy princess thing, but I was getting used to it, too.

"Please, don't worry about it," I said softly.

Finally, she gave me a small, hesitant grin, turned and gestured to the two girls behind her. "These are my girls, Ines and Tia."

I looked at them. They were smiling at me and both were nearly as pretty as Gloria (but not quite), and finally I said, "Hi."

They said, "Hi," back.

I was feeling weird. Then I realized this was because I was standing in Hector's t-shirt, tucked in Hector's side, in the middle of the night, with Hector's sister and her two friends in Hector's living room.

I wondered briefly why Hector's sister would break into her brother's house in the middle of the night, but I decided it was none of my business. I didn't have siblings. Who knew how they acted? Maybe this was normal.

I put my hand holding the cell phone around Hector's waist and waited for someone to say something.

No one did.

So I tried to figure out what was the nice thing to do in this situation and I settled on asking, "Should I make coffee?"

"Fuck no," Hector said immediately.

This jerked Gloria out of her Sadie Daze and she started snapping in Spanish at Hector.

Hector listened for about half a second then interrupted (thankfully, in English), "Gloria, no fuckin' way are you and the girls sittin' in my hot tub at fuckin' one o'clock in the fuckin' morning."

Hector had a hot tub?

"We'll be quiet," Gloria assured him.

"I don't give a fuck. What's in your head, breakin' into my house in the middle of the night? I could have shot you, for fuck's sake," Hector replied sharply.

"*Mamá* said you've been spendin' the night at Sadie's. We didn't think you'd be here," Gloria responded.

Blanca knew Hector was spending the night at my house?

How? Why? Again, *how?*

"That makes it okay?" Hector shot back, breaking into my crazed thoughts.

"You aren't using it!" Gloria snapped back.

"Jesus," Hector muttered, obviously at a loss to come up with a retort against his sister's (I had to admit) bizarre logic.

"Maybe I *should* make coffee," I broke in, trying to be peacemaker.

"Maybe Gloria, Ines and Tia should get their Mexican asses out of my fuckin' house." Hector didn't feel like allowing me to make peace.

Thus began a hot-blooded, Mexican-American sibling stare down that was so scorching, I felt even the latent Ice Princess shy away.

New Sadie, however, felt like marching straight into the fire.

I looked up at Hector. "Hector, let them sit in the hot tub."

Hector looked down at me, face still angry, but for some reason I knew he was not angry at me, and he started, "Sadie—"

"What's it going to hurt?" I broke in.

I watched Hector's teeth clench and a muscle leap in his cheek.

"That's okay," Gloria said, and Hector's and my eyes moved to her. "We'd have to use the bathroom to change and we'd have to come back in to dry off afterward. We'd probably be noisy," she explained, now smiling the Glamorous Chavez Smile at me (hers had a dimple, like Eddie's). "We didn't know you were here, Sadie, or we wouldn't have woken you up."

"No problem," I told her, wanting to laugh at her implication that if it had been just Hector at home they wouldn't have hesitated waking *him* up.

"We'll come back when you're here some other time. We'll *all* sit in the hot tub," Gloria invited herself over.

Hector's body went tight.

I was thinking I'd likely be in Crete by that time, licking my wounds and obsessively sketching versions of Hector's celebration tattoo, my father's skull, my beautiful rose, even though I didn't sketch. I'd have all the time in the world to teach myself.

Instead, I said, "I'll look forward to that."

"Jesus," Hector for some reason muttered again.

Gloria was close to laughing when her gaze swung to her brother. She said something to him in Spanish. His body grew tighter and Ines and Tia started giggling.

"You do that," Hector said, his voice as tight as his body, "there'll be retribution."

"Bring it on," Gloria returned, still smiling and not at all scared of Hector's threatened "retribution".

Then they hitched their bags over their shoulders, waved at me calling, "*Hasta luego,*" and they were gone.

Hector let me go and I watched him lock the door behind them. He flipped the light switch and came back to me. Throwing his arm around my shoulders again, he turned me and guided me up the stairs.

"What did she say at the end, before she left?" I asked as we walked up the stairs. I felt weird with his arm around me like that so I put mine around his waist and immediately didn't feel weird anymore.

"She told me she was gonna tell *Mamá* you're here."

Since, apparently, Blanca knew he was spending the night at my house, I didn't know why this was a big deal.

"Why is that a big deal?" I asked.

"She tells her, you'll find out," Hector said ominously.

Oh no.

We went back to his room. I crawled into bed while he put his gun away and then he joined me. He moved into me, turning me so my back was to his front and his arms were around me.

His heat seeped through me and I started to relax, feeling safe, snug, comfy, lovely when he called, "Sadie?"

"Yes?" I replied in a sleepy voice.

"Gloria gets you in the hot tub with her posse, they have any bright ideas, you ignore them and go your own way."

"What does that mean?"

"That means Gloria, Ines and Tia make Indy and Ally look like amateurs."

I blinked in the darkness. "Now, what does *that* mean?"

"Indy has her own police code," Hector informed me.

Oh my.

⌖

I woke to a cold, thus, I knew, empty bed.

I rolled, looked at Hector's side, but sure enough, he was gone. I sat up, pulled my hair out of my face and looked around the room.

No Hector.

Then I realized I had to use the bathroom.

I slid out from under the covers, walked out of the room and down the hall, looking into empty rooms. Two more bedrooms (neither of them refinished, one unused save to store more stacked boxes and furniture, the smallest one being utilized as an office), one bath.

When I got in the bathroom, I noticed Hector had already renovated it. A handsome, what looked like top-of-the-line (but what did I know, I was no plumber) bathroom suite and lots of warm, Mexican tile up the walls. Cobalt, mustard yellow and terracotta designs against a buttery-cream background.

I did my business and walked down the stairs in search of Hector. I found him in the kitchen.

At the sight of him, I stopped in the doorway.

He was still wearing his cutoff pajama bottoms but he'd added a dark-gray, long-sleeved, skintight thermal. He was standing by the sink on the opposite side of the room. His side was partially turned to the counter, hip resting against it, eyes looking out the window over the sink, coffee cup held aloft but forgotten in front of him.

His mind was on something.

I stared at him and thought for the millionth time that he never looked better.

The kitchen had not been renovated and it looked like an extension of the restoration efforts. Paint brushes and drying rollers lying out on rags on the countertops, buckets on the floor, bags filled with I didn't know what stacked in the corner.

I must have moved because Hector's eyes sliced to me. His thoughtful face warmed and he demanded softly, "Come here."

As if guided by their own personal brain, my feet moved me toward him as I watched him put his mug on the counter. When I got within reaching distance, one of his arms came around my shoulders, the other one around my waist and he curled me into his heat.

His head came down and he gave me a soft, sweet kiss (with tongues) that lasted until my arms slid around his waist and my body melted into his. Then he lifted his head.

"You want coffee?" he asked quietly.

Robbed of speech by the kiss, I nodded.

Before he could move, there was a clamor from the other room. A *loud* clamor.

Our bodies grew tight in unison before we heard Blanca call, "*Hola, mi hijo! Dónde estás?*"

"Fuck," Hector muttered.

I stared in horror at Hector's set face.

"Hector!" Blanca shouted.

"Kitchen!" Hector shouted back.

Oh no.

Someone, please tell me Hector didn't just tell his mother our whereabouts.

I was standing, in Hector's t-shirt, in Hector's arms, in Hector's kitchen, and Blanca (from what I could hear, carrying rustling bags) was headed our way.

183

My body prepared to flee. Hector's arms went tight. Blanca filled the kitchen doorframe.

She stared at us a second, then shouted as if we were across a football field and not across a room, "*Hola!*"

I was robbed of speech again, now for a different reason.

"*Mamá*, Sadie and I want a quiet morning."

"Bah!" Blanca exploded, bustling in and dropping six (yes, six!) bulging King Soopers bags on the counter. "Sadie needs breakfast. Do you cook, *mi hijo?* No, you do not cook. *Hola* Sadie." She smiled at me and then started to pull food out of the bags.

I watched as the food was revealed and I noted no breakfast-type items. It looked more like she was planning to stock the cupboards before the government announced rationing.

I found my voice. "Um, *hola* Blanca."

I felt Hector's eyes on me and I looked up at him. He was smiling.

Yes, *smiling!*

I shot him a glare. His body moved with laughter. I did *not* think this was funny. Instead, I found it mortifying. I pulled out of his arms and put some distance between us.

I'd never been caught in the morning by someone's mother. If I had dared to bring my boyfriends to my father's house and they wandered around in their pajama bottoms, my father would have had them executed (this might be a bit over the top, but my father *really* didn't like to share me and he had loads of suffocating ways to make that terrible fact perfectly clear).

Therefore, awake for approximately ten minutes, I found myself caught in a new predicament and I had no idea what to do.

New Sadie, however, surprisingly knew *exactly* what to do.

"Can I help?" New Sadie chirped to Blanca.

"Coffee. Black," Blanca answered.

Still annoyed at him, I shot another glare at Hector and then started opening and closing cupboards to find the mugs. His hand slid around my waist and pulled me into his side before he reached well beyond me and opened the cupboard over the coffeemaker. It was filled with mismatched mugs. I turned my head to give him another glare, but this effort failed when his mouth hit mine for a touch on the lips. Then he let me go.

I shrugged off his kiss and got down to the business of coffee. I was in the middle of finishing mugs for Blanca and me (*and* Hector, who slid his cup beside mine when I was pouring) and wondering how on earth I was going to get through this latest trauma (in a t-shirt, no less!) when I heard a man's voice call out, "Chavez?"

"Christ, is there a sign on my door that says come the fuck in?" Hector muttered.

I noticed at our latest visitor Hector instantly lost his good morning mood and it was Blanca's turn to shoot him a glare.

But my eyes flew to the kitchen doorway, wondering who this was now (and also wondering why my life couldn't be the *eeniest* bit easier) when Hector moved across the room and out of the kitchen.

"*Café, mi hija*," Blanca reminded me, and I stopped staring at Hector's departing back and brought her coffee to her.

"What else can I do?" I asked as I heard male voices in the other room. They were getting closer and my eyes went back to the door.

"Do you cook?" Blanca asked.

"Not really," I answered somewhat dishonestly. I'd never had to cook much, but I did know how to make coffee and toast, which was something.

"I'll teach you," Blanca assured me, moving around the room, putting away food and pulling out cooking implements.

I was feeling a weird, happy glow at Blanca offering to teach me to cook when Hector walked in. He was followed, to my horror, by the tall, handsome, dark-haired Ren Zano wearing a tailored suit (and wearing it really well, by the way). This making me *acutely* aware that I was wearing nothing but Hector's t-shirt and a pair of dove gray satin panties, which, luckily, you couldn't see as the shirt hung to mid-thigh.

Please, someone tell me, just… plain… no.

Ren's eyes scanned the room, coasting across Blanca with a quick, "Mornin'," and then coming to a halt on me. His face gentled, and without hesitation he walked to me, smiling.

"Sadie," he said softly.

"Ren," I replied.

To my shock (because he'd never done it before, not once), his arm slid around my waist and he pulled me to his body in a hug. After he was done with the hug, his arm loosened but didn't let go. I arched back over it, hands on his chest, and looked up at him.

Eyes on my face, he murmured, "Beautiful as ever."

Oh my God.

He'd never done that before either! What was *that* about?

I searched for the Ice Princess.

The Ice Princess never much liked coming out around Ren (although, of course, she did). But this time she flatly refused.

That was why New Sadie asked, "Are you well?"

"Yeah," he returned.

I smiled at him. "Good."

His gaze dropped to my mouth then his lips formed a grin. "Jesus, Sadie, never seen you smile," he remarked.

I cocked my head in confusion. "I'm sure you have," I replied.

His eyes moved back to mine. "Trust me, I would have remembered."

It was then I felt the electric current snapping through the room, right before I heard Hector, his voice not happy, saying in the form of a question but meaning it in the form of a demand, "Zano, you wanna step back?"

I realized Ren still had an arm around me right before he dropped it and stepped back.

Both Ren and I looked across the room.

Hector was standing, feet planted, arms crossed, eyes dark and looking beyond unhappy. So beyond unhappy, he looked downright angry.

No, one could say he'd gone right past downright unhappy to pretty extreme fury.

Blanca had a similar expression *and* she was holding a wooden spoon. A wooden spoon I thought she had a mind to use for something other than cooking.

"Chavez, you know Sadie's a friend," Ren told Hector in a low, placating tone.

"Yeah, but now she's a friend you don't put your hands on," Hector replied.

Oh my.

Why was he being so *rude*? This was Ren Zano we were talking about! Ren was a very nice man. There was no reason to be rude.

"Hector—" I started, and Hector's eyes cut to me. The minute I saw the look in them, for self-preservation's sake, I snapped my mouth shut.

"Coffee and we finish our talk in the other room," Hector told Ren.

"I'll get the coffee," I offered quickly and jumped to get Ren's coffee, needing something to do to keep my mind off the look in Hector's eyes. I asked Ren's coffee preference, hurried through the preparation and handed him his mug. He smiled his thanks, nodded to a still-frowning, closely-watching Blanca and walked from the room.

Then I gave Hector his mug, got scorched by a Hector glare that made my lungs burn and he walked from the room, too.

I picked up my own mug and tried to stop my hands from shaking and my heart from racing. I took a sip and realized I also had to stop breathing so heavily. I was panting like I'd just run a race.

That was when I noticed Blanca's eyes were on me.

"I think I made Hector mad," I blurted before I thought better of it.

Something flashed across her face. It looked like anger, warring with confusion, warring with compassion then she asked, "You *think?*"

"I…" I started, stopped, and walked the five steps to Blanca. "What did I do?" I finished on a whisper.

I watched her face soften as compassion won and she put a hand on my arm. "My Hector, he's a little hotheaded. You have to handle that boy with care. *Queridita*, first lesson, you don't let a man touch you, ever. If Hector's there to see it or he's not. But *especially* if he's there to see it. *Sí?*"

The light dawned. I might be fledgling New Sadie in my head. But in *his* head, I was *His* Sadie. Period, dot, the end.

I nodded to Blanca.

She patted my arm and went back to cooking. I grabbed my mug and went back to sipping, finding I was so uncomfortable with the idea of making Hector angry at me that it made my heart hurt.

Ren materialized at the door and jutted his chin at me. "Sadie, I'm leaving."

I decided my safest bet was to stay all the way across the room from him and this was exactly what I did.

"Bye, Ren," I said on a wave.

Ren grinned at me like he thought I was funny. His eyes moved to Blanca and he said his good-byes. Then he was gone and Hector was in the doorframe, his gaze was still scorching and it was on me.

"*Mamita*, a word."

It was not a request and he didn't wait for my response. He turned and moved away as I heard the front door open and close behind Ren.

I stood frozen to the spot. Then my eyes flew to Blanca.

She gave me a reassuring wink (which didn't reassure me) and gestured to the door with her spoon.

I pulled in my lips, put down my mug, took a deep breath and searched for Hector who was not in the living room, not in the cluttered other rooms, but upstairs in his bedroom. He was waiting at the door, and the minute I cleared it, he threw it to.

Blooming heck!

He opened his mouth, but before he could say a word, I launched in.

"He's never touched me before. I swear it. It weirded me out!" I cried. "Honest to God, I wouldn't even call him a friend. More an acquaintance. The Ice Princess always protected me from people getting near. When he hugged me, I tried to call her up but she was just *gone*. She keeps disappearing these days. Even when I need her. I'm used to having her around. I know you cannot imagine, but Hector, believe me, it's *beyond* annoying."

I stopped talking when I noticed that he'd stopped looking angry. Instead, his eyes had warmed and his mouth was doing the fighting-a-grin thing.

I replayed what I said, my hands clenched into fists, my eyes closed tight as my body went stock-still and waves of embarrassment flowed over me.

I'd done it. Now he knew everything.

How did I let *that* happen?

He was going to think I was absolutely, certifiably, *insane*.

Then I found myself snatched into strong arms, my soft body colliding with his hard one, and his face went into my neck. I opened my eyes as he turned me and started walking me backward toward the bed, his arms still locked around me.

Well, maybe he didn't think I was certifiably insane. But I was beginning to think he was.

His mood swings were just *bizarre*.

The backs of my legs hit the bed. He stopped us and his mouth moved to my ear.

"*Mamita*," his voice was rough with what sounded like laughter and something else altogether, "you think you could handle my mouth between your legs without freakin' out?"

The legs he wanted to put his mouth between turned to water.

"What?" I whispered.

His head came up. His eyes were burning into mine (now, in a different way) and my breath caught at the sight.

"I gotta have a taste of you and I gotta watch you come. I don't..."

My fingers at his waist dug in, and at that second if he let me go I'd collapse in a puddle at his feet.

"Your mother is downstairs," I breathed.

Hector's mouth came to mine. "The walls are thick."

"She'll wonder what we're doing!"

"No she won't," he returned.

"I won't be able to concentrate." I kept trying.

I felt his mouth smile against mine. "*Mi corazón*, you won't need to concentrate."

Oh my.

*That* got a stomach pitch.

Even so, I kept at it. "I can't. Not now. Maybe later."

His mouth moved away an inch. "Yeah?"

Oh my God!

What had I done now?

I had to keep at it. My hands went to his shoulders and my heart skipped a beat. I ignored my heart and nodded.

Before I could go back on my promise, he kissed me quickly and muttered, "Pack a bag, you're spendin' the night again. We'll try it. You can't deal, we'll stop and watch a movie."

"Okay," I said, but my stomach was twisting, my heart was in my throat and I was having difficulty breathing. This was partially panic, but it was also partially anticipation and I wondered which one would win that night.

Hector watched my face and his arms got tight. "Sadie, seriously, you can't deal, you tell me, we stop," he repeated in a way I knew he meant it.

The partial panic disappeared and before I thought better of it, I leaned into him, tilted my head back further and smiled.

His face warmed and his mouth descended. He gave me one of his slow, sweet kisses (with tongues) and my toes started curling when we heard a muted, "*Hola!* Anyone home?" and Hector groaned his frustration in my mouth.

His head came up briefly, but he leaned back in, gave me a quick kiss and told me, "Get dressed, *mamita*. That's my sister Rosa. Gloria's been busy."

I did not think this was a good thing, and the look on Hector's face confirmed it.

He let me go and I watched as he grabbed some clothes and left the room.

I dressed, but while I did so I heard two more "*holas*" (one male, the other female) and I searched for my Ice Princess, thinking maybe just a hint of her would get me through breakfast with the Chavez Family.

My Ice Princess was feeling lazy, so by the time I was dressed (all but my shoes; barefoot was the only way to go or I'd look like a snooty, Rich Bitch Freak), I knew it was just me, Sadie, who was going to face Hector's family.

And she was just going to have to do.

# Chapter 13

# Agent Chavez, oo, Agent Chavez

---

### *Sadie*

It was mid-afternoon and I was in Art.

Sitting on the edge of my counter was Daisy, legs crossed and mouth shouting her ideas (or, more honestly, her orders) at Ralphie and Roxie. They were both arranging paintings on the floor in the positions they would take on the walls when Ralphie and I installed them on Monday for the opening that evening.

I was behind the counter with Shirleen and Ava. The three of us were leaned forward on our forearms poring over the final catering menu I had to sign off and fax by three o'clock.

❦

That morning I had breakfast with Hector's very loud but very sweet family; all three younger sisters, Gloria, Rosa and Elena, and his older brother, Carlos. Carlos brought his girlfriend, Maria, and Eddie did a flyby mostly to show his face and pour warm coffee into his travel mug. He also gave me a one-armed hug and a kiss on the side of the head like he'd known me for years, not days (no kidding!).

During breakfast, I found out that Hector's Dad had died a few years ago. That Blanca was not happy at the snail's pace of Carlos and Maria's relationship (this somewhat alarmed me as they'd only been together two months and Maria was moving in with Carlos that weekend). And that Blanca and Jet's mother Nancy had made some decisions about Eddie and Jet's wedding that needed a *Reunión de la Familia*. Hector explained (by whispering in my ear, which, by the way, felt nice) that this was a family meeting and Blanca called them often.

After they left, Hector took me home and Ralphie was waiting to take me to the gallery. We were going to open late, but I didn't mind. The morning with Hector's loud, loving family in Hector's crazy, jumbled house was something I'd never experienced before in my life.

And I liked it. I liked it enough to take the time to memorize it so one day I could take out the memory and savor it.

Before he left, Hector told me he needed to give me something and I waited in the hall while he jogged back out to his Bronco.

I found I was nervous as to what he might give me. He hadn't had any time to shop. It wasn't like he was going to produce a bouquet of red roses or anything.

He came back in, stopped in front of me and held up a device. My eyes grew round with excitement.

"This is a——" he started but stopped when my hand whipped out and I snatched it from him.

"It's a stun gun!" I cried, so excited I was being nearly as loud as his family. "Veronica Mars has one of these!"

I lifted happy eyes to him and saw he was grinning. "Yeah, *mamita*, but be careful with that."

"Is it for me?" I trilled happily.

His hand went to the side of my neck and slid up, fingers in my hair, thumb at my hairline.

"Yeah. Keep it in your purse where you can get to it. It's got fresh batteries. You turn it on and touch the prongs to your target. A one second touch causes an incapacitating jolt, Three seconds, it'll take someone down."

I lifted the stun gun between us, stared at it in awe and murmured, "Aces."

I came out of my stun gun euphoria when I heard his soft laughter and my eyes went to him.

"What's funny?" I asked.

His fingers wrapped around my wrist, pulled the stun gun from between us and he closed in, his other hand sliding to the back of my head.

"You don't know, *mamita*, it'll be more fun to watch you figure it out."

Then he kissed me, another slow, sweet one (with tongues) that again lasted until I wrapped my arms tight around his waist and melted into him.

Then he was gone.

⋈

Ralphie and I went into Art, and at eleven thirty Ralphie picked up the phone and dialed.

"Jet, you pretty girl, I'm callin' in a delivery," Ralphie said into the phone as I watched in stunned surprise. "Sadie and I will simply *expire* if we don't have two of Tex's specials. Can you send someone over with them? I'd come get them, but see, Double H says I'm in charge of Sadie's safety during the day. We opened late. We can't close down just to get coffee and I can't leave her alone."

I stood beside Ralphie, still staring at him, wondering when Hector made Ralphie "in charge" of my "safety" while Ralphie nodded and said in the phone, "Un-hunh, un-hunh," then, "Oh, 'Double H' is Hector, stands for Hispanic Hottie'." I heard laughter through the receiver and he finished with, "Toodles," and put the phone down.

Then he turned to me calmly and said, "Daisy'll be over in ten with two specials."

At this point, I rewound my life back six weeks.

Six weeks ago, my father was in prison, my days were spent with Ralphie in Art and my nights were spent either at yoga class, a movie (by myself) or curled up with a book in my living room.

I had no excitement except a scary call or a buzz up from one of the Balducci Brothers. But that wasn't good excitement. That was bad excitement.

I was alone and, albeit frightened, my life was my own and my destiny was decided by me. Except for the Balduccis, I was in complete and total control.

Now I was never alone and I made no decisions for myself. When I did, they were circumvented. Ralphie thought he was my bodyguard. Blanca was going to teach me how to cook. Tom thought I was the reunited member of "the whole family". And Hector was going to put his mouth between my legs that night (and, by the way, the very thought made me shiver).

And then there was the imminent arrival of YoYo the pug, who was being delivered tomorrow night.

Instead of reveling in this which I should be doing, I was planning to disappear.

For a second, I wondered if I was crazy. Then it hit me that I wasn't.

First, a lot of people were going out of their way to make me safe, and that wasn't right or fair. They had better things to do, and furthermore, they barely knew me.

Second, even though they all appeared to like me no matter who sired me, I'd never forget and I'd always know I was the odd girl out.

Last, because Hector was a good guy (maybe even the best guy ever born), when he found someone, she should not be a *Belinda,* but she should also not be a drug dealer's daughter.

And she certainly shouldn't be the tawdry, broken, throw-around toy of the Crazy Balducci Brothers.

I knew I had to ride this out, keep my plans to myself, and when things were all ready, I'd sit down with Ralphie and Buddy and explain. Then I'd sit down with Hector and explain. Then I'd go and let them get back to their normal lives being good people and having nothing more to worry about than their Z Gallerie credit cards (not that Hector had a Z Gallerie credit card, more like Home Depot).

Daisy and Ava showed with the coffees, taking me out of my unhappy thoughts.

They stayed and gabbed.

When I said they "gabbed", I meant they filled in the gaps as told by the reporters and they shared with Ralphie and I the stories of how Indy got together with Lee. Indy was somehow mixed up with why Terry Wilcox disappeared. I knew Terry. He was a contemporary of my father's. He was creepy and I was glad he was gone (and my father had been *super* happy when he disappeared), but I was sorry he made Indy's life a misery before he left.

Then they told me how Eddie and Jet got together (Jet had nearly been raped, too, but luckily she was saved at the last minute).

Roxie "popped" around (said she was shopping at 16th Street Mall and she had about a dozen bags to prove her story correct). She found out what we were gabbing about and then *she* shared how she and Hank got together. She'd been stalked by an ex-boyfriend. He found her at Hank's house, beat her up and took her for a wild ride across three states before Vance, or Native American Hottie, found her. Eventually her ex got his hand shot mostly off (again by Vance) at one of Daisy's society parties (I'd heard about it, but obviously hadn't been invited).

Then they shared how Vance and Jules (the black-haired lady from the drag show) got together. Jules had gone on a vigilante mission to take down drug dealers (which meant I might not be her most favorite person) and she ended up getting shot twice (something, the girls told me, Hector blamed himself for; though I didn't get it, it seemed an honest, though heart-wrenching, mistake). Vance and Jules were the only other "Hot Bunch" (as Daisy called the Nightingale Men) and Rock Chick couple who were married and they had a newborn baby.

Finally, Ava shared how she and Luke got together. I found out she knew Ren too, and I also found out that Ren's cousin, Dom (who I knew too, but not as well as Ren; Dom used to be kind of a jerk, but I'd heard that he'd turned into a rather keen family man). Ava's story was kind of confusing, had to do with con men, and somewhere along the line she'd been violated too. Though not as bad as me, still. Did one put degrees on these things? Violation was violation, simple as that.

I already knew about Stella and Mace.

After they were done talking, I was seriously weirded out. But I also had food for thought. Mainly because it would seem I wasn't the first girl to catch the eye of one of the Hot Bunch who caused some significant worry, out-and-out scares and visits to the hospital.

While I was thinking this, Daisy, Ava and Roxie took off to The Market to get us sandwiches.

They came back with Shirleen, who was taking her lunch "hour" (an hour that lasted two), and they chipped in to help with the final touches for the opening. I asked Roxie for Jet's number and called her to warn her about the *Reunión de la Familia* (because that was the nice thing to do). She muttered some choice words, thanked me in a way that seemed very genuine (and even relieved). We hung up after agreeing to meet up sometime and then I turned to the catering menu.

≈≋≈

"You need some pigs in a blanket," Shirleen advised, casting a critical eye over the menu.

"You don't have pigs in a blanket at an art opening," Daisy said to Shirleen.

Shirleen's head popped up. "Sure you do. You just make 'em with those little baby sausages."

"It's an *art opening*. You need *vol au vents* or shit like that," Daisy said.

Shirleen turned back to me. "Ask 'em if they have pigs in a blanket. They wanna make it fancy they can wrap 'em up in Pilsbury crescent roll dough rather than biscuit dough. Trust me, people full of champagne and pigs in a blanket'll buy *a lot* of paintings."

"How do you know?" Ava asked.

"Because *I'd* buy a painting if someone gave me a glass of champagne and a non-stop supply of pigs in a blanket, especially if it was wrapped up in that crescent dough. Have you tasted a Pilsbury crescent roll?"

Ava nodded and smiled. "Yeah, there was a day when I'd bake and eat a whole tray of crescent rolls all by myself."

"Not hard to do," Shirleen muttered with the voice of experience.

The gallery's phone rang and I was so wrapped up in thoughts of Pilsbury crescent rolls, and wondering how hard it was to make them, I didn't even think when the operator asked me if I'd accept the collect charges.

I just said, "Yes."

"Sadie?" my father said in my ear.

My torso snapped up and my mind shut down.

He'd been calling for months, the gallery and my apartment. He had to call collect and I never accepted the charges. A few months ago, Ralphie received a call, put his hand over the mouthpiece and asked if he should accept but I'd shaken my head "no".

At the time Ralphie didn't ask questions. Now, obviously, he knew.

"Sadie?" my father repeated.

Shirleen and Ava had come up with me. I felt their eyes on me as well as Daisy's. I couldn't do anything. My mind was still shut down.

"Sadie! Jesus! Are you there? I don't have all fucking day."

"Daddy," I whispered.

I hated calling him "Daddy". I always hated it, but it was the only thing he allowed.

At my word, the room electrified.

Shirleen's arm shot toward Daisy and I saw her fingers snap repeatedly, but Daisy was already digging through her purse. I watched as she pulled out her cell.

"There's talk," my father said in my ear.

"Talk?" I repeated.

"Talk. We'll get to that in a minute. Where have you been and why have you refused my calls?"

I blinked.

Was he nuts? Did I play my role *that* well that for twenty-nine years he actually thought I *was* the dutiful daughter? I'd always thought my father was smart (he even told me he was smart; he told me this *loads*), but it seemed apparent he was pretty fucking dumb.

Daisy jumped off the counter, phone to her ear, and as she stepped away, Ralphie and Roxie got close.

"What do you mean?" I asked.

"Visiting days, Sadie. Christ, I have things to go over with you. I've been here for months. There's business to attend to. Where the fuck have you been?"

"Working," I replied. Wheels had begun to turn in my head as I heard Daisy talking quietly on her cell.

"Working," his voice was terse, angry and disbelieving. "Your father is in prison and you don't…"

My back started to go straight, and as my eyes focused on Ralphie's concerned face, my father's voice kept on in my ear, but I didn't hear a word he said.

Something strange was happening in my chest. Something hard and hot was forming there and I realized it was anger.

In a flash, my mind reactivated. I lifted my chin and a New Ice Princess, one I'd never met before, one that had a whole different way of dealing with things, slid with a decisive snap into place.

"Excuse me," I cut into my father talking, my voice dripping icicles.

"What?" he asked.

"I said excuse me. You were talking, but I didn't have any interest in what you were saying so I wanted you to stop speaking so I could ask you why you're phoning. I have an opening in a few days and work to do."

My father was silent.

"Hello?" I called.

"Sadie, now's not the time to be funny," he warned.

"I'm not being funny. I'm being perfectly serious. Now tell me, is there something you need or is this a social call?"

"*Have you lost your mind?*" my father exploded.

"No," I replied shortly.

A brief pause, then with soft menace, "It's true. You're fucking him."

I blinked in confusion. "Pardon me?" I asked.

"Chavez. You're fucking Hector Chavez."

I wasn't "fucking" Hector, but it was close enough for my body to start shaking.

How could he know?

Obviously word got round, even in prison.

New Ice Princess replied for me, "I can't imagine why that would be any of your business."

"You're joking."

"May I ask, *father*, why you're phoning when you hear I'm fucking Hector and you *didn't* phone when I'm sure you probably heard that Ricky Balducci beat me senseless, broke multiple bones and *raped* me?"

My father displayed a one track mind and his response made my heart squeeze painfully.

"Hector? You call him *Hector?*"

"Well, I can hardly call out, 'Agent Chavez, oo Agent Chavez,' when he makes me climax, now can I?" I snapped, New Ice Princess gone, Attitude Sadie in her place, and I heard Roxie let out a surprised giggle.

"Sadie, you little—"

I broke in before he could finish. "We're done," I bit out. "And I mean that. We're done. Don't call back, don't write and don't come looking for me on that sorry day when they let you out."

With that, I took the phone from my ear (even while he was still talking), pressed the off button and slammed it down on the counter.

My gaze swung around my audience. Uncertain faces watched me. Daisy was back amongst the crowd and all their eyes were on me.

I wanted one of my Ice Princesses, new *or* old, to come to me.

Instead, Shirleen's hand touched the small of my back. At her touch, I lifted my hands, put them over my face and burst into tears.

Shirleen turned me into her arms and pulled me into her body. "Get it out, child. Get it out."

I pressed my face into her shoulder and cried, hard, fierce, body-wracking sobs.

I wanted a "Dad". Someone like Tom. Hell, someone like Tex would be fine by me. Both of them cared more that I was raped than my own *fucking* father did.

And I wanted my mom back.

"I want my mom back," I said into Shirleen's shoulder, and realized that somewhere between her pulling me in her arms and that moment, we were joined by the others in a group hug.

"Sh, child," Shirleen said, and someone's hand stroked my hair.

"I really hate him," I whispered.

"Sh," Shirleen responded.

The air changed, and the change was so strong my head come up.

The door had opened and Hector was there. He looked about ten times more angry than he did that morning when I'd been stupid and let Ren hold me a *shade* too long. Not that I could have even thought that was possible, but there it was, written all over him.

Alaskan Hottie was with him.

Hector stalked toward me and the girls and Ralphie dispersed. I stared and wiped my eyes as he crossed the room in long, angry strides.

"What did I do now?" I cried when he was close.

I put my hand up. He walked right into it and his arms went around me.

"I heard the call," he said, looking down at me, face still full of rage.

I blinked (yes, *again!*). "You did?"

"We bugged your phone."

Of course. They bugged my phone.

"Your father's slime," he continued, his voice vibrating with anger.

I couldn't refute him. He spoke fact.

"You okay?" he asked.

"No," I answered.

His arms got tighter, and my hand slid up his chest to his shoulder. My other hand joined it on the opposite side and I tilted my head back further. He watched me a second. That second turned to two, then to three.

Then his face lost some of its rage (though, not all), and he promised, "You will be."

My stomach pitched.

His arms got tighter, and I watched, fascinated, as the rage disappeared from Mr. Mood Swing's face. Warmth replaced it and his head dipped closer.

"Agent Chavez, oo Agent Chavez?" he teased, grinning.

I closed my eyes.

Please, somebody, kill me.

He gave me a gentle shake.

I opened my eyes.

His mouth went to my ear and he murmured, "I'll look forward to hearing that."

Before I could retort, his head came around. He touched my lips with his, let me go, then he was gone.

I stared at the door.

Shirleen appeared at my side. "I tell you, six weeks ago, you asked me to take my pick, I woulda picked Luke. Now I'm thinkin' I'd like me a little piece of *that* boy."

"Shirleen!" Ava exclaimed on a giggle.

Shirleen looked at Ava. "Your boy's still hot," she assured her.

I looked at Ralphie.

He was smiling at me. I smiled back.

Then I couldn't help it. I burst out laughing.

***

"So, have you gotten a *mi amor* yet?" Indy asked, her hip up against her father's kitchen counter, a cup of coffee halfway to her mouth, a dishtowel slung over her shoulder, a grin playing at her lips.

"No," I replied and put the last dried glass away. "But I've had a *mi corazón*."

"Oo, a *mi corazón*," Indy smiled.

"What's this?" Ally asked, putting her palms on the counter on either side of her and pulling herself up to sit by Indy.

"Spanish endearments. Sadie's graduated from *mamita* to *mi corazón*," Indy told Ally.

"What's that mean?" Roxie asked, coming to the group after putting some leftovers away and closing the fridge with her foot.

"She's gone from 'babe' to 'my heart'," Indy answered.

I saw Ally's dancing eyes moved to me. "Chickie, you are *in trouble*."

"Tell me about it," I muttered.

They all laughed.

***

We'd had dinner at Tom's.

By "we" I meant Lee and Indy, Hank (Lee and Ally's older brother; he was very nice and they all looked alike: tall, dark and gorgeous) and Roxie, Ally, Tom, Hector and me.

After dessert, Tom pulled out the photos.

There were *loads* of them.

I knew he went out of his way. Some of the photos were really old, from back in the days when my mom was in high school. He must have been up in his attic for hours.

I wanted to try to pretend the pictures didn't fascinate me, but I couldn't.

I remembered my mom as sweet and loving, but also quiet and subdued. The photos showed a different Mom, laughing and smiling and full of life. I couldn't help but pore over them and even laughed when the others told stories.

Lee, Indy, Hank and Ally didn't remember my mom, but they had funny (and slightly crazy) stories to tell about their lives while they sifted through other photos.

Tom, however, *did* remember my mom and he had funny (and slightly crazy) stories to share about her, Katherine and Kitty Sue.

There was one photo I stared at for longer than the rest. It was of the "whole family" (as Tom called them), but for some reason, my grandmother was in it, too.

My grandfather had died before Mom married my father. My father's parents were, as he described for as long as I could remember, "dead to me". However I knew when they both died within a year of each other when I was a freshman at Denver University. My mom's mom died when I was three.

I had no memory of my grandmother, but the photo showed her holding me, my mom's arm around her. Kitty Sue and Katherine close to them, Tom and Malcolm close to their wives, kids scattered around their legs.

My grandmother and Mom had their foreheads together, faces tilted down, smiles huge as they looked at me.

When Tom noticed my attention to the picture, he leaned toward me and whispered, "You can keep that one."

I should have said no. It wasn't polite to take it. But I didn't say no. I looked at him, knowing my eyes were moist, and nodded. Then I slipped it in my purse the first chance I got.

Not much later, the women went to the kitchen to do the dishes and I heard male laughter in the dining room as I heard female laughter all around me in the kitchen.

Dinner, the trips down memory lane, the laughter... it was nice.

But it was scary.

It was scary because I could get used to it.

※|※

"So, how are things going with you two?" Ally asked, eyes on me.

"Who?" I asked back.

"Who?" Ally repeated on a grin. "You and Hector, you idiot."

Me and Hector.

Oh my.

How to explain? Impossible!

So, I shrugged.

"Come on, give," Ally pressed.

"I'd give," Roxie whispered to me. "She's relentless."

I put my hip to the counter on the other side of Ally and sighed. "They're... good," I tried.

"Good?" Indy asked.

"Yes," I replied.

"That's boring," Ally muttered.

"Maybe Sadie needs boring," Roxie said to Ally.

"No one *needs* boring," Ally retorted.

"Maybe Sadie does," Roxie defended my need for boring.

Ally's eyes came back to me. "Do you need boring?"

I looked at her a second then shared, "I have to admit, I could use some boring. But when I say things are good, I didn't mean they were boring."

"What *did* you mean?" Indy asked, and they all leaned forward.

I briefly debated my options.

I could go Ice Princess and tell them nothing (which they were probably not going to accept; nobody was paying the least attention to my Ice Princess anymore). I could tell them everything (which would take all night). I could tell them what was going to happen when Hector and I got back to his place (which might be embarrassing). Or I could tell them about the tattoo.

I told them about the tattoo. When I was done, they all stared at me.

Then Roxie breathed, "Oh... my... *God*."

"I've just decided Lee needs a tattoo," Indy declared.

"No!" I burst out. "If you say something to Lee then it might get back to Hector."

Ally jumped down from the counter, put her arm around my waist and started to guide me to the dining room while Indy and Roxie followed.

"Learn fast, sister," Ally said. "Nothing stays a secret in this clan for long. And that tat is *way too good* to stay a secret."

Well, wasn't that *just great*.

We entered the dining room and I went back to my seat by Hector.

After dinner, during the photo orgy, he'd done the scooting-my-chair-close-to-his move. Now he was lounging with his arm along the back of my empty chair. I had no choice but to sit in it with his arm still there.

The minute I did, it curled around my shoulders and he got in close.

"Ready to go?" he asked softly in my ear.

No. No, I was not ready to go. No, I was not ready to go to his house and have him put his mouth between my legs.

Well, maybe I *was* ready to go and do that since it was almost all I thought about all day (except, of course, my *fucking* father, and also the photos, but it was *mostly* all I thought about).

I didn't think about it in an "Oh my God no way I can do *that*" way. I thought about it in an "Oh my God I can't wait and I hope I don't mess things up again" way.

However, I did have one matter of business I still needed to attend to before I went on to what would likely be the next trauma of my life.

I'd had an idea, and I had to get the wheels in motion before I headed off to Crete because I wasn't going to be going alone. So I put my latest plan into action.

I turned to Hector and said, "I need to talk to Lee."

Hector's brows went up.

"Why do you need to talk to Lee?" Ally asked from across the table, being nosy again and also loud.

Lee heard his sister, his head turned and his eyes came to me. "You need something, Sadie?" he asked.

Oh boy. It was now or never.

"Do you have some time to talk at your office, maybe tomorrow?"

At this point, Lee's body turned to me, but his eyes flicked to Hector before coming back to me.

"I'm right here. We don't need to be at the office," he replied on a (very handsome) smile.

"Well, it's kind of business," I told him.

"Business?"

"Yes."

"What do you need?" he asked.

"I need you to find my mother."

The air in the room instantly changed. It went supercharged with something I didn't understand.

The women were all looking at each other in confusion. The men were looking at each other with closed, set faces.

This I did not take as good.

I forged into the crackling silence. "You find people, don't you?" I asked Lee.

His eyes had locked on Hector, but they came back to me and he nodded.

"Well, my mom disappeared and I thought, maybe, you could find her."

"Sadie——" Hector said from beside me.

"I'll pay," I threw in, just in case Lee thought I was asking for a freebie.

"It's not the money, Sadie. It's——" Lee started, but Tom interrupted him.

"Tomorrow, we'll meet," Tom surprised me by announcing (and inviting himself to come along) and everyone's eyes swung to him. "Four o'clock, Lee's office." Tom looked at Lee. "Be sure Vance is there."

I looked at Tom, confused as to why he'd want Vance there when Hector said in a weird, low voice, "Tom."

I turned to Hector. His face was blank but his eyes were active, and I was sensing something unsettled in him. This I did not take as good, either.

"We'll talk," Tom went on and I looked back to him. "I'll be there, Lee, Vance, Hank, Eddie and you," Tom said to Hector.

"And me," I put in and Tom looked at me.

"And you, Sadie," he agreed.

"Thank you," I said to Tom.

My expression of gratitude made every man in the room look uncomfortable and every woman in the room look at me with concerned eyes.

This alarmed me. Like, *loads*.

"Is there something I should know?" I asked Tom.

"Tomorrow, four o'clock," Tom replied.

"Yes, but—" I started.

"Four," Tom said firmly but gently.

I pulled my lips in, wanting to push it. But he'd gone out of his way with dinner, photos, giving me the picture.

So instead of pushing it, I said, "Okay."

Hector shoved his chair back. "Time for us to go," he announced.

Oh my.

All thoughts of the weird conversation flew out of my head as Hector pulled me out of my chair.

I tried to give Tom a handshake, but he refused it and instead gave me a hug. The hug exchange continued throughout the rest of the group, including Hank (who I barely even knew!).

Then Hector led me out to the Bronco. He helped me in, got in the driver's seat, turned the ignition and we were away.

My overnight bag was in his backseat.

My knees were shaking.

My skin was tingling.

My stomach was in not entirely unpleasant knots.

Blooming heck!

# Chapter 14

# Sadie's Gift

***Sadie***

Hector dropped my overnight bag by the door in his bedroom, walked to the side of the bed and turned on the light.

His eyes came to me. "You need anything?"

I tried to think of something I needed.

Courage? A single personality that knew who she was and what she was about rather than multiple ones who had no idea what they were doing? The true ability to rewind my life and go back to the minute my father was shipped off to prison and move, right then and there, to Crete rather than waiting for my life to unravel and bring me to this scary pass?

"No," I answered.

He started to empty his pockets, dropping stuff on the nightstand.

In a nervous panic, I leaned over and unzipped my overnight bag.

I grabbed my pajamas (white camisole, multiple pastels in plaid on white background drawstring bottoms, more of Buddy's trip to Victoria's Secret) and my toiletries case.

"I'm just going to use the bathroom," I muttered to my bag and took off, out of the room, down the hall, to the bathroom.

Keeping my mind purposefully blank, I changed. Then I pulled my hair in a messy ponytail on top of my head, brushed my teeth, washed my face and put on moisturizer. Though makeup-free was likely not the way to go for the evening's festivities. But as I mentioned, I was keeping my mind purposefully blank, thus, obviously, not thinking clearly as I was not thinking *at all* and instead acting on autopilot.

Then I looked in the mirror and allowed myself a moment to think about it.

In other words, I gave myself a pep talk.

"You can do this, Sadie," I whispered in a barely-there voice so Hector couldn't hear me talking to myself. He probably already thought I was totally crazy after my Ice Princess Diatribe that morning. I didn't need him to hear me talking to myself. He'd have me committed.

I took a deep breath and continued my pep talk. "This is what normal girls do. They sleep with men. They enjoy it. Well, sometimes they enjoy it, if it's good and the guy knows what he's doing."

I was getting off track so I blinked at myself in the mirror, shook my head and got back to the matter at hand. "Anyway, it's natural, it's right. And this is Hector and you've wanted this since the minute you saw him and I'm pretty certain sure he knows what he's doing. At least I hope so."

I stared at my image until I semi-believed myself. Then I pulled in my breath, straightened my spine, lifted my chin, turned out the light and went back to the bedroom.

Hector was stretched out on the bed on top of the covers, back up on all the pillows, legs out, ankles crossed. He was wearing his dark-gray thermal and plaid, cutoff pajama bottoms. The TV was on and a game was playing.

My heart skipped a beat at the sight of him relaxed on the bed. I decided not to think about it (again!) and took in the room.

The clothes hamper was now devoid of clothes. The bed was made and it looked like there were fresh sheets on it. Hector's boots and shoes had disappeared. The closet door was closed.

He'd cleaned the room!

"You cleaned the room," I blurted before I could stop myself.

Hector's eyes moved from the TV to me. "No," he replied. "This morning, when you and I left, we left my mother in the house."

My eyes went wide. "Blanca cleaned your room?"

Hector's gaze went back to the TV. "She meddles," was all he said.

"But…" I started, stopped, then finished, "you're a grown man."

He looked back to me and his mouth was doing that fighting-a-grin thing. "You wanna tell *Mamá* what to do? Tell her to mind her own business?" he asked.

I thought about telling Blanca what to do.

Then I thought about telling Blanca to mind her own business.

Then I shook my head fervently.

He let the grin loose then said softly, "Come here, Sadie."

With nothing for it, regardless of my knotted belly, skipping heart and shaking legs, I went to the end of the bed and crawled up it toward him.

When I got to within reaching distance, his hands were on me and he rolled me so my shoulder and head were resting on his chest again. He put his arm around my midriff this time and...

And...

And *nothing*.

I laid there. Hector laid there.

Still, nothing.

What was going on?

"Hector?" I called.

"Yeah?"

What did I say now?

Oh, blooming heck.

"I thought we were going to, um..." I couldn't finish.

"We *were* going to. Until I asked you at Tom's if you were ready to go, your body got rock-solid and I knew you weren't ready. So, we'll wait." His arm did a squeeze and his voice got softer. "I'm thinkin' you need more time to get used to me. I'm okay with that, *mamita*. Take all the time you need."

Someone, please tell me that he did, actually, just say that.

Again, before I could stop myself, I lifted up, dislodging his arm and twisted toward him. He had the remote in his right hand resting on his abs. I slid it out, found the off button, twisted to the TV and flicked it off. Then I turned toward him again, reached across him and put the remote on the nightstand.

I pulled breath in through my nose, put my hand on his chest and looked in his eyes.

They were staring at me with that warm intensity.

I bit my lips, let them go and whispered, "I think I'm pretty used to you."

I watched the warm intensity in his eyes turn fiery hot, and without hesitation he did an ab curl. Both of his arms went around me and he twisted, me landing on my back and him landing mostly on me.

His head was up and he was still staring at me.

"You sure?" he asked quietly.

No, I was *not* sure.

Still, I nodded.

That was when he kissed me.

The kiss was hot, hard, wet and urgent.

His hands were not. They were on me, over my camisole, non-invasive, light and sweet.

The two put together were nice. My belly unknotted and happy tingles started to slide across my skin.

His mouth broke from mine and slid down to my chin, along my jaw and he touched his tongue to the skin just below my ear.

Then he whispered some stuff to me in Spanish. I didn't understand any of it except maybe one word, "*preciosa*" (which could only mean one thing, couldn't it?).

At his whispering in my ear, his hands still light on me, the tingles graduated to shivers.

I turned my head and tasted the underside of his jaw. I felt his stubble rough against my tongue. I liked that, too.

Apparently so did Hector. His mouth came back to mine for another urgent, wet kiss. His hand slid over my bottom and he pulled me to him. I felt he was already hard and I liked that I could make him that way. I liked it enough to tug at his shirt and pull it up. His mouth broke from mine. He arched his back and lifted his arms so I could yank the shirt off and toss it away.

He came back to me immediately, his body heat hitting me, his mouth and tongue all over my neck, throat, chest, everywhere. The tingly shivers graduated to tremors, then (shortly thereafter) panting and finally (shortly after that) squirming.

This didn't feel normal and natural.

This felt extraordinary and supernatural.

His hand came up my midriff, its heat hitting my breast as his fingers curled around and held me. I pressed into his hold, and the minute I did, his fingers uncurled but his palm stayed where it was. Then it did slow circles against my nipple through the fabric.

Oh my.

I gasped into his mouth.

"That's nice," I breathed against his lips.

I felt him smile against mine.

Then his fingers snagged the edge of my camisole and they pulled it down over my nipple, and all of a sudden, his mouth was there. Then his tongue was there. Then he sucked deep.

My neck arched, my back arched, my hips arched, *everything* arched as supernatural happy feelings shot from my nipple to between my legs.

Hector's mouth disengaged. He pulled up the camisole, covering me again, but pulled down the other side to do the same exact thing.

Heaven.

The squirming became writhing and my hands moved over the skin of his shoulders. Then I engaged my fingernails (I couldn't help it, it felt so darn good). My nails scraped up his skin, feeling his muscles tense, up… up… all the way up, straight into his scalp.

At the feel of my fingernails, he groaned against my nipple (that felt good, too) and came back over me to kiss me, hotter, harder, deeper. His hands were not light and sweet now, but urgent and hungry, and all I could think was getting more of him.

My fingers left his hair and my hands pushed between our bodies. I pulled my own drawstring on my bottoms and started to wriggle them down. Hector felt it, rolled off me, and *whoosh*, my pajama bottoms and panties were *gone*.

Before I could react to the cold of losing him *and* most of my clothing, his hands spread my legs and he rolled between them, tagged me behind the knees, lifting them to bent, then wrapping my calves over his shoulders and then (no kidding!) his mouth was *right there*.

No, his mouth, lips *and* tongue were (no kidding!) *right there*.

And he knew how to use them.

Blooming *heck* but it felt good. My fingers slid into his hair to hold him to me as supernatural, extraordinary happy feelings scored a path through what felt like every fiber of my being. They gathered, tightened and I felt it coming.

But in the very, very back of my mind, I knew I didn't want it that way.

And the very, very back of my mind, for once, didn't want to be ignored.

"No," I whispered between moans.

I would have thought he wouldn't have heard me, but immediately Hector's mouth disappeared. His body came over mine, and I felt his heat on me as his weight hit me.

He shoved his face in my neck.

"All right, *mamita*, we'll stop," he muttered there, voice rough.

"No," I repeated, my hands reaching for the waistband of his pajamas, my head turning so my mouth was at his ear. "I want it to happen with you," I breathed.

His head came up.

I didn't look at him. I was busy trying to push down his pajamas (I failed—what could I say?—he was taller than me, my arms didn't reach).

"Sadie?"

Our eyes locked, and at the look in his I knew I *really* wanted it to happen with him. His gaze was hot, dark and hungry. My stomach pitched at the sight and my body squirmed (but my hands were still trying to find purchase on his pajamas).

Finally, since he seemed frozen where he was, I said, perhaps with the *eensiest* bit of desperation, "Hector please, I want you inside me."

"Sadie," he groaned, but still, he hesitated.

My mouth went to his and I whispered, "Please."

Within seconds (I didn't know how he did it and I didn't care), he filled me.

Hector "Oh my God" Chavez was deep inside me.

And I'd never felt anything better in my whole *fucking* life.

Then he started moving.

And that felt *even better*. In fact, it felt *amazing*.

"That feels *amazing*," I panted in his ear.

His head moved and I caught his grin right before he kissed me again.

Hector was a good kisser, but all the other kisses he'd given me were nothing compared to how it felt to be kissed by him while our bodies were connected and he was moving inside me.

None of them were even close.

Eventually, I found I couldn't kiss him anymore. I was breathing too hard, my hips moving against his, my hands on his skin, my fingernails digging in.

He lifted my legs at the knees and drove in deeper.

It was exquisite.

I shoved my face in his neck as I felt the beautiful anticipatory tightness right before my mouth went to his ear.

"Hector…" I started to say something. I didn't know what, but I didn't get to finish because, right then it washed over me, fierce, fiery and *huge*.

Bliss.

When I was done, I opened my eyes slowly, coming down, feeling him still moving inside me, driving deep, grinding hard, and I saw he was watching me, his eyes as hot as his skin.

"So… fucking… beautiful," he whispered.

Then it was my turn to watch.

⊰⊱

After he was finished, I took his whole weight and found I liked him heavy on me, his heat beating into me, his weight pressing me into the bed, his body still connected with mine.

He started to pull away.

My arms tightened around him and my thighs pressed into his hips.

He stilled.

"I'm too heavy," he said into my neck.

"I like it," I whispered. He didn't say anything so I explained, "Your body's warm. I always feel cold. You make me feel warm, and I never felt warm in my life."

I decided not to share the "snugly, lovely, comfy, safe" part with him.

A second passed then he muttered, "Jesus."

Well, maybe he read in the "snugly, lovely, comfy, safe" part.

Blooming heck.

More seconds ticked by, then his head came up. His fingers slid into the side of my hair and his eyes scanned my face.

"You okay?" he asked.

I nodded.

I didn't share that I *did* feel okay. In fact, it might be the first time I felt "okay" in my life. In that bed, in that room, in that house with Hector, I felt I was where I was supposed to be.

Where I belonged.

The drowning sensation hit me, the warm water lapping at my body, threatening to cover me, and I had the strange desire to pull in my breath… and sink.

Before this could weird me out (and I did anything stupid), he rolled us. We disconnected and Hector ended up on his back, me on top, our legs tangled. His body bucked and he yanked the bedclothes from under us and whipped them on top.

I lifted my head and one of his hands came to my hair. He pulled out the ponytail holder and my hair fell down around us. He tossed the ponytail holder on the nightstand and his fingers went inside my camisole then stilled at my sides.

"I wanna take this off," he murmured.

As an answer, before I chickened out, I did the same thing he did earlier, arching my back and lifting my arms. He tugged off the camisole and threw it to the floor at the side of the bed.

I settled, skin-against-skin, chest-to-chest, and his heat was overwhelming, penetrating my body, warming me straight to the core.

He pulled the covers high over my back then his hands slid down to my bottom and cupped me there.

I tucked my face into his neck. His warmth and my sensation of okayness settled in my belly, then in my chest, right by my heart.

Softly, I whispered, "Thank you."

His hands moved from my bottom so his arms could wrap tight around my waist.

This was nice, except his body was moving as if he was laughing.

My body got stiff.

"What's funny?" I asked his neck.

"*Mamita*, you just gave me the best gift anyone's ever given me and *you're* thankin' *me?*" he replied.

Oh… my… *God!*

He didn't just say that.

*Did* he just say that?

"Are you for real?" I breathed. It came right out of my mouth and I knew I sounded like an idiot, but I really did want to know.

His arms got tighter and his body started shaking harder.

I lifted my head and looked at him. He was smiling, brilliant white and glamorous.

"What's funny now?" I demanded, my eyes narrowed.

His hilarity became vocal and he burst out laughing. I didn't find anything was funny (at all) so I slapped his shoulder. He rolled us to our sides and shoved his (still laughing) face in my neck.

"Stop laughing," I ordered.

He kept laughing.

"Seriously, Hector," I warned him. "I'm getting annoyed."

His face came out of my neck, and when I caught sight of it, he was still smiling.

"Well then, *mi cielo*, we'll have to do somethin' about that," he announced, rolling us again, him on top.

Then his hands started moving on me.

"What are you…?" I tried to pull away from him but one of his arms locked tight and held me close. I looked at his grinning face, but read his intent loud and clear.

He couldn't be serious. Could he?

"We can't have sex again," I told him in the Voice of Authority. "We just finished five minutes ago."

His mouth went to my shoulder then trailed up. He added his tongue when it got to my neck and I shivered.

At my ear, he muttered, "Is that a rule?"

"No, it's not a rule. It's physically impossible," I informed him, sounding vaguely Ice Princess, but Know-It-All Ice Princess this time.

His lips came to mine and he looked into my eyes.

His were warm and intense. *Really* warm and intense.

Oh my.

"We'll work up to it," he murmured right before he kissed me.

Then we did.

≈

I felt the slap of cold that didn't go away even when the covers were tucked tight around me.

When the tucking stopped, I opened my eyes and slightly lifted my head. It was still dark and I could hear Hector moving in the room.

"What's going on?" I whispered, my voice scratchy with sleep.

I felt the bed move when Hector's weight hit it. He sat, pulled my hair away from my neck and leaned in.

"Doorbell. I'll take care of it. Go back to sleep," he answered, kissed my neck right where it met my shoulder, then the bed moved again as he got up. I watched his shadow walk across the room while tugging on the thermal and he disappeared into the darkness.

Kristen Ashley

I rearranged the pillows (Hector was a serious pillow hog); two beneath my head, one I held tight to my belly. I settled in thinking that Gloria and her posse were back for another try at some hot tub action.

Then I thought that it might be fun to sit in Hector's hot tub with Gloria and her posse.

Then I thought it might be *more* fun to sit in Hector's hot tub with Hector.

Then I fell back to sleep.

The covers slid off my shoulder and I could feel the heat and soft touch of a hand taking them away.

"Sadie?" Hector called.

My eyes opened. "What?" I muttered.

"Wake up, *mamita*. The Zanos are here."

I blinked in the darkness. Then I got up on an elbow, holding the covers over my chest.

I wasn't thinking clearly. I was still half-asleep. I could have sworn he just told me the Zanos were there in the middle of the blooming, blooming *night*.

"What?" I asked.

"Get dressed. The Zanos are here," he repeated. "We gotta talk."

He *did* say the Zanos were there.

I sat up fully. I held the covers against me with one hand and pulled my hair out of my face with the other. Hector had moved from sitting on the bed. He was bent over, gathering my clothes from the floor.

"What are the Zanos doing here?" I asked.

Hector handed me my clothes. "Just get dressed, *preciosa*. We'll talk downstairs."

The serious tone of his voice meant I should probably not take this as happy news.

Though what middle of the night visits were *ever* happy news? Except, of course Gloria and her girls' bid for the hot tub. That wasn't exactly happy (for Hector), but I found it humorous.

I decided to do as asked. First, he'd just called me "*preciosa*", something I liked (a lot). Even though I figured I knew what that meant, I still added a call to Jet on my Mental To-Do List for the morning to see where that ranked in Span-

216

ish endearments. Second, I wanted to find out what trauma was about to befall me now so I could deal with it and maybe get some sleep before the next one.

Hector moved across the room as I put on my camisole then fought the sheets and comforter as I put on my panties while in bed. Semi-decent, I got out of bed and pulled on my bottoms.

All of this effort was for nothing. Hector was rooting around in his closet and I'd rounded the bed by the time he found what he wanted.

He joined me at the foot of the bed and offered me a shadowy piece of clothing.

"Put that on," he ordered.

I took it, saw it was a flannel shirt and shrugged it on. It was soft and it was warm, and I hoped it wasn't Hector's favorite because I instantly decided it was going to find its way into my overnight bag.

We walked down the stairs. The lights were on and Ren was standing in the living room with his uncle, Vito Zano, and his cousin Dom.

What in *the heck* was going on?

I hesitated, not knowing what to do. Even my father's incessant training in social niceties hadn't prepared me for a middle of the night visit from the Zano Family. In fact, I was certain sure that kind of visit could not be found in *any* etiquette book.

Then, as I had loads of practice at dealing with whatever weird situation came my way, I made a decision and walked to Vito.

"Mr. Zano," I greeted, putting out my hand.

He took my hand and used it to pull me into his arms for a warm hug.

"None of that 'Mr. Zano' business now that Seth's out of the way, little one. I'm your Uncle Vito now," he told the top of my head.

Well, that was *just great*. Now I had an "Uncle Vito" to add to my growing list of friends I never knew I had.

Did *no one* remember my Ice Princess? Was *everyone* determined to make it harder for me to cut ties and disappear?

Darn it all to heck!

He let me go. I pushed aside my mental tantrum and I looked to Ren and Dom.

Ren looked good (as usual), wearing jeans and dark brown turtleneck.

Dom Vincetti, his cousin, was wearing a long-sleeved, thermal henley and jeans, looking rough in a way that was a lot like Hector (but Hector did it better, in my opinion).

Dom had always been the wild one. He was good-looking too, and usually an outrageous flirt, sometimes not in a good way, in a way my father said was crass. Now, he wasn't looking at me like he usually did (as if he was mentally undressing me), but in a different way, intense, and bizarrely at the same time, soft.

Just like Ren was looking at me.

This time, I let Blanca's lesson take hold, and instead of moving toward either of them (which might involve some form of touching which might make Hector mad; something I wished to avoid at all costs), I moved to Hector.

Hector's arm slid along my shoulders as I said to Ren and Dom, "Hi, guys."

Dom blinked. Ren's eyes flicked to Hector then back to me and he grinned.

Hector tucked me in his side.

No one spoke.

I waited.

Still, no one spoke.

Finally, when I could take it no more, I asked, "What's up?"

Hector answered, "The Zanos got Ricky."

My body went solid. Then relief dripped through me and I sagged into Hector.

*Thank you, God.*

"Thank God," I whispered.

"No, Sadie," Hector said softly, and I looked up at him and saw his face was carefully blank, but his eyes were glittery hard. He kept talking. "You don't get it, *mamita*. They've got him, but now you need to decide what they're gonna do with him."

My relaxed body went solid again.

"What?" I asked Hector.

Uncle Vito spoke. "You got two choices, little one," he told me, and my eyes turned to him. "The first, we take Balducci to the police." He stopped talking. I nodded and he went on, "The second, Balducci disappears."

My body jerked.

218

"Disappears?" I repeated, my voice breathy and disbelieving.

"Disappears," Dom affirmed, and my gaze moved to him. "Gone. No one ever sees him again. Not you, not his brothers, no one."

I just stared at Dom, not comprehending what he was saying; or more accurately, trying not to comprehend what he was saying.

Dom continued talking, "He fights the charges, you have to testify and you have to go through it again. Or you can choose for him to disappear and we take care of it. No trial, no testifying. It's over, he's certain to pay, and you move on."

Were they telling me they were going to *whack* Ricky Balducci for me?

Blooming *heck!*

"I can't ask you to——" I started.

"We wouldn't do it," Uncle Vito interrupted quickly, eyes on Hector. Then they came back to me. "You ain't the only one who hates Ricky. We put the word out he's available, they'll come out of the woodwork. We chose the one who'll do the job right, we hand him over and walk away. We don't know what happens from there. You don't. Chavez doesn't. Neither does his brother or Nightingale. No one's the wiser and it'll be done."

I realized my body was shaking.

"Sadie," Hector called, and I looked up at him. For some reason, he changed the subject and informed me, "That blood and the hairs they found on your furniture, some of it was Ricky's."

I didn't know why he was telling me that, but I nodded anyway.

He kept talking. "Harvey went before the judge yesterday, bail was set. Donny and Marty left him in jail. They didn't post bond."

I just kept staring at Hector, still not understanding why he was telling me all this.

Hector's fingers squeezed my shoulder and he curled me closer to him.

"*Mamita*, I'm givin' you the information you need to make a decision. What I'm sayin' is, the remaining free Balduccis aren't feelin' any brotherly love. They aren't takin' care of Harvey, and if Ricky gets locked up, it's likely they won't bond him out either. That means, neither of those two'll hit the streets anytime soon. That also means the other two are happy to jockey for position with Ricky and Harvey out of their way. And you got enough to get a guilty verdict if Ricky's stupid enough to fight the rape charge."

Finally I got it, and I also had a good idea of which decision Hector wanted me to make.

So I said, "Okay."

He curled me closer, his other hand went to my hip and his face dipped low.

"No, Sadie," he said softly, reading my thoughts. "It's your choice to make. I'm just givin' you the full picture. It isn't me who'll have to sit on the witness stand and tell a room full of people what happened that night. It also isn't me who'll have to listen to whatever fucked up version of events Ricky'll produce as his defense. You got the opportunity to avoid that. I'm not gonna take that away, and no one in this room, or out of it, will judge. The Zanos are givin' you a chance to decide what form your retribution will take. Only you can make it, but you gotta make it now."

I didn't like this. At all.

On the one hand, I didn't want to see Ricky again, and even if all the evidence was stacked against him, he was crazy enough to fight it. That would stink.

It would also likely mean I couldn't move to Crete or I'd have to come back.

On the other hand, everyone in that room knew what Vito meant by "disappear". Which would mean, if I picked choice number two, I was worse than Ricky Balducci. It would mean I truly was my father's daughter. I wasn't New Sadie. I'd never be a New Sadie of any kind. I would be Seth Townsend's daughter and that was who I'd stay, forever and ever.

I uncurled from Hector and my eyes turned to Vito.

"Please take him to the police," I said.

Hector's arm got tight around my shoulders.

Dom muttered a frustrated, "Fuck."

Ren expelled a heavy breath.

Vito nodded.

"I knew she'd pick that," Dom muttered. "We should have—"

Vito interrupted in a low, warning tone, saying, "Dominic," but I was surprised Dom knew my choice even before I did.

Dom fell silent and Vito turned to Ren. "Make the call, tell the boys."

Ren nodded to his uncle and walked to me. Regardless of Hector standing there, he leaned in and kissed my cheek. He moved away, pulled his cell out of his pocket and left the house.

Dom, Vito and I looked at each other.

No one spoke.

I decided it was time to move on to a happier subject that didn't involve the Balduccis, my rape or anyone getting whacked. My gaze focused on Dom.

"I hear Sissy's pregnant," I told him.

Sissy was his wife. They'd had some hard times and were separated for a while, but word was, they'd got back together and were starting a family.

Dom stared at me, still angry at my decision, then his face went soft and he muttered, "Yeah."

"Congratulations," I told him on a smile. I'd met Sissy a few times. Though I didn't know her well, she always struck me as being really nice.

"Life!" Vito exploded, making me jump. "Up and down, good and bad, birth and death, celebration and devastation. If you got any balls at all, you roll with the punches and get the fuck on with it, pardon my French."

My eyes moved to Vito. He was watching me and I could swear (no kidding!) I saw admiration.

That was when I realized he thought I had "balls".

I felt another warm, happy glow starting when Vito clapped and put his hands up in front of him.

"We're through. I gotta get home. Angela worries."

He made a move and came to me. Hector let me go and Vito gave me another hug.

When Vito moved away, he looked at me. "She told me to tell you she wants you to come to dinner. She'll call. Bring Chavez and a big appetite. My wife, she cooks. It's what she does," he finished.

Oh my.

Dinner with Vito and Angela Zano.

Before I could wrap my mind around that thought, Vito looked over his shoulder and jerked his chin at Dom. He clapped Hector on the arm and took off.

Dom followed. He didn't clap Hector on the arm but gave him a chin lift, shot me a weird look (still clearly upset at not getting to help Ricky Balducci disappear), but he put up a hand to squeeze my shoulder. Then he took off, too.

Hector locked the door behind them and turned to me. "You okay?" he asked.

Without hesitation, I answered, "I'd give my trust fund to be living a life where every other second you aren't asking me if I'm okay."

He bit his bottom lip, and again I didn't know what that meant; if he was trying to bite back a smile or hide his frustration. He walked to me, *close* to me, and his hand hit my neck, fingers sliding up into my hair, thumb at my hairline.

"That day will come," he promised quietly.

My toes curled and my knees went weak at the look in his eyes. So weak, I had to grab on to his waist to stay standing.

His head bent and his lips touched mine.

Then his head moved a hairbreadth away and he said, "Let's go to bed."

# Chapter 15

# Severed Edges

---

*Sadie*

I woke again to a cold, empty bed.

I laid there (my head on one measly pillow) and allowed myself a lovely, snugly, warm moment at waking up in Hector's bed before I threw back the covers and replayed my actions of the morning before. This time, I had to put my pajamas back on (so I did, with the addition of Hector's flannel shirt). And, with my stuff there, I added brushing my teeth and washing my face.

By the time I hit the stairs, I heard men's voices coming from the kitchen.

I rounded the stairs and saw Hector through the kitchen door.

He wasn't in nightclothes. He had on jeans and a tight, black t-shirt, but no belt. His feet were bare and his hair was wet which meant he'd been up long enough to shower.

Now, how did I sleep through *that?*

Seriously, this was getting weird. I never slept through anything.

Maybe it was all the sex.

I saw he had a coffee cup in his fist and his eyes were on someone who was talking. But they cut to me when they caught me rounding the stairs.

Even from the distance of across the living room and kitchen, I saw his eyes go lazy and his mouth form a small grin.

At his look, my knees went weak.

Last night, after the Zanos left, we didn't go to bed to sleep. We went to bed and he made love to me (yes, for the *third time!*).

The first time had been amazing.

The second time, "working up to it", meant slow and sweet and even more amazing.

The third time, mostly (but obviously not totally) sated, Hector had taken his time. It was clear he felt like exploring, and he did. What he didn't feel like was allowing *me* to explore, so he didn't. His undivided and prolonged attention produced an orgasm unlike any I'd ever experienced in my life.

Amazing didn't do it justice.

The word to do it justice hadn't been invented yet.

On this thought, I walked into the kitchen but I did it on shaking legs.

Luke Stark was there, as was Native American Hottie, or who I knew now was Vance.

I walked straight to Hector.

This might have been rude. Perhaps I should have gone to Luke and Vance and offered my hand. Hector seemed in a mellow mood, but even though these guys were pretty badass, the whole Hot Bunch/Rock Chick crew was a rather huggy lot. I didn't want Luke or Vance to hug me in front of Hector. They were his friends, but who knew what Mr. Mood Swing's response would be. And after what happened yesterday morning with Ren, I wasn't taking any chances.

"Sadie, you know Luke. This is Vance Crowe," Hector introduced as his arm slid along my shoulders and he tucked me into his side.

I nodded and said, "Hi, Vance." Then my eyes moved to Luke. "Hi, Luke."

One side of Luke's mouth went up in a sexy, half-grin. Vance's mouth formed a smile that was so confident it was breathtaking.

I stared at them and it struck me that they were seriously hot. Tall, great bodies, clothes that defined their well-toned muscles. Vance had black, shiny hair pulled back in a ponytail at his neck. Luke had short-clipped black hair and a mustache that was shaved precisely down the sides of his mouth.

I decided that Luke's mustache was absolutely aces. Normally, a mustache like that on a man (in my personal opinion) would look pretty stupid. On him, it was fantastic.

"*Mamita*," Hector muttered, and my body jerked as I realized, belatedly, I was staring at Luke Stark's mouth.

Oh no.

I figured certain sure I was in trouble.

Slowly, I looked up at Hector, expecting to be scorched by a Hector Glare.

Instead, his lips were twitching and he looked like he was having trouble not laughing.

Since I'd been awake for about five minutes and hadn't had time to decide who I was going to be that morning (Ice Princess, New Sadie, Attitude Sadie,

Take Charge Sadie, or some other Sadie, perhaps After-A-Night-of-Loads-of-Amazing-Sex-with-Hector-Sadie), my personalities decided for themselves.

Attitude Sadie clicked in and snapped, "What's funny now?"

I watched as he began to lose the fight with his hilarity.

"You," he answered.

"What's funny about me?" Attitude Sadie asked sharply.

"Everything, *mamita*," Hector informed me, his eyes still lazy, his smile blazing white, Attitude Sadie having no effect on him at all, whatsoever. "You're hilarious," he added.

My eyes narrowed. "I am *not* hilarious. Especially not at six o'clock in the morning before I've had my coffee," I retorted, then for some bizarre reason, I ranted on. "No. Wait. Never. I'm *never* hilarious. So, for the last time, stop laughing at me," I finished on a haughty demand.

"Lover's spat." I heard Luke mutter, and *he* sounded amused, too. My eyes moved to him upon the unwelcome reminder that we had an audience and embarrassment edged Attitude Sadie into the background as Luke continued, "Time to go."

Both Luke and Vance were still smiling. Luke's half-smile had changed to engage his whole mouth and I tried not to look because, at the glance I caught, I knew a good look would definitely get me into trouble.

I decided to attempt to switch to New Sadie because Attitude Sadie was making me the laughingstock of the Hot Bunch.

Apparently *everyone* thought I was hilarious (except me).

"It's not a lover's spat. I just need coffee," I informed them, trying to sound casual and like I often wandered around in pajamas in a kitchen full of handsome men after a night of sex and a mini-attitude-rant.

Still going for casual and confident, I pulled out of Hector's arm and went to the coffee. I yanked out the pot, turned and held it up to the boys, asking sweetly, "Warm up? Luke? Vance?"

This gesture, for some reason, produced more amused looks.

Now, really, was it me?

What was so darned funny about offering coffee?

Finally, putting his mug down, Vance said, "Thanks, Sadie. Got shit to do."

Luke followed suit.

I wondered what "shit" they had to do at six o'clock in the morning.

Did these guys ever sleep?

I thought about asking the Rock Chicks, obviously they would know. Then I decided I didn't want to know because their answers might scare me.

They said their good-byes, so did I, and Hector followed them to the front door.

I made myself coffee and tried to get my thoughts in order so I didn't make an even bigger fool of myself.

I had no practice with this kind of situation, waking up after a night of sex and a nocturnal visit from the Zano Family only to find early morning casual company in the form of friends.

Who, I wondered, did? Except Hector, of course. If the last couple of days were anything to go by, this seemed normal for him.

My thoughts were nowhere near ordered (but my coffee was ready) when Hector came back into the kitchen.

I'd turned and leaned against the counter. The mug was mostly to my mouth, when, in another Smooth Hector Move, he got close, pulled the mug out of my hand and placed it on the counter beside me.

"Hey!" I said, looking at my coffee mug. "I was drinking that!"

My head moved around, and before I knew what was happening, Hector kissed me.

It wasn't a soft, sweet, morning kiss.

It was a fiery, hungry, urgent kiss, and apparently unable to fight it (though, I had to admit, I didn't try), I melted on the spot.

It went from kissing to kissing and groping. Then Hector pulled his flannel shirt off my shoulders and it fell to the floor. His hands went into my camisole at the sides then up my back, trailing heat everywhere they went.

I followed suit, putting my hands up his t-shirt at the back, my fingers roving his hot skin.

All of a sudden, his mouth disengaged. He stepped back and grabbed my hand, turning and dragging me behind him.

I should have said something, but I had to concentrate on running to keep up with his long strides. At the stairs, he took them two at a time, pulling me behind him.

Not surprisingly, I stumbled. He turned and caught me, lifting me up. An arm at my waist, one at my knees, he spun and my legs went flying as he hitched me more safely in my arms.

He walked directly to his bedroom and tossed me on his bed.

Yes, *tossed me on his bed!*

At this, I felt my nipples go hard and tingles flew through my body on a beeline between my legs where I felt an immediate, delicious wetness invade.

I watched, my breath coming fast, as he tore off his shirt.

I decided to follow suit and tugged off my camisole as he watched while undoing the top buttons of his jeans.

Once I tossed my camisole to the side, he leaned over, put one hand to the bed and the other arm slanted across my waist. He yanked me up and my back arched. His mouth came down on my nipple, and without leading into it, he sucked deep.

"Oh God," I breathed, pretty certain sure I was going to climax on the spot.

Instead, my hands went to the drawstring of my pajama bottoms and I tugged. Hector's mouth left me. He yanked down my bottoms, taking my panties with them and then shoved me back to the bed.

My behind hit the bed. I kicked off my clothes but leaned forward. My fingers coming up, I undid the rest of the buttons on his jeans and pulled them all the way down.

And I saw him, right there, in front of me.

I liked what I saw.

And I wanted it.

And it was fucking well *my* turn to explore.

So I scooted to the edge of the bed, head tilted back to look up at him. His eyes blazing into mine, I wrapped my hand around him and took him in my mouth.

"*Dios mio,*" he groaned, then said more stuff in Spanish, his fingers diving into my hair, pulling it away from my face and holding it behind my head in his fists.

He let me explore, let me taste him for what felt like a nanosecond (but was probably longer; it was just that I liked what I was doing and I knew Hector did, too, which made me like it all the more) then his hands went under my armpits, lifting me clean up into the air. My legs wrapped around his waist, my arms around his neck. He went forward, I went back, both of us landing on the bed.

Before I had a chance to get used to our new position, he was inside me, and not like last night. This was different. Harder, rougher, not in either of our control and therefore shocking in its intense beauty.

He pulled my legs up at the knees until they were tucked against his sides and he kept slamming into me, one of my arms wrapped around his back, the other hand in his hair.

We weren't kissing and I heard our noises drifting around us, his low, deep grunts mingled with my softer whimpers. His face was in my neck and he was groaning there, breathing hard. My face was in his neck and I was moaning there, breathing hard and alternately tasting him and even (no kidding!) biting the flesh at his shoulder.

Then, all of a sudden, he stopped moving, his body buried in mine.

"Jesus, fuck, Sadie," he muttered in my neck. "Fuck," he repeated, his arms going tight. "Give me a second."

I was blinking, rapidly, surprised that he stopped and wanting the movement, the pounding, even our noises back.

"For what?" I asked.

His mouth came to my ear and he whispered, "I don't want to hurt you."

I closed my eyes and my arms went tight.

"You aren't hurting me," I promised. I squeezed him with my thighs (and other parts of me besides) and I heard him make a noise low in his throat. The noise spurred me to coax, "Keep going."

"Hang on," Hector murmured, still fighting for control even as he ground deeper (which felt good; good enough for me to remember that I wanted more).

It was my turn to make a low noise in my throat then I repeated, "Keep going."

"Sadie—" he started, but my arm moved. My hand went to his fantastic behind, the fingers of my other hand fisted in his hair. My movements made his head come up and I pressed my lips to his.

"Hector, please," I whispered, my voice a mixture of begging and demanding, "Please… fuck me."

I watched his eyes grow dark. Then his head slanted, his mouth took mine in another wet, hungry kiss and he did as I asked, wild and rough, until, minutes later, almost at the same time, we both exploded.

It was hard and hot and so overpowering, I moaned deep into his mouth as my body convulsed beneath his.

It took what seemed like forever to come down, tremors coursing through me as I concentrated on Hector, his body still pressing into mine, his breathing on my neck, going slowly from heavy to soft.

His weight bore down on me and I realized, to my surprise, that after the intensity of what we just shared, I felt even more snugly, warm, safe and comfy than I ever had before when I was with him (which was to say, ever in my life).

And, obviously, that was saying something.

That was, I felt more snugly, warm, safe and comfy until he spoke, his voice deep, husky and utterly satisfied.

"This is who I wanted to find. The girl from that night. I knew she was fuckin' in there. I just didn't know I'd have her this soon."

It felt like he'd shoved an icicle in my heart.

No.

Please.

No.

That was not me.

There were loads of Sadies but that wasn't one of them.

Was it?

A brazen hussy, throwing myself at him and begging him to fuck me?

The Society Slut who went slumming?

Did he think that was me?

Was that what he wanted?

I didn't want him to want that.

Then it hit me.

The rose on his back which he wanted to put on his arm.

He had the broken heart from *Belinda* to remind him not to let the desires of his body cloud his judgment.

He had the skull to celebrate taking down my father.

Neither of these things were good, loving, comfy, snugly, warm things.

They represented a hard earned lesson and the victory of a hard fought, dangerous battle.

Maybe the rose didn't mean what I thought it meant.

Or, more accurately, what I wanted to *believe* it to mean.

Maybe the rose represented another challenge.

Maybe I was right weeks ago when he was in my hospital room.

229

Maybe he was with me to finish the job. The job he started that night in my father's study and would have finished if I hadn't walked away from him.

The job of conquering *me*.

That night, I'd walked away from him, disdainful and bitchy, leaving him hard and wanting, and he'd been furious. Furious enough to call me a cock tease.

Maybe it was payback time.

Well, he just paid me back. He'd spent a night paying me back.

And that was all he was going to get.

He could have his rose now and he could remember, every time he looked at it, that he won.

I knew he felt my change when his head came up.

He called softly, "Sadie?"

I looked at his throat and even I heard the change in my voice, betraying (damn and blast!) my feelings.

"I need to shower," I told him, my voice soft but tight.

Hector's body went tense. "*Mamita*, look at me."

My eyes moved to his.

His were searching.

I had no idea what mine were.

Then he murmured, "She's gone."

Well, that told me what he saw in my eyes.

"I'm right here," I lied in order to cover. I'd think about this later, maybe when YoYo was lying beside me in bed so I'd have something else to keep my snugly, comfy, warm (if not safe; I didn't think a pug could keep me safe).

Then again, I'd kidded myself when I thought Hector wanted to keep me safe.

He was just like everyone else. After something, using me to get what he wanted.

I watched as he shook his head and looked like he was getting annoyed. "You're gone."

I tried to soften my features, to make him believe he still had me until I was well away from him and somewhere safe.

"No, I'm not," I replied.

At my words, he no longer looked like he was getting annoyed. He looked like he was *definitely* annoyed, and I guessed my efforts at softening my features didn't work.

230

"Don't lie to me, Sadie."

Well, now he *sounded* like he was definitely annoyed, too.

Then he clipped, "Why?"

Yes, definitely annoyed.

"Why what?"

"Where'd she go and why'd she go?"

"I don't know what you're talking about."

"You know exactly what the fuck I'm talking about."

I decided it was time to try a stare down.

This failed.

Then I decided to try something new and pushed at his shoulders. "Hector, get off. I have to get to work."

This failed, too.

"You have to fuckin' talk to me," he returned.

"About what?" I asked, fear and desperation making my tone short and clipped.

Hector stared at me then muttered, "Goddamn it," as he gave up and rolled to the side.

I lost his weight, his warmth and the connection of our bodies.

I felt this loss somewhere so deep, so important, it penetrated like a blade, changing something. Something crucial to my world. Severing it in a way I knew would never heal.

"At least tell me you're on the pill," Hector finished, and the wound intensified, the severed edges of it cauterizing because I knew then.

I knew.

He wanted no connection to me. Once this was done, whatever challenge he'd set for himself was won, he wanted no connection. Once he had his fill, he'd be gone, and like my mom, like my father, like any friend I'd ever had and both my ex-boyfriends, I'd lose him too.

"I'm on the pill." I whispered then rolled, wondering if I could make it to my clothes without dying of mortification.

I barely got to my side, definitely not up on an arm, before he tagged me at the waist and yanked my back into his heat.

His mouth at my neck, he warned, his voice low and angry, "Whatever Sadie I'm talkin' to, all of 'em have to know, this isn't done."

My heart sunk.

I was afraid of that.

⌖

"Wait here a minute," Hector said, his still-annoyed gaze slicing from me to Shirleen. Then he walked to the door that led to the inner rooms of Nightingale Investigations.

I looked at Shirleen, who was sitting behind the reception desk. Her gaze was resting on the door closing behind Hector. Then she looked at me and her brows went up.

⌖

I'd spent the day keeping busy.

After the fantastic "fuck me" sex, and the heartbreaking incident afterward, getting ready for work at Hector's house was an *eensy* bit uncomfortable.

This was because Hector was seriously angry (I didn't know what *he* had to be angry about; I wasn't using *him* as a difficultly procured notch on *my* bedpost after which I'd tattoo something on *my* arm—I didn't know what I'd tattoo to remind me of Hector but I was thinking a black panther because that's the only thing that would do him justice).

I knew he had his anger in check because he wasn't throwing cell phones into margarita pitchers (or the like). However, I also knew he *barely* had it in check, so I decided to stay well out of his way.

This proved the wrong decision. The more I tried to avoid him, the less he seemed in control of his anger. I didn't understand this reaction, but for obvious reasons I didn't ask.

He dropped me off at the brownstone and I thought, considering his temper still hadn't cooled, that would be that. However, that wasn't that because he kissed me at the door.

Yes!

*Kissed me!*

This was not like any other kiss he'd given me. His fingers drove into my hair, cupping the back of my head, tilting it up and using it to pull me forward. I fell into him, my hand at his chest, and his mouth came down on mine hard.

It was an angry kiss, and because of that, so hot and intense, it stole my breath and my ability to stand on my own two feet.

When my hand was clutching his shirt at his chest, my other arm was wrapped around his waist and my torso was plastered to his, his head came up and he scorched me with a Hector Glare.

"Ten to four, I'll pick you up at the gallery. Don't make any fuckin' plans tonight," he ordered, his voice deep, low and vibrating with unhappy emotion.

Before I could remind him about YoYo's arrival and my plan to be there when we got the dog, he was gone, leaving me swaying unsteadily in his wake.

"Holy Hot Blooded Latinos, sweets. What on *earth* was *that* all about?" Ralphie asked, wide eyes on the door.

My head was beginning to pound. Three nights of interrupted sleep and weeks of intense emotion were getting to me. After all that fantastic sex (four times!), I should have been relaxed and lose enough to do gymnastics. Instead, I was wound up tight.

"I don't want to talk about it," I told Ralphie.

And I really, *really* didn't.

"But——" Ralphie started.

I shot him a pleading look. "Please, please, Ralphie. I need quiet. I need peace. And, above all, I need time to get my head together."

Ralphie snapped his mouth shut, looking at me closely. I knew he was dying to know what was going on. Instead, he nodded, and to my shock, he left me alone all day to get my head together.

And get it together I did.

I formed several plans of action.

Depending on what Hector's next move was, mine would be a move to do one thing.

Protect myself until I could disappear.

And off to Crete I'd go. I'd tell Bex where to find me. She could tell Detective Marker how to get hold of me if the police needed me. But, other than that, I was gone.

As for finding my mom, well, Lee Nightingale wasn't the only private investigator in the world. There were others. I'd hire one of them, find Mom and bring her to me and she and I would eat souvlaki and pita bread (or whatever) and I'd work my way through all the Greek men on Crete who took my fancy, but I wouldn't give a single one of them my heart.

No fucking way.

My heart was for me and me alone. And, obviously, my mom (when I found her). And Ralphie and Buddy, who I'd keep contact with of course. And, maybe, Daisy and the Rock Chicks, if I could manage that without the involvement of Hector.

As for Hector, I knew the Ice Princess didn't work, so I settled on another strategy. I knew it would cost me but I was willing to pay the price.

There was going to be a *New* New Sadie. I was calling her Pretend Sadie and she was going to protect me.

It would make it easier in the long run, even though it would be far more difficult for the short one.

But I could do it. I lived twenty-nine years with my father pretending to be someone I was not. I could live a few weeks guarding my heart from Hector "Oh my God" Chavez.

And guard it I would.

⚑

At ten to four, Hector picked me up from the gallery.

I was kind of hoping that he'd cool off by the time he came, but one look at him told me this was absolutely not the case.

So be it.

I could work with that.

There was only one hitch on the way to the Nightingale Investigations offices. They were just around the corner from Art, maybe two blocks away. Still, Hector drove it, and as we approached the entrance to the garage, I audibly sucked in breath.

I'd forgotten about the garage.

My last time in the garage had *not* been a happy memory.

I wasn't ready to go back there again.

Hector heard me, muttered, "Fuck," under his breath, pulled out of his approach and rounded the block, parking on the street.

With effort, I forced my body to relax.

Before getting out, his hand wrapped around my neck and he turned me to face him. He was leaning toward me but not as close as he normally got. I noticed this and it made something ugly twist inside me. Something which I firmly set aside.

"I didn't think. The garage——" he said to me, his eyes were masked but his voice was soft.

"That's okay," I replied quickly.

He didn't let me go and his eyes scanned my face.

"Who's with me now?" he asked.

"Me," I answered immediately.

His eyes narrowed. "Which 'me'?"

"Me, me," I replied, as if there had always been only one (hardly!).

This answer didn't make him happy and that was when he got as close as he normally did.

I held my breath and braced (it was a good thing, too).

"If I didn't know it was worth it. If I didn't know from what happened last night *and*, whatever the fuck you thought it was, *mamita*, what happened this morning. And if I didn't like your hands in my hair holding my mouth to you, the smell of your fuckin' perfume when I'm buried inside you, and the way you lose that tight-as-shit control over every fuckin' move you make when you get excited and you use your nails and teeth on me, I'd give up. Because, *mamita*, you are one *serious* pain in the ass."

I hadn't planned for a speech like that (I ask you, who would?). Nor had I planned for how it made my heart race (damn and blast!), my stomach pitch (more damning and blasting!) or the area between my legs to tingle (damn and blast it all to hell!). Or, contradictory to all this, how it made me want to give him a good sock in the gut. So I thought my best bet was to pull in my lips and try to look ashamed of my pain in the ass behavior.

This didn't work. He shook his head in an annoyed way and let me go. We got out of the Bronco and walked up to the office.

However angry he was, he held my hand the whole way.

Now, how bizarre was *that?*

---

I took in Shirleen's raised brows but pretended I didn't see them.

Shirleen saw my pretending and thought it was bullshit.

"All right, tell Shirleen, what in *the fuck* is goin' on?" She lifted her hand and her thumb jerked to the door Hector just walked through. "That boy has been in a *foul* mood all day. Now, foul moods aren't unusual with Hector. He's moody but he's edgy. A boy's edgy, you gotta give him room for the moods. It comes with the territory. If he's good at his job, would put down his life for the boys and he ain't difficult to look at, like Hector, you do things like that. But this is different. Everyone's been givin' him a wide berth all day. Even Luke, Vance, Lee and Mace, and those boys ain't scared of nothin'."

I had to admit, I kind of felt better that badasses Luke, Vance, Lee and Mace also thought Hector's "foul" mood was worthy of a wide berth and I wasn't a *total* wuss.

I looked at Shirleen and realized she actually expected an answer.

"Um..." I hedged.

"Ain't no 'ums' with Shirleen. He's pissed way *the fuck* off and you look like, like... I don't know what you look like, but somethin' ain't right."

"Well..." I started, then I stopped.

She waited.

I stayed silent (really, what could I say?).

"That's it," she announced. I watched as she stabbed a button on her phone with a frosted-apricot fingernail and heard a dial tone coming from the speaker. Then she hit another one; the speed dial engaged and a rapid succession of tones could be heard. A ring, then two, then a voice came on the line.

"How's it hangin', sugar?" Daisy answered the phone.

"Shit's gone down with Hector and Sadie. Sadie's standin' here, cat's got her tongue and Hector's gone electric," Shirleen declared, and I was also quite pleased I wasn't the only one to feel Hector's angry electric current. It made me feel less of a freak.

"Oh shit," Daisy's voice said.

Boy, she could say that again.

"Powwow. Fortnum's. Tomorrow at noon. We're gonna get this shit *sorted*," Shirleen decreed, and I felt panic seize me as I hadn't planned for *this* either.

"But, I—" I started and Shirleen's hand whipped up, palm out to face me, and since she was scaring me a little bit, my mouth snapped shut.

"Gotcha. I'll get the phone tree activated," Daisy's voice said.

Phone tree?

The Rock Chicks had a phone tree?

Battle stations!

"Really, I—" I started again, but stopped when Shirleen's brows snapped together (so much for my puny battle stations) and Daisy's voice came over the phone.

"No back talk, comprende?" Daisy warned. "Be there or face Rock Chick consequences."

I had no idea what Rock Chick consequences were, but then again, I didn't want to know.

"Oh, all right," I gave in.

How bad could a powwow be?

I'd survived worse. Heck, I *was* surviving worse at that very moment!

The door opened and Hector came through.

"It's time, *mamita*," he announced.

See what I mean?

"Tomorrow, noon," Daisy's voice reminded me.

"All right," I responded, making my slow way toward Hector who was waiting for me, holding open the door.

"Noon," Shirleen repeated to my back.

That back went straight, my head whipped around, and for the sake of my pride, I snapped, "All right!"

This, for some bizarre reason, made Shirleen grin.

"Well, all right," she muttered through her grin.

Blooming *heck!*

Why was my life so *difficult?*

# Chapter 16
# Uglier and Uglier

*Sadie*

"Have a seat, Sadie," Tom said on a welcoming smile when I entered Lee Nightingale's office for the second time in my life.

They were all there: Tom, Eddie, Lee, Hank and Vance. They were all standing and they were all looking at me with carefully closed faces.

Oh boy.

Time for Pretend Sadie.

I stopped by one of the chairs in front of Lee's desk and I felt Hector close behind me. I took a deep breath, did a group scan, playing it safe, beginning the game and allowing myself a small, friendly smile.

Then I looked at Lee and announced, "I've changed my mind."

Lee's brows went up.

I continued, "See, I figure you won't let me pay you and that isn't fair. You and Hector and everyone are doing so much for me, I can't ask you to do more."

Lee smiled and I found myself momentarily taken out of my role and staring (he really had a nice smile).

Then he started talking. "Sadie, the Rock Chicks are a permanent red line item on my budget. They have been for months. We're used to takin' this kind of hit."

I had to admit, I hadn't prepared for *that* either, especially his assumption that I was a Rock Chick.

His assumption gave me one of those weird, happy glows. The kind I couldn't allow myself to feel or all would be lost.

Oh well, I had to power through.

"Even so, I think I'd prefer to hire someone else. This is making me uncomfortable," I replied what I thought was nicely but firmly. "So, if you have a recommendation for another PI, I'll give them a call."

Immediately I saw that my nice but firm didn't work.

Instead, Lee shook his head (still smiling) and Hector's hands came to my shoulders.

"Sadie, sit down," Hector said softly in my ear.

I twisted to look at him. "No, really, I—"

"Sit," he interrupted.

Sweet, Pretend, Guarding-Her-Heart Sadie slipped and I glared at him.

My glare deflected off his Cool, Collected, Macho Man Shields and pinged around the room, unnoticed by anyone.

"Sadie, honey," Tom said. I turned to him and saw he had his hand held out to me. "Come and sit."

Not wanting to be a bitch because Pretend Sadie was not a bitch, and anyway, he'd called me "honey" and that was so nice the weird, happy glow I was trying to ignore came back against my will, I walked to him. I put my hand in his and we both sat, facing each other.

"I need to tell you something," Tom informed me, keeping hold of my hand.

The weird, happy glow vanished.

Oh no.

I didn't like the look on his face and I didn't like that he felt he needed to keep holding my hand.

Furthermore, Pretend Sadie didn't like the vibe in the room *at all* and she wanted to run.

However, Ice Princess Sadie *never* ran. Ice Princess locked firm hands on Pretend Sadie's arms and held her in place.

With Ice Princess in control, I felt it safe to say to Tom, "Okay."

He squeezed my hand then he took a deep breath and launched in.

"Eighteen years ago, your mom came to me," Tom started.

I blinked and then stilled, knowing intuitively (from *years* of practice) that this innocuous statement was going to get worse.

Way worse.

I wasn't wrong.

Tom continued, "Lizzie knew what your father did and she didn't like it. She didn't want you growing up in that life. She also saw your future and she didn't like that either. She wanted to get you, and herself, out. She told me the only way to do that was to put your father in jail. She told me that she couldn't run, taking you with her, because he'd never let either of you go. She knew this because she tried on several occasions, but he always found you both and brought you back."

I pulled in my lips and felt myself starting to breathe heavier, my heart beginning to hammer in my chest, something hot and hard forming there.

My mom had tried to escape.

She'd tried to escape!

And she wanted to take me with her!

Oh my God!

I couldn't believe it!

Tom went on, cutting into my fevered thoughts, "She wanted to inform on your dad, to give me what I needed to take him down. I tried to talk her out of it. Your father wasn't as powerful then as he was when Hector got him. But he'd done well. He was top man for Luther Diggs and what she wanted to do was dangerous."

I couldn't believe this either.

My sweet, quiet mom an informant?

Impossible!

And I remembered Luther. He'd been around a lot back then. I also remembered never liking Luther, as in *never*. Luther was my first lesson in how to spot bad people, because in Luther's case, he was *very* bad people. He reeked of it. Luther had always scared me.

I was glad when Luther went away about a year after my mom disappeared. What I wasn't glad about was knowing, even at twelve, that my father had assumed Luther's elevated place in the crime world.

Tom kept talking, "She wouldn't be swayed. Even Kitty Sue tried to talk her out of it, but Lizzie was determined. She said if she didn't work with me, she'd go to someone else. I thought, if she had to do it, it was better if she worked with me. I thought that I could keep her safe—"

He stopped talking, his eyes closed tight and he looked away, but not before I caught the pain that slashed through his gaze.

My heart was in my throat, clogging it. That hot, hard thing in my chest started burning.

I knew where this was going and I didn't like it.

Not one bit.

But, for some reason, I still squeezed his hand and kept squeezing it until his eyes opened and came to me again.

"Go on," I encouraged softly.

He stared at me a second then took in another deep breath. "At first, she couldn't get me anything I could use. When she saw it wasn't working, she started taking risks."

I felt the tears hit the backs of my eyes at the thought of my mom doing the same thing I did with Hector. I knew how scary it was and I knew the consequences. And knowing now that she took the same risks, felt the same fear, all of it for me, made the burning in my chest intensify.

I found I was still squeezing Tom's hand. This time not to encourage him to go on but because I had to.

Tom reached out and took my other hand, holding both of our hands between us.

"She started to get some good stuff, found someone in Diggs's network that didn't like your father, didn't like Diggs. They started to work together, not just to take down your father, but also to take down Diggs. She never told me who it was. I asked but she wouldn't give. Then, one day, she was supposed to meet me. She said she had something for me, something she thought was big, important, but she never showed." He hesitated. I clenched my teeth, waiting for it, knowing it was coming, then he went on, "I never saw her again."

There it was.

"Please, no," I whispered before I could stop myself.

Tom gave me a hand squeeze.

"I looked for her. Malcolm and I did it together. We had to do it on our own time. Your father never filed a missing person report. He told everyone she left you. I knew she didn't. I knew she'd never leave you. Never Sadie. Never."

He shook my hands so I knew he meant what he said. I nodded, biting my lips, knowing he thought this might make me feel better, at the same time knowing it didn't make me feel better. Not even a little bit.

He went on, "Malcolm knew that, too, so we looked for her."

"What did you find?" I asked, but I wasn't sure I wanted to know.

"Leads, lots of leads. All of them dead ends. We searched for over a year, but, Sadie, we found nothing. The leads dried up and with nothing to go on, I'm sorry, honey, so, so sorry, but we had no choice but to stop."

I nodded.

I didn't blame him, he tried. He tried to protect my mom and he tried to find her when she disappeared. He was a good person, I knew that. I had no doubt he did the best he could.

But what he was saying meant that someone made my mom "disappear", just like Uncle Vito wanted to make Ricky disappear. And that meant my mom had been scared and alone. That meant my mom was never coming back. That meant that someone had taken her away from me.

And that someone might be my *fucking, fucking* father.

On that thought, something in my brain exploded. Pain sliced through my temples, I tore my hands out of Tom's and shot out of my chair.

"Sadie—" Tom stood with me, but I whirled.

"I've got to go," I muttered.

No friendly smiles now. No alternate Sadies to help me deal. It was just *me*, and I needed to get out of there, go somewhere. I didn't know where. I didn't care where. It could be anywhere, but I had to go there and scream at... the... top... of... my... *lungs.*

If I didn't let out the hard, hot knot of pain that was in my chest, I knew it was going to burst. And it was so ugly, so huge, if it burst, it would kill me.

In my blind escape, I ran smack into Hector's solid body and his arms closed around me.

I looked up at him.

"I've got to go," I told him, sounding desperate and not caring.

I *was* desperate.

At that point, I forgot about all my father's lessons never to let any weakness show. I didn't care that everyone in that room knew I was desperate.

I didn't care about anything but getting out of there.

"Hang on, *preciosa*," Hector murmured.

"*I've got to go!*" I screamed in his face and watched him wince, and his head jerked like the raw emotion in my voice was a physical thing; a hard, sharp, painful slap.

I struggled.

His arms went tight.

I pushed against his chest, putting my bodyweight into my hands while staring at them, willing my efforts to work, fighting the pain in my chest, feeling my heart beating in my throat, all the while begging, "Please. Please. *Please.*"

"Sadie, listen to me." Hector's arms separated. One stayed tight at my waist, pulling my lower body to his heat. One went up my back and into my hair, giving it a gentle tug so my head tilted back to look at him. When I caught sight of his face, I noted he was no longer annoyed and moody. His face was soft, his eyes were warm and intense, but this didn't help either. "Vance is a tracker. He's good. Tom and Malcolm kept notes on everything they did. Vance is going to pick up the—"

I shook my head and started laughing.

He stopped talking because the sound of my laughter was far from amused. Instead it was harsh and bitter and so ugly it scratched my own ears.

"I'm not stupid, Hector. It was eighteen years ago. There's nothing to pick up and if there is, I don't want to know what he's going to find."

"*Mamita*, you don't know. Give it a chance," Hector encouraged softly, but I shook my head and twisted my neck to look at Tom.

"You knew her. You said she'd never leave me, right?" I asked Tom.

Tom was watching me, looking pale and concerned, but he nodded.

"So, if she felt she had to leave anyway, she'd have come back. Or she'd have found a way to talk to me. She could have used you or Kitty Sue or *anyone*," I went on.

"Honey—" Tom started.

But I interrupted him, and with a forceful tug, I yanked out of Hector's arms and twirled to face Tom.

"And now he's gone. He's been in prison for ages and she hasn't come back. If she *could* come back, she would. Wouldn't she?" I demanded then repeated on a shout, "*Wouldn't she?*"

"Sadie, come here," Tom replied softly, his arms coming up and out toward me.

"He killed her," I announced in a flat voice, ignoring Toms arms, feeling nothing but that hot, hard thing burning in my chest. My body went ramrod straight, my hands clenched in fists at my sides. "My father found out what she was doing and he *fucking killed her!*"

"Hector, get her," Eddie warned, but I took off.

Not to escape, but pacing swiftly around the room, agitated and unable to stand still. Thoughts thundering in my head, pain pounding in my temples, striking there like jackhammers.

"This is *unbelievable*," I got out, taking a half a dozen steps before Hector caught me and pulled me to him again. I stopped, looked up at him and cried, "*Unbelievable!*"

"*Mi corazón*, calm down," Hector muttered.

"Calm down?" I snapped, eyes narrowing on him. "This is my *father*,

Hector. His blood flows through *my* veins and he's a killer! My grandmother died when I was practically a baby, did he kill her, too? And his parents, he kept them from me, but I knew they died when I was nineteen, within a year of each other. Did he kill them, too?"

I was on a roll, ranting in front of an audience, unconcerned about what they might think, who they might see, what I exposed by the words that came out of my mouth. The only thing I knew was the more I talked, the less that thing in my chest hurt and I had to get it out before it destroyed me, so I kept right on going.

"And my boyfriends. I knew he warned them off, but I've never seen them again, never ran into them at, say, a movie or the mall. How bizarre is *that*? You always run into people, especially your exes, exactly when you don't want to see them. Did he whack them for daring to touch me?" I asked. Then my mind flew in another direction. "And Greg! The guy who worked for him who flirted with me, my *fucking* father saw it and I never saw Greg again. Did he off him, too? Poor Greg, daring to flirt with Sadie Townsend. *That* was a mistake. King Death strikes again!" I shouted, totally hysterical now. Then I demanded to know, "When's it going to end? *When?* What's next? Am I going to find out my *fucking* father ran over my cat, Cleopatra, when I was eight? He said it was a neighbor who did it. It was probably *him!*"

"I'm sure your father didn't run over your cat," Hector told me gently.

"You're sure? Well I'm not. He probably drove around neighborhoods in his spare time, aiming for cats just for kicks!" I snapped back.

Hector gave me a gentle shake. "*Mamita*, you got to calm down."

I looked up at him and all of a sudden I remembered where I was, who I was with, what I was saying and I pulled in my breath.

He was right. He was *so* right.

I had to calm down.

So, I had filth running through my veins instead of blood.

So what?

I knew that. I'd always known it.

This just proved it irrevocably.

It proved I had no business standing here with these good people.

It proved I was *exactly* the kind of girl Hector could conquer then throw away without looking back.

It proved that wasn't only true, but I *deserved* it.

I had to get out of there, pronto.

"I need to go," I told Hector. "I need to get back to the gallery. I have work to do."

"I'm thinkin' that's not a good idea," Hector replied.

"What do you suggest I do instead? Sit in a dark room and reflect on my pitiful life? My mother who probably died trying to protect me? My squished cat?"

"Sadie—"

I shook my head and lifted my hands to pull my hair away from the sides of my face, leaving them there. "No, I need to do something normal. I need to be around pretty things in my gallery. I need Ralphie. I need Buddy. I need to go back to the brownstone and play with YoYo. I need Veronica Mars. I need to do everything I can do to forget all that is my *fucking hideous* life."

Something flashed across his face. Something so strong it penetrated my hysteria. I wasn't certain sure, he hid it as quickly as it came, but I could swear it was disappointment.

I realized then that of all the things I told him I needed, he wasn't one of them.

I'd inadvertently scored a direct hit and I should have been glad. But I was absolutely not.

I sallied forth. There was nothing else I could do. In my life, sallying forth was my only option and it always had been.

I dropped my hair and put my hands on his biceps.

"Please, Hector, take me back to the gallery."

Finally, his arms dropped. He stepped back and I lost his heat.

And I saw that I also lost him. I could see it in his face closing down and his eyes going blank. And I knew it because he didn't touch me, he didn't slide his hand in my hair and he didn't stay close.

And this hurt. It hurt so much I felt that hot, hard thing in my chest grow and spread. Up my throat and down to my belly, until I found it difficult to breathe and I was certain sure it was going to suffocate me.

Even though I lost him, he still quietly replied, "All right, Sadie. I'll take you back to the gallery."

I let out a breath and found that didn't help at all.

⌛

## *Eddie*

Eddie Chavez watched the door close behind his brother and Sadie and something about both of them made him feel unsettled.

Then Tom spoke and Eddie's eyes moved to him.

"Seth Townsend is a piece of shit," Tom announced. "But he loved Lizzie. It was an obsessive, smothering love, but he loved her. He didn't kill her."

Lee leaned against his desk.

"You sure about that?" he asked.

Tom nodded. "None of the leads took us close to Seth. I don't even think he knew she was talking to me. Malcolm and I figured Diggs found out what Lizzie was up to and ordered the hit."

"Any chance she's still alive?" Eddie asked, crossing his arms on his chest.

This time, Tom shook his head.

"Sadie's right. Lizzie would have found a way to keep in contact with her or she would have come back. Furthermore, Lizzie was loaded. Still is. She had a trust, she was an only child and she inherited everything when her mother died and they had a large estate. The money is still sitting in her accounts. She never touched it. Seth never went after it either, didn't try to have her declared dead so he could get his hands on it, never claimed desertion so he could get it for Sadie. Nothing. I'm not even certain Sadie knows it exists. If Lizzie found a safe place, she could have taken the money and she and Sadie could have lived their lives without ever lifting a finger. Eighteen years ago, Malc and I talked to Aaron Lockhart, Lizzie's family accountant, and we told him our suspicions. His loyalty was to Lizzie and Sadie and he watched that money like a hawk, *and* he would have done what he could to see Lizzie and Sadie safe. I called Aaron this morning to check and not a penny of that money moved, not in eighteen years. If Lizzie was alive, there would have been a time when she needed it. It never moved."

"Any point pursuing this?" Vance asked. "Sadie's got a new wound now, and by the look of her, she has no intention of letting it heal. She intends to keep it licked raw. After eighteen years, that trail's cold. I manage to find something, what purpose would it serve?"

Eddie looked at Vance. "At least she'd know her father didn't kill her mother."

Everyone knew that was so thin, it was practically useless.

But for Sadie, who had nothing but still managed to lose more, thin was better than nothing.

Because of that, Vance gave a jerk of his chin and muttered, "I'll look into it."

Hank moved to Lee's desk and used his hands to pull himself up to sit on it. "We got another problem," he announced when he'd settled.

Eddie felt the air in the room get heavy and his body tensed.

"Play the tape," Hank said to Lee, and Lee reached out and hit a button on a recorder on his desk. Sadie and Seth's phone conversation from the day before filled the room. When it was over, Lee hit the stop button.

Hank's eyes went to Eddie. "He said there's business to attend to."

Eddie clenched his teeth.

Hector had said Sadie had a will of steel. He hoped to fuck his brother was right because if Seth Townsend was doing business from prison, she wasn't free of him. Not yet.

Lee spoke, "Hector heard the conversation. We played it back half a dozen times yesterday. He didn't look happy at what he heard. I figure it was for more than the obvious reason, but he didn't share. We got somethin' else to deal with here?"

"No idea," Eddie replied truthfully, and he saw Lee's eyes cut to Hank before he continued. "Hector told me she knew what her father did. He also told me she slipped him information when he was on the inside."

All eyes came to him at this surprising revelation.

"You're fuckin' kidding," Vance murmured.

Eddie shook his head.

"Little Sadie?" Tom whispered.

This time, Eddie nodded.

"What are we talkin' about here? What did she give him? Was she involved, in a position to know?" Hank asked.

"No. Hector said the information was worthless, but she didn't know that. He wasn't in the place where he could tell her without putting them both in danger and it doesn't matter. She did it all the same. Still, I'm thinkin' Townsend figures family ties bind and she could help him keep a hold while he's in prison. There was shit the Feds knew existed but they couldn't find it. We know he's still got men loyal to him and he's keepin' himself informed. Now, he knows she's strayed and he obviously isn't happy about it."

"Where's the link?" Vance asked. "If she wasn't involved while he was active, why the fuck would he involve her now?"

Eddie shook his head because it was beyond his comprehension why a father would want to drag his daughter into a life of crime.

Then he looked at Lee. "Brody needs to do a hack, find out what the Feds got and what they didn't and if they're still keepin' an eye on him. I'll talk to Hector. We got more than the Balduccis to worry about. We need to keep Sadie clear of her father. By the sound of it he's lookin' to suck her in."

"She hates him," Tom put in. "She's not getting involved."

"That's not what I mean," Eddie told Tom. "His daughter has taken up with the agent who brought him down. We all know Seth Townsend sure as fuck isn't going to stand for that, even if he's behind bars."

"I'll get Brody on it, you talk to Hector," Lee said immediately.

Eddie took in a breath. He didn't like what he was going to have to say next. He didn't like to owe markers to anyone who was dirty, but he knew he had to say it.

His eyes moved to Lee. "You need to go to Marcus and Vito. They need to make their protection of Sadie official. Townsend and any of his crew that are out there need to know what they're up against if they're thinkin' retribution against Hector or Sadie."

Lee simply nodded.

"This just keeps getting uglier and uglier," Hank muttered.

Hank was right, but Eddie, thinking about his brother's woman, her mother dead, taking her life in her own hands to be free of her father, ending up beaten and raped by one of his competitors and Sadie's response to this latest news, still hoped Hank was wrong.

As for the unsettled feeling he had about Hector and Sadie, the way they behaved and the way he saw them looking at each other, Eddie knew it was time to talk to Jet.

## *Buddy*

"Double H is here," Ralphie whispered from his position at the window, and Buddy looked to his lap.

Sadie's head was there, her magnificent hair fanned out everywhere and she was asleep. YoYo was on her side and asleep too, tucked in the crook of Sadie's lap, Sadie's hand on the dog's belly.

Sadie had come home from work with Ralphie, her face pale, her eyes dead, a look that seriously alarmed Buddy. It didn't help that Ralphie was giving Buddy faces saying, nonverbally, all was even *more* unwell in the World of Sadie.

She'd tried to make a go of it, pretend excitement for YoYo's arrival (as was her way). But Bex showed up with the dog, took one look at Sadie and asked, straight out, "Oh God, Sadie girl, what's happened now?"

Sadie pulled in her lips, trying for control (this lasted about a second). Then she snatched YoYo out of Bex's arms, cuddled the dog against her face and burst into tears.

Through her blubbering, she told them a crazy story about her father killing her mother, something about "amazing 'fuck-me' sex" with Hector (she said they had sex four times, which had to be a crazy story; four times in one night and all of them "amazing" was impossible, and if it was true, Hector Chavez was legend material) and ended on some incomprehensible nonsense about her need to learn Greek.

They calmed her down, made her eat, and then Buddy gave her two Tylenol PMs and sent her to the couch with Veronica Mars.

When Bex left, Buddy and Ralphie followed and they all had an impromptu conference on the front stoop about what to do.

Ralphie had a plan.

It was a bad plan.

Buddy and Bex didn't like it, but Ralphie was adamant and he talked them both around (as was *his* way).

Then Ralphie called Hector and told him to hold off coming over until they knew Sadie was "visiting dreamland" (Ralphie's words) and they could talk.

Hector didn't like it, but Ralphie was adamant and talked him around.

Now Hector was there and Buddy *still* didn't like the plan. But he'd been watching Hector closely now for over a month.

Buddy didn't know Hector well but there were a few things he *did* know.

He knew (because a friend of his at Denver Health told him) that Hector had spent the night in her room in a bedside vigil after she'd been raped. Hospital gossip spread it around that this hot Hispanic guy had brought her in, gone berserk when they'd tried to separate them and ended up having to be physically removed from her examination bay. He'd lied to the staff, telling them he was her partner. After that was over, he and his friends had spent a month sitting outside the brownstone, making a statement to anyone who might want to come after Sadie. When he finally deemed it time to make his move, he went against what Buddy was certain was his nature and took it slow, showing patience, restraint and understanding. But also, Buddy noted, a sense of humor, consideration and a gentleness that Buddy thought was almost unreal.

Ralphie adored him, and talking with Bex about it, she agreed with Buddy's assessment of Hector's behavior. She admitted she even trusted him and Bex didn't have a high opinion of men, what with working at a rape crisis center that was a job hazard.

Even so, they were about to break Sadie's confidence and Buddy didn't like doing it.

And he hoped to all hell that they weren't about to break her heart.

Buddy moved Sadie's head, slid out from under her and carefully tucked a pillow in his place, hoping he wouldn't wake her. She moved. Buddy sucked in breath, but she just curled her knees up higher, pinning YoYo, who didn't mind and simply snuggled closer. She tucked her hands under her cheek in prayer position and stayed out.

Buddy let out a sigh.

At that point, Ralphie and Hector walked in the room.

Hector's eyes immediately went to Sadie.

"She's asleep," Buddy whispered then, "Kitchen."

Hector's gaze sliced to him and he didn't even try to hide his look of tender concern.

At his look, Buddy knew.

*Thank Christ*, he thought.

They went into the kitchen and Ralphie closed the kitchen door as Buddy got three Fat Tire beers from the fridge.

He opened the beers while Hector asked, "How is she?"

"A fucking mess," Ralphie answered, and Buddy shot him a killing look. "What?" Ralphie responded to the killing look. "She's been crying her eyes out and blathering on about learning to speak Greek. What's *that* all about?"

"Learning to speak Greek?" Hector asked and Buddy slid him a beer.

They settled on stools at the island and Ralphie kept going, "Yep. Greek. She's lost it. Says her father killed her mother and she's got to learn to speak Greek. If that isn't the hallmark of losing your mind, nothing is."

Hector stared at Ralphie a beat and then put his elbow on the island, pressed his three middle fingers to the area between his brows and rubbed hard.

Buddy watched Hector, his heart clenching, then asked, "*Did* her father kill her mother?"

Ralphie's head snapped around to look at Buddy, then he went pale and his gaze swung to Hector.

Hector took his fingers from his brow and took a long swig of beer.

Then he leveled his (fucking fantastic, Buddy had to admit, the color was so intense and those *lashes*, Jesus Christ, divine) black eyes on Buddy and said, "She got bad news today. Her mother's likely dead. It's an outside chance, but her father could have done it. He had motive and opportunity."

"No, please no," Ralphie breathed then shut his eyes tight.

"I knew about it but didn't want her to know," Hector told him. "The boys agreed with me, Lee, his brother Hank, my brother Eddie," Hector explained. "She forced my hand, asked Lee to find her mom right in front of Tom. Tom knew her mother. He's a friend of her family she didn't know she had. He wants her back in the fold. He wants to protect her like he feels he should have been protecting her since her mom disappeared. To do that, he wants her trust so he wanted nothing between them. I didn't like it, but I agreed. It was the wrong choice, at least now. It was too fuckin' soon."

"Not much more she can take," Buddy decided.

"Nope," Hector agreed.

Buddy and Hector stared at each other unhappily.

Ralphie's eyes reopened.

"What are we going to do?" he asked.

"What you been doin'," Hector answered simply.

"I'm not sure *Auntie Mame* and Veronica Mars are going to soothe the soul of a recently raped girl who just found out her father might have killed her mother. That's beyond the powers of Tinseltown," Ralphie informed Hector.

Hector stared at Ralphie, likely, Buddy thought, wondering how he, as macho and heterosexual as they come, found himself sharing a beer in the kitchen of a gay man who just used the words *"Auntie Mame"*, "soothe the soul" and "Tinseltown" in two sentences.

Buddy decided it was time to get down to business.

"You need to know a few things about Sadie," Buddy said, and Ralphie's head snapped to him again, this time with the addition of narrowed eyes.

"What are you doing? I'm going to tell him," Ralphie announced.

Buddy looked at his lover. "Ralphie, I'm tellin' him."

"I'm telling him. It was my idea," Ralphie returned.

"Maybe so, but he needs it straight. No exaggeration," Buddy replied.

"I wouldn't exaggerate!" Ralphie snapped.

Buddy gave him the look he deserved for uttering such a lie.

Ralphie glared back.

"Would someone tell me? I don't give a fuck who," Hector cut in, losing patience.

"What do you drink?" Buddy asked immediately, taking charge.

Hector looked at the beer in his hand then back to Buddy.

"No, stronger. Bourbon, vodka, gin…?" Buddy explained.

Hector's eyes went intense and Buddy pulled in breath at the power behind his look.

Then Hector muttered, "Shit."

"Shit is right," Buddy muttered in return.

Hector sighed then said, "Bourbon. Jack, if you've got it."

Ralphie went to get the Jack Daniels and three glasses.

They had three more beers and made a major dent in the bottle of Jack by the time they were done explaining what Ralphie called The Night of A Thousand Horrors Accompanied by Lemon Drops.

A night neither of them thought that Sadie fully remembered.

A night where she explained about her mom, her father and her life.

This, Hector didn't seemed surprised about, so Buddy figured he knew.

A night where she talked about Daisy, the Rock Chicks, going to see Lee Nightingale, Hector being there and how that made her feel.

This, Hector also didn't seem surprised about, but his mouth got tight and his face went dark, likely, Buddy figured, with guilt.

A night where she talked about having no friends and living her life as an Ice Princess.

This, Hector took in without giving anything away. But still, the air in the room changed, almost like it had gone electric.

A night where she described, in detail, what had happened with Ricky Balducci.

After what little Buddy shared (but clearly it was enough), Hector's entire body got visibly tight. His face went scary dark and Ralphie cautiously removed all bottles from his reach.

"Hold it together, Hector," Buddy warned. "She's in the next room."

Hector jerked his head in what was supposed to be a nod while a muscle jumped in his cheek. He looked away and threw back a shot of Jack, pouring himself another the minute he was done. He threw that back, too.

Buddy looked at Ralphie.

Ralphie bugged his eyes out at Buddy.

Buddy finished on the part of the night where Sadie shared about Sadie. The part she shared at the end of the night. The part they both figured she didn't remember sharing.

It was who she thought she was, who she wanted to be, how she didn't know how to be that and what she thought that Hector thought she was after what happened "that night in my father's study".

Hector stared at him.

"She thinks I think she's a society slut out slumming?" he asked, looking angry.

"She says *you* said that," Buddy corrected him.

Hector looked away and threw back another shot of Jack.

"Jesus," he muttered after he swallowed. "I never called her a slut. I told her I was *glad* she went slumming. She had to know I wanted her. Fuck, I had her against the wall with her skirt around her waist, my hands in her pants, for fuck's sake."

This was *way* more information than they needed, but Buddy figured it was Jack Daniels Magic. As good (if not better) than lemon drops.

Hector kept talking as if to himself, "She knew who I was. She'd been feeding me information on her father for months. And I knew what kind of woman she was. She knew I knew. What's in her fuckin' head?"

"That episode didn't, um... end well, did it?" Ralphie asked carefully, and Hector's eyes sliced to him.

"No," Hector replied tersely, then his teeth clenched. The muscle leaped in his cheek again and he looked away. "*Fucking hell*," he hissed (again, to himself), sounding even angrier. "Fucking hell," he repeated, looking up at Buddy, something dawning on him. "She didn't know. We talked about it the other night. I told her I knew she was my informant and she didn't know I knew. Fucking hell, I've been so wrapped up in all her shit, I didn't put it together. I said something to her that night when she walked away and it wasn't nice. I was pissed as hell. I figured she'd get that, understand why and get over it, like I did, because I thought she went cold on me, walked away, because she had to, to protect both of us. Jesus, if she didn't know—"

"She's confused," Ralphie said quietly. "She thinks she's marked by her father, less of a person because of who he is. She spent years enduring a life of fear, playing a role, hating every minute of it without a single person to turn to, to trust. She had a chance to become someone else, but instead she was stalked by four crazy brothers and then interrupted in the effort of finding herself when she was raped by one of them. She doesn't think like normal people. She's never had a normal life. But now, she's on the edge, Hector. She's holding it together, but she's teetering. We can't let her fall off."

Buddy took over. "What's happening with you two, it isn't your normal boy meets girl, boy asks girl out—"

"I fuckin' know that," Hector clipped, interrupting Buddy, eyes narrowed and angry and clearly having had his fill of sharing.

Buddy pushed it. "I know you do. What I wanted to say was, in a normal relationship, it would be too early to ask this question, but we have to know your intentions."

"What are you sayin'?" Hector's voice was still clipped.

Buddy kept at it. "I'm asking you your intentions. Far as we can see, Ralphie and I are the only ones she trusts. We're taking that seriously. We figure you're not in it for a casual—"

Hector leaned forward, and at his threatening posture and drawn brows, Buddy stopped talking.

"I'm gonna say this once, out of respect for what you've done for her, and then we're done here. There's nothin' casual about this. Got me?"

Okay, it was safe to say, Hector Chavez was done sharing.

And Hector Chavez's feelings were far from casual when they came to Sadie.

Buddy thought that was good to know.

"Got you," Buddy assured him.

"I got you, too." Ralphie smiled happily then turned to Buddy. "I told you. I told Sadie too. Double H is—"

"Christ," Hector muttered, interrupting Ralphie, tossing back the last of his third beer and standing. "I'm takin' Sadie to bed. Which room is hers?"

"Top of the stairs to the right. She has her own bathroom. Are you staying?" Ralphie answered and asked.

"Fuck yeah, I'm stayin'," Hector replied.

"You need to borrow some pajamas?" Ralphie offered.

"Ralphie," Buddy said in a low warning.

Hector stared at Ralphie a beat, then two. Finally he said shortly, "No."

Ralphie flicked out his hand. "Our casa is your casa, or however it goes. Make yourself at home."

Hector's glance cut across the both of them, which Buddy figured was his way of saying "goodnight", and he started to move from the room.

He stopped when Ralphie called, "You know, some of that amazing 'fuck me' sex Sadie was going on about while she was freaking out this evening wouldn't be amiss in this situation. Stress relief."

Hector's eyes slashed to Ralphie, and Buddy could swear he looked like he didn't know whether to throw something or laugh out loud.

"Ralphie, shut up," Buddy said.

"I'm just saying," Ralphie replied.

"Shut up," Buddy repeated.

"*I'm just saying*," Ralphie repeated, too.

Hector gave up and left the room, closing the door behind him.

Ralphie gave Buddy a look and then tiptoed across the room to the door.

"Get back here," Buddy hissed, and Ralphie put his finger to his lips, carefully pulled open the door an inch and peeked out.

Buddy wanted to be the better person, but he couldn't help himself.

He made it in time to peer out the crack in the door, bending under Ralphie to do it. Then he saw Hector's back walking away, Sadie in his arms, her head resting on his shoulder, face tucked into his neck, her arms linked around his shoulders.

"Mm, that boy looks *good* from behind," Ralphie whispered.

Buddy's eyes rolled to the ceiling then, since they were there, he said a little prayer.

# Chapter 17

# It Was Organic

*Sadie*

I woke up in my bed in Ralphie and Buddy's guest room.

This was a strange sensation. Firstly, I hadn't slept there in days. Secondly, I knew immediately Hector was with me. I could feel his heat all down my back and his arm was wrapped around my midriff, elbow cocked, forearm tucked under me, hand at the side of my breast.

Oh my.

Now, how did I get in *this* predicament?

I didn't have time to rewind my night. It was too late to try to figure out how I ended up in my bed with Hector. It was time to extricate myself, pronto.

I prayed he was asleep and started to slide forward so I could escape.

His arm went tight.

"You're awake," he said into the back of my neck.

Damn and blast!

"Yes," I replied, and wondered if I should have feigned sleep.

"Good," he muttered, his body pressing closer. Then his thumb (no kidding!) started to stroke the side of my breast. "Before you get a chance to put your defenses up, *mamita*, we're gonna talk."

This was *not* good.

I'd been awake five seconds. I could barely think, much less talk, with Hector, *with* Hector's heat at my back *and* Hector's thumb stroking my breast.

I definitely should have feigned sleep.

It was time to form an upon-waking escape plan so I could go somewhere and get my multiple personalities together where we could confer and decide who was going to take on this latest challenge.

"I, um, need to use the bathroom," I tried.

This failed.

"In a minute," he responded firmly.

"I'm not sure I want to talk," I told him, trying again.

This failed, too. Miserably.

"That's good, too, because you aren't gonna be talking."

Oh no.

A talk without me talking.

That *definitely* was not good.

"Hector—" I started and tried to turn, but his arm got tight. His body fitted itself close to my back and I couldn't move.

"Sadie, quiet and listen," he ordered.

I could just *not win.*

I hadn't even been awake for two minutes and I had another life trauma on my hands!

Oh well, so be it.

I willed my body to relax, but mentally braced for what was to come next.

Hector felt the tension leave me and his thumb went back to stroking (this, I had to admit, felt super nice, but I told myself to ignore it; this didn't work, but at least I tried).

Then Hector started talking.

"I grew up in a house full of family; brothers, sisters, a mother, a father. My dad was a prosecuting attorney and he worked long hours. *Mamá* was a part-time guidance counselor at our high school. We weren't rich, but they managed to give us everything we needed, even if we didn't have most of the shit we wanted. They worked, but they were around. They were good parents. In our business, in our faces, providing guidance but letting us fuck up enough so we could learn. Some of us took advantage, fucked around, caused them problems. They never gave up hoping we'd eventually do the right thing and made sure we knew that."

Now, why was he telling me this?

In a perfect world, of course, I would want to know all about Hector's life.

But this was far from a perfect world.

And, I wondered, was Hector one of the ones who "fucked around, caused them problems"?

I didn't get a chance to ask (not that I would), because he kept talking.

"I don't know how you grew up, but I watched you with your father when I was on the inside, *mamita*, and, at first, I didn't understand it. When I did, it turned my stomach."

I drew in breath and held it.

I didn't know what I expected from this first thing in the morning talk where I didn't get to talk, but *that* wasn't it.

I had forgotten, or chosen not to remember, how much he'd been around. My father kept him close. He liked him, trusted him. He even told me he was grooming Hector for "big things". In the end, Hector had been around loads.

It didn't occur to me what he would see or even that he was watching. It *really* didn't occur to me that he'd have any reaction to it. No one cared about me or what I was going through. Not only did I suspect they didn't care, I also I didn't tell anyone, and I hid behind The Ice just in case anyone got close.

But, somehow, it appeared Hector had seen through all that.

And furthermore, what he said meant he cared.

I didn't know how that made me feel except the weird, happy glow was trying to push through.

Then, I felt his mouth touch my neck. He kissed me there and it took an immense effort of will to hold the glow back because him kissing my neck could only mean one thing, and I couldn't allow myself to believe in it. Believing in it would set me up as the fool. Or worse, let him get close and that couldn't happen.

"That isn't family, Sadie," he told me softly, obviously unaware of my inner turmoil. "I don't know what it is, but it sure as fuck isn't family."

With no choice (other than to suffocate), I let out my breath on the word, "Okay."

His arm gave me a squeeze. "I don't know what you got inside you that helps you deal. I don't know, growin' up with that, how you managed. But I'm thinkin' your mother gave you some of it and the other part comes from you. Or at least the you I had yesterday morning."

At his reminder of yesterday morning, my body went tight and so did his arm.

"Don't fuckin' shut down on me," he warned and he sounded like he meant it.

Oh my.

I forced my body to relax. It was difficult, but I did it so I could get this over with and fast.

When my body relaxed, so did his arm.

"Now, we got a situation. I don't have many choices in this situation and none of them are good. But I made a decision and you gotta know what it is."

Oh my, oh my, *oh my*.

Hector's made a decision.

This, I figured, did not bode well for me.

I wasn't wrong.

"I want you," he said into the back of my neck, his hand moving up to curl around my breast in a way that was so possessive, I found myself holding my breath again while he went on. "I've wanted you a long time, longer than you know. Before you came into your father's office that night, well before. I lost control that night, fucked up, let things lie the way they were. I should have talked to you. I didn't. I didn't think it was safe. After your father went down, I should have come to you. I didn't. It was the wrong choice. Now, something shitty has happened to you and I felt I needed to proceed with caution. I couldn't come on strong, not after what Ricky did to you. I couldn't push it. I didn't want you thinkin' you were movin' from under your father's thumb to under mine. I could have stepped back, but that would mean *I* wouldn't be where I wanted to be, which is right here."

His fingers at my breast squeezed and I felt my stomach perform a happy pitch. I tried to ignore that, too (and failed).

He kept talking, "I felt I was makin' progress until yesterday morning. Now, you got some fucked up idea in your head about what happened and you gotta get this Sadie, so listen. It's important. Because I want *that* girl. That's who I'm doin' all this for 'cause that girl is the real you. The one who loses control and takes what she wants and gives back without racking up the debt. And she doesn't give a fuck about what her actions say and what people will think."

I was breathing heavily now, wanting to block out his words. But with him there, all around me, I couldn't.

He kept at me.

"So, I've made a decision. I'm not fuckin' around with this anymore."

He wasn't fucking around with this anymore?

What did *that* mean?

Had he been fucking around before?

He kept going, "I want the real you. To get that, I'm givin' you the real me. I'm not gonna hold anything back."

Oh my God!

He'd been holding back?

How could he be holding back?

He kept talking, "And I'm bettin' that the real you'll be able to deal. We'll ride this out and get to the other side."

Oh no.

No we wouldn't.

No... we... would... not.

Unfortunately, he wasn't finished.

"You try to shut down, you try to hold back, you try to push me away, to take off, fair warning, *mamita*, I won't like it and I won't allow it. You feel that's me puttin' you under my thumb, I can live with that. You'll learn the difference between how your father treated you and how I'm gonna treat you. Do you understand what I'm sayin' to you?"

What did I say to that?

"Sadie, answer me. I gotta know you understand."

"Yes," I replied.

I understood and it scared me more than anything had scared me before.

"You got anything to say?" he asked.

I thought about it then I made an effort at protection.

In other words, I lied (badly).

"I'm not sure there's something here. I don't think I feel about you the way—"

He interrupted me, "You feel what you're wearin'?"

I didn't understand the question. Then I thought back to the night before and all I could remember was falling asleep on the couch.

My hand went to my waist and I felt soft flannel bunched there.

Damn and blast him to perdition!

I'd stolen Hector's flannel shirt the day before, shoved it in my overnight bag, all ready to take it with me to Crete as a reminder never to get myself in another fool situation *ever again*.

Now, somehow, I was wearing it.

Which meant I was in another fool situation *right now!*

"How...?" I started, but stopped when his head moved. His mouth came to my neck, lips sliding up to the back of my ear.

"Carried you to bed last night. Went for your pajamas in your bag, found my shirt. You don't feel about me the way I feel about you, why'd you steal my shirt?"

Blooming *heck*.

With no other choice, I decided to go for attitude. "You shouldn't have rooted through my stuff."

"You shouldn't have stolen my shirt," he returned.

This was true.

"You can have it back," I snapped.

I felt his body move. I lost his heat, but only so he could put his hand to my belly and press me to my back. He came up, elbow in the pillow, head in his hand and looked down at me, grinning.

I glared up at him.

"I don't want it back," he said.

"I don't want it anymore," I lied.

The grin widened to a smile, his head bent and he kissed me softly.

"You want it," he murmured against my lips.

I did. I wanted it. I wanted it to remember not to be a fool. I also wanted it for those times when I would pretend I could be a normal girl with a normal boyfriend having a normal relationship. I wasn't sure flannel was *de rigueur* on Crete, but I also didn't care.

That was when I remembered Pretend Sadie and what she was going to do for me.

And I realized I needed her even more than I thought I did.

Because she was going to get me free, with my heart guarded. But she was also going to get me the memories I'd need in order to go on, alone, without my mom, without anyone.

"Oh all right," I gave in, blowing out a huff of air. "I want it."

That was when Hector's eyes grew dark, warm and intense, and I stared in order to memorize that look so I could hold it with me for a long, long time.

While I was staring at his face, he pulled the covers down to my thighs. He watched me as his fingers moved to the buttons of the shirt and undid them (he'd only done up two) and he spread the shirt wide.

I pulled in breath and started to cover myself when he mumbled, "Don't."

It was hard, but I made my hands settle and his eyes went to my chest. His hand followed, and slowly it trailed down my chest, between my breasts, over my ribcage and midriff to my belly. The whole time, his eyes watched his hand, and when his hand rested at my belly, that belly melted.

This was because his face got this expression, an expression I'd never seen on him before. It was more intense and warm than normal. But it was also soft and bizarrely, at the same time, hard. I got the impression it was like him cupping my breast. It signified possession.

At that realization, I couldn't help it, my bones went liquid.

"Hector——" I breathed.

His eyes came to mine. His fingertips moved across the top edge of my panties and his head descended.

That was it. I gave in because it was Hector. I wanted him (he was right, obviously). I wanted the memories of "us". And I wasn't disappointed.

It was just as amazing as before.

It was a mixture of hot and urgent, but slow and sweet, and the only difference was, when I tried to shrug off the shirt, he wouldn't let me. He made me keep it on, even when we were ready, breathing heavily, kissing hard, my nails scraping at his skin and he rolled to his back, taking me with him. He yanked up my knees so I was straddling him, guided himself inside and pushed me up so he filled me.

It felt *great*.

I started moving, our eyes locked. His hot on me, mine had to be the same because my body felt hot. Everything felt hot. My eyes *had* to look as hot as his.

His hands moved on my body under the shirt. I put mine over his and his kept going, taking mine with them. Then one of his hands went between my legs, shifted, pressing my own fingers to me and manipulating them.

"My God," I breathed, tingles shooting from between my legs down the tops of my thighs as it started happening, the tingles gathering, getting tight.

I bent forward slightly, resting my free hand on the bed, giving me more leverage to move faster, grind down harder. His free hand went to my jaw, his thumb trailed my bottom lip and at his touch, I parted my lips. Touching my tongue to his thumb then my teeth tagged it, biting softly before I sucked it inside my mouth.

The minute I did that, his face went darker, his eyes went hotter and everything happened at once.

I came, hard and delicious. At the same time his hand left mine between my legs. His arm sliced around my waist and he threw me to my back and started pounding into me, prolonging and intensifying my orgasm as he took my moans in his mouth. Before I was finished, his groans mingled with mine.

When we were done, while my hips jerked softly under his in the aftermath, my hands moved along the skin and muscle of his back, I replayed the last fifteen minutes, burning it into my brain to carry with me forever.

"You still with me?" he asked, his voice gruff.

"Yes."

"Don't shut down on me," he muttered, and I felt guilt slide through me that he'd even think that but it was my fault. In a short time I'd conditioned him to it.

My hands stopped roving and my arms got tight.

"Okay," I said.

He rolled to the side, rolling me with him but keeping my leg around his hip with a hand behind my knee. Then his fingertips slid gently from the back of my knee to my bottom and back again and again and again.

I tucked my face in his throat and memorized the feel of what his hand was doing, too.

"You wanna talk about yesterday?" he asked quietly.

"What about it?"

"In Lee's office."

My body went tight and I immediately shook my head.

He stopped stroking my leg and his arm went around me.

"That's okay, *mamita*. You don't need to talk about it."

I relaxed.

Then Pretend Sadie asked, "Can you do me a favor?"

It was his turn for his body to grow tight.

"What?"

I tipped my head back to look at him and his chin dipped so his eyes could lock with mine.

He looked great after we had sex. His eyes still intense, but his expression satisfied. It was his best look *ever*.

"The Rock Chicks have called a powwow," I told him. "Do you know what that is?"

He shook his head, but I felt his body relax and his mouth twitched.

"I don't either, but I've been ordered to attend. If Ralphie's not invited, can I call you? Will you take me there? It's at noon."

The intensity in his eyes faded and they went soft.

"I can do that."

Pretend Sadie relaxed into him and she smiled.

Real Hector smiled back.

Real Sadie's heart clenched so hard it hurt.

Then she memorized his smile, too.

⋙⋘

"You aren't allowed here. Go!" Daisy demanded, pointing at Hector the minute he, YoYo and I walked into Fortnum's.

"Daisy!" I snapped.

"What a cute dog!" Roxie cried.

Daisy's ignored Roxie (and YoYo) and her glare settled on me. "This is a Rock Chick Powwow. The rules of a Rock Chick Powwow are, you gotta be a girl, a gay, Duke or Tex. No one else is allowed."

"Why are Duke and Tex allowed?" I asked, bending over to pick up YoYo and cuddle her to my chest. This, unfortunately, gave her access to my throat and chin which she licked exuberantly as her little, chubby body wiggled happily in my arms.

Daisy, still ignoring YoYo, answered, "Who knows? Who cares? It just happened. It was organic. But now it's Rock Chick Law."

Rock Chick Law?

They had a phone tree and laws?

Blooming heck!

"Can I get a coffee?" Hector asked in an amused voice.

The arm he had slung around my shoulders curled and he pulled me and YoYo mostly into the front of his body (this gave YoYo the added target of Hector's throat, something to which Hector seemed totally oblivious). I looked up at him and his face was blank, but his eyes were dancing like he found Daisy hilarious but dared not laugh out loud.

"Can I play with your dog?" Roxie called, and my gaze slid to her for a smile before Daisy started speaking again.

"Coffee and leave," Daisy clipped at Hector then she turned to the couches where all of the Rock Chicks, plus Mace (who was sitting on the arm of the couch by Stella, her back turned to him and resting against his thigh), were lounging.

"You too," Daisy ordered Mace. "Vamoose."

Mace's eyebrows went up, but other than that he didn't move a muscle.

"I'm not kidding, Mace. These talks get deep. There's usually detailed descriptions of Hot Bunch on Rock Chick sexual activity. Do you wanna know how you compare to Hector? I don't *think* so," Daisy went on.

My eyes got huge. Not only because of what she said, but because she had an audience. And that audience not only included Indy, Ally, Jet, Roxie, Jules, Ava, Stella and Shirleen, but also a bunch of customers I'd never seen before *in my life*.

Not to mention, she was telling Mace what to do. I knew Daisy was a little bit crazy and over the top, but I suspected that was taking her life in her hands.

"Fucking hell," Hector muttered over YoYo and my heads, clearly thinking along the same vein.

"You can say that again," I whispered, staring at Daisy.

He caught my whisper, his eyes scanned my face and his arm gave me (and YoYo) a little squeeze.

Then Hector decided to intervene.

"You're not talkin' to Sadie about our sex life," he told Daisy. My body went tense and Daisy whirled.

Then her eyes narrowed.

Oh no.

That might not have been the right thing to do.

YoYo yapped at Daisy or Hector, I didn't know which, she was wiggling so much. She could be yapping at a random customer, how would I know?

"Hector—" I started, trying to control YoYo and the flow of conversation.

"I don't care if you are a badass mother ex-DEA Agent hot guy," Daisy snapped, interrupting my attempt to smooth over the situation. "You can't control the Rock Chick Powwow. The Powwow goes where it goes. We just follow."

"Sadie's had a rough few weeks," Hector reminded Daisy.

"You think I don't know that?" Daisy shot back.

"Whatever the fuck this is, you aren't gonna fuck with her head. She's got enough fucking with her head," Hector warned.

Daisy's eyes bugged out and her brows went to her hairline.

"We're not gonna *fuck with her head!*" Daisy screeched.

"Can we *not* say 'fuck' so loud in front of the customers?" Indy threw in a request.

Jet and Ava looked at each other and let out small giggles.

"I get back and she's shut down, I'm not gonna be fuckin' happy," Hector clipped out, ignoring Indy's request to avoid the f-bomb.

"The point of the Powwow, Hector, is not to shut her down but to *sort her out,*" Daisy threw back.

It was time to step in before the Battle of the Badass and Southern Diva escalated any further. I put YoYo down and she immediately ran to Roxie, who was bent over, clapping and making kissy noises.

"I don't think I need to be sorted out," I put in.

Daisy's Mother-Hen-on-a-Rampage eyes focused on me and she snapped, "Shirleen said there were problems."

Shirleen, sipping a latte, calm as could be, chimed in from an armchair opposite Stella, "Looks to me like it sorted itself out. The girl's been laid. My guess, fairly recently. Guessin' again, good and proper. Next problem!"

I closed my eyes.

Someone, please tell me that Shirleen didn't just announce to the entire store that I'd been laid "good and proper".

I opened my eyes again, looked up at Hector and whispered, "Please, tell me Shirleen didn't just announce to the entire store that we've had sex."

Hector bit his bottom lip and again I didn't know whether he was biting back a smile or anger.

If it was my choice, it would have been the latter.

"Hate to say it, *mamita,*" he said, eyes scanning the crowd, some of whom were surreptitiously watching us, others settled in and openly enjoying the show, "but it seems she did."

"Are they always like this?"

I could tell now he was fighting back a grin. "Far's I can tell, yeah," he replied.

"Why is my life so *difficult?*" I blurted out before I could think better of it.

I watched as Hector's eyes went gentle and he replied, "This isn't difficult. And Sadie, it isn't bad. They don't mean you any harm. They just care."

I knew he was right.

But still.

Everyone in the entire store knew I'd been *laid*.

His hand went to my neck and slid into my hair, his thumb against my hairline.

"Looks like the Powwow is a bust. You wanna go back or you want a coffee?"

"Coffee," I answered. "I should get one for Ralphie, too."

"I'll get 'em," he told me, and his face dipped and his mouth brushed mine.

Then he was off to the coffee counter, leaving me affected deeply (yes, even by his brush on my lips!) and teetering without his body to support me.

"Sit down before you fall down, child." Shirleen called.

I decided to do as she suggested before I caused an even bigger stir and took a seat in a big, comfortable armchair amongst the crew.

"I cannot *believe* you have a small dog wearing a cute sweater accessory!" Ally exclaimed. "Chickie, you got it goin' *on*."

"YoYo's not mine. Buddy, Ralphie and I are watching her for a friend," I told Ally.

"It's still a cute sweater," Roxie said, rubbing YoYo's body all over and YoYo was loving it, wiggling in Roxie's lap, showing her belly.

"The sweater's not YoYo's, exactly. It's Ralphie's," I explained.

All eyes came to me.

"Don't ask, it's a long story," I went on.

All lips formed grins.

"Everything all right?" Jules asked, her eyes on me, her arms holding her new son Max.

I surprised myself by saying, "No."

Now why did I say that?

I didn't *share*.

Ever!

"No?" Ally asked quietly.

"I got bad news yesterday," I shared again.

Yes, shared.

Yes, again!

What was happening to me?

"Your mom," Indy said softly and I looked at her. "Lee told me."

"Eddie told me," Jet put in.

"Hank told me, too," Roxie added.

"You should know, they told the rest of us," Ava finished.

I feared I was about to hyperventilate.

"You don't have to talk about it," Jules said immediately, watching me closely for a second. Then her eyes sliced to Ally, but it was Stella that spoke with her super cool, throaty, sexy voice (no kidding, Stella's voice was aces).

"She doesn't, Ally, so lay off."

"I didn't say anything," Ally defended herself.

"We should let Sadie control what she wants to share," Jules replied, and I decided I liked Jules, *loads*.

"It just felt like I lost her all over again."

That was me too!

It just came out.

I could no longer control my own mouth. I was blurting out private thoughts willy-nilly!

"That's understandable," Ava told me.

"She was trying to protect me," I went on, still unable to stop myself, and they all had their eyes on me.

Normally, I wouldn't like that.

Normally, it would make me uncomfortable.

Normally, I would call my Ice Princess.

But their faces were open and their eyes were kind. Instead of feeling uncomfortable, it felt like they were open because they wanted me to give it to them so they could take it away. Even though it was bad stuff, *really* bad stuff. But that way, I wouldn't have to hold it inside anymore.

Now, how bizarre was *that*?

I put my hands in my hair, pulling it away from my head and looked at Mace's boots.

Then my hands dropped and I whispered, "I can't stop thinking about it. Thinking that she died scared. I hate it that I'll never see her again, because I always thought..." I stopped, then took a deep breath and started again, "But I hate it more that she probably died scared."

Then all of a sudden, that big, hard, burning thing came back into my chest and it started choking me. I even made a choking sound *out loud*.

"Oh blast! I'm going to fucking cry *again*," I announced, then my hands went over my face and I burst into tears.

Within moments, I felt fingers curl around my wrists and strong hands pull me out of my chair. Then I was up against a rock-hard body that, for a second, I thought was Hector's. But it was bigger than Hector's body, taller and the arms that wrapped around me were different.

I looked up and was shocked to see Mace through wet eyes.

"I'm sorry," I whispered.

His hand went to the top of my head and slid down my hair to my neck. He put pressure there until my cheek was against his chest.

"Don't be." His deep voice sounded over my head and rumbled in my ear.

My arms slid around his waist and I held on to him and he held on to me, and I cried silently against the chest of a man I didn't know at all, except his name. And I did it in a bookstore, full of people. Some I knew. Most I didn't.

And I didn't care, not even a little bit because, as I cried, I felt that hard, hot ball in my chest start to shrink and fade until, after a while, it was nearly gone.

Then I was shifted, turned and Hector was there. His arm went around my shoulders and he tucked me in his side, curling me to face him. His hand went to my face, his thumb wiping at the wetness there.

"You okay?" he murmured.

"Stop asking me that," I replied.

He grinned and his fingers formed a fist. His knuckles slid across my cheekbone gently before his hand fell away.

"You're okay."

I put my temple to his shoulder then saw a big mug with foamy milk on top thrust into my line of sight.

"Drink that, woman," Tex ordered, and I looked up at him as I took the mug. "Shee-it. Someone get her a Kleenex, her makeup's runnin'."

My hand not holding the mug shot to my face to wipe away mascara.

"Don't bother. It's all over the place. You need a mirror," Tex told me with brutal honesty. Or I should say, Tex *boomed* at me with brutal honesty, so perhaps the one person on the other side of the room who hadn't witnessed my meltdown could be in on the show.

I still wiped. Tex still stared. Hector still kept me tucked tight to his side.

Daisy handed me a Kleenex and then Tex spoke (or boomed) again, "Don't know your Ma. Figure she was good people, she did what Indy says she did. Do know, she was here, she'd be fuckin' proud. You been through what you been through and you're still standin'. Lotsa women wouldn't only bend, they'd break. But you didn't do either and you're still standin'. You were my daughter, I'd be so fuckin' proud, I'd shout it from the rooftops. I figure, so would your Ma. And you can take *that* to the fuckin' bank."

Then he was gone and I stared in the space where he was for several, speechless, open-mouthed seconds, letting his words penetrate my brain.

And then something else hit my chest. It was that weird, warm, happy glow, but it was so intense, so invasive, so overwhelming that it made the painful, burning, hot ball that had been there before seem puny.

Then I burst into fresh tears, these loud and wailing.

Smooth Move Hector divested me of my coffee cup, handed it to the waiting Daisy and pulled me into his arms.

I shoved my face into his chest, wrapped my arms around his waist and bawled like a baby.

And I didn't care who saw that, either.

Finally, I said into his chest between sobs, "After this, if I cry again, shoot me."

"No fuckin' way," was Hector's (unhelpful, in my personal opinion) response.

I looked up at him. "Seriously, Hector, shoot me! My mascara's ruined! It's going to take me hours to unpuff my eyes enough to put makeup on again!"

Through my watery, mascara-clogged eyes, I watched his brows draw together. "You want me to shoot you because your mascara's ruined?"

"Yes!" I cried.

He burst out laughing.

"I'm not being funny!" I wailed, smacking him on the shoulder.

Hector's head descended and he gave me a light kiss on my quivering lips.

His mouth moved away half an inch and he said, "*Mi cielo*, you're hilarious."

"Holy crap, we need a party," Ally announced behind my back before I could retort.

I turned in Hector's arms.

"You're partying at my gig tonight. Bring Sadie," Stella put in.

"We'll all put on sparkles!" Daisy shouted.

"Oh shit, white man rock 'n' roll and sparkles. Fuck," Shirleen muttered.

"Pre-gig margaritas and girlie dress up at the loft!" Ava declared.

"I'll get Nick to babysit," Jules threw in.

"I'll bring my guac and chips," Jet offered.

"Rock on!" Indy shouted.

"You got *that* right, sister," Roxie added, and, for some bizarre reason, they all burst into fits of giggles.

Hector stopped laughing and murmured, "Fucking hell."

I looked up at him, not crying anymore, and whispered (with a small tremor in my voice), "I think I'm in trouble."

At that, Hector's head bent to look at me, and slowly, he smiled.

# Chapter 18
# Eighties Rock Video Bimbo

*Sadie*

"Yeah?" Luke's voice sounded over the security speaker by the elevator to his and Ava's loft.

"It's Hector and Sadie," Hector replied.

My heart clenched at those words.

He said, *Hector and Sadie.*

Hector and Sadie!

Oh my God.

We were Hector... *and*... Sadie!

"Elevator's on its way," Luke said through my freak out, clearly not seeing anything wrong with a "Hector and Sadie'.

Then a different panic seized me, and without a word, I turned and started toward the door.

I got three steps when an arm sliced around my waist, Smooth Move Hector caught me and turned me into his body.

"Where you goin'?" he asked, his brows drawn, his eyes scanning my face.

"I can't do this," I blurted. Pretend Sadie gone. Ice Princess Sadie enjoying a cocktail by an imaginary pool. Take Charge Sadie getting a facial. It was just me and I couldn't do this.

No way.

I was no Rock Chick. I'd never been to a rock concert in my life.

My favorite recording artist was Madonna, for goodness sake!

"Why?" Hector asked.

"I like Madonna," I told him, unable to stop myself.

Hector stared at me like I'd just announced my devotion to Engelbert Humperdinck.

"What?"

"Madonna!" I cried as the elevator doors opened. "Like a Virgin? Confessions on a Dance Floor? You know, Madonna!"

His face cleared and he started grinning. "I know Madonna."

"Well then, there you go. I'm not a Rock Chick. I'm a Pop Chick. Pop Chicks aren't cool. They don't go to *gigs*. They don't rock out! They go to clubs and dance! And I didn't ever do that, either!"

He ignored my rant, turned us, arm firm around my shoulders, and guided us toward the elevator.

I struggled.

With little effort, Hector controlled the struggle and got me in the elevator.

"Hector!" I snapped. "Didn't you hear me?"

"You'll be fine," he said as he leaned to the side, taking me with him and tagging the button.

"I won't be fine."

"You will."

"I won't!

The doors closed and Hector curled my solid body into his arms.

He was still grinning.

"I see I gotta loosen you up," he told me, his eyes dancing, but they were warm and intense.

Oh no.

I knew *that* look.

"Hector—" I started, but he didn't listen. Instead, he kissed me.

In about a nanosecond, he loosened me up all right. So much, we were full-on necking when the elevator doors opened.

"Yowza, get a room!" I heard Ally call.

I pulled free of Hector's arms, looked into Luke and Ava's cool LoDo loft and felt my face go flush as my eyes bugged out.

Everyone was there, including two guys I'd never seen before. There were margarita glasses scattered amongst bowls of chips and guacamole with the bizarre addition of loads of tubes, tubs, brushes, combs, sprays, bottles, jars, mirrors and hair dryers.

The Rock Chicks were all in various stages of... I didn't know what. Their makeup was way over the top, their hair teased out to maximum volume and they were all dressed like, well, there was no nice way to put it... skanks.

"We've decided to go groupie!" Ava announced happily.

"Not groupie, Eighties Rock Video Bimbo," Indy corrected her (like there was a difference).

Eighties Rock Video Bimbo?

Were they nuts?

Regardless of this alarming announcement, which would make anyone in their right mind turn and flee, Hector moved me into the loft and Luke got close to us.

"You got a choice, babe," Luke said, and my eyes turned to him when I realized he was talking to me. "You can stay here and get skanked or you can go out tonight with Hector and me. We'll probably get shot at but I'm thinkin' it's the better choice."

My mouth dropped open and my heart started beating harder before I realized he was teasing me.

Still, teasing or not, I turned to Hector and said, "I don't want you to get shot at."

Hector was grinning. "I'm not gonna get shot at."

I was not deterred. "You get in a situation where you even *think* you're going to get shot at, you exit said situation, pronto," I demanded.

"Oowee, listen to Little Miss Bossy," Shirleen called.

I cut my eyes to Shirleen and she laughed at the ice rays I sent darting in her direction.

Yes, *laughed!*

Whatever.

I had bigger fish to fry.

I looked back at Hector. "Promise me."

"Sadie—"

"Promise!" I snapped.

"Shit, you're cute," Hector said rather than promising.

I narrowed my eyes. "I'm *not* cute and I'm *not* being funny. Now, promise."

He curled me to his front and his mouth touched mine.

When he lifted his mouth from mine, he murmured, "Promise."

"Well," I breathed. "Thank you."

He smiled.

I stared.

"I remember those happy days when it was all soft kisses and promises," Ava said.

I turned out of Hector's arms and caught Luke giving Ava a brows raised look that made his own unique promise, and his look was nearly as hot as the ones Hector gave me. My eyes moved to Ava and I saw her face had gone soft, but her teeth were biting her lip and I knew she knew she was in trouble. But the good kind.

"All right, enough of this. Hot Boys, out. Rock Chicks, T-minus thirty minutes to Stella and The Gypsies. We got *work* to do," one of the guys I didn't know said and I recognized his voice.

It was Tod. And, out of Burgundy Rose drag, he was tall, slim and had a crew cut.

"Hi, Tod," I called. I pulled away from Hector and walked a few steps into the loft.

"Hi, girlie." Tod smiled. "This is my other half, Stevie." He gestured to the handsome Hispanic man who was mixing a pitcher of margaritas and smiling at me. "Stevie, this is Sadie."

"Hey, Sadie. Welcome to the madhouse," Stevie said, and I couldn't help it. He was so right, I smiled at him and gave him a wave.

"Babe, we're goin'," Luke told Ava, and without hesitation she moved to him.

I watched as he took her in his arms and put his lips to hers, but he didn't kiss her. I couldn't hear, but he whispered something to her, his mouth moving against hers and whatever he said made her smile and melt into him.

I felt jealousy, pure and acid, burning through me before Hector cut off my line of sight.

"You come to me when you're done," Hector ordered as his hand went to the side my neck and up, fingers sliding into my hair.

I looked up at him, the jealousy still burning but my stomach pitched all the same.

"Okay."

"I don't know how long this thing will take Luke and me, but I probably won't make it tonight. Lee, Eddie and Hank are designated drivers. They're goin' to the gig. Tex and Duke both said they were goin', too. If Mace isn't workin', he's always at Stella's gigs and tonight is one of those nights. You stay close to one of them, close enough to touch 'em. All night. Got me?"

I nodded.

His face dipped to mine and he murmured, voice so soft, I barely heard him, "Now, kiss me good-bye."

I blinked. The jealous acid drifted away and the stomach pitch turned to a belly melt.

"What?" I whispered.

"Kiss me," he repeated.

Regardless of my melted belly, the Ice Princess had finished her cocktail and decided to take over. "I think we've already made enough of a spectacle of ourselves."

His eyes went warm and intense. "All right, *mamita*. I'll kiss you."

Then he did, hot and hungry and just as quickly as it started, his mouth broke from mine and he was gone.

I stared, my body swaying without his close as the elevator doors closed on him and Luke. Hector stared at me, too, his face soft and knowing. Then the doors shut him from sight.

"All righty then," Ava called. "Sadie, get over here. We've got work to do."

Slowly, I turned and everyone was smiling at me.

Oh my.

꿈

"I wanna be you!" I shouted, drunk on margaritas mixed with Fat Tires as Stella and her band stood in a Rock Chick huddle during one of her breaks.

Her eyes turned to me. "Funny, until you came in tonight, looking all groupie slut, I wanted to be you. I love the way you dress." Her eyes did a full body sweep and she gave me a meaningful, but smiley, look.

I knew what she was talking about. Seconds after Hector and Luke left, Daisy informed me that she, Roxie, Tod and Stevie had gone shopping. Since I was shorter and smaller than the rest of the girls, I couldn't share clothes. So they'd bought me my Eighties Rock Video Bimbo outfit. It came complete with a torn up black T-Shirt with "Stella and The Blue Moon Gypsies" across the breasts (so torn, it was falling off one of my shoulders, exposing my thin black bra strap and the two "o's" in "moon' were blue moons), a shorter-than-short (or even decent) denim mini-skirt with a ragged hem, a wide, black belt with a heavy, oval buckle with a rose stamped on it (they'd heard about Hector's tattoo, of course) and a pair of black motorcycle boots.

Yes, *motorcycle boots*.

Yes, Seth Townsend's perfect Ice Princess daughter was tramping around Denver in *motorcycle boots*.

Replete with square toes and silver hoops connecting straps that went up from the soles and around the ankle.

The boots were *aces*.

My hair was teased out to uber-volume, all waves and ringlets going up, out and down, and my makeup was so beyond heavy, I felt it on my face like it weighed a ton.

And I didn't care.

I didn't care that I looked like a bimbo groupie from hell.

Because *I loved rock 'n' roll!*

"I love rock 'n' roll!" I shouted at Stella.

"Join the club, sister," Ally shouted to me, laughing.

"Good Lord," Shirleen muttered and Daisy giggled.

"Will you teach me to play guitar?" I asked Stella, knowing I was pushing it. She was a big star. Well, in Denver anyway, if the crowd was anything to go by. And she had a recording contract. They were going on the road soon to promote their new album.

"Sure," Stella replied on a smile.

"I'll pay," I promised.

Her smile got bigger. "Friends and family discount," she said then leaned in and whispered, "which means free."

"Cut your teeth on Guitar Hero, it's the only way to go," Annette, who I'd met when the Rock Chicks came to my gallery weeks ago and who also ran a head shop across the street from Fortnum's, advised.

"Guitar Hero!" Buzz, Stella's bass guitarist snapped, sounding (and looking) affronted. "Fuck Guitar Hero!"

"Guitar Hero's the shit," Annette shot back.

"Guitar Hero's for pussies," Buzz returned then looked at me with a smile. "*I'll* teach you guitar," he offered.

"I'll teach you drums. Drums are where it's *at*." Pong, Stella's drummer, moved in.

"Fuck the drums, I'll teach you the sax. You blow a horn, you know cool." Hugo, Stella's saxophonist, got close.

"Yay!" I shouted and clapped, too excited to turn any of them down.

An arm went around my waist and I found my body moved back several feet from the band. I looked up and saw Eddie had hold of me.

"Maybe you can decide to learn to be a rock star when you aren't shit-faced," Eddie suggested, eyes on the band.

"Okay," I agreed readily, even though I'd already decided I was going to be a rock star.

Forget Veronica Mars.

I wanted rock 'n' roll!

Eddie's eyes moved to me. He looked at me a second and I saw him smile, dimple and everything.

"I like your dimple," I told him.

His eyes flashed then they got all glittery (which was hot!), and, just like his brother, his body started shaking with laughter.

Finally, his eyes moved to Jet.

"You wanna take over here?" he asked her.

Jet looked at Eddie then her gaze moved to Daisy, then Ava, then to me.

"Let's go to the restroom," she announced and didn't wait for me to reply. She just took my hand and dragged me to the restroom.

When we got into the restroom, no one used the facilities. Just like the girls on *Sex and the City*, they all turned to the mirrors and started fixing their lip gloss.

I'd always wanted to go to the restroom with my girlfriends and fix my lip gloss.

And here I was, *doing it!*

Wasn't that *great?*

"I love Eddie. He's my favorite of Hector's siblings," I informed Jet magnanimously, turning to a mirror and digging my lip gloss out of my pocket (Indy had taught me how to go purse-less at a rock gig: lip gloss, ID, money and credit card in front pocket, cell phone in back).

"I'll let him know." Jet smiled at me.

"You have a beautiful smile," I told her. "You're really pretty. But when you smile, I swear to *God*, you're so beautiful, you make my heart squeeze."

I saw Jet blink like this surprised her (and how bizarre was *that*? she had to know she had a beautiful smile; if she didn't she was *blind*) but I was too happy to be putting on lip gloss in the restroom with my girlfriends to take too much notice.

"Eddie likes you, too," Ava told me, and I saw through the mirror her eyes were on Jet.

"Aces!" I cried, excited that Eddie liked me. Heck, excited that *anyone* would like me.

Daisy giggled her Christmas bells giggle.

Jet got closer to me. "He's a little worried about you, though."

I finished with my lip gloss and looked at her as I shoved it back in my pocket (this was hard, my skirt was *tight*).

"Worried?"

"Yeah," she replied, and I realized with some surprise that she was being serious.

"Why on earth is he worried?" I asked, forgetting, for one shining moment, that my life was one devastating trauma after the other.

"He doesn't know, can't put his finger on it," Jet explained. "He talked to me about it and he wanted us to make sure you're okay."

Daisy and Ava got closer and I looked at them. They all looked serious now and my happy buzz slipped a notch.

"You know, sugar, I been through what you been through," Daisy told me.

My confused eyes moved to her.

"You have?"

She got closer. "Was workin' at Smithie's, it's a strip joint. Marcus part-owned it back then. I didn't know him, but I saw him come in every once in a while. After a show, one of the customers raped me behind Smithie's. It wasn't as bad as what you went through but it was bad."

At this announcement, I felt my face pale as my happy buzz vaporized.

Daisy went on, "Smithie and Marcus found out and they flipped. Smithie doubled up on bouncers and made it policy that all the girls were escorted to their cars after we closed. And Marcus, well... that's when Marcus and me got together, kind of. It wasn't like he asked me out, but every day after it happened he sent me bouquets of daisies. Every day. For weeks. Until my house was so filled with pretty flowers that it was hard to keep my mind on ugly thoughts."

I stared at her, my heart hurting for her. Then I whispered, "I *knew* I liked Marcus."

She smiled at me, reached out, caught my hand and held it tight.

"When he decided the time was right, he came at me. It was tough on me and I made it tough on him, but he never gave up. He kept comin' until I gave in. And I'm glad he did."

"You have to know," Ava put in before I could process what Daisy said. "That what it is with these guys is different than what it is with other guys. It's different than what it is with the kind of guy who would hurt you, either what that man did to you or how other men can tear you down. They come on strong because they *are* strong, not because they're jerks or anything."

I didn't know what to say, so I said, "Okay."

"Hector's a good guy," Jet told me, and I looked at her.

It hit my drunken brain what they were saying and I felt my shields go up automatically.

"I know," I replied.

"You have to let him in." Daisy squeezed my hand.

Oh no.

Just.

No.

They didn't get it. They probably couldn't. They weren't me.

There were two sides to this coin. The one side was me and the fact that Hector was likely too good for me. The other side was life as I knew it, that I couldn't trust anyone and that nothing worked out for me. It couldn't. I was who I was and I deserved whatever Hector had in store for me, using me then leaving me behind.

Maybe a girl who'd had friends, whose mother hadn't been murdered while protecting her, whose father hadn't kept her imprisoned in a beautiful mansion her whole life, a girl who hadn't been brutally raped, could trust, could understand.

But that girl wasn't me.

I couldn't tell them *any* of that.

I wanted to.

But I couldn't.

Because they wouldn't get it.

"We're okay," Pretend Sadie promised on a smile.

They all stared at me.

"No, really," I said.

"You're holdin' somethin' back," Daisy accused.

"No, I'm not," I lied. I was drunk but not drunk enough to share. I'd done enough sharing. Sharing was only going to get me in deeper and I was deep enough as it was.

Ava looked at Daisy then at me. "You'll want to run, to keep yourself safe. I know the feeling, we all do. Listen to the voices of experience and move beyond this faster than we did. It's worth it, I promise." I nodded, but she got closer. "Seriously, Sadie, it's worth it. I promise," she repeated.

I knew she knew that, the way Luke held her that night. And I was glad she had that. She was sweet.

But that was never going to happen for me.

I wanted it, more than anything in the world, to know Hector was putting his arms around *me*. But he wasn't. There was no "me". He was either putting his arms around "His Sadie", a creature that didn't exist, or his latest conquest.

Simple as that.

These were good women. They'd never been taught that lesson.

And I hoped they never learned.

I pulled in my lips and pretended to think about it.

Then I nodded.

"I don't—" Daisy started, staring at me closely.

"Let her alone," Jet cut her off.

"But—" Daisy went on.

"Give her time to think," Jet interrupted again and looked at me. "You need to talk, anytime, day, night, whenever, you call one of us. We're here, Sadie. Always."

I pulled my lips in and didn't have to pretend or force the tears that were shining in my eyes at what she said. I was wishing this could be real, could be my life, but I knew it couldn't.

Unable to speak, I just nodded again.

"We're done here," Jet told Ava and Daisy.

"We're not done," Daisy pushed.

"We're done," Ava announced firmly.

Daisy dropped my hand but only to cross her arms on her chest.

"I'll be watchin' you," she warned.

I decided to set this firmly aside and go back to the enjoying the drunken portion of the night.

"Okay," I told her like I could care less.

Jet smiled at Ava.

Daisy narrowed her eyes at me.

We heard Stella's voice and I knew the band was going to start again.

"Rock 'n' roll!" I shouted, whirled and used that as my excuse for escape.

I threw open the door, flew out of the restroom, got two steps into the hall and slammed into something solid.

Hands came to my upper arms. I looked up and all my breath left me in a rush.

"Jerry?" I whispered, not believing my eyes or my fucking terrible luck.

I mean, seriously!

Why me?

Out of the frying pan and into the fire!

I looked again, but my eyes did not deceive me. It *was* Jerry, one of the henchmen in my father's gentleman army. Tall, blond-haired, blue-eyed, good-looking, and normally, mostly silent. He'd disappeared the minute the DEA moved in and I hadn't seen him since.

"Sadie," Jerry replied.

"Who're you?" Ava asked from beside me.

"Stand back. Now." Daisy didn't care who he was, and at her words all the girls got close to me.

Jerry ignored Daisy. "Your father's got a message for you."

My eyes went wide.

Then my back went straight and my chin went out.

All right.

I'd had *enough*.

This was *not* happening.

I'd had a tough day. A tough week! A tough fucking life!

I was going to take no more.

"Is that so? Well I have a message for him, too," I snapped back.

Jerry's hands went tight on my arms. So tight, they hurt.

"Quiet and listen to me."

"Last warning, stand back." Daisy got in closer.

I ignored her and leaned in. "No, you listen to me. No messages, no nothing. My father doesn't exist anymore. You tell him that." Then, for good measure, I used one of Hector's badass lines, "Got me?"

Jerry ignored my fairy princess/bimbo groupie badass and returned, "Sadie, I'm warnin' you, Seth is losin' patience with you."

Ice Princess gave him a Chill Factor Sub-Zero Glare. "Do I look like I care?"

He leaned in and we were nose-to-nose right before he said threateningly, "Girl, you better care."

"Take your hands off her." I heard Eddie say from behind Jerry.

I looked around to see him standing there, feet planted wide, arms loose at his sides and looking unhappy.

Jerry let me go and turned to Eddie. Then he gave an amused hoot.

"Detective Chavez," Jerry said in an ugly voice. "Now I'm confused. I thought it was your brother who was tappin' her ass."

I gasped.

"Uh-oh," Ava said from beside me as Eddie's body went visibly taut.

Jet, Daisy, Ava and I huddled as Eddie warned Jerry, "You got one second to disappear."

"Yeah?" Jerry taunted, pretending to look around. "You sure you wanna try to get a piece of me? I don't see Nightingale at your back."

"Eddie, let's just go," Jet put in.

"Move away," Eddie told Jet, not taking his eyes from Jerry.

"Eddie—" Jet kept trying.

"Jet," Eddie clipped, and that was all he had to say. Jet shuffled us all back. We moved as one in our Rock Chick huddle, all of our eyes locked on Eddie and Jerry.

"Fuck, you think you can get a piece of me." Jerry sounded amused.

Eddie didn't say a word. He didn't move. His eyes didn't leave Jerry.

"This is gonna be fun," Jerry went on and Eddie still didn't reply, pushing Jerry to ask, "You gonna stare at me all night?"

Eddie still didn't move.

But he did speak.

"No, I'm gonna ask you what Townsend would think if he knew you been meetin' with Donny Balducci."

*What?*

Jerry and Donny?

No way.

Jerry's eyes narrowed. "You been watchin' me, spic?"

I gasped again, this time angrily.

"Oh Lord," Ava muttered.

"What did he just say?" Jet asked, her voice trembling.

"Stand down, Jet, I think Eddie's got this covered," Daisy told Jet, pulling the huddle back another few steps.

Eddie had gone silent again, but the air had changed. It became heavy and very, *very* scary.

Jerry waited for a reaction to his racial slur, and when none was forthcoming, he (stupidly, if you asked me), decided to create one.

His arm reached out. He planted his hand in Eddie's chest and I saw him give a shove.

I stared and my mouth dropped open.

I was certain he'd given a shove, but Eddie's body didn't move.

No kidding, it didn't move an inch.

Solid as a rock.

I watched surprise slide across Jerry's face, surprise I was pretty certain sure was mingled with a hint of fear as Eddie encouraged in a low, menacing voice, "Keep goin'."

"Fuck you!" Jerry clipped and immediately threw a punch.

Quick as a flash, Eddie ducked but came up. Body cocked to the side and swinging, he landed a fist in Jerry's stomach and I heard Jerry's awful grunt.

"Oh for goodness sake, we're missin' Stella," Daisy grumbled as if Eddie's fight with one of my father's henchmen was akin to an annoying traffic delay on the way to a movie and I looked at her, mouth still open. She was digging in her purse (not all Rock Chicks went purse-less) and she came out with a stun gun.

Oh boy.

This was getting worse by the second!

Jerry threw another punch. Eddie's chin jerked back, and again, Jerry missed his target. But Eddie moved swiftly and landed another blow, this time to Jerry's kidneys, and this time Jerry's grunt was filled with pain.

"Give me that stun gun! I want to stun that jackass!" Jet cried, her hand going out to wrap around Daisy's wrist and the now crackling stun gun.

That was when Jet and Daisy started to scuffle, both trying to get control of the stun gun.

And there it was.

The night got even worse!

My eyes swung from Jet and Daisy to Jerry and Eddie as Jerry went at Eddie, advancing quickly. Eddie was retreating but he was weaving almost casually (not joking, casually!) while Jerry tried some one-two combinations, but none of them connected.

We had an audience now. People were amassing in the hall to watch, but no one seemed to want to get involved. That was, no one except a big blond man who was shoving his way through from the back.

"What the fuck?" Tex asked when he made it to the front, right when Eddie stopped retreating and weaving and landed another savage body blow, causing another grunt of pain from Jerry. "That's it, Chavez, fuck him up!" Tex boomed his approval. What he did not do, I noticed immediately, was intervene. Then he threw back his head and gave out a wild catcall.

Really!

These people were *nuts!*

"This is *just great*," I snapped to no one as Daisy and Jet were grappling for the stun gun next to me, Ava was trying to stay out of their way, Eddie and Jerry kept at it and Tex settled in for the show. "Can't I have one trauma free night?" I went on complaining (again, to no one).

At that moment, I had a stroke of luck and Daisy dropped the stun gun.

Without thinking and fed *up*, I bent down, picked up the gun, and Ice Princess in total control, just like I'd done it dozens of times before, I walked right up to Jerry, reached up and touched the hissing prongs to his shoulder.

Hector told me a second would give an incapacitating jolt, three would bring him down. He wasn't wrong. After the third second, Jerry was at my feet. But I was bent over and I kept the stun gun on him even as his body jerked around on the floor with the bolts I was zapping into him.

Around about the seventh second, Eddie pulled me away.

"I think that'll do it, *chica*," Eddie said in my ear, his arm around my waist, my back against his front.

I looked up at him, nodded, then looked down at Jerry.

"Tell your lord and master to fuck off," I said to the blinking but otherwise unmoving Jerry. "I mean it. I'm done with him, done with you, done with that life. You can tell Donny when you see him next to fuck off, too. Get this straight, Jerry, tell them both to... *fuck... off.*" Jerry just kept blinking at me, and I decided to take that as his agreement to deliver my message.

I took a deep breath and shoved Jerry and my father mentally aside (for the time being). I turned in Eddie's arm. It went loose and I smiled up at him, deciding to mix New Nice Sadie with Pretend Happy Sadie and get on with the *good* part of the night.

"Thanks for fighting for me," I said breezily. "You want me to buy you a beer?"

Eddie stared at me blank-faced for a second then his eyes went warm and the dimple came out.

What he didn't do was answer.

"Okay then," I decided for him in order to move past this latest fiasco (which I had, again, somehow survived, and luckily so had everyone else). "Beer for you," I told Eddie and went on. "Shots for the girls. Come on!" I yelled, turned, stepped over the prone Jerry and started to head to the bar.

Then I stopped, turned back around and leaned down to Jerry again. "One more thing. I know I zapped a bunch of your brain cells just now, but the word you were looking for has *three* syllables." I lifted my fist, shoved it close to Jerry's face, my fingers flicked out and I counted them off as I spoke, "His... pan... ic, you moron."

Then I straightened and saw Jet, Ava and Daisy grinning at me, but I whirled on a flounce and stomped away on my new motorcycle boots.

I was shoving through the people (not really getting very far) when they parted like I was Moses and they were the Red Sea. Tex's hand came to the top of my head.

"I'll take a beer, too," Tex said to me, his hand leaving my head, but he didn't leave my side.

"I'll buy you a beer. Heck, I'm rich. In fact, I'm totally loaded. I'll buy *everyone* in the club a fucking beer," I answered.

Tex boomed out a laugh.

"She's not buyin' the house a round," Eddie said, materializing close to my other side and making me jump. I hadn't even felt his approach.

"She's rich, what's there to do with money but buy a round?" Tex asked good-naturedly.

"She's not fuckin' buyin' the house a round," Eddie returned sharply.

"All right, badass, stand down. Shee-it," Tex gave in.

I would not be denied some form of generous gesture, however. "I'm buying you both a beer," I told Eddie, stopping at the bar.

"I'm drivin', no beer," Eddie looked down at me.

Blooming heck, but being nice was not easy.

"Well then, I'm buying Tex a beer and the girls shots," I returned.

Eddie grinned. "*That* you can do."

I gave him the Ice Princess Icicle Ray of Death Glare.

"Well, thank you," I said coldly.

His arm came around my shoulders, he tucked me into his side and he kissed the side of my head.

*Unbelievable.*

Was the Ice Princess, like, *invisible* to these people?

"Yo!" Eddie called.

The bartender trotted up and Eddie gave my shoulder an affectionate squeeze as indication I should give my order.

Apparently, she was.

Oh well, so be it.

I decided to skip the fancy stuff and ordered straight tequila shots.

What the heck.

Right?

⚓

"I can walk to the door," I told Lee as he walked beside me up to Hector's front door.

Lee looked down at me and smiled. "I know."

I weaved a little bit.

Seriously, he had a *great* smile.

And at that moment, I decided that he should be made aware of this fact.

"You know," I informed him (yes, I was drunk, or more drunk, or, say, *uber*-drunk), "I don't know if anyone's ever told you this but you have a *very* handsome smile."

He slung an arm around my shoulders (what *was* it with these guys and the arms around the shoulders? not that I was complaining; it was nice, but still, how touchy could you be?).

"It's been mentioned," he replied, his head coming up to look at the house and his chin gave a jerk.

My eyes followed his and I saw Hector standing inside his open front door. He was dressed: jeans, boots, white t-shirt under a buttoned-up but untucked flannel. The flannel was bunched up around the gun that was on his belt at the side of his hip.

I decided at that moment that Hector looked good wearing a gun.

Then again, Hector always looked good.

"Hi," I called and waved to Hector as Lee and I walked up the front steps.

Hector just stared at me. Then his eyes cut to Lee.

It was then I realized Lee's arm was still around me.

I looked up at Lee when we stopped in front of Hector and informed him helpfully, "You might want to take your arm away. Blanca tells me Hector doesn't like men touching me."

"Blanca told you that?" Lee asked, his smile (and arm) still firmly in place.

"Yes. She's known Hector, like, his *whole* life, so I think she's in the position to know."

Lee nodded, his smile somehow bigger like he was trying not to laugh. Then his eyes moved to Hector and he said, "I tried to stop it."

Hector looked at Lee, then looked at me and he muttered, "Oh fuck."

"It was Ally's idea," Lee told Hector.

"What was Ally's idea?" Hector asked Lee.

"It was *not* Ally's idea!" I cried.

"It wasn't!" super-power-eared Ally yelled from the open back window of Lee's Explorer. "It was Sadie's idea. I just was offering moral support."

"Shut up, Ally!" Indy shouted out the open passenger side window.

"I will not shut up! I'm not taking the fall for this one!" Ally shouted back.

I turned to the car, dislodging Lee's arm. I lifted both my hands and pressed down. "No one's going to take a fall. Everyone calm down. It's all okay. *It's rock 'n' roll!*" I screamed.

"*Righteous!*" Ally screamed back.

"*Rock on, sister!*" Indy screamed, too.

"It's rock 'n' roll?" Lee asked, sounding as amused as he looked.

"You all wanna quit screamin' at three o'clock in the mornin' in my fuckin' neighborhood?" Hector suggested.

Mm, well maybe we were being an *eensy* bit loud.

"Time for beddie by," I announced (sounding like Ralphie). I got up on tiptoe, kissed Lee's cheek (like Ralphie and Buddy would do to me), turned and gave Indy and Ally a double devil's horns (like Ava taught me), and shouted, "Rock on!"

They shouted back in unison, "Rock on!"

"Christ," Hector muttered, but I ignored him, walked into the house and headed toward the stairs.

I was in his bedroom. I'd turned on the light by the bed and was sitting on its side when he arrived.

"What did Lee try to stop?" Hector asked when he hit the room.

I leaned over, yanked off a boot then held it up to him.

"Look at this boot!" I cried, "Isn't it *aces?* Daisy and the gang bought it for me. They bought me my whole outfit!" Then I threw the boot at him, thinking it was so cool, he might want to get a closer look.

He caught it, stared at it for less than a second, then tossed it toward the pile that had somehow sprung up in the short time since Blanca's tidying effort.

"Hey!" I snapped. "Don't throw my new boot. It'll get scuffed."

Hector advanced, saying, "It's a motorcycle boot. It's supposed to be scuffed."

Oh.

I didn't know that.

Boy, I had a lot to learn about being a Rock Chick.

I was going to have to start taking notes!

I leaned over and pulled off the other one while he stopped in front of me. Then I hesitated.

Oh, what the heck.

I threw it in the pile and took off my socks.

"Can I ask you to do somethin' for me?" Hector asked.

I looked up and saw he had his hands on his hips and was towering over me. I couldn't read his expression, mainly because it was unreadable.

I decided I didn't like him towering over me. I also decided I didn't like so many clothes on him. He looked *far* better naked.

So I stood up and started to unbutton his shirt.

"What?" I said to his shirt, concentrating on my task.

"Burn that fuckin' skirt."

My hands stilled and my head snapped back.

"Excuse me?"

"That skirt. Burn it."

I was confused. I liked my skirt. No, I *loved* it.

"Why?" I asked.

His hands came to my shirt and he pulled it up. My arms went with it and he whipped it off.

"*Mamita*, just don't wear it again."

I decided to give in and not wear it in front of him, but not burn it. I could wear it on Crete and he'd never know.

"Oh, all right," I agreed, but I didn't sound happy about it (because I wasn't).

His hands came to my hips and mine went back to his shirt.

"Now, what did Lee try to stop?" He went back to his earlier subject.

I'd kind of lost track of things so my mind rewound the evening and I remembered Eddie's fight with Jerry, which Lee didn't even see, and I got confused.

"Me stun gunning Jerry, my father's henchman?" I guessed as I finished with the buttons, lifted my hands and pulled the shirt off his shoulders.

His hands left my hips when I leaned into him and tugged the flannel down his arms. Then I whipped it around, shrugged it on and started to button the two buttons at my breasts while his hands came back to me. This time to the front button and zip on my skirt.

"Nope, Eddie called, told me about Jerry. Lee knows I know about that. What else happened tonight, after the fight?"

I pulled in my lips and tried to think as Hector slid down the zip on my skirt (and thinking was not easy to do). I decided to help him and lifted the hem of the flannel to get it out of his way. He slid the skirt over my hips and pushed down. It fell to my ankles, but Hector's hands, and body, froze.

Then he moved. One hand went low on my right hip. The other one went to the side of my belly by my hip and he framed the bandage that was at my hip bone with his hands.

"What the fuck?" he muttered, then his eyes cut to me.

"Oh yeah!" I yelled, even though he was right there, barely a foot away. "I got a tattoo."

Hector's brows went up and I smiled at him.

"That must be what Lee was talking about," I informed him. "He didn't think it was a good idea. Neither did Eddie. Or Hank, for that matter. Tex thinks I'm a nut. Duke and Mace liked it, though, and the girls thought it was *aces*. So do I. Look!"

I bent over and peeled the bandage away, exposing the brand new tattoo, it and my skin glistening with tattoo goo.

It was a black panther, fierce, graceful and snarling.

I *loved* it.

"It's a black panther," I informed Hector unnecessarily as his hands were still framing it. His body was leaned slightly to the side, his head cocked and his eyes were locked on my hip. "I thought my idea was lame at first. But I couldn't think of anything else that represented you." I noticed his head jerk and his eyes slice to me, but I didn't process it. I kept talking, "Then I told the artist guy about you, that you had black hair and black eyes that could go really intense and you were a badass and I liked the way you moved, graceful and in control, like a cat. He sketched that and me and *all* the girls, even Shirleen, thought it was *perfect*. So, I said—"

I stopped talking because Hector's hands moved away from my hip and they closed around my waist, tight. So tight, his fingers were digging in and that got my attention.

He'd straightened and those black eyes I told the tattoo artist about *were* intense. Beyond intense. They were burning right into me.

"How fucked up are you?" he asked.

I thought this was a strange question, so my head tilted to the side and I asked back, "What?"

He let me go, but only so he could pull off his t-shirt and he did this fast.

At the sight of his chest, my breath left me in a whoosh.

"How fucked up are you?" he repeated. He unclipped his gun from his belt and threw it on the nightstand, all the while looking at me. "Sadie, fucked up. Shitfaced. Trashed. Loaded. *Drunk*. How fucked up are you?"

I was still confused, watching him, feeling his heat, his intensity and something hungry about him. Seriously hungry. Therefore, I was watching him, confused, yet getting turned on at the same time.

*Way* turned on.

He leaned down and pulled off his boots, sending them, in turn, sailing across the room.

Then he hands came back to me, his thumbs went into my underwear, hooking into the sides. He shoved them down until they fell to my ankles.

Oh my *God*.

Did he just do that?

"Sadie, answer me."

"Um, on a scale of one to ten?" I asked, unsure how to answer. Unsure what to do. Not even sure I still remembered how to breathe.

He lifted me up. I let out a surprised gasp and my arms and legs wrapped around him.

"What are you doing?" I cried.

"You put my mark on you. To show my appreciation, I'm gonna fuck you until you scream my name, and I wanna make sure you remember it. Now, how fuckin' drunk are you?"

My heart was beating wildly, my belly had melted to oblivion and I was pretty certain sure I'd had a mini-orgasm.

What I wasn't was drunk. Not anymore.

"I'm not drunk anymore."

"Good." He put a knee to the bed but didn't put me down. "Now, *mamita*, where the tat is, I can't be on top so you got two choices. Either you ride me or I get creative. Your choice, but choose now."

I swallowed.

"Hector—" I started.

He cut me off, "Now."

Oh my.

He meant business.

And I liked his business.

So, I whispered, "Creative."

He grinned, slow and sweet.

Then he got creative.

# Chapter 19
# Ibuprofen and Midol

### *Sadie*

"*Preciosa*, wake up."

My eyes opened and I saw Hector sitting on the side of the bed. He had on jeans and a tight-fitting, navy t-shirt and he looked awake and alert.

I glanced at him through slitted eyes.

He had worked last night, until late. Then he'd vigorously shown his appreciation for my tattoo just like he said he would.

And, really, how bizarre was *that*? It was *my* tattoo. But apparently Hector was more excited about it than I was. As in *loads* more in a macho-man, badass, fuck-me-until-I-screamed-his-name type of way, of course.

Though, I didn't scream his name when he made me come, but I gasped it, and I did this *loud*.

Nevertheless, *he* hadn't tied one on last night, mixing margaritas with Fat Tires and tequila shots. *He* was likely not hungover like I knew I was at that very moment. *He* was not having a life filled with daily multiple-traumas. And lastly, *he* didn't have an opening at his gallery tomorrow night.

So *he* could be awake and alert on a Sunday morning.

*I* was hungover. I felt it in my stomach and my head. So *I* was going to sleep.

To communicate all of that, I mumbled, "Sleep." Then turned and burrowed into the pillows.

Once I did this, the covers were pulled down and I made a peeved noise. But he ignored this. His hands went to my waist. He twisted me, pulling me up and across his lap, settling me there and his arms came around me.

I decided to ignore his latest smooth move and shoved my face in his neck, burrowing into his heat and hoping he'd get the message.

"Sadie, look at me," he murmured, and the way he did made my heart squeeze painfully.

I took a deep breath, wondering what was happening now. I pulled my face from his neck and looked at him.

"Jimmy's downstairs," he told me.

I let out the breath.

That was it?

Another visitor?

Boy, Hector was a popular guy.

"Jimmy?" I asked.

"Detective Marker."

My body went tight.

Hector's hand went to my neck and slid up into my hair.

"Harvey Balducci was murdered last night."

All of a sudden, I felt even sicker.

"Oh my God," I whispered.

"Jimmy wants to talk to you."

That was when I understood and I felt something lodge in my throat. So big, it threatened to choke me.

"I didn't do it," I blurted, and as I was concentrating on swallowing, I didn't notice Hector's brows draw together.

"Sadie—"

I cut him off, beginning to feel panic slide through my system. "I didn't do it. I swear. I didn't."

The arm Hector had around me got tight and I watched his eyes start to narrow.

"What the fuck?"

I kept on, "I don't like Harvey. He's a jerk and I want him to stay away from me, but I didn't kill him, Hector. I swear."

I'd begun to tremble, my body shaking. Hector's hand came out of my hair and locked around my waist. Then he gave me a gentle but firm shake. I stilled and looked at him. His eyes were now fully narrowed and he looked angry.

"What the fuck are you talkin' about?"

"You said Detective Marker is here to talk to me—"

"Jimmy's here to make sure you hear it from someone who gives a shit. He's here to make sure you're okay. He's here to let you know Ricky got bonded out this morning. And he's here to ask you a few questions. He's not here because you're a suspect. Your phones are tapped, practically every move you make is followed by cameras, and you're never fuckin' alone. Even without that, no one would think it was you. Jesus, Sadie, what's in your fuckin' head?"

I felt fear replacing the panic in my system at the first part of his speech, so I missed most of the other stuff he said.

"Ricky was bonded out?" I breathed.

I watched, fascinated, as the anger slid out of his eyes and a different kind of anger replaced it (don't ask me how I knew this, I just knew). Then I saw a muscle leap in Hector's cheek.

"Yeah," he said. "I guess Donny and Marty were moved to brotherly love once Harvey'd been poisoned while on the inside."

I closed my eyes.

The doorbell rang.

Hector muttered, "Fuck."

I opened my eyes again and he was looking at me.

"Get dressed and come downstairs. We'll talk later about what was in your fuckin' head," he finished.

Great, *just great*.

He stood up, taking me with him and putting me on my feet.

I was realizing for the first time that I was naked as the day I was born when both of Hector's hands came to my neck, fingers sliding up in my hair, thumbs on the undersides of my jaw and he tipped my head back to look at him.

He touched his mouth to mine softly, eyes open the whole time, and when his head moved back half an inch, he said, voice low and powerful, "He isn't gonna fuckin' touch you."

He watched me until I nodded, my head moving against his hands.

Then he was gone.

I pulled my head together and quickly got dressed (in the forbidden skirt, but I shunned the Stella tee and put on Hector's flannel because it covered more). I ran to the bathroom and let out a surprised, muted scream when I looked at myself in the mirror.

Eighties Rock Video Bimbo was scary the night of, but she was hair-raising (literally) the morning after.

And Hector had seen me like that!

*And* kissed me!

Oh... my... *God!*

I took a deep breath and calmed the mental flip out. I washed my face, found Hector's brush and was tearing it through my wild, bimbo-groupie, morning after hair when there came a knock at the door.

Before I called, it opened and Hector came in. I just stared at him as he walked up to me and put a cup of steaming coffee on the side of the sink. He turned to me, grabbed my wrist, opened my palm with his other hand and planted four white pills in it.

"Hangover cocktail, ibuprofen and Midol. Don't ask, it works. They give you salve for the tattoo?" he asked.

I was staring at the pills, but I looked up at him and nodded.

"Douse it before you come down. You gotta keep it moist so it doesn't fade." He reached beyond me, opened the medicine cabinet, rooted through it and came out with a package of new tops for an electric toothbrush. He handed them to me without a word, touched my lips with his again and he was gone.

I kept watching the door, not knowing what to feel.

After my mom left (or, I should say, was murdered), whenever I was sick, my father sent one of our maids to take care of me. They did it because it was their job, not because they cared about me.

But no one had brought me a hangover cocktail in my life.

No one.

Shakily, I sucked down the pills, pulled his electric toothbrush out of its charger, found his toothpaste and went to town on my teeth. Once done, I dug the tattoo balm out of my skirt pocket, pulled up my skirt and peeled back the bandage to salve the tattoo. While I was righting everything, I heard the door-bell ring again.

I sighed, wondering what now. I wiped the goo off my hands with a towel, grabbed my mug and walked downstairs.

I stopped at the foot of the stairs.

The living room was filled with people. Detective Marker was there, and so were Jet and Eddie, Indy and Lee, Hank and Roxie and Daisy and Marcus.

Someone had uncovered and moved a couch and a coffee table into the living room. There was a box of donuts opened on the table. Everyone had a mug of coffee, apparently courtesy of Jet, who was holding the empty coffeepot and on her way back to the kitchen.

"Mornin' sugar, I brought hangover donuts," Daisy called, waving a glazed in my direction.

"How's the tattoo?" Roxie asked, sitting by Daisy on the couch and leaning toward the donut box.

I came unstuck and walked into the room.

"It's okay," I answered Roxie as she pulled out a long, glazed cinnamon twist. Then I looked around. "What are you all doing here?"

"Eddie heard the news. We had to come up to the Highlands anyway for *La Reunión* so I came with him," Jet told me on a smile then lifted the pot. "I'll make more coffee." And she exited the room.

"Lee heard, too," Indy said. "I came because you left your purse in the Explorer and because I'm nosy." Then she scrunched her nose, took a bite of a powdered sugar, chocolate icing-filled donut and grinned.

"Hank heard, too. I thought I'd come to introduce you to Shamus, our chocolate lab. He's out in Hank's SUV," Roxie added.

"Marcus heard, too. I decided to bring the donuts," Daisy finished.

That was super sweet of her, of all of them, because I knew they weren't there because of Family Meetings, returning my purse, being nosy, wanting to introduce me to family pets or bringing donuts. They were there for me.

This felt nice. *Super* nice.

Though, the very thought of donuts made me queasy.

I looked at Roxie.

"Why's Shamus in the car? Why didn't you bring him in?"

"I didn't know if you'd want me to, but I can go get him now," Roxie answered, her eyes lighting up.

"That'd be great," I smiled.

Before Roxie could move, Detective Marker cleared his throat.

"Maybe you can meet the dog in a minute, Sadie. If you don't mind, we need to talk."

Oh darn.

I minded.

I minded *loads*.

But my father taught me *never* to procrastinate. Get things done in a timely manner and do the tough jobs first to get them out of the way.

I'd much rather meet Shamus. But instead I blew out a sigh (even though it was rude) and said to Detective Marker, "All right."

I walked into the room and sat on the arm of the couch next to Indy.

"Hector told you Harvey was found dead last night?" Detective Marker asked me.

I nodded. "What happened?"

"We don't know. We're investigating. It looks like poison," Detective Marker answered.

"How could someone poison him in jail?" I asked.

"Don't know that either. They're lookin' into it. You know Donny posted bond for Ricky?" Detective Marker carried on.

Indy's hand went to my knee. She squeezed there and her hand went away.

I took in a deep breath, weirdly fortified by Indy's knee squeeze, and nodded at Detective Marker.

"You been in contact with your father recently?" Detective Marker asked.

So, this was what this was all about.

I looked around the room and noted everyone was watching me.

The daughter of a killer, sitting in their midst.

I felt bile fill my throat and swallowed it down.

I looked back at Detective Marker. "It can't be him. He's in prison."

"Have you talked to him? Does he know what the Baluccis've been doin' to you?" Detective Marker pressed gently.

"I got a call from him a few days ago. He didn't mention it, but I did," I answered. "Not Harvey, just Ricky and the rape. Still, I think he's got a way of staying informed."

"He didn't say anything about Harvey or Ricky?" Detective Marker pushed.

I shook my head. "He was more concerned about why I haven't been in touch, why I haven't visited him. And he'd heard about Hector and me and he wasn't happy."

Detective Marker nodded.

"Do you think he did it?" I asked softly, trying not to think of everyone in the room and what they might be thinking of my father, of me, of what this all meant.

"Lotta folks would do Ricky. He's not got a lot of friends. Marty and Donny, I could see them being put on hit lists, they're not friendly guys either. Harvey was just a dumb fuck, annoying and stupid. He rubbed people the wrong way, but he wasn't a threat to anyone. Makes the list of suspects shorter," Detective Marker told me.

"So, you think it's my father," I answered for him, my heart sinking.

"No, we're lookin' into every possibility. Including Marty, Donny and Ricky. Their brother might not have been a threat to anyone else, but he fucked up, forced your hand, put himself and Ricky behind bars. Him bein' stupid meant he was a liability. This wasn't the first time he fucked up, weakened the family position. Those boys'd eat their own young. I don't put anything past them."

This was true. The Balducci brothers weren't only insane. They were mean and insane. I knew that better than anyone.

"I'm not sure I can help you. I'm trying not to have anything to do with my father," I told Detective Marker.

"I know that, Sadie. That's why I'm gonna ask you to do somethin' that might not be easy."

Blooming heck.

He was going to ask me to do something not easy.

My whole life was something "not easy".

"What?" I asked.

"Eddie tells me one of your father's boys tried to pass you a message last night. I know you two are estranged. Still, he's your father, so I understand this might be tough for you. But, if he contacts you, however he does it, I'm askin' you to let me know he's done it and what he said."

Oh.

Was that it?

"Certainly," I replied immediately.

Detective Marker blinked and I felt a strangeness fill the air in the room.

"Sadie, I know this is hard—" Detective Marker went on.

"It's not hard," I answered easily. Then I offered, "I try not to take his calls. Do you want me to take them and get him to talk?"

Detective Marker blinked again, then his head turned and he looked at Hector.

I followed his gaze and saw the Hot Bunch settled around the armchair. Hank was sitting on the arm of the chair, Lee opposite him, standing, arms crossed on his chest.

They looked almost like twins, except Lee had chocolate brown eyes and Hank's were the color of whisky.

Hector stood by Hank, hands on his hips. Eddie at his side, arms like Lee's.

They almost looked like twins, too, except Eddie's hair was only maybe one week past needing a cut and Hector's was at least two (probably three).

They were all looking at me, but Hector was watching me with that warm intensity, this time mingled with what I could swear was approval, and I felt that weird happy glow start to light in my chest.

"You willin' to do that?" Detective Marker asked me, and my mind moved off the happy glow and my eyes moved back to him.

I shrugged. "Sure. I might need some coaching or a script or something so he won't cotton on, but I could do it."

Something flashed across Detective Marker's face before it went soft. "You been through a lot, Sadie. This would be—"

I cut him off, "This would be nothing, Detective Marker. I've been playing a game all my life around my father. This is just a new game and I simply need someone to explain the rules. Give me some coaching. My phones are already tapped so it's all good."

Detective Marker kept staring at me then he said, "Sadie, if it's your father exacting vengeance for what they did to you that means Ricky is probably next."

"And?" I asked.

Detective Marker didn't answer.

"You think I'd rather not stand in his way if he's going to whack Ricky," I answered for him (again).

"I'm just—" Detective Marker started, but I interrupted him as my back went straight.

"My father taught me a great deal, Detective Marker. He'd had a hard knock life and he was generous with those life lessons. He's a criminal and he did bad things, but his lessons were good. He didn't hide who he was from me, but part of his teaching didn't include how to be a killer. Either be one or be an accessory to one. If he killed Harvey and plans on killing Ricky, those sins are going to be on *his* soul, not mine. So if you're asking me if I'd impede, even if that impeding meant standing aside and doing nothing, the investigation into the murder of the man who assaulted me or the planned murder of the man who raped me, the answer is no." After delivering my speech, I stood, back ramrod straight and finished, "Can I meet Roxie's dog now?"

Detective Marker's lips twitched (now, what did *he* find amusing? really, I didn't get it) and he said, "Yeah, Sadie, we're done."

"Good," I replied shortly, leaned down and picked out a chocolate-covered yeast. "C'mon Roxie, I want to meet Shamus," I called, swept the room with a glance noticing that the entirety of the Hot Bunch had the lip twitch going on, except Hector, who was grinning straight out.

Seriously, what, *exactly*, was so fucking funny?

I decided I didn't care. I ignored them and sashayed out of the house in my indecently short bimbo skirt that Hector made me promise never to wear again (ha! take that!), bare feet (thank goodness it was warm, even for early Autumn) and Hector's huge flannel.

It wasn't until Daisy and Indy joined us, Jet had come out with the fresh pot to give us all a warm up and Roxie was holding my coffee and donut while I threw a Frisbee for the adorable, cuddly, soft, seriously-over-happy Shamus that I realized that I'd spent the entire morning as me.

No Ice Princess, no Attitude Sadie, no Take Charge Sadie and no Pretend Sadie.

Just me.

And I didn't know what to think of that.

But I did know it brought the weird, happy glow back.

And, incidentally, Hector was not wrong about the ibuprofen and Midol. It worked like a charm.

⌇⌇

## The Best Day of Sadie Marie Townsend's Life

Except for the morning, that Sunday was the best day of my life.

Better than any of the days when my father was away "on business" and I could pretend I was free.

Better, even, than any of the waning memories of being with my mom.

Simply the best.

⌇⌇

At first, I thought it was going to go from bad to worse.

Because, after the men held a meeting inside while the women drank coffee, played with Shamus and picked over Hector's response to my tattoo (at length and in some detail) outside, Detective Marker left. So did Indy, Lee, Roxie, Hank and Shamus.

Eddie, Jet, Daisy and Marcus stayed, but only so Hector, Marcus and Eddie could go over what they wanted me to try to get my father to talk about and how I should do that.

Once they were through, I smiled and said, "Easy."

Eddie and Marcus looked at each other, not in a friendly way though. They didn't appear to like each other much, but instead they seemed to be putting up with each other for the sake of whatever was happening (now) with my father.

Hector kept looking at me. "Not easy, Sadie. You're gonna have to stay sharp and on target and listen to any cues he gives you that he knows what you're up to."

"No problem," I responded.

Hector bit his lip and shook his head, then he said softly, "*Mamita*, I know you been playin' your father your whole life, but when you were, you weren't sleepin' with the guy who put him in prison. He doesn't trust you now. You're safe, no one can get to you. But you want to get anything out of him, you gotta be smart, not cocky."

Someone, please tell me Hector didn't just call me cocky!

"I'm not being cocky!" I snapped.

"You're bein' cocky," he returned.

I gave him a glare. "Trust me, Hector, I know what I'm doing."

"Just listen to what I'm sayin' to you," Hector returned calmly.

I kept glaring.

He kept watching me.

We went into a stare down.

I became aware of the other people in the room and I thought it was probably rude to continue a stare down so I gave in.

But I didn't like it.

"Oh, all right."

His mouth moved like he was fighting a smile.

I looked at Daisy and rolled my eyes.

She let out a Christmas bells giggle.

Then Jet said something that threw me.

"We better go. I promised Blanca I'd help her get ready for *La Reunión*." She looked at Eddie. "Are we all going together?"

Even though Jet asked Eddie, Hector answered, "Sadie's gotta change."

My heart leapt into my throat.

"Change for what?" I asked.

Hector's eyes came to me. "*La Reunión*."

I blinked, thinking I knew what he was talking about, but hoping I did *not*.

"Why do I have to change?"

"*Mamita*, you aren't wearin' that fuckin' skirt out of the house unless it's to walk out to the Bronco and walk into the brownstone to get changed before goin' to *Mamá's*."

My heart in my throat grew to about ten times its size.

"I'm not going to your mother's," I whispered.

"You are."

My eyes went wide.

"I'm not. It's a Family Meeting, I'm not family."

The air in the room went electric. Hector's eyes grew dark and his body went tense.

Sensing the change, Eddie, Jet, Daisy and Marcus cautiously moved away.

"You shittin' me?" Hector asked, oblivious to our audience.

Now, I was confused.

"No," I answered honestly.

"*Mujer*, your mark is on my back, my mark is on your hip, and you're sayin' you aren't family?"

Oh my.

Mr. Mood Swing looked angry.

And I didn't know what *mujer* meant but it didn't sound as good as, say, *preciosa* or *mi cielo*.

"Um…" I replied, because I didn't know what else to say. The Scorching Hector Glare was burning straight into my brain, making my mind go blank.

Hector's eyes sliced to Eddie.

"We'll be there after Sadie changes."

Eddie (wisely, in my personal opinion) silently nodded and everyone prepared to leave.

I took Daisy and Jet aside on Hector's front porch and I whispered to Jet, "What does *mujer* mean?"

Jet bit her lip before saying, "It means 'woman' and it usually isn't bad, but I think Hector's kind of mad."

Kind of?

She'd obviously not been seared by The Scorch.

I looked at Eddie, Marcus and Hector, who were all standing by Eddie's shiny, red Dodge Ram and talking.

"Does he think I'm family?" I breathed.

"Oh Sadie, Blanca calls you *mi hija* and Hector's a Chavez through and through. They work fast. Even if Hector decided to give you a break and let you out of *La Reunión*, Blanca would hunt you down. No doubt about it."

I stared at her.

How did *this* happen?

"This must be what he meant by not fucking around anymore," I told them.

"What does that mean?" Daisy asked, and still reeling from all that was happening, I shared our conversation from the morning before. Or Hector's conversation, since I wasn't allowed to talk (I told them that, too).

Daisy and Jet grinned at each other. Not like something was funny, but like something made them really, *really* happy.

Then Daisy said, "Sugar, count your lucky stars he gave you a week of fuckin' around. Now that he's serious, you're his. No ifs, ands or buts, just plain ole *his*. Comprende?"

"But—" I started.

"I say this to all the girls, even though they never listen, but I'll say it again. Don't fight it," Jet cut in.

"But—" I tried again.

Daisy giggled at Jet. "Now we get to the fun stuff."

Fun?

Were they plumb crazy?

This was *not* fun!

Before I could say more, they hugged me and left.

Leaving me alone with Angry Hector.

Blooming heck.

His long strides took him from the sidewalk to me in no time at all. He grabbed my hand and dragged me into the house.

"Choose now. We shower here or we shower at your place," he said, not breaking stride as he pulled me up the stairs.

*We* shower?

*We?*

"Hector—"

He turned unexpectedly and tugged me into the bathroom.

"We shower here. Ralphie and Buddy might be at your place. Here, you can make all the noise you want."

Noise?

I was going to make noise?

Why would I…?

Then it came to me.

Oh no.

"Hector—"

His hands went to the hem of the flannel, up, and then it was gone.

"Hector!" I snapped.

His blazing eyes locked on mine. "*Mamita*, we don't have a lot of time, don't piss me off. Pissin' me off is gonna take time."

My mouth dropped open.

Then I snapped it shut.

"Don't… don't…" I stuttered, then demanded to know, "Why are you angry?"

He put his hands to both sides of my neck, pulled me close and tilted his head down to look at me.

"I don't know," he replied sharply. "Maybe it's because your first thought this morning was that anyone would think you were a murderer, even me. Fuck, you sat in my fuckin' lap and swore to me you didn't do it like I would think for one fuckin' second that you would."

"But—" I tried to cut in, but he kept talking.

"Or maybe it's because, no matter what I do and what *you* do, you aren't fuckin' cluein' into what's happenin' here."

"And what, *exactly*, is happening here?" I shot back.

His eyes got dark (or, I should say, *darker*) and he said quietly, "Now you're pissin' me off."

I threw my hands out to the sides, exasperated. "Why?"

His eyes narrowed. "Are you payin' attention at all?"

"Yes!" I snapped, totally over it, and then I went straight into a rant. "But I don't get it. Excuse me, Hector Chavez, but you saw how I grew up. You *know!* I've never been to a Family Meeting! I've never put on lip gloss in the restroom of a club with my girlfriends! I've never sat around a dinner table looking through photos and reminiscing! All this is happening while the Balducci brothers are assaulting and threatening me, my father is freaking me out and I'm having conversations with police detectives. Not to mention, you've decided not to 'fuck around anymore', whatever *that* means, and I have an opening tomorrow! So, if I'm a little slow, you'll have to cut me some *fucking* slack, all right?"

Somewhere during my rant, Mr. Mood Swing decided he wasn't angry anymore (really! how was I supposed to keep up with this guy?) and his face went soft. His eyes went so warm they were hot and his fingers drifted up into my hair.

As his head descended, he murmured, "All right, *mi corazón*. I'll cut you some slack"

"Well, thank you," I said, sounding snippy, which was hard when his mouth had settled on mine.

"Now I'm gonna do you in the shower then we'll get you home. You can get changed and get your stuff because you're spendin' the night tonight, and we'll go to *La Reunión*."

My heart flipped, my belly melted and my irritation disappeared.

"*Do* me in the shower?" I breathed.

His tongue traced my bottom lip and that felt so nice, my knees buckled right out from under me. So badly I had to grab on to the material of his tee at his waist to stay standing.

His eyes were open and looking into mine.

"Yeah," he said against my mouth.

"I think I'm not over my rant."

His hands left my hair. He pulled my skirt up around my waist, his thumbs hooked into my panties and I gasped against his mouth as he pulled them down.

"You can yell at me while I'm fuckin' you."

Oh my.

That was it. I wished I could say I was stronger, held out a little longer, but I melted.

And, incidentally, *we* showered. He *did* me in the shower, my back against the tiled wall, my legs wrapped around his waist, my hands everywhere they could touch. And I didn't yell at him while he was doing it.

⌖

The rest of the day weirded me out. So much I couldn't handle it, so I decided to ride with it and memorize every last second so I could carry it with me forever.

We went to the brownstone and I did my business, with the addition of Buddy begging Hector and me to take YoYo, even if she was spending the night at Hector's. This was because, he explained, Ralphie was becoming so attached to the dog, Buddy feared there would be a dognapping.

We loaded up my stuff (Hector told me to "pack heavy", which meant more than a night's worth, and after my rant, I didn't have it in me to put up a fight so I did as he ordered), YoYo, YoYo's doggie paraphernalia (under Ralphie's maniacal dognapper-in-the-making glare) and we headed off to Blanca's.

Jet and Eddie were getting married imminently and Jet was barely holding on to her dream vision of a wedding. She'd given into the whole Catholic Mass thing (for Blanca), but for a reception, she'd hired a barn somewhere in the mountains, replete with a hog roast, hayrides, a bonfire and s'mores at the end.

Bizarrely, at the same time, Blanca and Nancy had rented the local hall. Blanca's cousins were catering and Nancy's neighbor was going to croon lounge music during a sit down, four course meal.

And, apparently, Blanca and Nancy's vision included *loads* of lavender bunting.

After a gut-busting lunch, Nancy and Blanca ganged up on Jet.

I sat with YoYo in my lap and noticed right away that Jet was going *down*.

First off, Eddie was removed, entirely. In fact, he looked like he thought the whole thing was funny and didn't even flinch when Jet glared daggers at him. Hector and Carlos stayed silent, but they also appeared to find the whole thing amusing. Gloria, Rosa and Elena were also silent. I could tell they were commiserating with Jet but they didn't have the guts to jump in. Carlos's girlfriend Maria sat silent too, but she looked scared out of her mind (probably exactly what I looked like). Tex, on the other hand, was busily eating through the leftovers on the platters of food on Blanca's table, and it appeared he didn't even know the meeting was happening at all.

So it became apparent that it was going to have to be me.

I thought about how to do this without Blanca's house exploding under the force of a Full Blown Blanca (and Nancy) Hissy Fit.

Then I came up with a plan.

"I've never had roasted hog," I announced during a lull in Jet's browbeating.

Everyone's (surprised) eyes came to me.

Even though they were scaring me (particularly Blanca, but also Nancy), as per usual I sallied forth.

"And I've never taken a hayride." I looked at Jet and informed her in a chirpy voice, "I've always wanted a s'more but my father never let me go to camp. Or take a hayride. Or go to a hog roast. He was weird that way, you know, being kind of suffocating and not letting me be social or have friends." I glanced across the table and declared, "Sounds like fun!"

So I was manipulating the fact that they were nice people and trying to make them feel sorry for me.

It was the only card I had to play, and for Jet, I played it.

Jet was smiling at me, beautiful and huge.

Eddie wasn't smiling, exactly, but I could see his dimple.

Hector was shaking his head, but his eyes were warm and intense in a new way that was mixed with humor and affection, and *that* brought back that lovely, snug, comfy feeling.

Tex's head snapped in my direction.

"Fuckin' A, woman. You've never had a s'more?" he boomed.

I shook my head.

"Christ, everyone's gotta have a s'more before they die. Fuck that shit, I'll build a fire in my backyard tonight and I'll stop by Kumar's on the way home to get the stuff. Everyone can come by——"

Damn and blast!

Tex was being really nice, but he was *ruining* everything!

"No," I cut in quickly, "I can wait until Jet's wedding."

"There's no waitin' for s'mores," Tex boomed back.

"But——" I started.

"No lip!" Tex boomed again.

"Sadie and I have plans tonight," Hector put in smoothly, and Tex's eyes went to him. They narrowed, then I watched as the light dawned, and slowly he sat back.

"I'll make you a s'more latte so you'll have somethin' to go on until Jet and Eddie's wedding," Tex told me, then his eyes moved to Jet. "Now, where's this fuckin' barn and do I have to wear a fuckin' tie?"

The power, I could tell, had shifted.

I could tell this because Nancy and Blanca went thin-lipped.

"Yay!" I shouted as my finale, hoping to shift the balance irrevocably to Jet's side. To do this, I clapped, YoYo yapped happily in my lap and maybe I went a little OTT. "Roasted hog!" I cried happily. "Hayrides! Bonfires! *I... can't... wait!*"

Blanca and Nancy looked at each other.

I held my breath.

They stayed silent.

That's when I knew we won.

They didn't like it, but they didn't push it.

I let out my breath and sat back.

My work was done.

And, believe it or not, Jet gave me a look of such shining gratitude, no kidding, I almost cried right there on the spot (I, of course, did not).

Before we left (believe it or not again!), she asked me to be a bridesmaid.

Me!

A bridesmaid!

For a second, I was so excited at the prospect of being a bridesmaid, I forgot I was moving to Crete and I couldn't stop myself from hugging her and saying yes.

Then it hit me. But I didn't take it back. I wanted to live that one glorious moment, and even if it made me selfish, I didn't care.

I wasn't going to give it up.

No way.

I promised myself I'd call her and explain everything.

I'd just do it... later.

Shortly after, I was still in the moment when Hector and I left. But we didn't go to his house. We went to the grocery store.

Sadie Townsend, daughter of a fallen Drug King, and ex-DEA Agent Hector "Oh my God" Chavez *grocery shopping.*

If my father saw us (or when he heard), he'd have a kitten!

Since I was in the moment and enjoying said moment, I didn't fight it.

Instead, I went with it.

Even when Hector put his hands on the cart handle beside mine, which meant the heat of his body was pressed against my back, his chin was resting on my shoulder and we walked a whole aisle that way (a whole aisle!). Even when Hector laughed at me when I asked him where the Pilsbury crescent roll dough was (what was funny about that, I wanted to know, but I didn't ask). Even when he ran into some guy he knew, a handsome, African-American, off-duty police sergeant named Willie, and he introduced me. Even when they chatted, all the while Hector had his arm wrapped casually around my neck, me tucked firmly into his side, making me feel like a real girlfriend, someone who actually *belonged* tucked firmly into his heat while he chatted with a friend.

Yes, even through all of that.

The moment continued when we got to his place, unpacked the groceries and he asked me if I wanted to watch a movie. In turn, I asked him if I could help him on his house by sanding his floors. His chin jerked at my request and he looked at me funny, like I surprised him, but he agreed.

He patiently showed me what to do and we spent the afternoon in the living room sanding his floors. Him using this big sander thingie and me on my hands and knees using a small handheld sander close to the wall and in the corners. Other than doing dishes, laundry and cleaning my house once in a while (I had a cleaning lady; what could I say? I was rich), I'd never done manual labor in my life. And even if it made me a freak, I didn't care...

There was nothing better than sanding Hector's living room floor with Hector.

Nothing.

Okay, maybe there were some things, but those involved Hector, too.

At that point, I was beyond "the moment". I was living the dream and I fell into it, letting the warm, lovely, snugly, comfy waters sweep over my head, sucking me down.

Happily, gratefully, I let myself sink.

We finished sanding the floor and took another shower (yes, together!), got dressed and Hector barbecued pork chops outside on the grill while I made a salad (I could cut up vegetables, no problem), boiled some new potatoes (boiling! easy!) and baked Pilsbury crescent rolls (they ended up perfect, absolutely delicious; all you had to do was follow the directions!).

Since it was still warm(ish), I put on his flannel and we ate in the backyard at his outside table by his huge hot tub with YoYo sitting on one of the other chairs and me feeding her tidbits with my fingers.

When we were done eating, I was rinsing the dishes and loading up Hector's rickety old dishwasher and Hector was outside at the grill again. YoYo was with him, racing around the yard, and I watched through the window as the flames went high.

Then he came back inside and disappeared into the house. He reappeared with a wire hanger and a tool and grabbed some stuff out of the cupboards. Then, without a word, he tagged my hand and pulled me back outside.

He positioned me by the still flaming grill and started to cut the hanger with some wire clippers.

"What are you doing?" I asked.

He picked up a bag of marshmallows and tossed them to me.

I caught them but kept looking at him.

"S'mores," was all he said.

My breathing went funny.

So maybe I *was* slow. He bought the stuff with me at his side in the grocery store. But how was I to know what he had planned? I just thought he was a man who liked marshmallows, chocolate bars and graham crackers in the house. I'd personally never had all three in my house at once, but each item individually, sure!

I decided not to make a big deal of it, like burst into tears, throw myself in his arms and declare my everlasting love for him.

Instead, I asked, "Did you ever go to camp?"

He grinned, and it was a new grin. An *effective* new grin, because it was so wicked, it made my belly melt. "If you count three months in juvie when I was fourteen then, yeah. But we didn't have s'mores."

My mouth dropped open.

Then I asked, "You, Agent Hector Chavez, did a stint in juvie?"

He was straightening out the hanger and still grinning. "Yeah."

It was too much, I couldn't help it.

I burst out laughing.

My eyes were closed so I didn't see him move until his arm was wrapped around my neck. I was yanked against his body so hard, I slammed into him, and he kissed me, hot, wet, open-mouthed and long enough for me to melt into him (and then some).

Then his mouth broke from mine. He touched his forehead to mine for a nanosecond before he moved away and I felt my breath catch at the sweetness of it.

"Like it when you laugh, *mamita*," he said quietly.

I stared at him then I swallowed.

He didn't wait for a response, maybe didn't need one. I didn't know and didn't ask. Instead, he handed me the hanger and took the marshmallows from me, opening the bag with his teeth.

"What'd you do?" I asked.

"Probably better to ask what I didn't do."

I let out another small laugh as he made me hold my hanger up to his hand and he fed some big, fat marshmallows on it.

"Okay, what didn't you do?"

He gave me one of his glamorous smiles. "I never killed anyone."

My body started shaking with laughter.

Through my laughter, I said, "So I take it you're one of the ones who fucked around enough to cause your parents problems."

He guided my hanger over the grill and dumped the bag of marshmallows on the side shelf but kept his arm wrapped around my neck, his eyes trained on my marshmallows.

"Carlos, Rosa and Elena were the good kids, Eddie, Gloria and me... not so good."

I felt this somewhere deep and the laughter left my body.

Hector's arm gave my neck a squeeze. I knew he wanted my attention so I looked up at him.

He was watching me closely.

"Now what's in your head?" he asked softly.

"She loves you all the same. The good and the not so good," I whispered, referring to Blanca.

"Always has," he replied.

Immediately, I replied, "You're very lucky."

At my words, he curled me so my front was against his and his face dipped to mine.

I saw that look in his eyes. The warm, intense, eyes-soft, face-hard, signifying-possession look, but something else was there. Not pity, but maybe understanding that he had something beautiful that I had not. I knew instinctively he didn't feel sorry for me, but he felt something.

"I know," he murmured, and there was a great deal of feeling in his soft words.

Perhaps sensing I'd had enough, perhaps wanting a s'more, he showed me how to make them and we ate them. Then we made out by the grill in the now-chilly Autumn air, our mouths tasting of s'mores (Hector's kisses were amazing, but when he tasted of s'mores, they were simply *heaven*).

After s'mores, we walked upstairs and lay, fully-clothed (but shoeless) on his bed and watched a movie (*The Big Easy*; I hadn't seen it in years and forgot how good it was).

Then, likely inspired by the movie (thank *God*), Hector played out a certain part. But his effort lasted longer, was a bit more creative, included more than just fingers (moving on to lips and tongues), and it finished a whole lot differently.

Before he snapped out the light, he put balm and a new bandage on my tattoo.

Then he tucked my back to his front. YoYo snuggled close into the crook of my lap, Hector held me tight and I laid there, listening to him breathe (and YoYo snort) until I knew he was asleep.

Then I rewound my day from start to finish.

Then I rewound it again.

Then I did it again.

Then I felt the wetness slide silently down the sides of my eyes, soaking into the mound of pillows I shared with Hector. I put my arm on his at my waist and linked our fingers.

In his sleep, his fingers tensed until they held mine tight.

Only then did I fall asleep.

Kristen Ashley

## *Hector*

Hector felt Sadie's fingers relax in his and he knew she was finally asleep.

He took in the scent of her expensive perfume, knowing and liking the fact that it was on his sheets.

His arm wrapped tighter around her waist, pulling her deeper into his body.

Her head tilted forward. His went with it, he buried his face into her hair, but he felt the wetness her tears left on the pillow against his cheek.

His eyes opened in the dark.

"Fucking hell," he muttered.

# Chapter 20

# Bon Bons

*Sadie*

Art was filled, shoulder-to-shoulder, with people.

I'd never had an opening this huge.

Even before my father was arrested for trafficking drugs and half my contacts shunned my openings (the other half only continuing to come to drink my champagne, look down their noses at me and feel superior), no opening had been this popular.

My artist, Lisette (who painted unbelievable watercolors), was beside herself with the turn out.

I didn't have the heart to tell her it was not prospective buyers, but the ever ready to party Rock Chick/Hot Bunch crew, complete with Hector's entire family, Indy's Dad Tom, Tod and Stevie, Tex and Nancy, and Duke and his wife Dolores. Even the Zano clan came, Uncle Vito and Angela, Dom and Sissy and Ren and some woman I didn't know.

Indeed, every single Rock Chick and their respective Hot Bunch Guy was there. All the girls looking glamorous, all the men looking knockout gorgeous wearing suits and shirts with collars opened at the neck.

That said, Duke had dressed up how I guessed any Harley biker guy would dress up. He still had the bandana around his forehead and the leather vest, but his black t-shirt had long sleeves and no saying emblazoned on the chest and he'd switched to black jeans. Tex, on the other hand, didn't look any different and was wearing jeans and a plaid flannel shirt.

I didn't even know they'd been invited (Ralphie's doing, no doubt). But I had to admit, I was happy they were there.

It felt different with them there. Good. Safe. My openings had not only never been that crowded, they'd never been that filled with laughter.

"I told you pigs in a blanket would be a hit," Shirleen said from beside me, nabbing (at my count) her fourth gourmet "pig in a blanket" off a passing tray and shoving the entire thing in her mouth.

She wasn't wrong. The blanketed pigs were going down a treat. Everyone seemed to love them.

"You were right Shirleen. I promise I won't have another opening without pigs in a blanket," I assured her, crossing my heart and putting up two fingers so she'd believe me.

"Damn straight," she replied, her tawny eyes smiling. Her gaze moved across the room and she went on, "Hector sure cleans up good."

I looked at Hector.

She was not wrong.

I'd gotten ready at his house that morning and he'd dropped me off at Art. The day had been busy, hanging the paintings and going over everything one last time, even though I didn't have to. I was obsessively organized, never procrastinated, always checked and double-checked every detail and was a list maker. The entire thing was ready to roll with no hiccups days in advance (as usual). Even the installation had gone easier than normal because Daisy, Roxie, Stella and Ava came to help.

Hector had stayed away all day. He didn't even call. It felt weird being away from him that long. Since Ralphie let him in the brownstone over a week ago, it seemed like he was always around, or at least never far away.

When I said it felt weird, I meant I didn't like it.

At all.

I liked having him around.

And that meant I was seriously in trouble.

After we were done with the hanging and everything was ready, Ralphie took me home so we could dress for the opening.

Hector told me that morning he'd meet me at the gallery. He showed up half an hour after the festivities started wearing a suit. One look at him and my heart stopped.

His suit, at first, I thought was black. But, on closer inspection, I realized it was a very dark gray. He also had on a tailored, collared shirt that was one shade lighter than the suit and black cowboy boots. That's it. It seemed simple, but on Hector, it was highly effective.

Sometime during the day he'd had his hair cut though. And he'd had it cut in a way that now it looked sexy, messy, long-ish and still in need of imminent cutting, but it looked good on him. Way good. *Too* good.

Honest to God, he never looked better.

However, he was very far away from me and over the last two hours, had stayed that way. When he arrived, he'd come to me and kissed the top of my head but that was it.

At first, this weirded me out.

I was still living the dream. The dream of Hector and Sadie together, sanding floors and making s'mores and owning a pug that raced around the backyard.

Him staying away made me think I'd done something wrong.

I'd reverted to my designer armor (it *was* an art opening and I *did* own the gallery; I couldn't exactly wear flannel, like Tex).

I was wearing a slim-fitting, brush-the-knees, ecru skirt that was covered in opalescent beading. My top was stretchy, ecru, knit silk, long-sleeved and off the shoulders, but very snug. I had a velvet ecru ribbon tied as a choker around my neck, pointed-toed, spike-heeled, ecru satin mules with bugle beads stitched on the toe and my hair pulled back severely from my face and fastened with another velvet ribbon at my nape. It was definitely an Ice Princess outfit.

I knew Hector didn't like my armor and I thought it pissed him off.

But even though he stayed away, I knew he knew where I was at all times (don't ask me how, I just did). Sometimes, when my eyes would stray to him, I saw he was watching me. Sometimes, his face would grow soft. But other times, he looked like he was trying to figure me out (those times were *not* my favorite times; I didn't want to be figured out, no way).

I tried not to think about it and instead did my job making sure the champagne flowed, the trays of hors d'ouevres were plentiful, and above all, I mingled.

It was about an hour after he arrived that I understood why he stayed away. He stayed away because I was working and he was giving me space.

And, at that thought, I quit panicking and I also quit sinking down in the warm, comfy water where the possibility of a "Hector and Sadie" had taken me. Instead, I executed a below the surface back flip.

I turned away from Hector, who was now standing talking with Tom and Hank, and looked at Shirleen.

"Hector's the most handsome man I've ever laid eyes on in my life," I told her bluntly, and I didn't even care what she thought about me saying it.

"Mm-hmm," Shirleen agreed, her eyes still locked on Hector. "Never fancied me a brown boy, but given the chance, I wouldn't say no to Hector Chavez. No fuckin' way."

After she said that, she tore her gaze from Hector, looked at me and I grinned at her. She grinned back then her eyes flicked over my shoulder and her grin died.

"Shit. Society bitch, three o'clock and closing in. Gotta go," Shirleen whispered and then, *poof*, she was gone, disappearing in the crowd.

Dazed at her quick disappearing act, I turned around and watched Monica Henrique bearing down on me.

Oh no.

What was *she* doing there?

She'd hated me since the whole Nanette thing went down!

And she was *definitely* not on the guest list and hadn't been since The Daisy Incident.

And there was no way Ralphie would invite her. She'd come before and Ralphie instantly loathed her.

"Sadie!" she screeched, fake smile on her face, throwing her arms out straight in front of her like we were best friends reunited after years apart.

Before I could escape, she grabbed my upper arms and pulled me in for air kisses. First one cheek then the other, then she leaned back, still with her hands on me.

"Oh my *God!*" she continued to screech (loudly), her eyes on my cheek. "What happened to your face?"

Someone, please tell me she did *not* just say that.

I felt people turning to look at us and I wanted to cut and run.

Of course, I did not.

My back went straight, my chin jutted out and I ignored her unbelievably insensitive question.

"Monica. Lovely to see you," I said in a voice that made it clear I felt the opposite.

She ignored my tone and let go of my arms, but only to get close to my side and link her arm with mine.

"Sadie, I don't know if you know this," she whispered conspiratorially. "But *Daisy Sloan* is here." And she said Daisy's name like it tasted bad.

My body stayed frozen stiff, but my head turned slowly to look at her.

"I know," I said. "Daisy was *invited*." I stressed the last word to make my point. But it flew directly over Monica's head. Or more likely, she ignored it because she was a bitch.

A look went across her face like she was thinking about this then she came to a conclusion and carried on, "Well, her husband *is* loaded. And you've got paintings to sell, now that your situation has, um... changed." I stared at her, shocked even further that she brought up my father, but she didn't notice it and went right on talking. "We must do what we must do."

I felt the saliva gather in my mouth.

Instead of spitting it at her (which I really wanted to do), I swallowed it. Because right then, I knew why she was there.

I knew.

She was there to rub my nose in my own misfortune.

See! Total bitch!

My mind started whirling to try and hit on something (anything!) that would make her let me go without causing a scene and make her just plain *go* without, again, causing a scene because I did, indeed, have paintings to sell. A scene might hinder that effort.

Before I could come up with a plan, her eyes caught on something and her head came up.

"Don't I know him?" she asked, and my head turned in the direction where she was looking. I saw Hector, his handsome face carefully blank, but his eyes were on me and I could see, even across the room, they were alert.

I turned back to Monica and opened my mouth to speak when her eyes went squinty like she was looking into the sun.

"I think he works for my yard company. He's one of those, you know... immigrant workers or whatever. What's he doing *here?*"

My head jerked back like she slapped me right before my hands formed into fists.

Now, someone please tell me she did *not* just insinuate that Hector "Oh my God" Chavez was an immigrant yard worker crashing an art opening.

She kept going, oblivious to my tense posture and what had to be a deadly vibe emanating from every pore in my body.

Her eyes still on Hector she said, "God, Sadie, he's staring at you. I don't know, he's definitely good-looking, if you like that kind of thing, but... oh dear, he's heading our way!"

She jerked my arm as if to pull me away, but I stood rooted to the spot.

I yanked away from her and stayed where I was, but my head turned to watch Hector walk the last six feet to my side.

The minute he did, I moved in.

I put one of my hands on his abs and leaned up on tiptoe to kiss his down-turned lips.

"Hi, babe," I said softly and saw something warm flash in his eyes but I ignored it.

Somewhere along the line, something had exploded in my brain and I was powerless to control my own actions. That was to say, I was beyond worrying about causing a scene. Or, I should say, I was about to cause *the* scene that would end *all* scenes.

I leaned my body into him until his arm slid along my waist and I turned to Monica.

"Hector, this is Monica Henrique. Monica, this is Hector Chavez. Hector used to be an agent for the DEA, which is why you probably recognize him because he was undercover in my father's operation for over a year before he brought him down. So, obviously, he used to be around a lot. Now, we're sleeping together, and let me tell you, he's *amazing*."

I felt Hector's body grow tight and I saw Monica's face pale, but I kept on talking.

"Hector," I flicked my hand out to Monica, "Monica never worked a day in her life. She hasn't slept with her husband in five years, but she *has* slept with the guys who work for her gardener, *loads* of them. She also gets Botox injections. So much, I think it's affected her brain because she thought you worked for her yard company. I'm guessing, wishful thinking?" I asked Monica sweetly.

Now Monica's mouth had dropped open.

"Sadie——" I heard Hector say in a low voice from beside me.

But I ignored that, too, and kept my eyes on Monica even as I saw people approaching from all sides.

"And, just to set the record straight, I don't sell paintings because I have to. I'm rich, my mother was rich, my mother's mother was rich, my mother's mother's *mother* was rich. My family struck it big in the gold boom and we've been fat cats in Denver for years before you crawled out from the underbelly of whatever scaly, reptilian, dragon queen that spawned you. I don't have to work. I sell paintings because I'm good at it."

Vaguely, I heard a gasp that might have been Daisy, but I didn't have time to look. I was on a roll and kept going.

"And I got this cut on my cheek when I was beaten and raped a month ago. You know that, everyone knows it, and you're just being a screaming bitch by bringing it up."

Hector's hand got tight at my waist and he repeated, "Sadie——"

I continued to ignore him and ranted on, even as more people approached our group.

"And I'll finish with this little nugget, and Monica, I want you to listen well. Don't you dare waltz uninvited into my gallery and disrespect me, my friends and my boyfriend. You do it again, I'll drag you out of here by your hair. Got me?" I snapped.

Monica sputtered once then twice then breathed, "I don't believe——"

I leaned in and interrupted her, "It was a yes or no question."

Her eyes narrowed, she sucked in breath and (believe it or not!), she hissed, "You'll never sell another painting in Denver again!"

Now, how unoriginal was *that?*

It was the worst comeback ever!

"Oh well, I guess I'll just sit on top of my big pile of money and eat bon bons," I returned casually. Then, quick as lightning, I morphed to not-casual-at-all, leaned back toward her and clipped, "Now get out of my gallery."

She pressed her lips together, gave me a squinty-eyed look, transferred the look to Hector, then back to me, and she turned and marched out.

It was at that juncture I realized I was breathing heavily.

Hector's dark gray shirt came into my vision and I looked up into his black eyes.

"What the fuck was that about?" he asked.

"She's a bitch," I answered.

"I gathered that, *mamita,*" he told me, and I could hear the amusement in his voice.

And it was at *that* juncture I realized he was fighting a grin.

And I knew not one single thing was funny about this particular situation.

I got closer to him as it hit me that we had an audience, and likely had one for some time.

"This isn't funny," I whispered to Hector, ignoring the people gathered around.

His body started to shake with laughter. "You just told her you were gonna sit on your big pile of money and eat bon bons. Sadie, seriously, do you not get that that's funny?"

I opened my mouth to speak, but didn't get out a single sound when I heard a woman's voice call, "Sadie?"

I looked to the side and saw the whole gang gathered around. Rock Chicks, Hot Bunch, family and friends, all of them obviously getting what was funny because they were all smiling.

But there were two new people there I'd never seen before except in pictures. A man and a woman. They were both tall, slim, dark-haired, and I knew they were Hank, Lee and Ally's parents, the Nightingales.

"Sadie," the woman whispered, tears shimmering in her eyes. She walked right to me and pulled me in her arms for a fierce hug. I felt her head turn and she murmured in my ear, "My God, sweetheart, you look exactly like Lizzie."

Oh my.

This, I knew, was Kitty Sue, my mom's best friend.

While Kitty Sue hugged me, I looked at the man at her side. He was smiling down at me.

And that was Malcolm.

Before I could wrap my head around this, she pulled away. When I looked at her I saw she had herself together. She was smiling from ear-to-ear and the tears were gone.

"It's so good to see you," she told me and turned to her husband. "Malc, doesn't she look just like Lizzie?"

He leaned in and kissed my cheek.

Yes.

*Kissed my cheek!*

I hadn't seen him since I was three!

"Spittin' image," he said when he moved away.

I wondered what I should do in this situation (again, the etiquette books didn't cover this topic), but I didn't have to wonder long. Kitty Sue took over.

"I hope you don't mind, we crashed your party. But I couldn't wait to see you. Malc and I just got back from Hawaii last night. I wanted to call but we totally crashed. Jetlag. Serious. Crazy. Have you ever been jetlagged?" she asked but didn't wait for an answer. "Anyway, you and I have *so* much to talk about. I hear Tom showed you some pictures, but I have more..." She blathered on, hand on my upper arm, fingers squeezing affectionately.

I was staring at her, lips parted, stunned silent (not that I could get a word in edgewise) when she was interrupted and someone new called my name.

She dropped her hand, looked over my shoulder and so did I.

There stood Aaron Lockhart, leaning on a cane, liver-spotted, mostly-bald head shining in the lights of the gallery.

Blooming heck!

"My dear," Aaron said and then it was his turn to lean in (or up, as Aaron was kind of stooped) and kiss my cheek.

What was going on?

Aaron was always invited but never came (his wife didn't like to socialize much).

"Aaron, how are you?" I asked. Ever the hostess, I took his hand and gave it a squeeze before dropping it.

"In a hurry," he answered. "Berta's out in the car with the five dogs," he told me then looked up at Hector, and for some reason, shared, "Pomeranians. Five Pomeranian dogs. One is too many. Five is the definition of living hell. I told her that I'd named our son as my life insurance beneficiary, but I *still* think she's trying to kill me."

There were chuckles all around, but again, I didn't find anything funny. This was because I was getting a bad feeling about his visit *and* our audience.

"Aaron, do we need to go somewhere and talk?" I asked.

"No, Sadie. This will be quick. Just popped by to give you the good news that you're in luck. Mrs. Burnsley's family is moving her into assisted living at the end of the month so the London flat will be available. It's coming to outside season so the property in Crete will be open in a few weeks and it'll stay that way until mid-February. The booking company has plenty of time to move people around before next year so you're free to go to either place."

My body went solid and I heard the chuckles die away.

"Are you going on vacation, Sadie?" Ralphie materialized close by and his voice sounded confused.

I looked at him and opened my mouth to speak, but damn and blasted Aaron got there first.

"Not vacation. Moving," Aaron answered.

I heard gasps, but worse, I felt a fierce electrical current whipping all around me, and I knew what *that* meant.

Aaron, somehow oblivious to the current (and the gasps), went on, "Which brings me to my next subjects. Taxes, health insurance, residency visas. I'm looking into them and I'll get the information to you by the end of the week. I'm advising Crete, better weather, and London is expensive, would be difficult for you on a fixed income, even yours. The exchange rate is certain death. Also, I'll need to get into your storage locker so the auctioneers can have a look at your belongings and give you a quote for selling them."

"Moving?" Ralphie butted in, and I looked at him.

He was pale and I felt that hard, hot thing start forming in my chest again.

"Moving," Aaron (again!) answered.

"You can't... I don't understand——" Ralphie stuttered.

"Ralphie, we'll talk about it later," I said quietly, trying to ignore the thing in my chest and the current in the air.

"Ralphie? Is this Ralph Mankowicz?" Aaron asked.

"Aaron, please, maybe we can go——" I tried damage control.

"Yes, I'm Ralph Mankowicz," Ralphie answered, ignoring my effort at damage control.

"I have some paperwork for you to sign, son," Aaron replied. "It's in the car, I'll just——"

"No!" I cut in, "Aaron, can we——" I started again, but Ralphie interrupted me.

"Paperwork?"

"Yes, to sign over the gallery," Aaron, ever informative, answered.

The air in the room was now heavy, tense *and* electric, and I knew everyone was watching, listening and not liking what they heard.

Why, I will ask again, was everything in my life so... *fucking... difficult?*

"Sign over the gallery?" Ralphie repeated.

"Yes, to you and a Mr. Leon Simmons," Aaron told him, and his gaze came to me, heavy, wiry, white eyebrows raised in question. "Isn't that right?"

I didn't answer Aaron because Ralphie was looking at me. His eyes were wide. There was confusion written plain on his face, right alongside what looked an awful lot like hurt.

My heart squeezed.

"Ralphie, we'll talk about this later," I tried again, my voice quiet.

"Later? You want to talk about it later? You're moving and signing over the gallery to Buddy and me and you want to talk about it later? What's this all about?" Ralphie didn't feel like letting me try. He felt like being dramatic (as usual) and angry (not as usual).

"Let's go somewhere else—" I tried yet again.

"No, I want to know, right now, what this is all about," Ralphie replied, arms crossing on his chest.

I swallowed. Then to get it over with I told him on a rush, "I'm giving you and Buddy the gallery as a thank you for all you've done for me."

He stared at me, face shocked. Then I watched as his eyes went hard.

I thought he'd be pleased.

He was absolutely not.

"You're joking," he breathed.

"No. I want you to know how much I appreciate everything… all that… just everything."

"You could do that by not moving to fucking *Greece,*" he snapped back.

I blinked.

"What?" I asked.

"I don't want your fucking gallery. I want you and not via e-mail from your new life on the Med. I want you here. Close. Where we can drink lemon drops and watch Veronica Mars."

I couldn't think what to say. I thought certain sure he'd love owning the gallery. He was good at what he did. The best. He'd be his own boss. He'd make loads more money.

He must not get it.

"Ralphie, I'm not sure you understand. I don't just own the gallery. I own *the building.* You and Buddy will get it all. This is LoDo, prime real estate," I informed him.

That was when Ralphie leaned in and shouted, "Fuck the building!"

I winced.

Apparently he got it.

He just didn't want it.

"Ralphie, please quiet down," I whispered.

"I will *not* be quiet. I cannot *believe* you're moving to Greece. That's... that's *insane*."

Now hang on a second!

"It's not insane," I shot back.

"It is! Who moves to Greece? Do you know a single soul who's moved to Greece?" He didn't give me a chance to reply before he continued, "No? Me neither. No one moves to Greece. Goes there. Yes. Gets laid. Definitely. Drinks ouzo. Lots of it. Gets a sunburn. Of course! But you don't *move* there!" He was still shouting. "And giving me a *building? A building!* Are you nuts?"

Seriously, this was getting right on my nerves!

Why wouldn't anyone let me be nice?

"I owe you so much, I had to do something!" I shouted back.

Ralphie threw his hands high into the air. "You *are* nuts," he yelled. "This is what friends do! There is no 'owe'. Someday, my precious Momma's going to die or I'm going to get a hangnail and you'll be there for me. That's how you give back. You don't give out lavish Christmas bonuses, expensive birthday gifts and buildings, for fuck's sake!"

Oh my God!

"I thought you liked my birthday presents!" I yelled back.

"I do. But only if they're given from the heart, not to buy my friendship," he shot back.

It felt like he slapped me right across the face.

I flinched and took a step back. That step forced me into something solid, and breathing heavily, my heart beating in my throat, the hot knot burning in my chest, I turned and looked up to see Hector.

Oh my.

The muscle was jumping in his cheek. His face was stony but his eyes were on Ralphie.

"You done?" he clipped at Ralphie.

"No," Ralphie snapped.

"You are for now," Hector replied, and without hesitation he leaned in, took my hand then dragged me through our stunned audience, through the rest of the crowd, down my back hall to my office.

He threw open the door, flipped on the switch and pulled me in with a controlled violence that sent me flying several steps into my office. He slammed the door behind us.

I stopped in the middle of the room, turned and looked at him.

That knot in my chest expanded, searing painfully wider through my chest and lungs and *just this close* to my heart.

Hector stood in front of the door, eyes beyond scorching. I didn't know what beyond scorching was, but whatever it was, his eyes were doing it.

"Were you gonna tell me?" he asked, voice low and vibrating, but his words were enunciated perfectly clearly.

"No," I answered, and his eyes flashed dangerously. "Yes," I went on quickly, and there was another flash. "I couldn't make up my mind," I finished lamely.

"Why?" he snapped.

"Why?" I asked.

"Sadie——" His tone held a warning.

I realized I was trembling, deep body shakes, and my hands went to my cheeks, rubbing and pressing at the same time, shoving my skin toward my ears.

Then I decided that it was time.

It was time a week ago, but I'd given in. I'd been weak. I'd wanted to live the dream.

Now, it was definitely time.

"I know what you're doing," I told him.

Without hesitation, he shot back, "Yeah? What am I doin'?"

I dropped my hands and straightened my shoulders. "I know how you felt that night in my father's study when I walked away from you. You were angry. You weren't even angry, you were livid. A woman doesn't do that to a man, not a man like you, not without some kind of..." I stopped then started again, "I know you were angry and now you're paying me back."

I stopped talking.

I did this because the voltage of the electric current whipping around intensified so sharply, if I'd looked, I would have sure as certain seen white hot sparks crackling around the room.

"A man like me," he said slowly.

I swallowed.

He continued.

Kristen Ashley

"A man like me who'd use your body and abuse your heart to exact fuckin' retribution just because you walked away leavin' my cock hard?"

Well, since what he said sounded kind of stupid, I realized belatedly I might have been wrong about that.

"You think that's the kind of man I am?" he pushed.

"Hector—"

It was then he lost control of his anger and the room went wired.

"Answer me, goddamn it! You think I'm that kind of man?" he barked.

I jumped and stepped back.

He advanced.

That knot in my chest spread to my belly and my heart, burning through me so I couldn't breathe.

"Don't touch me," I whispered.

"I wouldn't touch you, Sadie. Not that way." He stopped just short of me and looked down at my face. "I'd like to knock some fuckin' sense into you, but that's not the kind of man I am."

At his words, my stomach clenched. Painfully.

"Maybe I was wrong," I said quietly.

His head cocked to the side and his eyes flashed again. "Maybe?"

I reached back with both hands and grabbed my hair at my ponytail, my hands fisting in it.

"I'm confused!" I cried, "I don't have a lot of experience—"

He interrupted me, "*Mamita*, I'm warnin' you. That excuse is wearin' thin real fuckin' fast."

My breath was coming in quick bursts. I dropped my hands and said, "You don't understand."

"Explain it to me."

"You still wouldn't understand."

"*Explain it to me!*" he roared.

I shook my head, or more like, jerked it from side-to-side.

I couldn't take anymore.

Not one more second.

I couldn't breathe, my stomach hurt, my head was pounding and that thing in my chest was threatening to explode.

I had to go, get out of there, go far, far away.

I rushed around him, got to the door and threw it open, but only took one
step into the hall before his fingers wrapped tight around my upper arm and he
swung me around.

"Take your hand off me!" I shouted.

"We're not fuckin' done."

"We're done!"

"No we fucking well are not!" he yelled.

Then it all came out in a humiliating, painful burst.

I couldn't control it. I had to get it out. The burning hot knot would kill
me if I didn't.

"*I'm protecting you!*" I screamed, "Don't you get it? I'm protecting you!"

He blinked, slowly, his brows coming up in surprise, but I kept going and
I did it loudly, shouting at the top of my lungs.

"You deserve better than me, Hector Chavez! You're a good man from a
good family surrounded by good people. My father was a Drug King. He kills
people! It's what I am, he *made* me. And Ricky Balducci raped and brutalized
me. You know it. You saw it. *You were even there!*" I screeched, out-of-control,
breath coming fast, eyes stinging with tears. "You saw me! You told me you'd
never forget. You saw me! You're better than that and I know it. You deserve
more than that. You don't think you do, but you've got a tattoo on you that
reminds you to think with your head, not your body. I don't want to be the next
tattoo you get when you learn your lesson one day and realize what you've done.
That you could have had better. That you could have had more. That you could
have someone good and clean and right. Someone who belongs at your side. Not
someone vile and ugly and tawdry and used that you should have never, ever,
*ever* settled for!"

He pulled me closer, muttering, "*Mamita.*" And I saw it in his eyes. They'd
gone so warm they burned a hole straight through my heart.

With superhuman effort, I yanked my arm out his grasp, whirled and ran.

"Don't follow me," I shouted over my shoulder as I saw him advance into
the hall. I stopped and turned again. "*Don't!*" I shrieked, my voice so shrill, it
was like a physical thing, clawing through the air.

Then I whirled again and ran, blind, mind blank, heart beating so hard I
thought it'd hammer out of my chest.

I pushed through people, felt hands on me, heard calls, shouts, even grunts. But I ran through it all, straight to the counter. I yanked open a drawer and pulled out the keys to my apartment.

People got in my way. I heard their voices speaking to me urgently but nothing penetrated.

I dodged, ducked, yanked my body away. I heard a gravelly voice say, "I got her," but I was gone, out the door into the cold night air, running.

After a block I bent double, pulled off my shoes and threw them in traffic. Then I sprinted like the devil was at my heels, the second block, then the third, then the fourth. On the fifth I was at my apartment building. I threw open the outer door, punched in the security code, yanked open the inner door and darted into the lobby.

I hadn't been there since the rape and I didn't think about it. I ran straight to the stairs, stitch in my side, breath rasping in my throat, up the four flights then out into the hall and to my door. With shaking hands I tried to unlock it. It took me three tries and then I was in, and I stopped, looking around in the dark, feeling the emptiness, remembering...

My nails went to my scalp and I ripped them through my hair, felt them, painful and harsh, as I dragged them along my scalp, down the back of my head, pulling the ribbon free.

I couldn't be there.

I couldn't go to Art.

I couldn't go to Ralphie and Buddy.

I couldn't go to a Rock Chick.

I couldn't go to Hector.

I couldn't go anywhere.

There was no where I belonged.

Nowhere safe.

I went to my bedroom. Quickly walking through, the memories of the night when Ricky broke in stabbing at my brain. I walked straight to the sliding doors that led to the balcony. I closed the door behind me and stepped out into the cold. Then I plastered my back against the stone wall and drifted down. My shirt and skirt snagging against the stone, down I went until my bottom hit the concrete. My knees were up. I put my cheek against them and I tried to find one of my Sadies to help me.

But they were gone.

Not on vacation, not having cocktails, not getting facials; my Ice Princess, Attitude Sadie, Take Charge Sadie and Pretend Sadie had all vanished. They didn't exist anymore. They weren't there to be called.

It was just me.

Only me.

I was all there was left.

I wrapped my arms around my legs. The cold night air crept into my bones. I kept my cheek to my knees and I sat there in the dark stillness of the night.

Alone.

⚘

The sliding glass door opened.

I heard it and kept my cheek to my knees, my face turned away, my body so cold I was shivering.

A hand slid along my lower back, another one under my knees.

I twisted as the arms lifted me. I turned to fight and stilled at what I saw.

I thought it would be Hector.

It wasn't.

It was Duke.

He carried me into my bedroom, set me on my feet and turned to the sliding door, pushing it shut.

Then I watched in stunned silence as he came to me, and when his arms were wrapping around me, pulling me tight to his big, warm body, I heard a violent noise coming from outside the apartment, like a body had thudded against the door.

I jumped and my head snapped around.

"Hector," Duke said over my head. "He's out there, the boys are with him. They're holding him back so I don't have a lotta time."

My lungs seized at his words, and even though the warmth of his body was heating me, I still shivered.

"Knew your mom," he went on. "Didn't know her well. I was a student then, gettin' my Master's but I hung out at Ellen's store. Ellen was Indy's Grandma. She gave the store to Indy when she died."

I didn't reply. I stood in his arms and tried to keep my mind blank, but his words came at me and I had nothing left in me to fight in order to keep them from penetrating my brain.

"I used to study there, made friends with Ellen. Katie, Indy's Mom, Lizzie and Kitty Sue came in all the time. So did your dad."

I sucked in a shocked breath at this announcement and waited.

"Loved your mom, your dad did. Thought she hung the moon. You could see it every time he looked at her. I didn't get a good feelin' about the guy, but Ellen thought he was special. 'Sharp as a tack, big heart.' She told me. She had good instincts. She could sense things in people. She never shared much, but she did tell me things weren't happy at home for your dad. It wasn't a good place for him to be. So he spent all the time he could with Lizzie."

I was blinking, rapid and uncontrollable, as he kept sharing.

"Things happen, life is shit, decisions are made, paths are chosen. Your dad chose the wrong paths. But I suspect he chose them for good reasons, thinkin' he was doin' the right thing, wantin' to give you and Lizzie a better life than what he had. I know this, Sadie, he loved your mom. And she loved him. Back then, he was her world. So, I suspect what made you was love. They loved each other, Sadie, and that's what made you. It might have gone wrong. It might have gone bad. But that's the way it started, that's where you came from and that's who you are."

I heard my own breaths escaping my nostrils in sharp bursts and another violent noise sounded in the hall.

"Somethin' else darlin'," he went on quickly, and his voice lowered. "Your mom was here, she saw what I saw at your gallery, heard what I heard you say, it'd tear out her heart. Girl, it would just kill her to think you thought that of yourself. She made the ultimate sacrifice for you. Don't let it be for nothin'. Take hold of life and live it beautiful like she wanted you to do."

I gulped down a sob, but it tore through and now I was shivering for a different reason, tears flowing down my face. I pressed my cheek against his chest and wrapped my arms around his girth.

"Now, darlin', there's a man outside who's likely to do somethin' he'll regret to men he respects if you don't get out there and stop it."

I pulled in my lips, but as I did it, without thinking and without hesitation, I pulled free of Duke, walked on my frozen feet through the bedroom, living room, straight to the front door which I yanked open.

Ten feet down the hall I saw the backs of the Hot Bunch (and Tex). Lee, Hank, Mace, Vance, Luke (and Tex) were all there. Their bodies held in a way that was just plain scary and the air in the hall was thick and hostile.

They heard the door, turned and parted. I saw Eddie and Hector, Eddie's back to me, body confronting Hector, Hector facing me.

Eddie turned. Hector's eyes sliced to me and I started walking forward.

Hector advanced.

I started running.

I ran straight into him and his arms closed around me.

I shoved my face in his chest, my fists gathering the material of his shirt by my cheeks and I cried hard, shoulder-shaking, uncontrollable sobs.

His arms went tighter and the heat of his body enveloped me.

"I'm an idiot," I said into his chest.

"You're not an idiot, *mi cielo,*" he murmured.

I shook my head, but kept his shirt in my fists so my face was rubbing against his chest.

"I'm an idiot," I repeated through my bawling.

"You're a pain in the ass, but you're not an idiot," he replied.

I tipped my head back and looked at him. I couldn't see much of anything. He was blurry through my tears.

"I told you that you were going to have to cut me some slack!" I cried.

He stared down at me. "You movin' to Greece?"

"No," I said immediately.

I felt the tension leave his body then one of his hands drifted up my back, up my neck, his fingers sliding into my hair.

His head dipped down and he touched my lips.

"Good," he said against my mouth. "Now let's go home."

# Chapter 21
# A Cooler and a Picnic Basket

*Sadie*

I woke in Hector's bed, feeling Hector's heat at my back, his mouth at my shoulder and his hands moving on me.

I sensed it immediately. The urgency and the tingles started.

"Hector?" I whispered.

He answered in Spanish, his mouth at my neck, words I didn't even understand causing the tingles to grow into shivers.

I turned in his arms, pressing into his body. He fell to his back, pulling me on top of him. One of his hands went into my panties, the fingers of the other one slid into my hair.

I put my mouth to his. His hand put pressure on my head, we kissed and I melted immediately as the kiss shot straight to hot, hungry and wild.

I'd gone to bed wearing my panties and one of his flannel shirts and both were gone within minutes.

Luckily, Hector had gone to bed naked.

I used my mouth on him, his throat, neck, down his chest, my teeth dragging across his nipples, my tongue outlining his tattoo.

Then down further, tracing his abdominal muscles with my lips, all the while my hand was wrapped around him, stroking, until, finally, I went down even further.

When I did, I heard his groan and his fingers slid in my hair, pulling it back. While I worked him, my gaze drifted up his chest. I saw him watching me, eyes blazing. A thrill shot through me and I felt the wetness immediately gather between my legs.

He allowed this for a while then pulled me up so I was on my belly at his side. Before I could turn, he did an ab curl, and all of a sudden, he was over me, between my legs, lifting my hips so I was on my knees. H positioned me and drove inside.

My head flew back. I came up to my hands then lifted my torso, reaching out to grab the headboard as he pounded into me. One of his hands went to cup my breast, finger and thumb doing an amazingly effective nipple roll. His other hand went between my legs, finger honing in on the target. His torso was bent to mine and his face was in my neck. I turned my head to him.

"I love," I panted, too turned on by what we were doing to think about my words, "being connected to you."

As an answer, he drove in deep and stayed there, grinding hard, his finger between my legs creating magic.

My head went back again, colliding with his shoulder as the glorious tightness gathered, intensified and exploded. It was so immense, it took me out of time, out of my world, into the world of a real Hector and Sadie. Together. Connected. And everything about them very, very right.

⚔️

After he finished, he gently pulled out, fell to his back, positioning me on top of him. One of his arms wrapped lightly around my waist, the fingers of his other hand traced mindless patterns on my bottom. My face was in his neck.

"*Take hold of life and live it beautiful like she wanted you to do.*" Duke's words sounded in my brain.

"They're gone," I whispered.

His arm at my waist tightened, his other hand stopped moving and cupped my behind.

"Sorry?" he asked, his voice rough, probably from what just happened, and I felt that roughness somewhere happy and deep.

"My Sadies," I explained quietly. Embarrassed and unsure, I kept my face in his neck, and taking a deep breath, I powered on. "See, like I told you, to get through, I needed the Ice Princess. But these last few weeks, trying to find my way, I created more of them, Attitude Sadie, Take Charge Sadie, Nice Sadie... I tried to find them last night to help me, but they're gone."

He gave me a squeeze and ordered softly, "Look at me."

I didn't want to. No, I *really* didn't want to. So I didn't.

"I don't think I can," I told him. "You probably think I'm crazy."

He gave me another squeeze, waiting a moment and then he spoke.

"*Mamita*, they're not gone. They've always been there. You just discovered them. They're who you are."

His words surprised me, mainly because they made sense, and I lifted my head to look at him.

"Do you think so?" I asked.

He rolled us so he was mostly on top and his eyes scanned my face.

"Yeah," he answered. "You're the most complicated woman I've ever met."

My brows drew together in confusion.

"Is that good?"

He grinned and his eyes went warm.

"Fuck yeah," he told me through his grin. "Gotta tell you, *mi cielo*, you missed a few."

This time, my brows went up.

"I did?"

His mouth touched mine, but his eyes stayed open, staring at me. Then his head moved away an inch.

"Yeah. Crazy Sadie. Sweet Sadie. Funny Sadie. And my favorite, the Sadie who just let me fuck her the way I wanted and she got off on it, even more than me."

Someone, please tell me he did not just say that.

My eyes narrowed.

"I did *not* get off on it more than you."

This time he smiled and it was his wicked smile. So, even though I was angry, my belly still melted at the sight.

"You did," he said.

"I did not," I retorted.

His hands started moving on me and his mouth came back to mine. Not to kiss me, but instead he murmured against my lips, "*Mamita*, don't you think I can feel you? You're so wet, you're slick. You feel like silk. You came hard. You always come hard. I know it, I can feel it. When you do, you get so fuckin' tight…"

Oh my God!

Even as his words were turning me on (yes, again!), I interrupted him.

"You think a lot of yourself, Hector Chavez," I snapped, lifting my hands to push at his shoulders. He moved away a few inches, but his smile got bigger, whiter and far more glamorous.

"Yeah, and you do, too."

I gasped, outraged.

He bit his lip, watching me, then said, "I see I got Attitude Sadie now." Then his head bent and he nuzzled my neck. "I like her, too."

At his words, for some bizarre reason, ice water flooded my veins and my body froze.

"Don't make fun of me," I whispered.

Immediately, his head came up and I noticed his smile had vanished.

He stared at me a second, eyes dark, then he spoke.

"I'm not makin' fun of you, Sadie. I'm teasin' you. There's a big fuckin' difference."

I watched him and realized belatedly that his smile had not only vanished, Mr. Mood Swing was getting downright angry.

He kept talking, proving me right.

"*Mujer*, you're gonna have to learn, pretty fuckin' quick, to trust me. I'm not like the people you know, the society bitches, the assholes your father recruited. You don't have to shut down. You don't have to put those fuckin' shields up. Christ, I *want* you to be who you are."

Yes. I was right. He was downright angry.

My heart lurched.

I did it again. I insulted him. Not as badly as last night, but not good either.

"Hector—" I started.

"This is your gig, Sadie. I can't help you. You're gonna have to figure it out, and fast. I'm not walkin' on eggshells wonderin' what fuckin' reaction you're gonna have to everything I say. I'm gonna say this once so pay attention. I'm not passin' the time here, enjoyin' a sweet, hot piece for the fuck of it. If you don't get it yet, I'll give it to you. What we got, it means somethin'. Do you understand?"

My heart lurched again, but this time it felt nice and that warm, happy glow hit my chest.

"I understand," I whispered.

"You better fuckin' understand," he bit out.

I closed my eyes tight then opened them again.

"I'm sorry." He stared at me silently and I continued. "About just now, and about last night. I was horrible. I said horrible…" I stopped and then started again, "I'm working through it, I promise."

He kept staring at me a second then two then his fingers slid into the side of my hair and I saw his mood swing again. But not fully; he was holding on to some of his anger. I could see it.

"Jesus, you're a pain in the ass," he muttered.

"I'm sorry about that, too," I said instantly, and I meant it.

His thumb came out of my hair and started sliding along my temple.

"I'll make up for it," I told him.

His eyes were watching his thumb, but at my words, they came to mine. "Yeah?"

"I'll buy you a building," I offered.

His body went tight and his eyes narrowed.

"Or, an island somewhere," I went on quickly. "I don't know how much islands cost, but there has to be one in my price range."

It was then I felt him relax. His mouth did that fighting-a-grin thing. I knew he finally let go of his anger and the happy glow settled in.

Since what I was doing appeared to be working, I kept talking. "It might just be a beach and a palm tree, but what else do you need on an island?"

He lost the fight with his grin, his head descended and I carried on, even when his lips were against mine.

"We'll bring a cooler and a picnic basket…" I stopped talking because he started kissing me, open-mouthed and sweet.

His body settled on mine and his arms were sliding around me when his cell rang.

He lifted his head and I saw right away that he'd morphed again, this time looking frustrated.

He pressed into me as he reached to the nightstand to nab his phone.

"This is over, *mi cielo*," his eyes came to me as he flipped open his phone, "*I'm* takin' *you* to a fuckin' island." Then he put his phone to his ear and clipped, "Yeah?"

My gaze was on Hector's face. My thoughts were on being on an island with Hector, and in the very, very back of my mind I figured my mom would like that. I mean, I wasn't altogether certain my mom would be thrilled about Hector's creativity in the sack (or my response to it), but what he did to me *was* beautiful in its way, and he made me feel good so she had to approve of that.

Right?

Then I saw his face grow tight and thoughts of my mom's approval of Hector disintegrated.

Oh no.

What now?

"No joke?" Hector asked into the phone, his eyes moving to me.

I did not like what I saw. Not at all.

"Right," he went on. "We're comin' down."

Without saying good-bye, he flipped the phone shut, tossed it on the nightstand and then stared at it, his face still tight, body now tense.

"Hector?" I called.

His chin dipped and he looked at me.

"Maybe we'll go to an island today," he murmured.

Damn and blast!

"What?" I asked.

His face went soft and he muttered, "Shit, Sadie."

"*What?*" I snapped.

He rolled us. Once he got to his back, he did an ab curl, his hands tugging at the backs of my knees so we were sitting with me straddling him. His head tilted back, mine down, my hands on his shoulders, his arms loose around me.

"Your gallery has been torched," he told me.

Convulsively, my hands moved to his neck and my fingers squeezed.

"Oh my God," I breathed.

"Fire started at five this morning. It's out now. They don't know how much damage yet, but it didn't spread." He paused then asked, "You insured?"

I was speechless so I nodded. For some reason, all I could think of was my lovely gift wrap and organdie ribbon, now probably reduced to ash.

And Lisette's paintings!

I closed my eyes tight, and not even thinking about it, I dropped my head until my forehead was resting on Hector's.

"Lisette's paintings," I whispered.

His arms tightened and I opened my eyes.

"You wanna go down there?"

"No," I told him. "But I'm going to go."

His hands went to my waist. He lifted me off him and to the side. He came over me, off the bed, hands back to my waist and he pulled me out of bed and set me on my feet.

Without a word, he tagged my hand and led the way to the shower.

⇒╪⇐

After Hector and I had our (yes, *our!*) shower, I called Buddy and Ralphie to give them the news.

Buddy answered and I felt weird. After last night, I thought they'd be mad at me. But Buddy's voice was its usual soft and sweet.

"You okay, sweetheart?" he asked.

"Yes. Did Ralphie—?"

"He told me. He's upset, thinks he hurt your feelings," Buddy interrupted.

"He didn't hurt my feelings. I was worried I hurt his."

"No, he gets what you were trying to do. He overreacted, as usual."

"It wasn't his fault."

Buddy changed the subject. "Are you really movin' to Greece?"

"Not anymore," I answered.

Silence for a second then, teasing, "Damn, there went my vacation plans."

I smiled into the phone, relief rolling over me for a brief shining moment, then my smile faded and I said, "I've got bad news."

More silence, then I told him about the gallery.

Then he shouted, "*What?*"

I winced.

I heard him cover the mouthpiece and even though it was covered, I heard Ralphie's shrill scream.

Buddy came back to me. "Ralphie, YoYo and me'll meet you there."

"See you soon," I said and we disconnected.

I dressed in my Lucky jeans, a slimfit, long-sleeved white t-shirt, the black belt with the rose buckle and motorcycle boots that Daisy, Roxie, Tod and Stevie gave me. I left my hair long to dry in crazy, natural waves and ringlets and did a half-assed pass with blusher, shadow and mascara. Though, I spent more time on my lip gloss. You had to be careful with lip gloss, even when you were about to view your burned out building. If you didn't you'd look like a clown.

Hector and I climbed into the Bronco and headed into town.

We hit LoDo and I saw Hector avoid the Nightingale garage which would be the perfect parking opportunity.

"You can park in the garage," I told him as he navigated early morning downtown traffic.

His eyes came to me briefly then went back to the road.

"I'm thinkin' you've scaled enough mountains for now, *mamita,*" he muttered, and his casual kindness made that happy glow grow a smidgen wider.

He drove until he found a spot on the street three blocks from the gallery and parallel parked.

Then Hector and I walked hand-in-hand toward the gallery.

As we approached, I saw the crowd forming a U in front of what was left of Art. Traffic had been diverted. There were barricades up in a wide arc in front of the gallery. The fire trucks and police cars were still there and people were standing around the barricades in the street.

Without apology, Hector shoved his way through the crowd to the barricades and walked right through.

A uniformed officer looked at him and gave him a chin lift. Hector and I walked into the opened area where firemen and police were milling about.

I stared at my building. The brick on the outside was blackened. The windows had shattered; the inside was blackened, too, and water was everywhere.

Hector walked us to Detective Marker who was standing watching us approach. We got close and stopped.

"Jimmy," Hector said, dropping my hand, but his arm slid around my shoulders and he pulled me into his side.

"Hector," Detective Marker greeted then his eyes came to me. "Sadie."

"Detective Marker," I replied and looked back at my gallery.

My heart sunk at the same time my body sagged despondently into Hector's side. In response, his arm curled around my neck and tightened.

"Donny Balducci's a firebug," Detective Marker remarked, his gaze never leaving the building.

"Yeah," Hector agreed, his eyes also locked on what was left of Art.

My head tilted back to look at Hector.

His face was stony.

My gaze drifted to Detective Marker.

He looked a weird mixture of angry and resigned. In other words, he had what could only be called a Cop Look.

Then Hector started talking again.

"Jack's sending the tapes by courier to the Station. We got them on the cameras. Jack saw 'em break in and called it in. Said he saw Donny with the gasoline, either Marty or Ricky with him. He didn't get a good look at the second guy but he knew it was a Balducci. They made fast work of it. The place was ablaze and they were gone before anyone got here."

"I hope its Ricky," Detective Marker replied, fishing his phone out of his suit jacket.

"Yeah," Hector said. "I'm thinkin' arson is probably a violation of his bond."

I was no longer listening. A thin film of red had descended over my eyes and there was a buzzing in my ears.

My sagging body went tight and I put my hand on Hector's stomach. I pulled slightly away and looked up at him.

"Why didn't you say anything?"

Hector's chin dipped and his eyes came to mine.

"Parceling out the bad news, *mamita*," he said softly. "You can only take so much at once."

I blinked at him and then took in both Hector and Detective Marker.

"Let me get this straight," I said, my voice trembling, something strange happening to me.

It was *not* my weird, warm, happy glow (not even fucking *close*).

It was *not* that hot, hard, painful knot in my chest.

It was something else altogether.

When I had both their attention, I kept talking. "First, for weeks, all the fucking Balduccis call me, stop by the gallery only when I'm alone, show up at my apartment day and night, doing crazy shit, saying crazy things and freaking me out. Then Ricky fucking Balducci breaks in, beats me up and rapes me. Then Harvey fucking Balducci assaults me and tries to kidnap me. *Then* Marty fucking Balducci threatens me over the phone and calls me the c-word, *twice*. *Now*, Donny fucking Balducci has burned down my gallery?"

I was shouting, people were looking at me and I didn't care.

"You have *got* to be *shitting* me!" I yelled.

Hector got in my line of sight.

"*Mamita*, calm down," he muttered.

I looked up at him and grabbed onto his tee, fisting it in my fingers and giving him a shake (well, trying to, but he didn't move, just his tee did).

"*You* be calm! I'm pissed right the fuck *off!*" I screamed.

"This is gonna end, soon, Sadie, trust me."

"Yeah, it's going to end soon. I'm gonna hunt those motherfuckers down and—"

Hector's hand came over my mouth and I finished my shouted threat so it sounded like, "Kff thff."

Hector shuffled me back, arm still tight around my neck, hand over my mouth, until we were away from Detective Marker and everyone.

Then his head came close. "*Mamita*, he knows you're emotional and don't mean it. Still, not good to threaten homicide in front of a cop."

I just glared at him over his hand on my mouth.

"You in control?" he asked.

"No!" I said under his hand but it came out, "Nff!"

His body started to shake and I knew he was laughing.

My head prepared to explode.

Now, really, seriously, there was *nothing* fucking funny about *this*.

"This is not fucking funny," I said under his hand, but again it came out, "Thff if nf ffing ffny."

I knew he was about to burst out laughing, which would mean I'd have to kill *him* right in front of Detective Marker (or not kill him because I liked him, but at least do him some bodily harm) when we heard, "We're with them."

Hector and my heads turned to the side and we saw Ralphie and Buddy with YoYo on a leash trying to get by a uniformed officer.

Hector dropped his arms, letting me go and called, "Joe, it's all right."

"Joe" looked at Hector, nodded and stepped aside. Ralphie and Buddy forged through, both of them walking slowly, their heads turned to the side staring at Art. YoYo strained at her lead, tongue lolling, bugged out eyes on me and Ralphie let her go. She scampered across the space. I leaned down and picked her up. She decided she needed to bathe my neck and jaw with her tongue so this was what she did, squiggling in my arms, all happy puppy.

"Stop," Hector suddenly clipped at the pug.

YoYo went still immediately and stared at him.

At his tone, so did I.

"She's just happy to see me," I explained to Hector.

"Only tongue on your neck is mine," he returned.

My eyes bugged out as far as YoYo's.

"You're jealous of a dog?"

"Fuck no," he answered, staring at me like I had a screw loose. "But I might have a mind to put my mouth on you and I don't want to do it after a dog."

Well.

Had to admit, he had a point.

And it was an interesting point.

And the thought of his mouth on me made me forget all about the crazy, mean, fucking, Balduccis.

Ralphie and Buddy made it to us and they gave chin lifts to Hector, (Ralphie's came with a, "Hey, Double H") and hugs and cheek kisses to me (Ralphie's hug was tighter than normal, longer, and after, he looked into my eyes until I smiled at him; only then did he move away).

"Lisette is gonna freak. She'd been working on that collection for over a year," Ralphie said, his eyes now on the blackened building, and my thoughts went right back to the crazy, mean, fucking Balduccis.

"Hector said it was Donny Balducci," I informed them, and in unison, they looked at me. "I know. But you aren't allowed to threaten his life, not in front of the police, or so Hector says."

"Can I threaten to beat the crap out of him?" Buddy asked.

I looked at Hector to assess his response to this.

He was fighting a grin but he shook his head at me.

"Probably not," I told Buddy.

"Well!" Ralphie cried (loudly). "Life gives you lemons, you make lemonade. We're insured against loss of income, this means vacation. This means shopping. This means trips to the spa. This means learning how to make that complicated lemon soufflé."

"You don't cook," Buddy cut in.

"Well, I'm gonna learn," Ralphie shot back. "And that means Sur La Table, Cherry Creek Mall, after breakfast. Maybe Williams Sonoma. I'm calling the Rock Chicks. I'm thinking Mercury Café." He turned to me. "You call Lisette, and after I'm done calling Daisy, I'll call the insurance people. We eat then we're shopping for kitchen implements."

"We don't need any kitchen implements," Buddy cut in again.

"One *always* needs kitchen implements," Ralphie returned.

"No shopping and no breakfast with the Rock Chicks. Unless I can get a man on Sadie, she's staying at the offices today," Hector entered the conversation.

"That's all right, Double H, I'm on the case," Ralphie assured him.

Hector's face went a weird mixture of hard and soft and I realized why when he started speaking in a voice that was the same as his face.

"No. I want a trained man on her. Buildings are burning. The Balduccis are feelin' pressure. I want her covered by a professional."

I stared at Hector, cuddling YoYo closer to the warm, happy glow in my chest because at that point it hit me not a lot of macho badasses would hang out with Ralphie (maybe Buddy, but never Ralphie). They wouldn't watch TV with him. They wouldn't have dinner with him. They certainly wouldn't be nice to him when they knew what they said could hurt his feelings.

And that was when I knew.

Right then and there, watching Hector be careful with Ralphie's feelings, I knew.

It had happened.

I *was* living the dream.

The dream of a good man who would save me. The dream of a man who would sweep away my bad life and take me to a jumbled bungalow (though Hector's house wasn't a bungalow, but still) and make me safe. Make me happy. Make me so warm, I'd never feel cold again.

The force of this realization caused me to take a step back as if it was a colossal weight that landed on me and I had to hold it up but couldn't quite manage it.

Hector, Buddy and Ralphie's eyes all snapped to me.

"Sadie?" Buddy asked, but Hector got close.

"*Mamita?*" His hands came to my neck.

I looked up at him. "I'm okay."

He scanned my face and his brows drew together.

"You're shuttin' down," he said, but immediately, so he wouldn't think that, I shook my head and got closer, a lot closer, crushing YoYo (who didn't seem to mind) between us.

I tilted my head back further.

"You don't get it," I whispered to him. "I'm okay."

He stared at me and I went on.

"My gallery is burned beyond recognition. I'm estranged from my father. Crazy men are after me. I had the freak out to end all freak outs in front of friends and most of my clients last night but... I'm okay."

I felt his fingers squeeze my neck as I watched his eyes grow warm, and I knew mine were the same.

"Finally!" Ralphie cried. Hector and I lost the moment and turned to look at him. "Told her to enjoy the ride, Double H, *ages* ago. She didn't listen. Finally, she's learning to enjoy the fucking ride!"

I shifted and pressed my side against Hector's front.

His arm curled around my neck.

Then I felt his lips kiss the top of my head.

I mentally pried my hands off the safety bar that was tucked, tight and secure, across my lap and lifted them straight in the air.

⋙⋘

"Do you ever file a thing?" Kitty Sue asked Shirleen from her hands and knees on the floor.

Daisy and I were with her, alphabetizing a mountain of paperwork in twenty-six piles across the Nightingale Investigation's reception area.

"It's not in my job description," Shirleen replied from her seat behind the reception desk, currently engaged in the difficult task of painting her nails a frosty grape.

Kitty Sue sat up so she was on her knees. She planted her hands on her hips, twisted to Shirleen and glared.

"You're the receptionist!"

"Yeah? So?" Shirleen asked, not taking her eyes from her nails.

"Receptionists file," Kitty Sue retorted.

"Filing people file. Receptionists answer phones and guard the door," Shirleen returned.

Daisy looked at me and giggled. I pulled my lips between my teeth and tried not to laugh. Kitty Sue didn't look like she thought anything was funny.

"This is my son's livelihood," Kitty Sue said as she got to her feet. "What if he needed something urgently and couldn't find it?"

Shirleen threw her head back and laughed for a long time.

"That's funny," she declared (unnecessarily) when she finished laughing.

"What's funny? I'm being serious," Kitty Sue shot back.

Shirleen leveled her amused gaze on Kitty Sue. "I practically gotta chain Lee to his chair to get him to fill out reports, type out notes and whatever other shit he's gotta do. He *hates* paperwork. All the boys do. Badass mothers get fuckin' grumpy when Shirleen rides their asses to get them to put pen to paper, or worse, fingers to keyboards. If it wasn't for me, our invoices would be six months late goin' out and no one would get paid. Including Shirleen. And Shirleen likes to get paid. I got two growin' boys who eat me out of house and home and are always takin' bitches to the movies and shit like that. I don't get paid, I'm fucked and Roam and Sniff'll look like beggars in front of their babes. Not... gonna... happen."

"Well," the wind, I could tell, had gone out of Kitty Sue's sails, "the least you could do is help us now."

"I will help you," Shirleen replied. "I'll tell you you missed a pile." And she nodded to a pile of papers at the end of her desk that was at least a foot high.

"Shit," Daisy muttered.

That was when I giggled at the same time the door opened and Ally and Indy walked in, laughing.

I sat back on my calves and smiled at them as they called, "Hey," to everyone.

Not two months ago, I walked into this office feeling the frosty air, knowing they hated me and wishing I was one of them.

Now I was sitting on the floor, sorting through Lee and The Boy's confidential paperwork, having spent the day getting to know Brody (the computer geek, and I mean *geek*), Monty (the guy who managed the surveillance room, where I was a bit weirded out to see they monitored Fortnum's, which meant my meltdown there was witnessed by even more people than I knew at the time) and Shirleen.

Kitty Sue had come by with lunch. We ate. We chatted. She told me great stories about my mom that only a best friend would know and she apologized about seven million five hundred thousand times about not "protecting" me throughout my life and not coming to see me after my father was put behind bars.

"I kept trying to figure out how to do it. What I should say," she whispered to me, holding my hand. "I didn't know what to say."

I squeezed her fingers. "It's done now. Over. Don't think about it." I blew it off as if it was nothing so she would stop beating herself up. Then I changed the subject. "You told me about my mom, now will you tell me about Katherine?"

She smiled, let go of my hand, sat back and told me great stories about Katherine.

Later, Daisy came around, Kitty Sue spied the paperwork and we all got busy.

"What in *the hell* are you doing?" Ally asked, staring at the papers all over the floor.

"Filing," I answered.

Indy turned to Shirleen. "I thought that was your job."

"Do I look like a file clerk to you?" Shirleen's eyes narrowed, clearly becoming frustrated with this topic.

"You're sitting behind a receptionist desk," Indy returned.

"Maybe we shouldn't talk about this anymore," I cut in, trying to help.

"Does Lee know you don't do the filing?" Indy, apparently, didn't need my help.

Shirleen grinned. "That's it. *You* talk to Lee about paperwork. *You* give him lip about paperwork. Now *that* I'd like to see. Make sure Shirleen's around when you talk to Lee about paperwork. He *loves* to talk about paperwork."

At this juncture, wisely, Kitty Sue decided to intervene, "Ally, get that pile from the end of Shirleen's desk and you and Indy help sort. Shirleen, move out from behind the desk, Sadie's going to type labels on the computer and make up folders. Daisy, start with the A's, file what already has a folder in the cabinet, give Sadie the rest so she can make folders. Come on girls," she clapped her hands, "let's go."

Boy, you could tell Kitty Sue was a mom. Even Daisy and Shirleen did as she ordered, which meant Shirleen moved to the far more comfortable couch and kept polishing her nails.

I found the folders and labels and started typing. Daisy started filing. Kitty Sue, Indy and Ally kept on sorting.

In an hour, we were done. The last label typed. The last folder put away. Kitty Sue closed a drawer with her foot and swiped her hands together like she was brushing off dust.

"Oowee, world's put to rights, Lee's paperwork is filed. I'll call the mayor," Shirleen announced from her reclining position on the couch, her head coming up from her perusal of *Us* magazine.

Daisy, Ally, Indy and Kitty Sue all went red in the face and glared at Shirleen.

"Why don't we go to dinner? My treat," I offered before anyone could commit a violent act, or worse, say something they regretted.

"Can't," Shirleen said, sitting up. "Orders are you stay here unless one of the Hot Bunch is around to escort you. They're all tied up. You're stuck."

"Then we'll order pizza," I decided.

Shirleen nodded and grinned. "That'll work. I got Famous on speed dial."

Of course she did.

"I'll call the girls. The Hot Bunch are all working tonight so they're all free," Indy put in.

"Tell Jet to stop by Pasquini's and pick up dessert," Ally threw in.

"Tell Jules to bring Max. I haven't seen him in *ages,*" Kitty Sue said.

"Tell Roxie to pop by the liquor store and get beer," Daisy finished.

I moved out from behind the desk to give Shirleen room and walked to the side of the couch to pick up my purse so I could call Ralphie and Buddy to see if they wanted to come around.

I grabbed my phone, dropped my purse to the couch and turned, back to the door, to face the girls, all of whom were across the room.

"I'll call Ralphie and Bud—" I started but didn't finish.

The door opened behind me. I didn't have a chance to turn, but I did see Daisy's face grow pale, her mouth opened to say something, but I felt something *very* unpleasant touch my neck.

I dropped the phone and everything went black.

# Chapter 22

# He Taught Me How to Make S'Mores

## *Sadie*

It was well past dawn when the door opened, the lights went on and Jerry walked in.

I'd been up for hours watching the sun lighten the dark room as it peeped through the closed curtains at the window.

I did not spend this time scared.

I spent it angry.

I was over this.

Over.

This.

*All* of it.

The fact that it was Jerry who'd kidnapped me right out of Nightingale Investigations reception area and not one of the crazy, mean, fucking Balducci Brothers didn't make me any happier.

This was only partly because I was over all the shitty, terrible traumas that kept making my life so fucking difficult. It was also because I knew Hector (and everyone, for that matter), were probably scared out of their minds that I'd been gone all night.

And them being scared pissed me right off.

I yanked my hand which was handcuffed to an iron bedstead so that it made an awful clink and I glared at him.

"Uncuff me," I snapped.

"No fuckin' way. You get uncuffed after you talk to your dad," Jerry replied, putting a mug of coffee and a bowl of cereal on the nightstand. The room I was in was clean, drab and had no personal items. Just a double bed, dresser and two nightstands.

"Where am I?" I demanded, taking a different tact.

"Your father's safe house. The Feds never found it," Jerry replied, standing several feet away from the bed, arms crossed on his chest, looking down at me.

"Where is it?"

"You're spreadin' your legs for an ex-Fed PI, Sadie," he returned, his tone ugly. "I'm not gonna tell you where your father's safe house is."

I decided to ignore his rude words.

"How did you get me?"

"Stun gun. You went down. I dragged you out. Your bitches came after me. I fired warning shots, they backed off. Got you in the car, Nightingale's operations man, Monty whoever-the-fuck came after me, I shot out his tire. You started to come around, I gave you a different kind of shot. Nightie night."

I felt my breath catch. "You *shot* at them?"

"Warning shots."

I yanked my hand against the cuffs and got up on my knees.

"I swear to *God*, Jerry, you hurt any of them, I'll fucking *kill* you!"

He grinned like he thought I was hilarious. "Much as I'd like to put a bullet in Nightingale's piece or his fuckin' sister, who's a pain in *everyone's* ass, you Dad's orders were to get you. No collateral damage. That's what I did."

That made me feel better, but I still spat at him, "You're a pig."

At my words, his face went hard. "Rather be a pig than a traitor." He leaned in and his face started to turn ugly. "You make me sick. The idea of that asshole's hands on you, his mouth on you, his dick in you. Christ, your father trusted him and Chavez fucked him. He fucked all of us. Now you're lettin' him fuck you. Can you imagine how that makes your dad feel?"

"My father feels? Wow, Jerry, thanks for sharing. That's news to me," I retorted sarcastically, too beyond angry to stop myself.

His face twisted with fury. "It was me you fucked over that way, I'd let the Balduccis play with you. Not Seth. 'Take 'em down, one-by-one, make it hurt,' he says to me. 'Keep an eye on Sadie, Chavez falls down on the job, make sure she's safe,' he says. Fuck."

My body had gone solid.

*Make sure she's safe,* he said.

My father wanted to be sure I was safe.

And, if I read it right, he was resigned to Hector having that job.

I couldn't wrap my mind around it and I started to tremble but luckily Jerry didn't notice.

"Eat. Your father'll call. He'll talk. You'll fuckin' listen, then I'll take you back to your fuck buddy," Jerry finished our tête-à-tête and turned to go.

In desperation, before I could stop myself, I blurted, "I need to call Hector."

Jerry stopped and grinned again, then his eyes got weird in a way I *did not like*.

"Like the idea of seein' what you'd do to get that call, Sadie. Maybe I'd make you let me fuck that smart mouth of yours." My heart started beating harder just as my eyes narrowed but he kept on, "But I like the idea of Chavez tearin' Denver apart lookin' for you more."

Then he was gone.

I stared at the door, giving it my Icicle Ray of Death Glare, which didn't work no matter how hard I tried. Then I ate my cereal, drank my coffee and waited.

Jerry came back, stun gun in one hand, keys to the handcuffs in another.

"Bathroom. You got one minute then I come in," he threatened.

I didn't fight and did as he asked.

I just had to wait. He said I had to listen to my father, and for Detective Marker this was what I was supposed to be doing. I didn't pretend to be happy about the circumstances, but I wasn't going to do anything stupid either. Jerry was mean and I didn't want to test him. I wanted to get through this latest trauma alive and breathing and go on. I was noticing the bad parts were interspersed with good parts. And of those good parts, some of them were great, some of them were fun and all of them gave me that warm, snugly, safe feeling.

If all I had to do was talk to my father to get back to all that, that was what I'd do.

After my bathroom break, Jerry cuffed me to the bed and disappeared again.

I tried not to think about Hector tearing Denver apart looking for me (which I was pretty certain sure he was doing) or the rest of my friends worried about me (again!). Instead, I decided what color Hector's living room should be painted (a dusky gray, like the thermal he owned that I liked so much). Then I decided he should install an island like Buddy and Ralphie's in his kitchen (I figured that would work, if it was an eensy bit smaller).

It might have been an hour, maybe longer, when Jerry came back.

He had a cell to his ear and he was nodding.

"She's right here," he said into the cell. He stopped by the bed and handed it to me.

I took it and put it to my ear.

"Sadie?" my father said.

I thought about my coaching from Hector, Eddie and Marcus and I snapped into the phone, "You had me kidnapped."

"Sadie—"

I interrupted him and clipped, throwing Jerry right under the bus (where he belonged, in my personal opinion), "I asked to make a phone call and Jerry told me he wanted to fuck my smart mouth!"

Silence.

Or I should say, scary silence.

As usual, I sallied forth. "Is this how we spend father and daughter hour now, *Daddy?* Any time you want to speak to me, one of your henchmen kidnaps me and threatens me with sexual violation before you and I have our chat?"

"I'll have a word with Jerry," my father said.

He sounded angry and I looked up at Jerry who now looked pale.

Ha!

"Make it two. I think *two* words with Jerry would probably be better," I retorted, my eyes locked on Jerry.

That was when Jerry's handsome face twisted in that ugly way again, and even though deep down inside it scared me half to death, I just kept glaring at him.

"Sadie, there are things I have to go over with you. I don't have a lot of time so I need you to be quiet and listen."

"Well, *Daddy*, seeing as I'm handcuffed to a bed in a room in a house where I don't know where the hell I am, I've got nothing better to do. So fire away."

He sighed then he said, "I need to tell you where the money is."

This surprised me. I had no idea what he was going to say, but I didn't figure that would be it. Giving me grief about Hector, yes. Money, no.

My chin dropped and I blinked at the bedclothes.

"What money?"

"My money, your money, our money."

"I know where *my* money is. Aaron takes care of it."

"That's your grandmother's money. This is our money. The money I earned, the money the Feds didn't get. It's in your name in an account in the Caymans."

I felt my heart lodge in my throat.

He was joking.

Right?

"Do you need me to get it for you?" I asked stupidly.

What was he going to do with it?

Unless he was planning a prison break.

Someone, please tell me he wasn't planning a prison break!

"No," he answered, and I let out a quiet, relieved breath. "I need to know you can get to it if you need to."

This surprised me, too. More than before. Down to my core.

My heart slid to the side, lengthwise, threatening to choke me.

"I don't want your money," I whispered.

"Sadie, you need to get gone, until the Balduccis—"

"Hector's taking care of me," I cut in.

"Yes, I can see that. He's doing a stellar job. That's why you're cuffed to a bed," my father shot back impatiently.

Oh no, he was not going to lay this on Hector!

"Only because Jerry shot at the Rock Chicks!" I cried.

"You think one of the Balducci boys wouldn't shoot at those girls? They wouldn't think twice and they wouldn't intentionally miss."

He was probably right about that.

I, of course, was not going to tell him that.

"Even the Balduccis wouldn't be fool enough to walk into Lee Nightingale's office and nab me. Jerry's fucked. Hector's probably livid and the Nightingale Men are going to freak."

"You think I don't know that?" he asked sharply. "I need Lee Nightingale breathing down my neck like I need a hole in my head. Sadie, you forced my hand, put me in a situation where I had to put one of my men at risk just so I could talk to my own goddamned daughter."

I steeled myself so his words wouldn't affect me.

"Are we done here?" I asked, sounding like I was definitely done.

"No. I need to give you the name of the bank, the account numbers—"

"I think I already told you I don't want your money and I'm fine where I am."

More silence. This stretched longer, became scarier, then my father said in a low voice, a voice I knew very well, the voice he used when he meant to be listened to and obeyed.

"We need to talk about Chavez."

I fought against my conditioning to listen and obey and said fake-breezily, "Talk away."

"I don't like you with him."

"Well, I didn't suspect you'd be leaping for joy, but I also don't care. I like him. He taught me how to make s'mores."

Silence again. This time it wasn't scary, it was something else.

"S'mores?" he asked, and I could swear my always unruffled father sounded confused.

"Yes, those graham cracker sandwiches where you roast a marsh—"

"I know what s'mores are, Sadie."

"Well, he taught me how to make them. He found out I'd never had them and always wanted to make some and he made sure I had them. And we sanded his floors. And his mother likes me. She's going to teach me how to cook."

The scary was back. "He's got you, *my daughter*, sanding his floors?"

"I asked to do it. Hector wanted to watch a movie."

"Jesus Christ," my father muttered.

At this point, in order to speed things up and get the hell out of there, I channeled Hector and explained, "I know you don't have a lot of time and you're not getting this so I'll give it to you. See, a good life is about sanding floors, making s'mores and laughing while you do the dishes. It's about putting lip gloss on in the restroom with your girlfriends during a rock gig. It's about being able to say things that aren't smart or do things that are really stupid and people forgiving you. It's about looking after each other. That's a good life. Ralphie and Buddy, my friends, gave that to me. Then Hector came into my life and made it even better. I've had that life for..."

I stopped, counted and then went on.

"Five weeks and five days. I like it. I'm not giving it up. I'm not going to the Caymans and living the big life off your drug money, surrounded by pretty things, eating the finest foods, drinking champagne, but being totally alone and utterly lonely. I'd rather paint Hector's living room which is what I might do today, if he lets me. Now, can we stop talking so Jerry can take me home and good people can stop worrying about me?"

Apparently, he didn't listen to a word I said.

"It's my job to take care of you, I'm your father," he told me.

"Well, if it's your job, you're fired," I replied calmly, proud of myself.

Who would have known I had it in me?

But there it was.

Silence again, then, "This isn't done, Sadie."

It was my turn to sigh. "I didn't figure it would be. But can it be for now? I need a shower."

Then he surprised me again, he did this by giving in.

My father *never* gave in.

Ever!

"Give the phone to Jerry," he ordered.

I smiled with saccharin sweetness (through my surprise) at Jerry and held out the phone.

"Daddy wants to talk to you." I told him.

Jerry gave me a glare. He took the phone, turned his back to me and walked out of the room.

Minutes later, he came back, holding a funny looking gun.

I stared in shock at the gun.

"Lights out," Jerry said and the last thing I saw were the Taser prongs coming at me.

⌦

I came to strapped into the front seat of Jerry's BMW and he was driving. I didn't know how long I'd been out, but it took a while for me to get my faculties together.

I figured I'd chatted enough with Jerry. He wasn't a great conversationalist so even when I had myself sorted, I kept my mouth shut.

After a while, Jerry, unfortunately, felt like talking.

"I'm gonna stop for a second. You're not clear of the car, I run you down. You try something smart, I go for payback. I'll be nicer to you than Ricky. Blood would put me off getting off. Who knows? Maybe you'd even enjoy it."

Seriously.

What a jerk!

"Swine," I mumbled, breaking my vow not to speak to him.

He kept on, clearly unhappy about me throwing him under the bus (or maybe he *was* swine).

"Don't mind sayin', all the boys had a thing for you. Chavez wasn't the only one. He just hid it better than the rest of us. You, Christ, all haughty, bitchy and ice cold. We spent a lot of time talkin' about how you'd feel if we got a piece of you. If our cocks would freeze off or if you'd finally let loose and be a wildcat. Your dad's still got power, but you try me, I figure it would be worth his retribution to have a crack at you and find out."

I turned to Jerry. "You *do* know I was raped, don't you? You *do* know that every word out of your mouth makes you lower than low, slimier than slime, scumier than scum? Don't you?"

He didn't answer.

I saw we were getting close to the Nightingale Offices and I knew that was where he was going to let me off.

I unbuckled my seatbelt, put my hand on the door handle and kept my mouth shut until I had just enough time to say exactly what I wanted to say.

Then, when the time was right, I said it.

"Just to appease your curiosity, Jerry, I like it fast, hot, hard and rough *and* I like it slow, gentle and sweet. I like it any way Hector wants to give it to me and he gives it to me *loads*. So, you can tell those assholes, being pansy-assed and afraid of my father, they missed out because I *am* a wildcat. And that's why Hector's getting it. Because he's not pansy-assed or afraid of *anything*."

And before he came to a full stop or could say a word, I threw open the door, put my feet to the pavement and ran.

I didn't look back. I went straight into the building and to the stairs not bothering with the elevator.

I rounded the landing on the first flight and slammed right into Mace.

Without a word, he took my hand and dragged me up to the third floor, into the hall and directly into the offices.

Shirleen was standing behind her desk, phone to her ear, eyes—full of relief—on me.

"Hector?" Mace asked Shirleen.

He didn't break stride. He kept dragging me through the reception area.

Shirleen put her hand over the mouthpiece nodding.

"On his way," Shirleen replied.

Mace punched a code into the keypad by the inner door.

"I'm okay," I told Shirleen.

"Thank God, child," she said back.

Mace dragged me through the door.

"Call Detective Marker," I shouted as the door closed behind me.

Mace dragged me straight to Lee's office and pulled me in.

Tom Savage, Malcolm Nightingale and Monty were all at Lee's desk. There was a mess of papers on it, papers that looked like maps and floor plans.

Their heads came up and they stared at me.

Then Tom broke away from the rest and came at me muttering, "Christ Jesus."

Before I knew it, he had me in his arms.

"Christ. Jesus. Jesus Christ," he whispered over my head.

So lightning wouldn't strike him for taking the Lord's name in vain (repeatedly), I said into his chest, "I'm okay. It was my father. He had one of his men kidnap me. He didn't hurt me. My father just wanted to talk."

Tom leaned back and looked at me. "We know it was Jerry. Daisy recognized him. We just didn't know what your father had planned."

I saw the relief written all over his face, and even though it was unhappy circumstances that gave him that look, for some reason somewhere deep it made me happy. So happy, I slid my arms around his waist, pressed my cheek against his chest and hugged him.

I don't remember hugging anyone like that of my own accord (and not in the middle of a major flip out) since my mom was killed.

"I'm okay," I repeated.

He hugged me back. "Thinkin' about givin' up Mexican food, girl. At least until we know you're safe. You nearly gave me a heart attack."

I pulled away and looked up at him.

"That's sayin' a lot, Tom likes his Mexican food," Monty called from his spot by the desk.

"I wouldn't want you to give up something you liked," I told Tom.

He smiled at me as Malcolm asked Mace, "Someone call Hector?"

"Shirleen," Mace replied.

"The girls?" Tom asked.

"Shirleen," Mace repeated.

"Prepare for a Rock Chick invasion," Monty muttered.

I looked at Monty, then at Mace, and finally at Malcolm and Tom.

"I'm sorry to worry you. I—"

Malcolm cut me off, "Didn't hear Kitty Sue, Indy or Ally say you waltzed out with Jerry, arms linked and laughin', so stop apologizin'."

I nodded.

Then, even though it probably sounded stupid, it was true, I said to Mace, "I really could use a cup of coffee. Do you guys have a kitchenette?"

"I'll get Brody to make a pot," Mace told me.

"Shit no!" Monty exclaimed, moving away from the desk. "Brody's coffee's thicker than custard. One cup'll keep you awake a week. I'll make it."

"Thanks Monty," I said to his back. He didn't turn around. He just lifted up a hand, flicked out his index and middle fingers and walked out.

"Shit to do," Mace mumbled. He tagged me with a hand behind my head and brought me close. He leaned low (Mace was really tall), kissed my forehead, then he was gone.

Monty made coffee and Shirleen, who didn't file but apparently did serve coffee, or at least she did to recently returned kidnap victims, brought it in with milk, sugar and mugs.

I had just taken my first fortifying sip (Monty made excellent coffee) when the door opened and Hector was there.

He looked at me, his face as dark as thunder.

I smiled at him.

For some reason, his face stayed dark and his gaze moved to the room.

"Get out," he told everyone.

My smile died.

"Hector!" I snapped.

No one seemed offended by this and everyone moved to leave. There were smiles and Monty even chuckled.

I didn't think this was funny.

Hector was being rude!

"You don't have to leave," I told them, putting my mug on the desk, but they were gone, the door closing behind Tom. But right before it did, I saw him turn and wink. Then he disappeared from sight.

I glared at Hector.

"That was rude," I told him.

He was three feet away from me.

Then, without apparently moving, he was right there, his arms around me, crushingly tight. My body plastered against his, his mouth came down hard on mine.

His kiss took my breath away. The only thing I could do was put my hands to either side of his neck and hold on.

He tore his mouth from mine and touched our foreheads for a nanosecond before moving back an inch.

His eyes were blazing hot. Not with desire or anger, but with something else that *still* made my knees go weak.

"Scared the shit out of me," he told me.

At the depth of feeling in his voice, all my organs at once ceased working.

"Hector," I whispered.

"Don't remember the last time I was fuckin' scared. I don't fuckin' *get* scared. That's why I used to find trouble. Would do anything, try anything, fuckin' fearless. Drove *Mamá* up the wall. Even undercover for the Agency. I fed off the danger. Loved every fuckin' minute of it. Never felt fear. Not once. Not until last night."

Oh… my… *God!*

Did he just say that?

He went on, "I didn't like it, Sadie."

Yes, he just said it.

My fingers tightened on his neck.

"I'm sorry," I said quietly.

"This has got to end," he told me, and I really didn't like the tone of his voice. I didn't like it so much my fingers went even tighter at his neck.

"What does that mean?" I asked.

"That means Plan B."

"What's Plan B?"

"Plan B means this ends."

My heart started tripping over itself (but at least it was now beating).

"What are you going to do?"

"Was toyin' with 'em, the Balduccis, pittin' them against each other. I wanted them to feel the fear. Trip up. Get angry. Turn their attention from you to each other so they'd implode. I wanted them to do stupid shit so we could get them and they'd go down. They took it beyond my expectations, poisoned their own fuckin' brother. Then they branched back out your way, torched your gallery. In the meantime your father stepped in, and if we don't shut him down, he's gonna fuck everything up."

I was stuck on his earlier point.

"Do you think they poisoned Harvey?" I asked.

"Poison isn't Seth's style. He doesn't mind mess. He likes to make a statement."

He was talking about my father and his words made my blood run cold.

Hector went on, "Marty has a chemistry set. We know he roofies girls he wants to fuck who won't give him the time of day. Likes to do the same to adversaries, makes it easier to kick the shit out of them. Word is, he's got an interest. He does research, plays around with pharmaceuticals just to see what they'd do. Eddie says there were two deaths by poison last year, both enemies of the Balduccis."

I stared at Hector.

Veronica Mars had been "roofied". In other words, slipped a date rape sedative so she'd go incoherent before she passed out. When she did, the creepy, weak, homicidal high school kid had his way with her (her cute, sweet high school ex-boyfriend did too, but he had an excuse: he'd also been roofied; it wasn't a good night for our plucky Veronica).

"That's gross," I said to Hector.

"That's Marty," Hector said back.

"What's Plan B?"

"You don't have to know what Plan B is. But while it's happenin', you aren't outside touching distance of me or one of the boys. Clear?"

"Clear," I agreed. "But I think I want to know what Plan B is."

He shook his head.

"Hector—" I started.

"You agreed I'd take care of you, I'm takin' care of you. That's all you need to know."

"Hector!"

He gave me a squeeze. His eyes went narrow and then, obviously because this was important, for good measure, he gave me a shake.

"Sadie, I'm askin' you to trust me."

I pulled in my lips, bit them and stared at him.

I'd made this bed, I'd tested that trust, I'd let him know it and now I was lying in said bed.

Blooming heck!

I had only one choice.

"Oh, all right," I gave in and watched his face start to relax. "But only if you let me paint your living room whatever color I want."

It was his turn to stare.

And he did this for a while.

Finally, he said, "*Mamita*, you're a little crazy."

Maybe I was.

But I was also on a mission.

"Do I get to paint your living room?" I asked.

He sighed then rested his forehead against mine. This time, he kept it there.

Then it was his turn to give in. "Just not pink."

"I'm not going to paint your living room pink!" I yelled, pulling my head away. "I can't believe you'd even think that."

At my outburst, his face went warm, and for some bizarre reason, he muttered, "Will of fuckin' steel."

"What?" I asked.

"Shit keeps comin' at you. Bad shit. Rape, your mother's murder, arson, kidnapping and you're standin' here wantin' to paint my living room. You got a will of fuckin' steel."

I didn't know what to say to that so I didn't say anything. But Hector did.

"And before you ask, *mi corazón*, that's good," he told me quietly.

My belly went into melt mode. He touched his lips to mine, soft, sweet and way too short.

I decided to change the subject from my "will of steel" (even though I liked that he thought that about me; it felt good).

"I need to talk to you about what Jerry and my father said."

"You had breakfast?"

"Jerry gave me a bowl of cereal."

He let me go and stepped away, but curled his arm around my neck and headed us to the door.

"I'll feed you. You tell me, then we'll go to Home Depot, get you some paint."

I smiled at him. I couldn't help it because there it was again.

I had a trauma.

I survived it.

Then Hector made life better again.

I stopped our progress to the door by planting my feet, putting a hand to his stomach and pressing into his side. I leaned up on tiptoes, and this time, *I* touched my mouth to *his*.

"Thanks, babe," I said softly against his mouth.

At my words, I watched, close up, as his eyes flared. He curled me fully to his front, his mouth came down on mine and he gave me a kiss that was so far from a touch on the lips, it wasn't even funny.

When he was done, he lifted his head. I was leaned into him, arms around him, unable to hold myself up and he had that possessive look in his eye.

"There she is," he whispered.

"Who?" I asked.

"*My* Sadie."

And, indeed, there I was.

And being there, Hector's Sadie smiled.

# Chapter 23
# Fred and Wilma

*Sadie*

I felt warmth at my neck. It moved up and then fingers sifted into my hair.

This was such a pleasant sensation, my mind decided to come awake. I opened my eyes and looked up.

"Hi," I said softly to Hector who was sitting on the edge of the couch. I was on my side, hands in prayer position under my cheek, my knees bent, and his hips were in the crook of my lap.

"If I didn't see it for myself, *mamita*, I'd ask if you got any paint on *the wall*," he said right before his hand left my hair, and his index finger slid across my cheek and down the side of my mouth. I knew he was tracing a paint mark, just one of many.

I ignored what his soft touch did to my body and got up on an elbow, one hand pulling the hair away from my face and getting stuck in the paint-clogged tangles.

"Painting's kind of messy," I informed him.

His eyes gave me a hair, face and torso scan. "It's not *that* messy."

I grinned and pushed all the way up. Going behind him, I got to my feet. I leaned in, grabbed his hand, pulled him up and invited, "Come look."

I dragged him from the north room to the south room and we stood in the middle.

I was thrilled with the results. The dusky gray went *great* with the dusky gray-blue of the other room. There were all sorts of ways to tie the rooms together. Toss pillows, throws, pictures, the mind boggled with the options (at least mine did). It was perfect.

I dropped his hand and pointed to the bottom of the walls.

"You said don't worry about the skirting boards; you were going to put wood ones in. Look!" I cried happily. "Matt helped by yanking off the old ones. He threw them in a pile in the backyard."

Hector wasn't looking at where the skirting boards used to be. He was looking at me.

"Matt was here to watch you, not help renovate the room," Hector told me.

I waved my hand in between us. "I know. That's okay. Duke came by and helped him. They never left me alone. Promise." Then I looked around. "Where's Matt anyway?"

"I let him go. I'm on duty now."

"Oh! Okay!" I chirped. Then I put my hand to his shoulder and turned him toward the fireplace. "While they were doing that, since we couldn't paint, Roxie, Ava, Stella, Ralphie and I stripped the wood on the fireplace. Isn't that wood fantastic? Who in their right minds would *paint* wood like that?" I asked and didn't wait for an answer. "As you can see, we couldn't get in some of the grooves. But Duke said there's some goo you can brush on to loosen it up and scrape it out. He's going to bring some by tomorrow."

Hector was looking at the fireplace, but his arm slid along my shoulders and he pulled me to his side.

"I've got the 'goo'," he said to the fireplace, but I saw his lips twitching. "It's in the kitchen."

"Fantastic!" I cried, clapping my hands then I threw out an arm. "We all painted. We did the ceiling white, like you did in the other room. Ava did the edging because she's an artist and she has a steady hand. It didn't take any time at all with the five of us, and we even did two coats. I think it looks *fab*. Don't you?" I tilted my head to look up at him. He was watching me, eyes amused, and he nodded. I smiled and went on, "Duke says we got the order wrong. We should have painted before we sanded the floors. Now I have to sand the paint splodges off."

Hector curled me into his front and looked down at me. "*We* didn't get the order wrong. You didn't ask to paint. You asked to sand the floors."

I blinked at him as I slid my arms loosely around his waist. "Oh. You should have said."

"You seemed all fired up to sand. I didn't want to disappoint you," he explained.

My belly went into melt mode (yes, over Hector letting me sand his floors!).

How bizarre was *that?*

I shook it off. Too excited by the news I had to impart on him, I couldn't think about my melted belly.

"Anyway, Duke's coming over tomorrow to stain the floors and he's going to show me how!" I announced like Duke promised a one-day, comprehensive course in the intricacies of neurosurgery.

Hector grinned, but said, "Not to put a damper on your good time, *mamita*, and as much as I appreciate Duke's help, I wanna walk on *my* floors, not Duke's."

Oh. Wow.

He wanted to refinish his own floors.

That got a belly melt, too!

Seriously, I was so weird!

"No worries," I told Hector, again ignoring the belly melt. "I'll break it to Duke."

He bent his head and touched his mouth briefly to mine. "We get your business done, this weekend, we'll finish the floors. Then we'll have somewhere to sit other than the bed."

I leaned further into him, liking that idea. Liking it *loads*.

It was not a surprise that got a belly melt, too.

"Okay," I said softly.

His eyes went over my face and hair again, then he informed me, "Takin' you out to dinner, get showered."

"Okay," I repeated. I smiled at him, pulled away and headed to the stairs.

I was up three steps when Hector called, "We're goin' to Lincoln's." I stopped, looked at him and he went on, "It's a roadhouse. You wear your designer armor, we're likely to get ejected."

I didn't answer. He was grinning at me and I knew he was teasing. I just shook my head in a non-verbal "whatever", trying to suppress my own grin (and failing), and headed upstairs.

I took a shower, scrubbed off the paint and thought about my day.

Outside of waking up kidnapped and the hours after that were in Jerry the Swine's company, that day had been the second best day of my life.

Hector and I had breakfast at a greasy spoon and Detective Marker joined us for coffee at the end. I told them both about Jerry spilling that my father told him to take down the Balduccis one-by-one, and I told them about the money.

Even though I'd been convinced this wouldn't faze me, it did. There was something about knowing my father ordered Jerry to protect me, he was avenging me against the Balduccis and he wanted me to be comfortable, money-wise, that made me feel that *eensy* bit like the traitor Jerry called me.

On the other hand, he'd had me kidnapped, maybe murdered my mother, and as Hector put it, "didn't mind mess". So, even though, way in the back of my mind, I wondered if I was doing the right thing as a daughter, I, at least, didn't have to wonder about being a good citizen.

During my story, Detective Marker and Hector exchanged some knowing glances, but didn't share with me and I didn't push it. They both told me I did a great job and they also told me (weirdly) no matter what, I was not to let my father give me the Caymans account information.

For the most part, Hector listened without reaction except when I told them some of Jerry's threats and commentary. Those little nuggets made his eyes go dark and that muscle leap in his cheek (so I didn't share half of it; I thought that was wise).

Then, as he told me he would, Hector took me to Home Depot and we went to the paint section. I picked the color. Hector approved. The paint guy squirted some dye into cans, shook the big buckets in a killer, wild, shaking machine that I liked so much, I told Hector I wanted to buy one.

This made Hector burst out laughing for some reason I did not get. Okay, so I probably didn't have that much paint to mix, but seriously, anyone could see it was a cool machine.

Matt (a.k.a. Surfer Dude Hottie) was waiting on Hector's porch with Ralphie and YoYo (Ralphie holding a s'more latte from Tex) when we got to Hector's house. Then Hector gave me a hot, long, leg-buckling kiss and took off. Ava, Stella and Roxie (called by Ralphie) showed up ten minutes later, Duke (called by Roxie) half an hour after that.

Then the fun began.

It might be a little weird that I liked painting, sanding and all that, but I didn't care.

Not even a little bit.

I finished the shower and put some goo on my scabbed over tattoo. I swiped my face with powder, went a bit heavier than normal on the blusher, took some time on shading my eyes with three different colors, slapped on mascara and did the lip gloss routine. I gunked up my hair with smoothing elixir, gave it a quick blow dry, gunked it up more with pomade and then left it loose to fall down my shoulders and back.

I went back to the bedroom and tore through my overnight bag. I'd packed heavy, but I had nothing to wear to a roadhouse. Even if I had my whole wardrobe handy, I'd still have nothing to wear to a roadhouse. In fact, I wasn't certain sure I knew what a roadhouse was.

Instead of calling downstairs and asking Hector (which might be embarrassing), I put on a pair of black, low-rider cords, my rose-stamped silver-buckled belt, a wrap-around lilac sweater with bell sleeves that showed some cleavage and my motorcycle boots. I figured the lilac sweater was pushing the boundaries of what was acceptable at a roadhouse, but the boots balanced it out.

Then me and my boots clomped downstairs. It was dark outside, but Hector had the overhead light on in the living room, and again, I admired the new walls. The difference was astonishing and it looked like our work took us leaps ahead in making Hector's house a home. There was actual physical evidence that I accomplished something and that felt nice.

I found Hector in the kitchen sitting on the countertop sorting through mail.

His head came up when I walked in. He did a full body scan, hair to boots then up again, stopping at my breasts.

His eyes lifted to mine. "You got a tank to wear under that?"

I looked down at myself. "Under what?" I asked stupidly, for where else would you wear a tank?

"Your sweater," Hector answered.

I looked out the window at the darkness. "Is it that cold?"

Hector didn't answer me so my gaze swung back to him and I saw his face was the same mixture of hard and soft it was when he talked to Ralphie yesterday.

"Come here," he demanded, and without question, I did.

When I got close he spread his legs and I took that as my cue and walked between them. When I felt his heat, I stopped, put my hands on his hard thighs and his hands came to my neck.

"I forget, with all the shit that's gone down, we don't know each other that well so I'll explain somethin' about me you gotta understand."

Oh my.

I didn't have a good feeling about this.

I decided to gird.

It was a good decision.

"What?" I asked.

His thumbs started circling on my neck which felt nice, but even so, I did my best to pay attention when he started talking.

"You were just a beautiful woman. Now you're *my* beautiful woman. What you got under your clothes is for me. No one else. They don't look. They don't touch. That's the deal. Yeah?"

I stared at him, speechless. Which was a good thing because if I had words, I would have said them so loudly the neighbors would hear.

"Now," he went on, either not feeling or not caring about the badder than bad vibes emanating from me directly toward him, "go put on a tank."

That was when I found my words.

"Maybe I should go put on my ragged white dress and stone necklace and you can put on your leopard skin tunic and we can pedal in our stone car to the roadhouse before you go bowling with Barney and I go shopping with Betty, Fred."

His thumbs stopped circling and his eyes narrowed.

"You wanna repeat that?" His voice was low with warning, telling me that, no, I didn't want to repeat it. I wanted to run upstairs and put on a tank.

This, of course, I did not do.

"I'm referring to the Flintstones who lived in the Stone Age."

"I know what you're referrin' to."

"My point is, Hector and Sadie are not Fred and Wilma. We don't live in the Stone Age. We live in the here and now, where women show cleavage and men don't tell their women what to wear."

"I asked nice."

"You didn't ask, you told."

"All right, I told nice."

I had no answer because this was true.

I still was not going to put on a tank.

Therefore, coming to a verbal stalemate, we locked eyes and went into stare down mode.

This lasted a long time. So long, I quivered internally and was about to give in when Hector blew out a sigh.

"You're not gonna give in, are you?" he asked.

"No," I lied. I was *so* going to give in.

He looked over my shoulder and muttered, "Fuck."

I tried hard not to smile. It would be bad sportsmanship.

Instead, I said, "Painting's hard work, I'm hungry."

His eyes came back to mine and I was pleased to see he wasn't angry, but I couldn't say he wasn't annoyed.

I could handle annoyed.

"Let's go." He pushed me back, jumped off the counter in front of me and tagged my hand, walking me to the back of the house rather than the front where he always parked his Bronco.

We went into the little mudroom off the kitchen that was full of more boots (yes, more boots!), more renovation equipment and other masculine detritus. He reached up on a shelf and pulled down two black visored motorcycle helmets and he handed me one.

I stared at the helmet in my hand then up at Hector, my heart beating a little faster.

"You have a bike?" I asked.

"Yeah," he replied.

My heart started beating even faster and I could feel my lips forming a smile.

"I've never ridden on a bike."

His hand came to my neck and he lost his annoyed look.

"Tonight's your night, *mamita*."

Then he put a hand to the small of my back and turned me to the door.

☙❧

"I'm gonna get us more beers," I told the table, which included Luke and Ava, who were at Lincoln's when we arrived. They'd only just sat down and got their drinks so Ava told us it was perfect timing. They did a seat shuffle. Luke sat by Ava at the tall table by the bar, her on the inside by the wall. Hector sat by me. I was across from Ava.

We ordered "Cajun Popcorn" as an appetizer (battered, deep-fried crawfish) and I got a meatloaf cheeseburger with fries. Even after the Cajun Popcorn, I ate every last bite of my burger and every single fry and I didn't even care. Manual labor made you ravenous. Blanca would be thrilled.

I loved Lincoln's. There were interesting people there, not just bikers but also urbanites, probably from the local neighborhood. It was worn in but not worn out, and the waitresses were super friendly.

I also loved Hector's bike, mainly because it meant I could get transported from one place to the other with my front plastered to Hector's hard, hot back, my arms around his tight abs and the wind hitting me everywhere. I decided the minute we hit the road and picked up speed there was nothing in the whole, wide world better than *that*.

I grabbed my wallet out of my purse and popped off the barstool, rounding Hector. But I only got a step away before I was halted by fingers curling into the waistband of my cords. I looked back as Hector pulled me to him and his mouth came to my ear.

"Give me your wallet and put it on the tab," he muttered in my ear.

"I've got money," I told him.

"*Mi cielo*, wallet." His tone didn't invite discussion.

I figured I was lucky to get away with the "Fred and Wilma" argument so I wasn't going to push my luck. I cocked my arm so my hand with the wallet was over my shoulder. He took it from me then kept talking in my ear.

"This end of the bar, I wanna be able to see you at all times."

I turned my head, nodded to him and he let me go.

I smiled to myself on the way to the bar, that warm, happy glow mingling with the lovely, safe, snugly comfort.

It felt good to be looked after.

"Four Fat Tires," I called to the bartender when he jerked his chin at me.

I felt a presence slide in beside me and I looked to my right then over the shoulder of the beautiful, dark-haired woman there to ascertain if I could still see Hector. I could so my body settled.

"I'm Natalie," the woman said and my surprised eyes went to her.

Wow. She was nice. Walking right up to me and introducing herself.

"Hi. I'm Sadie," I returned the niceness.

"Saw you with Hector," she said to me.

I blinked at her, not certain sure where this was going and thinking it might not be nice at all.

"Yes," I said hesitantly.

She leaned in. "Not bein' a bitch or anything, but, girl to girl, be careful."

I blinked again.

"What?"

"Hector. Be careful. He's a dawg."

"A dog?"

"A dawg," she repeated.

My eyes narrowed and my back went straight. "He's not a dog. He's a man."

"Not a dog. A dawg. D-a-w-g. Dawg. A player."

I knew what a player was.

I looked back over her shoulder at Hector. He was listening to Ava, however Luke, I noted, was watching me.

My eyes went to Natalie. "Maybe you're thinking of a different Hector," I tried.

"Nope. He's nailed me and half the women in this place. Girls look at him as a challenge. I know because I did it too. He's got the reputation for bein' good, as in *good*, which, by the way, he was, off the fuckin' charts. He's also got a reputation for not hangin' around, at all, not even spendin' the night in most cases. Every girl here probably thought she'd be the one to get a return visit, but far's I know, he never went back twice. Not to me, not to anyone."

After the words "nailed me" I felt like she started repeatedly punching me in the stomach.

Hector had sex with Natalie?

And *half the women in this place?*

I looked around the bar scanning the women. Luckily, the place wasn't packed, but it was relatively busy. Busy enough to mean, if this was true, *Hector* had been busy.

Again, I looked at Natalie and breathed, "You're joking."

She shook her head and I tried to read her face. She didn't look like she was being catty, just... real.

Natalie went on, "You look like a fairy princess who lives in an enchanted castle, not exactly a Lincoln's regular. We girls have to stick together. I'm just givin' you the heads up."

It was my turn to shake my head. "He's changed. He's different now."

"Yeah? He fucked me six weeks ago. No joke, it was so good, I remember when, where and every second of it. I'm not complainin', but just so you know, I called him three times and he didn't return a single call."

The bartender put my beers on the bar just as I grabbed on to the edge to hold myself up.

Six weeks ago was when I walked into Nightingale Investigations Offices right before I got raped.

And Hector had been in Natalie's bed.

Or, worse, she'd been in his!

She interrupted my crazed thoughts by putting her hand on mine on the bar.

"Listen, Sadie, I'm sorry. You look freaked. I gotta say, I been watchin' and he looks into you, *way* into you. Never seen him like that with anyone so maybe I'm wrong. Put it in the back of your mind. All I'm sayin' is, be careful."

Then she was gone.

I was so busy trying not to hyperventilate it took the bartender several tries to get my attention. I told him to put it on our tab, grabbed the beer bottles by their necks, and on shaky legs, I carried them to the table.

I saw Luke's eyes on me and I avoided them, scooted behind Hector, and taking great care, like it was a priceless artifact, I tucked my wallet, which Hector had set on my purse, inside.

"Everything okay, Sadie?" Luke asked and my eyes flew to him.

"Fine, great, wonderful," I lied, nabbed my beer and took a long swallow.

I felt Hector's eyes on me, but I turned my attention to tracing the label on my bottle with my thumb and trying not to let my hand shake.

"*Mamita*, look at me."

My eyes lifted to Hector.

His brows went together.

"You're not fine," he said.

From my peripheral vision I saw Ava and Luke look at each other, but I was too busy lying again to Hector to take much notice. "I think painting the living room just hit me. What with all the food and beer, all of a sudden, I'm tired."

"I'm going to the bathroom. Sadie, do you need to go to the bathroom?" Ava asked suddenly.

I shook my head, too freaked out to catch her hint.

Hector's hand went to the back pocket of his jeans.

"We'll get you home," he said.

My head jerked to him.

"No!" I cried. His narrowed eyes came to me and I made an effort to calm down. "No. You're having fun, everyone's having fun. I just got more beer. We'll drink them and go."

Ava looked at Luke, slid off her stool and headed to the bathroom. Hector pulled out his wallet and came of his stool, too.

"I'll pay the tab so we'll be ready to roll."

He walked to the bar. I watched him stop and I realized my happy glow was long gone and my heart actually hurt.

"Natalie was before you, Sadie," Luke said.

I tore my eyes from Hector and looked at Luke to find he was watching me. "What?" I asked.

"Don't know what she said to freak you, but I got a fair guess, and you gotta know, Natalie was before you."

I pulled in my lips. I was not talking about this with Luke Stark. Ralphie, yes. Daisy, yes. Any Rock Chick, yes. Luke Stark, absolutely not.

I took another sip from my beer and looked anywhere but at Luke.

"Hector didn't share what happened when he was workin' with your dad. We all figure, with the way things are now, you two had a thing. Whatever that thing was, the way you were in the offices that day, it wasn't on, which means it wasn't on when he was with Natalie."

I nodded to Luke, knowing, for whatever reason, this didn't make me feel even a little bit better, but unfortunately he wasn't done.

"You know I was there that night," he told me softly.

My heart tripped, I swallowed then said, "Please, Luke—"

"Never seen a man like that. Felt like it, with Ava, never seen it. He was not happy when you went unconscious and he was less happy when they wouldn't allow him to stay in your exam bay until you regained consciousness. That's all he asked, they refused. He lost it, got physical, and me and a security guard had to take him out. I figure, after seein' that, whatever he had with Natalie is shit compared to what he feels for you."

Somehow, I didn't know why and I didn't want to process it at that very moment (especially not with Luke), what he said made my heart hurt more.

"I think I was wrong about finishing the beer. I'm really tired. I'm going to ask Hector to take me home," I told Luke.

"Sadie—" he started, but I slid off the barstool and walked to Hector.

He had his back to me and he was talking to someone I couldn't see. I got close, lifted my hand to touch his shoulder but I stilled when I heard what the man was saying.

"... a fuckin' certificate for nailin' Townsend's piece."

Somewhere at the edges of my mind I realized belatedly Hector wasn't just standing at the bar. He was standing straight, his body rock-solid, at the bar.

The man I couldn't see went on and it also hit the edges of my mind he sounded more than a little inebriated.

The man hooted and practically shouted, "You're tappin' Ice Princess ass! Shit! Any time surveillance photos came in of her, we'd fight at the chance to make copies. She was the most jacked off on piece in history. And you're nailin' her. Chavez, that makes you a *legend*."

Both my hands went to my forehead, my fingers sliding into my hair. But I'd barely finished this maneuver when Hector's fist flashed out, connected and the man went down at Hector's feet.

Hector didn't like him down. He bent over, picked him up by his shirt and hustled him backwards until the man slammed against the doorframe to the other room. Hector pulled him away from the frame only to slam him brutally into it again. So brutally, his head cracked against the frame.

"What the fuck!" the man shouted.

I came unstuck and ran forward to Hector's left side. I saw Luke materialize on his right and a man wearing a black, Lincoln's long-sleeved tee was behind Luke.

Hector didn't notice us and put his face close to the man's.

"That's my fuckin' woman you're talkin' about," he growled and then stepped back, taking the man with him, and slammed him into the doorframe again.

"Hector," I whispered, putting a hand to his forearm, but he didn't even look at me.

The man put his hands on Hector's forearms too. "Christ, man, I was givin' you a fuckin' compliment!"

Hector did the slamming then getting into his face business again and snarled, "By tellin' me you jacked off to her picture? What the fuck's the matter with you?"

"Hector, stand down," Luke said in a low voice.

"Take it outside," the Lincoln's guy put in.

"What's going on?" Ava asked from behind me.

"Hector, let him go," I ignored Ava and got closer to Hector.

Hector didn't let him go and the man's face started getting red. Or *more* red.

"Fuck, I'm sorry. I didn't think you'd have a shit fit. Christ. I'm sorry, okay?"

Hector gave him a good, old, scorching glare and then stepped back with another solid push while letting go.

Then he turned The Scorch to me and ordered, "Get our shit. We're gone."

I thought my best move at this juncture was to "get my shit" and pronto. Which I did.

I grabbed my purse and waved good-bye to Ava and a bit more hesitantly Luke. Hector was bent over, nabbing the helmets out from under the table as I saw Natalie walk by, her face pale, her eyes on me. I could swear she mouthed the words, with the barest whisper of sound, "I'm sorry, I was wrong," and then she hurried away when Hector straightened.

I didn't have a chance to process this. Hector tossed me my helmet. I caught it and he moved in. His arm curled around my neck and he guided me firmly out to the bike.

"Maybe you should calm down before we get on the bike," I suggested when we stopped by his motorcycle and he took his arm away.

Hector's eyes sliced to me. "Next time we go out, I'm not bein' the nice guy and backin' down. You're gonna put on the fuckin' tank."

My eyes bugged out.

How did this get to be about *me?*

"Now this is about me?" I asked.

"You came up behind me, I smelled your perfume. You heard him talkin' about you. So yeah, it's about you. This whole fuckin' thing proves my fuckin' point," he shot back.

"That's very bizarre logic, Hector Chavez."

"It makes perfect sense to me."

"Well, perhaps you shouldn't be seeing me then," I returned. "Perhaps you should be seeing someone else that people *won't* talk about. How about Natalie? I met her tonight at the bar. She seems like a nice girl. No, wait, you've already fucked *her!*" I yelled.

Hector got close. I could feel his fury; I didn't have to see it, and I retreated until I felt bike.

"*Dios mio,*" he hissed. "Natalie. That's why you looked like someone ran over your puppy when you came back to the table."

"Heck yes!"

"What the fuck did she say?"

"To be careful of you, you were a dawg and that your dawg-ness was not ancient history, like I tried to tell her it was, since you nailed her six weeks ago."

His hand went up, he tore his fingers through his hair then his hand dropped again to his side.

"And this pisses you off?" he asked, sounding now both furious and perplexed.

I opened and closed my mouth twice before shouting, "Yes!"

"I hate to break this to you, *mamita,* but I wasn't a virgin our first time," he told me sarcastically.

"Count back, Hector. Six weeks. *Six weeks!*" I yelled.

"Yeah? So?"

"Six weeks ago, tonight, I was raped!"

His body went completely still.

Mine couldn't go still, I was breathing too heavily.

When he spoke, his voice was a lot quieter but I could still hear the edge of anger.

"Sadie, I wasn't fuckin' Natalie while you were bein' raped."

"The night before?" I snapped.

He shook his head but did it jerkily, still angry, but now his voice had a thread of impatience. "I don't fuckin' remember."

"She says you nailed half the women in there."

"She's probably right."

I leaned away from him and breathed, "Oh my God."

He got closer, taking away the minute space I'd gained. "Sadie, we got two choices. You can list for me all the men who got in your pants, which I don't wanna fuckin' know, and I can return the favor, which, trust me, *mamita, you* don't wanna know. Or we can go on from here, you and me, the past is fuckin' history. Choose. Now. I'm not livin' under the threat of this fuckin' time bomb either."

I turned away. "Take me to Ralphie and Buddy's."

His fingers curled around my bicep and he pulled me back to facing him.

"No fuckin' way. You sleep in my bed."

"Take me to Ralphie and Buddy's!" I yelled.

"No," he bit off.

I jerked my arm from his hand.

"Fine," I snapped. "Let's go home."

He leaned to the side and hooked his helmet on the hand grip of his bike. Then both his hands came to my neck.

I tipped my head back and glared at him.

"I said, let's go home," I repeated.

"You don't even hear what's comin' out of your own mouth."

"Yes?" I asked, saccharin-sweet. "Enlighten me. What's coming out of my own mouth?"

"You said, 'take me back to Ralphie and Buddy's' then you called my place 'home'."

At this canny, scary and life-altering observation, I took in an audible, very shocked breath, but he kept talking.

"How long's it gonna take for this shit to sink in for you?"

I decided my best bet was to keep quiet and simply glare, and this was exactly what I did.

Hector's hands went away from my neck. He angled to the side again and grabbed his helmet.

"Helmet up," he ordered, his voice sharp and still way beyond ticked off. "Don't give a fuck if you're hot, wet and panting or pissed as hell, you're sleepin' by me, in my bed, at *home*."

Without a decent retort (or, at least one that would compare to his) and with no other choice, I "helmeted up" and got on his bike behind him. He shot out into the street so fast, the loose hold I had on his waist was lost and I had to lean close and wrap my arms around him.

Wasn't this *just great?*

# Chapter 24

# Next!

### Sadie

I clomped on my boots into the house in front of Hector and stopped in the doorway of the darkened kitchen. He reached into me and flipped on the kitchen lights, then I clomped to the counter and slammed my purse on it.

I dug out my cell phone, shoved it in my back pocket, and without even glancing at him, I clomped out of the kitchen and upstairs to the bedroom.

I dragged out my pajamas (hot pink with tiny peach polka dots on the bottoms, peach camisole) and clomped into the bathroom.

I slammed the door.

Then I locked it.

Then I pulled out my cell, threw down the lid to the toilet seat and sat down.

I scrolled down to Jet in my phonebook and hit the green button.

She said I could call her anytime, day or night.

And she was marrying a Chavez man.

For these two reasons, on the ride back to the house, my mind whirling from one option to the next, I finally decided to call Jet.

I heard one ring, two then three then Eddie's voice saying, "Yeah?"

Great.

Just great.

Eddie answered Jet's cell.

"Hi, Eddie!" I chirped. "How are you?"

"Sadie?"

"Yes."

"You okay?"

"I think so. I haven't been kidnapped and no more property I own has been burned to a cinder... that I know of... so, yes. I'm okay."

I heard him chuckle.

"Can I talk to Jet?" I asked.

"Yeah. She's right here."

I crossed my legs, leaned forward with my elbow on my knee and jerked my foot impatiently.

Jet came on the line. "Sadie?"

"Hi, Jet."

"Is everything all right?"

I didn't really know how girlfriends did this kind of thing. Did they exchange pleasantries first and ease into it? Or did they just go for it?

I decided against easing into it.

"Heck no!" I replied.

Silence for a second then, "What's up?"

"You said I could call. Is it too late?"

"No, it's fine. What's going on?"

Still not easing into it, I told her.

Everything.

From Hector's demand I put on a tank, to the Fred and Wilma argument, to Natalie's revelations, to Hector going berserk and finishing on the conversation by the bike.

When I was done, there was a moment of silence then she asked, "That all happened in one night?"

"Yes. One night. Not even a night, a few hours," I told her. "You're marrying one of them. I figure you have to be an expert. Is Eddie like this?"

She laughed then said, "Um... yes."

Why was she laughing?

What, I must ask, was funny about this?

"Oh... my... *God!* How do you stand it?" I exclaimed.

"There's a lot here, Sadie. Maybe we should break it down," she suggested.

"Please do," I agreed graciously.

"First off, I wear what I want, but I don't go over that line that would send a hot-blooded Mexican-American man over the edge. It's just not worth it. A little cleavage, he has to get over it. The skirt you wore to Stella's gig, unacceptable."

"Hector told me to burn that skirt," I informed her.

She let out another laugh. "I'm not surprised. If Eddie saw me in that skirt, his head would explode."

I had to admit, the skirt was an *eensy* bit OTT.

Well then, one down.

"Next!" I cried.

I heard her laugh again then she said, "The girl at the bar—"

When she hesitated, I encouraged, "Go on."

"Well, that's harder. But, see, Indy told me Lee had a reputation, as did Eddie, both of them *bad*. Vance was considered a legend. Everyone knew he was a player. Luke even had a woman when he started with Ava. He blew her off the minute Ava came into his life. Hank, more discreet, but—"

I interrupted her impatiently, "You're telling me this because...?"

"I'm telling you his because you know them now."

Hmm.

This was a point to ponder.

They all seemed pretty devoted. In fact, if the stories were anything to go by, they'd gone above and beyond the call of duty to win the hearts of their respective Rock Chicks.

My foot stopped jerking and I decided it was time to get serious.

So I told her, "Jet, she was a nice girl. He didn't even remember when he slept with her."

I heard her sigh. "Duke explains this better, but it has something to do with the kind of men they are, the dangerous work they do, knowing who they are and what they want, recognizing it when they find it and not fucking around in making it theirs. Or... something like that. Anyway, whoever this girl was, she obviously wasn't the one because, Sadie, *you* are."

Oh *my*.

I didn't know what to say to that because what on earth did you say to that?

Then, for some reason, I blurted, "I saw him."

"What?" she asked.

I took in a deep breath and shared, "That night, when he brought me to the hospital after I was raped. I passed out and when I woke up in the emergency room, I saw them force Hector out of my bay. He didn't want to go. Luke told me tonight that Hector asked if he could stick around until I woke up. They said no and he lost it." I waited for her reaction to this announcement, and when none was forthcoming I pushed, "Really, Jet, how bizarre is *that*?"

"It doesn't sound at all bizarre to me," she answered quietly.

I shook my head, thinking she was not getting it, and sat up, pulling a hand through my hair and then dropping it into my lap. "You don't understand. We didn't know each other. I mean, we were around each other a lot when he was undercover, and one night we had a thing that didn't end well. But other than that..." I stopped then went on, "I don't get it."

"I don't either," she told me. "It even happened to me. One second, I was minding my own business, trying to avoid Eddie. The next second he informed me he was making me his business and the second after that, I was living with him. I watched it happen to Roxie, Jules, Ava, Stella, and I knew it happened to Indy. I don't know how these guys know. I don't know how their minds work. It just happens. They just know. I've stopped trying to figure it out."

Well.

It wasn't an answer but it was one.

Still.

It was time to get to the heart of the matter.

"What do I do now?"

Jet answered instantly, "Do what they do. Go with your instincts. It'll all work out in the end, I promise."

That didn't give me anything to go on.

"You okay now?" Jet asked.

I sighed then said, "No."

"You will be, honey," she replied softly. "It's hard. Then, when you trust it's for real, it gets a whole lot easier."

I answered, "Okay," but I didn't mean it.

She changed the subject to a much better one. "We need to get you fitted for your bridesmaid's dress. Can you do that tomorrow?"

At last. Something to look forward to.

"I think so. I'll have to check with whatever bodyguard I have."

She giggled. "Oh, I hope it's Bobby. I bet he'll *love* going to a bridal shop."

I smiled into the phone. Even though I didn't know Bobby, none of them were bridal shop type of men. Then I whispered, "Thanks Jet."

"Anytime, honey."

We disconnected. I did the getting ready for bed thing, gathered up my clothes and boots and walked into the bedroom.

The lamp was lit on the nightstand by Hector's side of the bed. Hector was sitting up against all (yes, *all!*) the pillows, chest bare, legs stretched out in front of him, ankles crossed, wearing a pair of gray, drawstring sweatpants that had also been cut off (poorly) at mid-thigh.

He looked better than ever, which at that moment I thought stunk.

A game was on TV, but his eyes sliced to me the minute I walked in.

It took effort but I ignored him. I wasn't quite finished being angry, though I wasn't certain sure what I was angry about anymore. And I wasn't quite ready to make amends and didn't know how anyway. So I dumped my stuff on my overnight bag and headed to the other side just as he angled off the bed and stalked out of the room.

I stared at his back until he went into the bathroom then I climbed in bed, stole two of the four pillows as should be my ration and propped them up on my side well away from his. I sat on the covers, arms crossed on my midriff, legs out, ankles crossed, and I locked my eyes on the TV.

I didn't watch sports, except tennis. Those tennis players had finesse— and nice legs—so the football didn't do anything for me. But I watched it like it fascinated me beyond imagining, even though Hector wasn't in the room (practice).

Therefore, when he came back, I kept my eyes glued to the TV and didn't look at him, except when he walked in front of the TV, of course. I didn't look at him when he got to his side of the bed and I didn't look at him when he resumed his position.

Then, all of a sudden, his arm sliced along the small of my back between me and the pillows. He yanked me across the bed until my body hit his then his arm bent so my front was against his side.

I put a hand on his abs to push away but his arm went tight.

"What are you doing?" I snapped, looking up, but he leaned across me and grabbed my pillows. Doing an ab curl, he shoved them behind him. "Hey!" I cried. "Those are my pillows."

"Settle, Sadie," he ordered in a low voice.

I. Did. Not. *Think*. So.

"Don't tell me to settle! You just stole my pillows!"

I pushed away.

His arm got tighter.

I pushed harder, putting my full body into it.

His other hand came to my hip and held on.

I wrapped my fingers around his wrist and pulled it away.

His wrist twisted and then his fingers wrapped around *my* wrist.

Thus began The Tussle.

I had no chance in heck of winning, but it didn't stop me from trying.

There was a lot of grunting (Hector and me), some sharp cries (all me), panting (mostly me), rolling (both of us), more rolling... still more rolling. Then it changed from being all about limb maneuvering, strategy and strength to being about getting as close as physically possible, tasting, touching, kissing and even biting (me again).

He yanked off my pajama bottoms and panties. I tugged off his sweatpants. Then we went back at each other like there were ten seconds left before the whole of planet earth was going to explode.

Finally, I ended up on my back, my legs wrapped around his hips while he drove deep inside me, our mouths touching, but we weren't kissing, just breathing heavily. The delicious anticipation was hitting critical mass in my body; my nails tore up his back, he groaned against my mouth at the same precise second his last, deep thrust caused the sweet tension to release and explode and I gasped against his lips.

When we were both finished, his weight settled on me, his heat surrounded me and he stayed deep inside me. We were both panting and he rested his forehead against mine, eyes closed.

Then his eyes opened and he said softly, "Christ, Sadie, puttin' up with you demonstrating how many more ways you can be a pain in the ass was worth every fuckin' second if that was the end result."

Someone, please tell me he did *not* just say that.

"You did not just say that," I said to him.

He didn't answer.

Instead, he abruptly switched topics. "Who'd you call?"

I blinked in confusion. "What?"

"In the bathroom."

Not that it was any of his business, I still answered, "Jet."

"She sort you out?"

I felt my eyes narrow. "Do you *want* me to be mad at you?"

His hips moved slightly, and I couldn't help it, I was still tender, I let out a little moan.

When I was done moaning, he grinned at me wickedly and muttered, "I'm thinkin', yeah."

I glared.

His grin died, face and voice now serious, he said, "We gotta get by this, *mamita*."

I kept glaring.

Then my mind flashed on the memory of Luke and the security guard forcing Hector away from me in the hospital when he didn't want to go.

And, even though if you asked me if I had any instincts, I would have told you no, I pulled them up from wherever they were lying latent and I went with them.

"Other than you, I've had two lovers," I announced and watched his face grow dark and begin to morph toward angry. "No. I don't want you to share yours. I'm just saying, neither of them... well, they weren't..." I stopped and then started again, "You need to know, I haven't let anyone close and tonight you found out why."

"Maybe you should keep talkin'," Hector told me. Not yet fully morphed into anger, not ready to break into a grin either.

"That man at the bar, who was he?"

Hector's head cocked impatiently at my off the subject question but he answered, "Knew him. Worked with him briefly. He's in the business."

I nodded then I lifted my hand to the side of his face and rested it there.

"What he said to you, about me, knowing you were with me, feeling he was okay to say that... Hector, even when they were beginning, I can't imagine anyone walking up to Lee and talking that way about Indy. Or Eddie about Jet. Or any of them. But me, Seth Townsend's daughter." My voice dropped to a whisper. "I'm fair game."

I saw an angry but understanding flare before he closed his eyes, and my thumb moved to trace his bottom lip. When it did, his eyes opened again and the anger was gone.

"Sadie—"

I talked over him. "Enter Ice Princess. She was the only way to get by when people thought about me like that, talked about me like that guy. Or *to* me, like Jerry did this morning. I knew it happened. They never said it directly to me because of my father, but I heard pieces here and there and I always *knew*. Until people forget, that's not going to change. They're going to think it's okay—"

"It's not fuckin' okay. It wasn't then and it isn't now," Hector broke in sharply, and my hand drifted down to cup his jaw.

"No, you're right, it wasn't and isn't. But they're going to think it is and you can't beat up every one of them."

He didn't say anything. He just stared at me.

So, as usual, I sallied forth.

"What Natalie said freaked me out," I went on and his gaze darkened again, but I shook my head, took my hand from his jaw and wrapped both my arms around him, squeezing his hips with my thighs. "Listen to me, Hector. It freaked me out because I was unprepared. I'd had a good day. I'd had a nice meal. I felt safe. I was happy. I wasn't expecting that. It threw me. If I'd had time to think about it, which I didn't, I would have worked through it on my own."

Again, he didn't respond, at least not verbally.

What he did was much better.

His head dropped and he nuzzled my neck with his nose then his mouth was there and my arms went tighter.

I turned my lips to his ear and whispered, "I won't wear that skirt again, but anything else, Hector, you have to let me be me. And the jerks can be jerks and they can think what they want. But we'll just come home and watch the game."

Again, he didn't answer.

Instead, his face came out of my neck and he kissed me, slow and sweet.

And, I figured, with his reaction, my instincts were right.

When his head moved away an inch, he looked in my eyes and asked softly, "Which Sadie is this?"

I felt my mouth form a little grin and I answered honestly, "I've no idea. I haven't met her yet."

He touched his forehead to mine a nanosecond. Then Smooth Move Hector did a push up. Our bodies disconnected, but his arm came around my lower back. He lifted me to him until my limbs wrapped tight around his body. His arm went away and he yanked down the covers under us and settled me in the bed. He joined me, snapping the covers back over us. His hands went into my camisole and he tugged it up and off and tossed it to the side of the bed. He finished by rolling us, him to his back, me tucked to his side, and he settled the covers up around his stomach and under my armpit.

I put my head on chest, wrapped my arm around his belly and fell asleep watching football.

⊰⊱

## *Hector*

Hector pulled gently away from Sadie's sleeping body. He got out of bed, leaned back in and tucked the covers around her.

He walked to the bathroom, took a shower, shaved and went back to the bedroom.

He dressed with his eyes on Sadie to make sure she didn't wake and because she looked cute when she slept, hands tucked under her cheek, her thick, soft, wild hair everywhere. Her scarred cheek was against the pillow, which Hector thought was a good thing. She seemed not to notice it anymore or she'd put it somewhere in her head where she didn't think about it. But every once in a while the sight of it and the reason it was there crept into Hector's consciousness and it would serve as an angry reminder. This was happening a lot less lately. But when it did, it didn't lose any of its intensity.

Once dressed, he leaned in and kissed the top of Sadie's head.

She didn't stir.

He went downstairs.

He made coffee, flipped the switch on the coffeemaker, wrote a note for Sadie and went upstairs and put it on the pillow. He was walking back downstairs when the knock came at the door.

He opened the door to see Bobby.

"*Hombre*," he said. Bobby jutted out his chin and stepped in. Hector closed the door and went on, "Sadie's sleepin'."

"Got coffee?" Bobby asked.

Hector led the way to the kitchen, poured a mug for Bobby and a travel mug for himself. Bobby walked with him to the front door.

"Cell contact okay?" Bobby asked.

"Yeah," Hector replied.

"You thinkin' positive thoughts?" Bobby went on.

"No," Hector responded.

His first errand that day was unpleasant but unavoidable.

Bobby nodded.

Hector walked out into the pre-dawn morning, got in the Bronco, started it up and drove to Vance's house.

Just before Max was born, Vance and Jules had moved from her small duplex to a three bedroom bungalow with a white picket fence that was four doors down from Indy and Lee's place, but still only a block away from Jules's Uncle Nick.

Hector parked in front of their house and had a hand on the door handle when he saw Vance exit the house and stop. Jules was there, holding a coffee mug and wearing a robe. Her hair was down and mussed and she looked half asleep. She lifted a hand to wave at Hector. He gave her a chin lift and settled back in his seat. Then she tilted her face to Vance, who accepted her invitation and bent his head to her.

Hector looked away.

Minutes later, Vance opened the door, slid in, put his travel mug between his knees and buckled up.

Hector took off.

"This gonna go well?" Vance asked the windshield.

Hector didn't take his eyes from the road. "I'm thinkin', no."

"How far you gonna push it?" Vance asked.

"As far as I have to."

Vance didn't respond and the conversation died, both men lost in their own thoughts.

It took an hour and a half to drive to the prison. Hector had called in a few markers, or a few *more* markers. This business with Sadie was draining his reserves, but he also didn't give a fuck.

They were met at the entrance and taken to a room. Bars on the windows, a couch, a table, two chairs. They stayed standing and waited, silent.

Less than ten minutes later, the door opened and Seth Townsend walked in with a security guard.

He took one look at Hector, not even glancing at Vance, and he turned to the security guard.

"Take me back."

The security guard's eyes moved to Hector before he closed the door and stood in front of it.

"Take me back," Seth repeated to the guard.

Hector studied him. Even with months inside, he looked good. Body fit, his prison blues wrinkle-free like he had them ironed, his hair cut neatly.

Hector tried to find some hint of Sadie in him, but it wasn't there.

Seth Townsend was tall, dark-haired with some distinguishing gray, and his body was made up of lean, muscled bulk. He was impressive, had a presence that was both magnetic and menacing, even in prison. How this man made Sadie, Hector couldn't begin to guess. If he hadn't seen the photos of Sadie's mother, he would have thought she was adopted.

"We gotta talk," Hector said.

Seth's gaze sliced to him but he was silent.

"I wanna cut a deal," Hector went on.

Seth's eyes flashed and he smiled. It was not an amused smile. It was a triumphant one. He walked further into the room.

"You want to cut a deal," Seth repeated.

"Yeah," Hector replied.

Seth put his hands in the pockets of his pants and rocked back on his heels.

"All of a sudden, I want to cut a deal, too," Seth said.

It was Hector's turn to stay silent.

Then, as if Vance nor the guard were in the room, Seth offered, "I'll make it worth your while to stay away from her."

Hector showed no reaction to this and remained silent.

"Good enough to fix up that house of yours, trade up to a better car, even afford a decent haircut."

Exposing his knowledge of Hector's living arrangements and vehicle mixed with the inference that Hector was beneath Sadie's notice, Hector knew Seth was trying to rattle him.

Considering he left Sadie naked and asleep in his bed, Hector remained unrattled.

Seth watched him closely then said, "No? Then I'll make it *not* worth your while to stay with her."

"This how you scared away Tracy and Brent?" Hector asked about Sadie's only two boyfriends. She didn't need to tell him about them last night. He already knew. He'd dug them up as a matter of course during the investigation and knew all about them.

"They took the first option," Seth replied without remorse.

"I'm waitin' for option three. The one where, once you get out, you invite me to Thanksgiving dinner," Hector returned casually.

Seth showed no response.

"We done with this topic?" Hector decided it was time to move on.

Seth shrugged.

"Sadie's bad business has to stop," Hector continued.

Instantly Seth retorted, "You *are* clever. You come up with that on your own?"

Hector ignored him. "You can carry on and fuck it up or we can work together."

Seth's eyes went hard. "You have got to be joking, Chavez. No way in hell we're working together."

"Then I got a choice," Hector replied immediately. "Vance here has been diggin' around Elizabeth's disappearance. Vance is pretty good at findin' shit out. So good, he found out she was whacked by Mickey Balducci. You remember Mickey Balducci?"

Hector watched with some degree of surprise as Seth showed a reaction. Before he could control it, pain sliced across his face. The one thing Seth had given Sadie was the ability to put up an impenetrable defense. This was a first.

Still, Seth didn't respond.

Hector kept at him. "Vance can share with Sadie what he knows or we can let her go on thinkin' you did it."

That was when Seth Townsend's magnetic, menacing, invulnerable aura cracked. His body jerked and his face went pale.

"She thinks *I* did it?" he whispered.

Hector nodded. Seth's hand came out of his pocket and up slightly as if it was going to tear through his hair. He realized quickly what this would expose, dropped his hand and he looked out the window.

Hector opened his mouth to speak when his cell went. He decided to give Seth a moment to reflect, dug it out of his back pocket and looked at the display which said "Sadie Calling". His eyes cut to Vance as he flipped it open and put it to his ear.

"Sadie," he answered, and he felt the air in the room grow dense.

She was whispering, voice panicked, "I got up. You weren't here. I was going down to the kitchen to find you. I was on the landing, looked downstairs and I saw a *man's legs* on the couch. They weren't yours. Hector, where are you? *Someone's in the house.*"

*Fuck*, he thought, anger gripping him at the fear in her voice.

Without hesitating and without giving a thought to his audience, he bent his head, stepped away and turned so his side was to the room.

"Calm down, *mamita*. That's Bobby. He's lookin' after you today. Didn't you see the note I put on the pillow?"

He heard her take a deep breath and then he heard her move. Finally, she sighed.

"Blooming heck, I'm sorry. It's right here. I didn't see it."

"You okay?" he asked immediately.

"Yes," she replied and she sounded okay, in an instant totally over her panic. Will of fucking steel. "Where are you?" she asked.

"Doin' some business."

She hesitated and he knew she was bracing before exposing herself. She did that a lot, and he figured, didn't know she was doing it. He wondered vaguely when it would stop when he heard her ask, "Am I going to see you today?"

He fought a smile. His head came up and he looked sightlessly out the window.

"Yeah, this won't take long, but I got other shit after this. No matter what, I'll be home tonight, take you to dinner."

"Maybe we shouldn't go out. We're not really good with going out. Maybe we should cook something here."

"Whatever you want, *mi corazón*."

"After we eat, you can take me for another bike ride," she told him and he bit his lip and shook his head.

"Gotta say, *mujer*, it's good you like the bike."

"Will you take me for a ride?" she pressed.

"I'll take you for a ride."

She didn't respond to this, but he heard the pleasure in her voice when she went onto a different subject like they had all day to talk. "I have to go with Jet to get fitted for a bridesmaid's dress today. Do you think Bobby would take me?"

The thought of Bobby taking Sadie to get fitted for a bridesmaid's dress made Hector lose the battle with his smile.

"Yeah."

She carried on, "I know you want to do your floors, but if I have time, can I goo your fireplace?"

He couldn't help it. He gave a short laugh. She made "gooing" his fireplace sound like it was the height of entertainment. He didn't know a single woman who thought "gooing" a fireplace was a thrill a minute.

"Yeah," he repeated, still smiling.

"Where's the goo?"

"Back room," he answered. "Listen, *mamita*, I'm in the middle of something."

"Oh! Sorry. You should have said."

"I just did."

When she spoke again, he heard the smile in her voice. "Okay, I'll let you go."

"You leave the house, you're never outside of touching distance from Bobby, got me?"

"Got you," she replied readily.

The tension left his body. "Later."

Then he heard her voice going soft and breathy like it always did when she said it, "Bye, babe."

And like it always did, he felt that soft, breathy word in his gut before he flipped the phone shut, turned back to the room and found Seth Townsend staring at him.

Something had changed. Hector couldn't put his finger on it, but he knew, before Seth spoke and confirmed it, that whatever it was, it was big.

"I was like you," Seth told him, voice hard, eyes active, body taut. "Just like you."

Hector's eyes narrowed.

"I doubt that," he replied scathingly.

"You're wrong," Seth returned, and then, voice still hard but his words were soft, "Just like you." He paused and went on, "You fuck her over, I'll kill you."

Vance moved. It was almost imperceptible, but the threat was not. Hector put his hand up toward Vance because he knew Seth had just given in.

Seth crossed his arms on his chest.

"You know about Mickey. What else do you know?" he asked Hector.

"That you avenged your wife by bringin' down Luther, who ordered the hit, and takin' Mickey out altogether. The Balducci boys didn't forget and have been tryin' to chip away at you for a long time. With you out of commission, they went after Sadie."

Seth's only reaction to this was lifting his chin then he said, "Tell me your deal."

Hector glanced at Vance then back at Seth.

"Jerry isn't your soldier anymore. He's pissed about me, he's pissed about Sadie and he's pissed about your instructions to look after her. In doin' so, forcin' him to put himself at risk with Lee, somethin' no one does of their own free will. Somehow he knows about the Caymans accounts and that Sadie's the only one who can get to the money. He's struck a deal. He's workin' with Donny now. You're playin' right into their hands. He's obeyin' your orders until Sadie gets the account information. She knows about the accounts, she's fucked. They got options. They could roofie her, they could threaten her, whatever. They take her to the Caymans, sedated or under duress, she hands them the money. They don't have a use for her anymore and they either play with her, take her out, or both. In the meantime, whatever power you got left takes another hit without that cash. You're weak, the Balduccis avenge their father's murder and you're as fucked as Sadie."

Seth did not look happy and asked, "I thought you boys had Donny on tape torching her gallery?"

"We're after him, the police are after him, but he's proving difficult to find," Hector replied.

At that news, Seth looked even less happy.

"What's the deal?" he ground out.

"You back off, let me handle it. That's the deal."

"You must be joking," Seth returned.

Hector shook his head.

"That's not a deal," Seth snapped.

"Only one you got," Hector shot back.

"You want me to stand back and—"

"No, you tell me everything, everything the Feds didn't find. The location of your safe house, any other property you own, where your money's comin' from, what soldiers you got left workin' for you, where I can find 'em. You keep tryin' to contact Sadie, but you get hold of her, you don't fuckin' tell her shit."

"And what, you hand this over to the Feds?"

"No, the boys go huntin'. The Balduccis are hidden, we figure Jerry's helpin'. They're usin' your own resources to fuck you."

"This doesn't make any fucking sense. The Balduccis want my business. They can't waltz around Denver being the big men now. They fucked up, got caught on camera committing arson. Ricky's—"

"Seth, they don't want your business. They don't intend to stay in town. They get your money, they live off your back for the rest of their lives knowin' they got everything you had, including bringin' Sadie low."

Seth stared at Hector then his mouth got tight.

"Goddamn it," he muttered.

"We got a deal?" Hector pushed.

Seth kept staring at Hector. His gaze sliced to Vance, then his eyes cut back and locked on Hector.

"Deal."

# Chapter 25
# Code One

*Sadie*

"Yahtzee!" I yelled, bouncing on my bottom on the couch that was situated in the front window of Fortnum's.

"Girlie, you're on a hot streak!" Stevie cried, leaning forward and giving me a high five.

He wasn't wrong. It was my third Yahtzee that game and I'd had two the game before. I was kicking Yahtzee *butt*.

"Three yahtzees in one game, two the game before. That's unheard of. Fuck this shit, we need to go to DIA and get a direct flight to Vegas. With the way Sadie's rollin', we hit the craps table, we'll all retire," Shirleen announced.

"I could go to Vegas," I told Shirleen, and I could. Why not? It sounded fun. I'd only been to Vegas once and that was with my father. It was a business trip and I had to entertain almost the whole time I was there. I'd been able to see a few of the sights, but I hadn't been able to gamble at all.

And I was on a hot streak.

I already had enough money to retire but more never hurt.

Right?

"You're not going to Vegas." Bobby frowned at me.

I looked at Bobby (a.k.a. Alaskan Hottie), opened my mouth to say something then decided to close it.

I'd only just met him that morning and practically the first thing I did (after drinking coffee and making toast) was make him help me goo the fireplace and scrape paint out of grooves.

He didn't mind this, but then I'd made him help me sand the whole fireplace down (by hand).

He didn't mind this either.

*Then* I'd made him sit in a bridal shop with Jet, Nancy, Blanca, Tod and Stevie.

He minded that.

Tod and Stevie, I found out, were the officially unofficial Rock Chick Wedding Planners; or, at least, Tod was (and, by the by, Tod didn't like the idea of a hayride either, but, he declared magnanimously, was going to "work with it").

Jet had chosen the color, but all her bridesmaids could pick their style. I'd decided which style I wanted immediately but Tod made me try on seven more dresses, just in case.

Then they made Nancy and Blanca try on mother-of-the-bride and mother-of-the-groom gowns, even though Nancy and Blanca both were going to get something at a department store (Tod changed their mind about this and all three of us ordered gowns that day).

We then got into a complicated discussion about accessories. Tiara, veil or both? Gloves, yes or no? If yes, full length, half length, only hand? And if gloves at all, fingerless or not?

Needless to say, I was not Bobby's favorite person at that moment.

After the three hour bridal shop session, Nancy and Blanca had gone their separate ways and Jet, Bobby, Tod, Stevie and I went back to Fortnum's to play Yahtzee. Tex, Indy, Duke and Jane (another of Indy's employees; she was a painfully quiet, equally painfully thin and even more painfully shy woman of indeterminate age) were working.

Once we arrived, Indy and Jet mostly played Yahtzee with Tod, Stevie and me. Jane disappeared into the shelves with an armload of books only to come back and get another armload and disappear again. Tex stayed at his post behind the espresso counter with a steady stream of customers he was supremely ungracious to (but, bizarrely, they didn't seem to mind). Duke played wingman behind the espresso counter or manned the book counter when a book was sold. Finally, Shirleen had arrived half an hour ago and joined the Yahtzee marathon.

Ralphie phoned in between Yahtzee games four and five to tell me he was cooking dinner for Double H and me the next night and since this was his cooking premiere, if we didn't show, he was disowning us (his words).

Not wanting to be disowned, I called Hector to ask him about Ralphie's invitation. He accepted without reservation, even after I explained to him that Ralphie was most definitely not the cook in the family. I also let him know I was hanging out at Fortnum's.

Between my turns with the fake velvet lined Yahtzee cup (it was, Tod informed me, the Yahtzee "Deluxe" edition), I was struggling with the decision of which was my second best day ever, yesterday or today.

Trying on bridesmaid dresses and looking at tiaras and veils was fun and I'd never done it. And, with Tod taking charge and Nancy and Blanca not scaring me, it was good spending time with them. It was neat watching Jet with Nancy. The mother/daughter banter, the familiarity, the way they made it obvious they were close. But what was almost better was the way Blanca was with Jet. How it was clear she was already a member of the family, accepted, loved and even, sometimes (I noticed), precious.

That last part, and the hope I held in the very, very back of my mind that I'd have that too (one day), edged out yesterday as my best day.

Especially when I thought of my phone conversation with Hector that morning.

Just the thought of that phone conversation gave me goose bumps, the good kind.

I'd let my guard down. I'd let him in. I'd shared my secrets. I'd opened a small door to a little place inside me, and he'd slid in. I found he not only fit, he seemed comfortable there and I liked it.

But, better, it seemed he liked being there. Not just a little, a lot.

And sensing that, the severed edges torn apart in my heart that I thought would never heal felt whole again.

"No time for Vegas," Jet said, taking me out of my thoughts. I glanced at her and she was looking out the window. Then her eyes came to me. "Double H is here," she finished on a grin.

I rolled my eyes at her use of "Double H", turned in my seat and looked out the big front window to see Hector slamming the door on the Bronco. Fortnum's was on a corner and he'd parked on the cross street opposite the store.

I watched as he caught the light just right and started to jog across the four lanes of Broadway.

He looked good jogging. Natural, cool, casual, his body at his command and I liked watching him. So much, I felt my heart start to beat a little faster and my mouth began to form a smile.

That was when the shots rang out.

I froze, heard startled cries, but my eyes stayed riveted on Hector as his body jerked. He bent over, now running. His hand going to the back of his jeans, I saw him pull out a gun.

That was all I saw.

I was lifted bodily from the couch. This surprised me and I let out a little scream, not only because of the surprise, but because I was being carried away and I couldn't see Hector around Bobby's big body.

"Put me down!" I yelled, squirming in his arms until I could see around his massive shoulders. I caught a glimpse of Hector crouched in front of a car in front of Fortnum's. He pulled up slightly, arms cocked and out in front of him, pointed upward, gun hand resting in his other palm, and he fired once.

I lost sight again when my bottom was planted on the book counter, and without hesitation Bobby put a hand in my chest and gave me a shove. As I fell backward, arms wheeling around to regain balance, I noticed movement all around the store. Indy was shouting at customers to stay in the store and move to the book aisles.

Before I fell, strong hands came to my waist and I was yanked over the other side of the counter. My feet hit the floor and Duke pressed into me until we were both hunkered down, Duke's big body mostly covering mine.

I heard pounding feet, more cries, more gunshots, and in a panic, I tried to surge up but Duke kept solid.

"Stay still!" he ordered.

"Hector!" I shouted toward the floor (which was my forced vantage point; Duke had my head tucked down with one of his hands) and I continued to push against Duke's bulk.

"Still!" Duke repeated, pressing into me.

"Shots fired. Fortnum's bookstore, Bayaud and Broadway." I heard Tex boom from across the room, obviously on the phone, then in a louder boom, "Loopy Loo, don't worry about the customers, get to cover, *now!*"

"Oh my God," I breathed and Tex continued.

"Hector Chavez is the target. He's outside with Bobby Zanzinski, both are returnin' fire."

"Oh my God," I breathed again.

I felt movement, Duke was jostled and I was able to lift my head a bit. I saw Jet shove a customer behind the book counter with us. They both got low, sat on their behinds, knees up, backs to the shelves.

"Bobby's gone out," Jet told Duke, her face pale.

I looked at Duke and saw his mouth grow tight as more gunshots could be heard.

My eyes moved back to Jet.

"This isn't happening," I told her stupidly because it was... fucking... *happening.*

"Stay calm, darlin'." Duke's gravelly voice came at me and my eyes sliced to him.

"*You* stay calm!" I snapped, again trying (and failing) to push at him. "*My* boyfriend's out there!"

"He knows what he's doin' and there ain't no way you can help him," Duke shot back.

My heart racing, I glared at Duke, knowing he was right. Then I glared at Jet, then at the trembling female customer who was huddled next to Jet and who looked like one of those grunge rock band people who needed a shower and shampoo.

Without any option open to me, I did the only thing I could do.

I made an empty threat.

"All I can say is, if this is a Balducci, I'm hunting him down and I'm going to rip his heart out with my bare hands and use it as a soccer ball!"

The Grunge Customer stared at me and slid a little closer to Jet.

I heard sirens and noticed that there weren't any more gunshots.

"The shots have stopped," I told Duke immediately.

"Stay low," Duke replied.

"We need to see if Hector and Bobby are all right," I went on.

"Sadie, stay low," Duke repeated.

Even though I really didn't want to, I stayed low and tried to deep breathe. This was hard.

My eyes locked on Jet's. She nodded reassuringly to me, put her arm around the trembling customer and pulled her close. I nodded back and pulled in more breath, but no matter how deep they were, I couldn't seem to get enough oxygen in my lungs.

We waited what seemed like four days.

Four *long* days.

Finally, I heard Bobby say from the front of the store, "Tex, Duke, Shirleen, we're movin' Sadie out."

Before I could react to Bobby being back, Duke hauled me up and hustled me out from behind the book counter.

I saw Bobby, alive, no bullet holes or blood visible, seemingly fit as a fiddle standing at the door, gun in his hand. The black Nightingale Explorer was pulled up on the sidewalk right outside the front door.

"Hector?" I asked Bobby.

"He's fine," Bobby answered.

I pulled in more breath and finally felt oxygen hit my lungs.

Then, as if she couldn't hear Bobby, I shouted toward the book counter, "Jet, he's fine!"

"I heard! Get gone!" Jet's voice shouted back.

"Indy?" I yelled.

"I'm fine, go!" I heard Indy yell back from behind the espresso counter.

"Tod, Stevie?" I called.

"Girlie, go!" Tod called back from somewhere in the bookshelves. "We're fine."

Before I could do any more, Shirleen, Tex and Duke got close and hurried me out while Bobby kept his gun up and his eyes peeled. In seconds flat, I was out the door, in the back of the Explorer and the door was closed. Shirleen climbed into the passenger side, Bobby behind the wheel and we took off.

"Where's Hector?" I asked, buckling up.

"With Ricky," Bobby replied.

It felt like a ten ton weight hit my chest and I stopped breathing entirely.

Luckily, Shirleen spoke for me. "What'd you say?"

"It was Ricky Balducci shootin' at him. I drew his fire, Hector rounded the building, climbed the fire escape and got him," Bobby answered.

Visions of Hector choking the life out of Ricky (or worse) filled my head. I started breathing again (more like hyperventilating) and yelled, "Go back! You can't leave Hector with Ricky! He's going to—"

"He had him disarmed, cuffed to a door and he's got a gun on him," Bobby interrupted me. "The cops were approachin' when I left. Ricky's facin' rape, arson and now attempted murder. Hector assaults him, he fucks it up. Hector's a wild man but ain't no way he's gonna fuck this up, no matter how much he wants to kick Balducci's ass."

This made sense and it made me stop hyperventilating.

Then another thought occurred to me.

"Why did you move me out?"

"Hector wants you at the offices," Bobby answered.

"Why?" I pressed.

"I didn't ask. I don't care. He wants you there, I take you there. I follow orders and I don't question them. Ever," Bobby returned.

I decided (since Bobby had just been in a gunfight), that maybe now was not the time to be asking any more questions.

He took us to the offices and parked in the underground garage. I didn't have time to have an emotional drama that I was back in the garage for the first time since I'd careened in there after being raped. Shirleen and Bobby hustled me out of the car, up the stairs and into the offices before I could blink.

Shirleen stayed in the reception area, but Bobby took me straight through the door to the back rooms and into the surveillance room, which was filled with a couple of desks, monitors, equipment and the big, muscular bulk that was Jack.

Jack turned to us. His eyes did a professional full body scan of me then they moved to Bobby.

"Got the call," he told Bobby.

"Code One?" Bobby asked.

"Yup," Jack replied.

I looked between them, wondering who would explain.

"I'm off," Bobby said. Then he was.

The door closed behind him. This I took as Bobby not being the one to explain.

Therefore, I turned and asked Jack, "What's Code One?"

"Sit. Watch the monitors," Jack responded.

I sat in a swivel chair in front of the bank of monitors, six across, four rows, each with what looked like a DVD recorder under it. I trained my gaze on the screens and repeated, "What's Code One?"

"Do as I say, when I say, no matter what you see on the monitors," Jack answered.

Though this wasn't really an answer I didn't quibble. I didn't suspect that now was Quibble Time. Quibble Time was after whatever Code One was was over and I was innocently playing Yahtzee with my friends again.

"Should I be worried about whatever's happening?" I went on.

"Nope."

"You're sure?" I pressed.

"Yup."

I didn't really believe him, but as I mentioned, it was not Quibble Time.

We watched the monitors.

Then I asked, "What are we looking for?"

"Anything."

"What kind of anything?"

"Anything, anything."

I was feeling ill-equipped to be Jack's Monitor Helper, but I decided to stop asking questions about my assignment. It was not only not Quibble Time; it was probably not Question Time either. Except for things looking like they'd gone back to normal at Fortnum's and a bunch of people in the pool hall doing pool hall type activities, nothing much was happening.

I decided on a different subject. "Can I call Hector?"

"Nope."

Blooming heck!

"Can I call him in, say, fifteen minutes?" I tried.

"You can shut up. That'd be good."

My back went straight, but my eyes didn't leave the screens.

"Did you just tell me to shut up?"

"I see you didn't hear me."

"Hector was in a gunfight!" I snapped.

"Not the first, probably not the last."

Oh my.

*That* shut me up.

I decided not to think about that until I was, say, six hundred years old, and silently we watched the screens.

Then I saw something in the pool hall.

"Oh my God!" I cried.

Jack went on alert.

"What?"

"Look at her outfit!" I pointed at a girl in the pool hall. "Her tank top is skintight and she's not wearing a bra. And her skirt is shorter than the one I wore to Stella's gig!"

Jack was silent, but I felt he'd lost his intensity.

I peered closer. The girl on the screen bent over a pool table and I gasped when I was treated to a partial moon. "Blooming heck! She's wearing a *thong!*" I exclaimed, then went on, "Now, if you're going to wear a skirt that short, you really should wear proper underwear."

Jack remained silent.

I looked at him. "Don't you think?"

Jack's eyes remained on the screens. "I think Hector owes me big time is what I think."

Hmm.

Perhaps Jack was not the kind of man who discussed women's underwear choices, even after dramatic shootouts (or, perhaps, ever).

I decided that was my cue to stay silent again.

This lasted less than a minute.

"Why are we watching a pool hall?"

"The Balduccis own that pool hall."

I felt bile slide up my throat and I swallowed it down.

I thought that was apropos. The Evil Fitzpatrick clan hung out at a pool hall in Veronica Mars.

I didn't share this with Jack.

"Oh," was all I said, but I watched closer.

We sat in silence for a while, and then I saw Hector's Bronco enter the garage.

"Thank you, God," I breathed, watching him park.

He got out, started toward the door to the stairs and I felt my body begin to relax. But then I saw Hector stop and look toward the entrance of the garage.

Jack tensed.

I tensed.

Then I saw a BMW careening into the garage.

Hector pulled his gun out of the back of his jeans again and I automatically went into a squat, not standing, not sitting, and not sure what I was going to do.

"Sit," Jack ordered, not taking his eyes from the screen.

I sat.

I stared.

The BMW halted and Hector had his head cocked and his gun up, trained on the car.

I held my breath.

Marty Balducci got out of the BMW and my body automatically went into my ready to run squat again.

"Sit!" Jack repeated, louder this time, and I didn't want to, I really didn't want to, but I sat again.

Marty didn't look good and I felt the blood drain out of my face. I couldn't see all that clearly on the small screen but he appeared to be bleeding from multiple gunshot wounds to the chest.

Marty held on to the open car door to keep himself up, but I could tell he was struggling. He lifted his gun toward Hector, but he couldn't quite lift it far enough. I could see they were talking (or shouting) at each other. Hector, arms out, gun up, was advancing slowly.

Jack hit a button on the console and the room filled with the ringing of a phone.

Then, on another monitor, I watched as an Explorer entered the garage.

I stared, body tense, as it parked at an angle behind Marty's BMW and Lee and Luke got out, already armed, guns up and trained on Marty.

"What's happening?" I whispered, but Jack didn't answer. He had his hands on the console in front of us, close to both the phones that were pointed in his direction and a number of buttons and knobs.

"Nine, one, one," a voice said. "What's your emergency?"

"I need an ambulance. There's a man with multiple gunshot wounds in the garage under Nightingale Investigations..." Jack told the operator, speaking clearly, calmly, giving an address, his name, a telephone number.

While Jack talked, I saw Lee and Luke advance on Marty, just like Hector. They all seemed to be talking to each other and moving in slow motion.

Without warning, likely unable to hold himself up anymore, Marty suddenly went down.

"He's down," Jack said to the 911 operator.

Hector and Lee stopped moving slowly and rushed to Marty. Hector kicked Marty's gun away, shoved his own into his jeans, got down on his knees and bent over Marty, obscuring our view. Luke ran to the back of the Explorer.

Something caught in my corner vision and I looked to a monitor two banks up and to the right and at what I saw, I shouted (and pointed for good measure), "Jack! It's Donny!"

Donny Balducci and two men I didn't know were creeping along the hallway, which hallway I didn't know.

"We need cars," Jack barked at the 911 operator. "Squads. We got three men, all armed, in the building approaching the Nightingale offices. Same address as for the ambulance. We got civilians in here. We're on the fourth floor. Over and out."

Then he hit a button and immediately flipped a switch. "Lockdown. Three armed men approaching," Jack said but I heard it over a PA which seemed to be all around us.

I watched Shirleen jump up, open a drawer, pull out a gun and she ran to the front office door and locked it. I felt Jack's movements as he hit another button and the room filled with ringing again.

"Get out of there Shirleen, get out, get out..." I chanted, watching Donny and his gang approach the office door as Shirleen hustled toward the inner door.

"Stark." I heard Luke's voice fill the room and tore my eyes away from Donny to see Luke standing in the garage, his phone to his ear.

"Donny's in the building, two men with him, all armed in the hallway outside the front office door. We're in lockdown. Ambulance is in transit for Marty. I called squads. Over."

Jack was talking, but Luke was now moving, jogging toward the stairs, Lee breaking away from Hector and coming with Luke. Somewhere along the line someone had given Hector a first aid kit, but it was sitting next to him on the concrete unused and Hector was giving Marty CPR.

Then I saw Shirleen disappear from the reception area.

"Status. Over," Luke said.

"Shirleen's in the hall, Brody's in the back office. Sadie and me in the surveillance room. Everyone else out on assignment. Over."

"Shirleen goes in with Sadie. You're in the hall. Over and out."

Luke and Lee had disappeared from the screen because they'd hit the stairs. Jack pressed some buttons and the viewpoint changed on some of the monitors and I saw Luke and Lee on the stairs, taking them two at a time.

Jack got up, and when I turned to him, he had a gun.

"No matter what you see or what you hear, you do not leave this room. Got me?"

I nodded.

"Repeat it," he said.

"No matter what, I won't leave this room," I said quickly.

He nodded then he was gone, Shirleen passing him on his way out.

"Jack got the police comin'?" Shirleen asked, her eyes going directly to the monitors and she started scanning them as she took a seat.

"Police and ambulance," I replied.

"Holy shit, what's happened in the garage?" Her eyes were riveted on Hector giving Marty CPR.

"Marty drove in, got out of the car. He was filled with bullets. He collapsed. Hector's working on him. Lee and Luke are headed up here."

Shirleen was silent.

Then quietly she remarked, "They don't have vests."

"What?"

She looked at me then back at the monitors and muttered, "Nothin'."

It hit me she meant bulletproof vests.

I felt fear slice through me as I watched, mouth dropping open, as Donny gave up trying to force the door open with his foot, took a step back and drilled some rounds in it with his gun. Then he kicked the door open and they all surged in just as Lee and Luke rounded another flight of stairs.

"Why don't they wait for the police?" I shouted, coming into a squat again, and I wasn't going to sit down, no way. I didn't know how to sit anymore.

Visions, unbidden, forced themselves into my head. Lee and Indy's wedding picture in the paper. Luke taking Ava in his arms and talking against her mouth. Both of them teasing me.

It hit me that these were my friends and they were in danger.

Because of me.

I straightened out of my squat and stood.

"Child, settle," Shirleen said softly.

All at once, everything happened, on the monitors and in the office.

I heard more gunshots, these close, coming from Donny, who was firing at the inner door. The paramedics were running toward Hector. Uniformed police were running up the stairs, guns drawn. Lee and Luke were in the hall and jogging toward the offices.

"Stay back!" I shouted, leaning forward now, hands on the console, body trembling, eyes going manically from screen to screen.

Lee stopped outside the door and flattened himself against the wall, and with quick head jerks, he peered around the door, Luke beside him, as Donny pulled open the inner door.

"Jack," I breathed.

More gunshots. Shirleen and I sucked in breath as Lee then Luke surged around the door and into reception.

My body jerked as I heard shouts, gunshots, close. Very close.

I saw both Lee and Luke were inside reception, both moving and firing, just as I noted, on another screen, Hector running up the stairs, taking them three at a time.

Without thinking, I turned and bolted to the door.

Before I got close, Shirleen caught me in two strong arms and pulled me back.

There were more gunshots and I closed my eyes, put my hands over my ears and I heard Jack's voice, soft and reassuring, coming at me from my memory banks the night of my rape.

*It's okay. It's okay. You're okay. You're safe.*

The pain of fear for Jack sliced through my gut.

The gunshots and shouting stopped.

My eyes flew open and I looked to my left at the monitors. Shirleen and I stood, her arms wrapped around me, and we watched. Luke, the police and now Hector were in the reception area. Luke and Hector were advancing, both still armed, guns pointed to something on the ground, the police were moving around talking into the mouthpieces at their shoulders.

Lee had disappeared.

"Can we go out now? Can we go?" I asked Shirleen.

"Hang on, baby. Stay with me," Shirleen cooed softly.

"Lee. Jack," I whispered.

"Hang on."

We lost sight of Hector and Luke and Shirleen and I stood silently watching the monitors. It seemed odd and distressing that everything was normal at Fortnum's.

They had no idea.

No idea.

It could have been seconds, but it felt like hours before the door opened and Hector stood there.

Shirleen's arms dropped away and I surged forward, my body slamming into his, his arms closing around me.

"Please, please, please, please, please," I breathed into his throat.

"Jack got clipped, just a nick in the neck. He's fine. He'd had time to put on a vest," Hector said, and I could feel the vibration of his voice at his throat against my lips.

"Lee?"

"Lee's fine. He's seein' to Jack."

My body sagged into his. His arms got tighter and I felt, rather than saw, Shirleen squeeze by us and leave the room.

I tilted my head back and looked at Hector.

"Are you okay?"

He dipped his chin and his black eyes caught mine. "Yeah, *mamita*. I'm all right."

My arms tensed. "I'm so sorry. So, so, sorry."

I watched as his eyes flashed and he murmured, "*Cállate, mi amor.*"

"It's my fault," I went on.

"*Cállate,*" he repeated softly.

I blinked then my brows drew together in confusion. "What's that mean?"

"It means shut up."

Oh.

Well then.

"That sounds nicer than the English shut up," I told him.

His lips twitched. "It isn't."

I didn't have the time to worry about Hector being rude.

I took in breath and asked, "Marty?"

Hector replied immediately, "Not good. He should have driven himself to the hospital, not here."

I moved on. "Donny?"

"Donny and his boys were all down with officers workin' on 'em when I got here. But Luke and Lee got a lot of experience with this shit. They don't shoot to kill, just neutralize."

That might be so, but there was no way they had time even to aim.

So I told Hector, "What just happened was insane. They didn't have time—"

He interrupted me by saying firmly, "They had time."

I stared at him and realized he wasn't lying.

I decided to move on again. "Why did it all…" I stopped then started again, "What happened?"

His face dipped lower. He touched his lips to mine and he said, "We'll talk about it later. After we talk to the cops and after we're done sittin' in the hot tub."

Right away, this made me smile. I couldn't help it. Even with all the drama, the very thought of sitting in a hot tub with Hector sounded *great*.

No, *especially* with all the drama.

And there it was again.

Drama. Gunfights. Paramedics. Police officers. Fear. Panic. Life-threatening situations. Jack getting "clipped".

And Hector swept it all away with hot tub promises.

I snuggled closer, then my smile faded.

"I'm not allowed," I told him.

His head jerked with surprise right before his face changed and he looked like he was about to laugh.

Now, really, seriously, truly there was *absolutely* nothing funny about *this*.

"You're not allowed?" he repeated.

"My tattoo," I explained. "The tattoo guy said——"

He interrupted me again. "It'll be okay."

I cocked my head and asked, "You sure?"

One of his arms came from around me and his hand went to my neck then up, his fingers sliding into my hair. Instead of tilting my head back, he tilted it down and I felt his lips moving against the top of my head.

"I'm sure."

Then he kissed me there.

After that, he and I went out into the hall and I took over "seein' to Jack".

⌦⌐

"Back in the news today is Nightingale Investigations. Some months back, the private investigations firm achieved local fame while guarding the lead singer of a popular local band. This afternoon, on Broadway, a gunfight played out between——"

The newscaster was cut off when Hector pressed a button on the remote and the TV screen went blank.

I lifted my still wet-haired-from-the-hot-tub head from his chest and looked up at him.

"I was watching that," I protested.

He threw the remote on the nightstand. His body turned into mine and I found myself on my back with Hector mostly on top of me.

"I don't wanna watch the news," he told me, his eyes locking with mine. "I wanna fool around with my girlfriend."

My belly melted, even though we'd just "fooled around" in the hot tub not an hour ago.

"We just fooled around in the hot tub," I reminded him, as if he could forget. One thing was certain sure, *I* couldn't forget. Hot tub sex was *amazing*.

(Oh Lord, I hoped he *couldn't* forget).

He grinned wickedly (he didn't forget) and his head started descending. "Don't care."

"What if they said something about me on the news?"

His mouth hit mine. "Don't care."

"What if they said something about you?"

Since I persisted in talking, his lips left my mouth, trailed down my cheek, along my jaw to below my ear. "Don't care."

"What if they said something about my father?"

His tongue touched the skin below my ear, moved down and forward to my throat.

I shivered, then he said, voice deeper now, "Don't care."

"Hector," I called, my arms going around him, one hand going up into his hair. Truth be told, I really wanted to have sex (yes, again, but he *did* just call me his girlfriend and I liked it; I liked it *loads*, and I felt like I should get to celebrate). But, as hateful as it was, I had to know so I went on, "What happened today?"

He pulled up and looked at me. Then one of his hands came to rest on the side of my head.

Then he did something strange.

His thumb came out and slid across the scar on my cheek and his eyes, warm and intense, watched it move while I held my breath at this gentle, yet somehow weirdly profound, gesture.

His gaze came back to mine.

"Today, we got one step closer to this bein' over."

This surprised me.

"One step?" I asked, confused. "But Ricky's in jail. Marty and Donny are in the hospital under armed guard—"

His mouth touched mine and I quit talking, then he said, "One step, *mamita*. There's still more cleanup to do."

"What cleanup?"

He stared at me a second, then two, then on the third second he continued, "I just wanna make sure you're safe."

"But—"

His thumb moved from my cheek to my lips, effectively quieting me.

"One night, Sadie. One night just you and me and this bed and your body and none of this shit comes in. For one night, I wanna forget it. Can you give that to me?"

I pulled in my lips.

I really wanted to know what happened that day and why, with the Balduccis gone, he thought he still needed to make sure I was safe.

But I realized two things at once and they hit me with the strength of an oncoming train.

First, he'd never asked me for anything.

That wasn't strictly true. He'd taken things and he'd given things, but he'd never asked for anything except to take care of me, for me to trust him and to give him this and none of those things took anything from me. They just gave.

Second, earlier that day, he'd called me *mi amor*, "my love", according to Jet, the ultimate Spanish endearment.

Because of those two things, I nodded.

Then I watched, close up and fascinated, as his face went soft.

His mouth came toward mine.

Then we forgot everything and it was just him and me and our bodies in his bed.

# Chapter 26

# Christmas Dinner at the Big House

*Sadie*

I woke up, alone, the bedclothes tucked tight all around me.

I pulled some of Hector's pillow hoard under the covers with me, held them to my chest and stared at the wall for several moments, mind blank, still half asleep. Then I wondered if sometime during that day I'd be undecided in ranking it as my second best day ever against the day before, and the day before that (barring kidnappings and gunfights, of course).

Then I wondered if there would be a day when there were so many good days, I wouldn't be able to rank them anymore.

And somewhere in the very, very back of my mind, I had a feeling there would.

This thought made me smile at the wall.

I got up, still sleepy because Hector kept me up late. "Fooling around", I learned, was different than the other stuff we did. It took longer, *loads* longer—not that I was complaining (at all). I put on my pajamas and one of Hector's flannel shirts and shuffled into the hall.

I smelled bacon cooking and heard voices downstairs and I knew Hector had company (again).

I wandered downstairs, through the living room and into the kitchen.

Hector not only had company, he had loads of company. Tom, Kitty Sue and Malcolm were there. Blanca was at the stove. Vance was leaning against the counter. All of them had coffee mugs.

Hector was sitting on the counter and I smiled to everyone, gave them a little wave, but shuffled straight to Hector.

He opened his legs when I approached and I went straight in. My arms sliding around his waist, I pressed my cheek to his chest and one of his arms went around shoulders.

His other hand came to my chin and lifted my face. When I saw them, his eyes were soft and warm, which made *me* feel soft and warm as well as snugly, comfy and lovely.

"You okay?" he muttered.

I nodded and murmured, "Sleepy."

"You should have stayed in bed."

I grinned, cuddled closer, and my voice breathy, I said, "Babe. And miss the party?"

His face changed. It got that soft, hard, possessive look and his eyes went from warm to hot. If we didn't have an audience, I knew something would have happened, but instead he let go of my chin. I dipped my head and pressed my cheek against his chest again. He muttered some soft words in Spanish into my hair and then kissed me there.

I caught sight of Blanca, who was staring at us, bacon fork pointed up, coffee mug in her other hand.

I blinked then blinked again, but even so, the expression on her face didn't change. She was watching me with a feminine, motherly version of the same soft, hard, possessive look that her son had just treated me to. I didn't know what to make of that except it made that snugly, comfy, lovely feeling intensify.

"Blanca, can you teach me how to speak Spanish while you teach me how to cook?" I called to her.

Her body gave a start and she shook her head as if clearing it, then said, "*Sí, mi hija.*"

"*Gracias,*" I returned.

She grinned.

I grinned back.

Kitty Sue burst out laughing.

My eyes moved to her.

"What's funny?" I asked.

"I just think it's cute. After twenty-six years, you haven't changed. I'd be over at your mom's having coffee in the morning and you'd get up, all sleepy, and come in and give her a snuggle just like you're doing with Hector right now."

418

I was blinking again, that snugly, comfy, lovely feeling blossoming, the warm glow starting in my chest.

"Really?" I asked Kitty Sue.

"Really, honey," she replied. Her eyes shifted to Malcolm, to Hector, then to me, and, her voice pitched lower, she told me, "Though, if your dad was having coffee with us, you always went straight to him. Always."

At her words, my body went ramrod straight and Hector's arm went tight.

It occurred to my still waking brain that everyone being there wasn't a social call.

Instantly, I looked up to Hector and declared, "I'm going to Vegas. I was hot yesterday playing Yahtzee. I'm taking the Rock Chicks with me and I'm going to win enough money for them to retire."

"Not sure bein' hot at Yahtzee translates in Vegas, *mamita*," Hector told me.

"You weren't there, it was huge. I got three yahtzees in one game," I explained.

Hector grinned, but his thighs tightened around me and he said softly, "Sorry, *preciosa*, hate to say it but you're not gonna get out of this."

I sighed.

I knew it.

I just *knew* it.

So I was having some really good days.

But they were still mingled with some really bad times.

"That's what I was afraid of," I whispered to Hector. I turned my back to him and faced the room. Hector's arm went around my chest and he pulled my back to his front, and I was glad. His body was warm, hard and strong and I had a feeling I was going to need it.

Malcolm asked my preference then brought me a cup of coffee.

"All right, sock it to me," I said to the room after Malcolm handed me my coffee.

"After breakfast," Blanca decreed.

For some bizarre reason (lack of sleep, a latent bent toward danger), I decided to go head-to-head with Blanca.

"I'm sorry, Blanca, but seriously, whatever it is, I'd rather get it over with."

She gave me a good, long, Blanca stare.

I gave her a good, long, Sadie stare.

This lasted awhile.

Then she said, whirling the bacon fork in the air, "*Como quieras.*"

I had no idea if I won or lost so I twisted my neck and looked up at Hector.

"What'd she say?" I whispered.

"As you wish," he answered, his lips twitching.

I turned back to Blanca. "Oh. That's pretty. *Como quieras.* As you wish. Nice."

Blanca smiled and I felt Hector's body move with laughter. Vance was grinning his arrogant grin at me and everyone else was chuckling.

I twisted back to Hector. "Did I say something funny?"

He burst out laughing.

Apparently, I did.

Whatever.

It was time to get back to the matter at hand.

I looked back at the room. "Can we please focus, people?" I asked.

The smiles and chuckles died away, and immediately I wanted them back.

Too late, because Tom started talking.

"Sadie, you remember a few days ago when we talked in Lee's office?"

Oh my.

This was not starting out well.

Of course I remembered. How could I forget? It was when I found out my mother was probably murdered. Who would forget that?

"Yes," I replied hesitantly.

"Well," Tom went on. "Eddie asked Vance to look into things. Vance did and he found out what happened to Lizzie."

My body lurched and a hand went out to Hector's knee, fingers curling around it, gripping hard. Hector's arm around my chest squeezed.

I looked at Vance.

"I'm sorry, Sadie," Vance said softly, and I knew I wasn't going to get good news. Mom wasn't waiting for me in a small agricultural village in the mountains of Peru where news was brought on foot through treacherous mountain paths so she didn't know yet it was safe to come home.

I closed my eyes, and on the backs of my eyelids I saw my mom smiling at me.

I opened my eyes again and said to Vance, "Tell me."

Vance's gaze cut to Hector, came back to me, and without hesitating, he told me.

"Luther Diggs found out what your mom was doin'. He ordered the hit. Mickey Balducci was one of his men back then. He carried it out."

This hurt, like, *loads*.

I didn't let it show.

"Where is she?" I asked, and I was proud that my voice only held a little tremor.

Vance stared at me closely then asked carefully, "You mean her body?"

That hurt even more.

Her body.

My mom's body.

Dumped somewhere, in a river, in a shallow grave, alone, unmarked, undiscovered, gone.

These thoughts penetrated my heart like a million little, sharp daggers.

I didn't let this show either.

Instead, I simply nodded.

His eyes stayed gentle on me. "I don't know."

I nodded again.

"Your dad didn't know she was informing on him," Malcolm cut in, and my gaze moved to him.

"He didn't?"

Malcolm shook his head. "No."

"A couple of months after it happened, word got to Seth that Luther ordered the hit and why." Tom entered the conversation. "You remember Bernie Watson?"

I nodded yet again. Bernie had been my father's right hand man for years. He'd been around for as long as I could remember. Old enough to be my father's father, he retired to Florida five years ago. He'd always scared me a little, but I still always kind of liked him. We sent each other Christmas cards and he always sent me a birthday card, every year, with a five dollar bill in it just like he gave me when I was a kid.

"I remember Bernie. He sends me birthday cards," I told Tom.

"I talked to Bernie," Vance said to me and I looked back to him. "Bernie had a lot to say. About your dad, about your mom. About how your dad didn't give a shit about your mom informing on him, but he did give a shit that she'd been taken out. Bernie told me when he found out, your dad went cold. That was his word. Cold. He started takeover maneuvers against Diggs immediately. Took him down within ten months of finding out."

I realized I'd started trembling only when Hector's hand came out and took my coffee cup away. Then he leaned into me, his hands going down my arms, his fingers curling around my wrists. He wrapped both my and his arms around my body and rested his chin on my shoulder.

This should have helped. Somewhere deep I realized it felt nice. But it didn't help.

"He took care of Mickey Balducci, too. Didn't he?" I whispered. "The Balducci Boys aren't insane and mean, they were after revenge. Weren't they?"

Vance didn't say anything. He just nodded.

I twisted my head to look at Hector. His chin came away from my shoulder and his eyes caught mine.

"I don't know what to do with this," I said softly.

"Nothin' to do with it, Sadie, except know he loved her, he avenged her and he didn't kill her," Hector told me.

"I don't know what to do with that, either," I said back.

"Seth didn't come over with your mom. He wasn't social." Malcolm started talking and my eyes moved from Hector to Malcolm. "But we knew him. Sometimes he'd come out to dinner or pick Lizzie up from a barbeque and stay for a beer. He wasn't a mellow guy. He wasn't laidback, but he wasn't the man he is now. Not back then. Losin' her did that to him. I thought it then, I'm sure of it now."

I didn't have time to process that before Vance spoke again.

"I found her stuff."

I started blinking.

Yes, again.

"Her... *stuff?*" I asked Vance.

"Her stuff. Your dad kept it. It's in a storage unit in Aurora. The unit is filled with clothes, jewelry, shoes, photos, books. It isn't just filled, it's preserved. Every piece has been carefully packed away, the unit is temperature controlled, sealed against water damage and it's fireproof. Units like that cost a fortune."

"Oh my God," I breathed, my trembling body starting to shiver.

My father hadn't gotten rid of every memory of her. He'd kept it.

My father hadn't killed her. He'd avenged her.

My body went straight and I pulled away from Hector a bit and looked at Kitty Sue. "Tell me how I was again with my father."

Kitty Sue looked at Malcolm and she swallowed before looking back to me.

"Lizzie used to say she sometimes wondered if you knew she existed. She told me, when you were a baby, Seth used to get up and give you your bottles in the night because you'd cry if she went to you. But you'd settle if she handed you to him so he just did it all the time. She said he didn't mind. She thought he secretly loved it. Anytime you'd fall over, bang yourself on something, you'd always go running to him—"

I shook my head and Kitty Sue stopped talking.

That couldn't be true.

It was my mom. It was always my mom.

"No," I breathed.

I pulled fully away from Hector and took a few steps into the room.

"Sadie, come here," Hector called softly.

I turned to him and it all came to me, stuff I hadn't remembered in years.

I closed my eyes tight against the memories, the strongest of which was how he'd come in after Mom brushed my hair at night and kiss the top of my head, just like Hector.

He'd tuck the bedclothes tight around me and turn out the light.

"*Night, my beautiful, sweet Sadie,*" he'd whisper.

"*Night, Daddy,*" I'd whisper back.

Oh. My. *God.*

How could I forget?

How?

"I informed on him," I said to Hector.

Hector jumped down from the counter and came at me, but I backed away, putting up a hand.

"When you were undercover and... and... *just a few days ago!*" I shouted.

"*Mi amor,* come here."

I shook my head, still backing away.

"He wanted to be sure I was safe, taken care of. He asked Jerry—"

423

"He did make sure you were safe," Hector told me. "If he hadn't helped, we wouldn't have flushed the Balduccis out yesterday. It would have taken days, maybe weeks before we got them."

I stopped my retreat and stared at Hector, not sure I heard him correctly.

"What?" I asked.

Hector stopped too, but he kept talking. "Vance and I went to see him yesterday."

At this announcement, my mouth dropped open, but Hector kept going.

"Jerry had aligned himself with Donny. I told Seth that and he gave us everything. They were hidin' in one of his safe houses. He has three. Vance and I hit one. Lee and Luke another one. Mace and Monty hit the third, where they were stayin'. But they must have got word and they cleared out before Mace and Monty got there. Then they panicked. Ricky came after me. Thinkin' that Marty gave them up, Donny shot him. But he got away, came to us for protection. Donny followed, but knowin' they were fucked, he played out a last ditch effort at vengeance, guessin', correctly, we had you."

I was stuck on an earlier point.

"You went to see my father?" I asked.

Hector nodded. "Yeah."

"He talked to you?"

"He gave me everything."

I couldn't believe this because, frankly, it was absolutely, positively, *unbelievable*.

"He helped you?"

Hector nodded again, watching me closely.

"You?" I repeated.

"Me," Hector replied.

"For me," I whispered.

"For you."

I pulled in my lips and I felt the tears hit the back of my eyes, stinging there.

"I'm *not* going to cry!" I yelled. Then, damn and blast, blast, *blast*, I promptly burst into tears. "Fuck!" I shouted and found myself in Hector's arms. "I'm crying," I told Hector's chest unnecessarily, my arms wrapping around his waist and my body pressing against his.

"Cry, *mi cielo*. Who gives a fuck?" Hector said over my head.

"I do! I'm sick of crying! But he's been… he's been…" I choked then hiccupped. "He's been trying to get hold of me and I haven't even gone to see him!" Even though the last bout of tears hadn't yet gone stale, I burst into fresh ones all the same.

Hector's arms grew tighter.

"We'll go next visiting day. I'll take you."

I was shocked at this offer. So much, my tears ceased immediately. I tilted my head back, looked at Hector through blurry eyes and asked, "You will?"

I was pretty certain he nodded.

"I can't believe he helped you," I whispered.

"He helped *you,*" Hector amended. "He didn't help me and he didn't like seein' me either. It wasn't like he invited me to Christmas dinner at the big house."

I couldn't help it. What he said was funny, so, through my waning tears, I burst out laughing.

"Christmas dinner at the big house?" I repeated, still giggling.

One of Hector's hands came up and wiped at my tears. He grinned but he didn't respond.

"Do you think he knows I informed on him with you?"

Hector's gaze went from my cheeks to my eyes. "No."

"Why wasn't he angry that my mom betrayed him?" I asked, as if Hector would know.

Apparently Hector did know because he answered.

"Because he loved her. You love someone, you forgive a lot of shit. She wasn't exactly doin' the wrong thing, *mamita*. He was."

Hector was right.

I pulled in breath, looked at him a second, then two, then let the breath go and leaned into him, pressing my cheek against his chest and giving him a tight squeeze.

Then I moved, doing a circle so his arms were still around me but my back was to his front.

I looked at the room to see everyone was watching.

"I'm okay," I announced to the room, and surprisingly I was.

I looked at Vance and my voice went soft.

"Thank you," I said, and he gave me a chin lift which I took to mean "you're welcome".

My eyes skimmed across Malcolm, Kitty Sue and Tom and then rested on Blanca.

"Unless someone else wants to rock my world, I think we can have breakfast now," I told her. "Can I help?"

Blanca gave me a close look. Then she must have approved of what she saw because she smiled and declared, "Today, I'll teach you to scramble eggs."

I knew how to scramble eggs, but I decided not to tell Blanca that. It might spoil the fun.

And heaven knew, I needed some fun.

I felt Hector lean into me and he whispered in my ear, so only I could hear, "Will of fuckin' steel."

The warm, snugly, comfy, lovely feeling was back *with* the happy glow, and I knew part of it had to do with what I learned that morning.

And the fact that Hector had given me that, too.

Now, in my bizarre world of bizarre events that happened every day, that was the bizarrest of all. My boyfriend, who happened bizarrely to be the ex-DEA agent that brought down my Drug Kingpin father, also, in a bizarre way, brought my father back to me.

Blooming heck.

How totally bizarre was *that?*

I could be my own soap opera!

Instead of sharing any of this with Hector, I turned to look at him, leaned in and touched my mouth to his. Even though his arms flexed around me and his eyes flashed at my mouth touch, I gave him a small smile, pulled away and headed toward Blanca.

Kitty Sue grabbed a bag of bread and the toaster.

Tom moved to make another pot of coffee.

Then Blanca taught me something I already knew.

And after breakfast, I walked hand-in-hand with Hector, following Vance to the door, and I asked Vance if he had time that day to take me to my mother's stuff.

Vance said he did.

That was when I knew that day was *definitely* going to beat out yesterday and the day before as my second best day *ever.*

Though, nothing was going to beat The Day of Hector and The S'mores.

Nothing.

# Chapter 27

# Mr. Edge

*Sadie*

As all others around me clapped, hooted and screamed, I stood stunned with my mouth hanging open, staring at the darkened stage.

Roxie leaned into me and screamed, "She's the shit, isn't she?"

Still too stunned to look away from the stage, I just nodded.

＊

After the traumatic pre-breakfast events and relearning to make scrambled eggs with Blanca, Ralphie called and told me that the news of the Balduccis going down was so good, he'd changed that evening from a cozy dinner for four to "A Big Ol' Blowout" (Ralphie's words). All the Rock Chicks (plus Tod and Stevie, Duke and Tex) were invited to Ralphie and Buddy's for a "The Balducci Brothers Have Finally Been Brought Down Blowout". We ate Ralphie's hors d'ouevres (which were actually really good). Jet brought some chocolate, caramel brownies that were to-die-for, Indy brought a humungous bag of whole, salted cashews and the rest of the girls brought enough booze for fifteen Balducci Brothers Blowouts.

Hector and the Hot Bunch, all busy with other activities (likely cleaning up my problems—I still didn't know what this meant and didn't ask; not because I didn't want to know, because I'd had a hectic day, what with sorting through my thoughts, my mom's stuff and helping Ralphie and Buddy with the party), managed to show their faces, even if it was for a few minutes. They shifted through, eating, having a soda, toasting to one of the gazillion boisterous Balducci Brothers Have Finally Been Brought Down Toasts (the Rock Chicks started a competition for the best toast; Ally declared Shirleen the winner with her "Burn Motherfuckers Burn" toast) and then sliding out again.

Later, when we got bored with the toasts and were full up with food, it was time to consider alternate party activities and Stevie suggested a Yahtzee marathon (too many people). Ralphie suggested a Veronica Mars marathon (not active enough). Ally suggested traveling up to Fort Collins to see Stella's gig (we were drinking too much, it was too far away and the gig had already started). Then Jet suggested we go to Smithie's, a strip club.

Everyone agreed to Smithie's.

In my sheltered life, I'd never had cause to think of strip clubs or strippers, much less consider the possibility I'd ever go to a club and see a stripper. Since Daisy had stripped there in a past life, Jet had worked there as a cocktail waitress when her thing was going on with Eddie and the bad guys, and Jet's sister was currently the top dancer for Smithie, not to mention, Jet told me (with pride), she was the finest stripper in the Rocky Mountain Region, I thought it best not to pass judgment.

Though, I wasn't certain sure about hanging out at a strip club.

❦

At Indy's request, I phoned Jack at the offices to ask him to put a callout for rides to the club. We'd already been drinking heavily, and apparently the Hot Bunch didn't only act as protectors and bad business cleaner-uppers, they were also on call to be designated drivers when the Rock Chicks were tying one on.

This, by the way, was my fourth call to Jack that day.

This was how the last call went:

Me: "Jack?"

Jack (loud and angry): "Would you quit fuckin' callin'? I was just clipped. It took six measly stitches to close it up. For the last time, I'm fuckin' fine!"

Me (snappy and impatient): "Well! Don't blame me for worrying! No one has ever been shot keeping me safe before!"

Jack (after an angry sigh): "I'm beginnin' to wish I hadn't put on the vest."

Me (full of attitude): "Jack, you're just going to have to deal. It's like they do when someone saves someone's life and for the rest of that someone's life, the other someone looks out for them."

Jack (now angry and confused): "What?"

Me (just confused): "I don't know. I think it's Asian. Maybe the samurai?"

Jack (muttering): "Jesus. Chavez owes me big for this."

Me (deciding to move on): "Anyway, we need designated drivers. We're going to Smithie's."

Jack: "I'm on it."

Disconnect (without a good-bye).

Well!

---

Hector, Matt and Bobby showed up, everyone squeezed into SUVs (tightly) and we rolled out to the strip club. Hector took Ralphie, Buddy, Daisy, Ally and me in his Bronco. The men escorted us in, right past the long line outside that was standing at the velvet rope (without the doorman even looking twice at us) and through the doors. We'd barely cleared the doors when a big, on the good side of middle aged black man approached, and just like Tex, he cleared a path through the club and shoved some men away from tables at the front, left side of the stage. We followed in his wake.

"VIPs, fuckin' *move*," he shouted at the men at the tables, and they scurried immediately.

Wow, the Rock Chicks were something!

Jumping the velvet rope and front row seats at a strip club!

How bizarre (and cool) was *that?*

Then he turned to me and opened his mouth. But before he said a word, Jet was there.

"No, Smithie, she doesn't dance."

Smithie turned wide eyes to Jet. "What? You think I'm crazy? Askin' Seth Townsend's daughter to strip for me? He'd have my balls for dinner, battered and fried."

Oh my.

Me?

Stripping?

Oh.

My.

Jet looked like she was going to mouth off so I intervened.

"I'm Sadie," I told him unnecessarily, and put my hand out.

My small hand was engulfed in his big one and he squeezed.

"I'm Smithie, and I know who you are. Heard about you. Thought all the talk was bullshit, but you actually do look like a fuckin' fairy princess."

I smiled at him and leaned in. "That's nice, but I know it's not really true."

He'd leaned in to listen but leaned back, brows drawn, and said, "Bitch, look in a mirror. You're right out of a fuckin' movie."

I was a little shocked he called me a bitch, but by the way he spoke I didn't think he meant anything bad by it.

Then he leaned back in and proved me right when he went on, "It's too fuckin' bad they don't fry men for what Ricky Balducci did to you. He got the chair, I'd be happy to flip the fuckin' switch."

My eyes got big at what he said, but not the part about him obviously knowing I'd been raped. I'd realized by that time the Rock Chicks didn't keep secrets, not even personal ones. He pulled away again, dropped my hand and looked at Hector.

"You stayin'?" he asked Hector.

"Nope. Lenny on tonight?" Hector replied.

Smithie nodded, said (bizarrely), "He's on her." Then he left.

Hector curled me into his heat with an arm around my neck and I looked up at him.

"Boys're busy, but you'll have rides home," he told me. "Lenny is one of Smithie's bouncers. He's good. Lee tried to recruit him, but he couldn't work for Lee and study for his Master's at DU at the same time. Even though he's good, he's untrained. So don't make it tough on him. Keep him in sight at all times and don't let the girls talk you into anything stupid."

I nodded. Hector kept talking.

"I get done before you leave, I'll come get you. We'll sleep at my place. You get done before I get here, you go home with Ralphie and Buddy and I'll be there later."

I tilted my head to the side and asked, "Do you want me to wait up for you?"

He shook his head and answered with a demand, "Give me your keys."

I gave him my brownstone keys and the alarm code. He kissed me quick and hard and he was gone, leaving me swaying.

Then we sat. Lenny, a huge, tall, muscular, midnight-skinned black man materialized and positioned himself behind my chair. Shirleen talked me into trying appletinis (they were *fab*). We gossiped, giggled and sometimes watched the strippers.

I sat there thinking it was definitely my second best day ever.

Not just my friends and the Balducci Blowout party, but also because, that afternoon, Vance took me to my father's storage locker. Hector was busy, but at his arrangement (which, personally, I thought was ultra-sweet and super thoughtful and worth some sort of payback, but I'd have to think of something other than a building or an island; maybe something that involved lingerie), Daisy and Kitty Sue met us there.

Vance opened the locker, and with a hand on the small of my back, pushed me in, walking in behind me. He turned on the light, but it hit me before the unit was illuminated.

The smell.

My mother's perfume. White Shoulders.

I hadn't smelled that smell in years.

I took a step back and my shoulder ran into Vance's hard body.

I stopped, frozen for a moment, then twisted my head to look up at Vance.

"Her perfume," I whispered, tears stinging the backs of my eyes.

His hand slid up my back to my neck and his fingers curled there, giving me a squeeze.

"We can come back," he told me, his voice and eyes soft.

I took in a deep breath, shook my head and Vance and I walked in. The weird, warm, reassurance of Vance's hand didn't leave my neck until I dropped to my knees at the first box.

We stayed there an hour, all of us going through boxes (except Vance, who, after helping me through my initial weird out, stood outside). I cried a little bit and Daisy held me. Kitty Sue cried a little bit and I held her.

When we left, I had a list in my purse of the things I'd come back and get later.

But there were two things I took then.

I'd uncovered a framed photo. A photo I'd forgotten existed, but it used to sit, pride of place, on our mantel.

It was a picture unlike anything the Seth Townsend of now would allow. It was taken when I was six, out in our backyard, by a professional photographer. However the setting was casual, my mom's flower-filled garden in the background, and the pose was natural.

My father sat in a garden chair and had Mom in his lap, his arm around her waist, his fingers curled at her hip. Both her arms were around his shoulders and she had her cheek against his. I was standing, pressed into his other side, his other arm wrapped around my little kid body, my head leaning into his chest. Mom and I were laughing at the camera. I didn't remember why. My father wasn't laughing, but he was smiling. Not like something amused him, but like he was happy and *precisely* where he wanted to be.

I couldn't believe I forgot that photo.

Then, forcing myself to get over it, I vowed I'd never forget it again.

I also found something else I forgot. The necklace Mom used to wear all of the time. My faded memory banks were uncertain, but I thought she'd stopped wearing it a year or so before she disappeared.

It was a thin gold chain which hung to the dip in the throat, and linked on either side to a pendant that was a connected, scrolled, elegant "E" and "S". The top curve of the "E" and the bottom curve of the "S" each had a diamond in them.

When we left, I held the picture to my belly, the necklace in my fist, and I got in Vance's Explorer.

I asked Ralphie and Buddy and they let me put the picture on their shelves.

I put the necklace on for the party.

Then I helped my boys get ready for the party. The girls and guys came over, we drank, we toasted, we ate, we went to the strip club and we had a complete and total blast.

After a while, Jet's sister Lottie came on, and I forever would never cast judgment on strippers again. She was sultry. She was intoxicating. She could move so beautifully it was art, not stripping. She had me enthralled within seconds and on my feet (with everyone else) after moments. She danced for two songs and only took her fabulous, turquoise-and-peacock-blue-sequined bra off at the last minute, exposing perfect breasts for only a flash before the lights went black.

She was, as Roxie said, *the shit*.

No doubt about it.

"Oh... my... God!" I shouted to Roxie and Jet's eyes came to me. "I want to be her." I looked at Jet. "Do you think she'll teach me to dance?"

Jet grinned.

"Who you think taught her to dance, sugar?" Daisy asked me on a Christmas Bells giggle. "In my day, I had a velvet rope, too."

I stared at Daisy.

432

"Then you're the shit, too!" I screamed at her then looked back at Roxie. "I wanna strip!"

"Oh Lord," Shirleen groaned, sitting down. "First she wants to be a rock star, now she wants to be a stripper." Then she lifted her hand and snapped her fingers at no one in particular. "Somebody, get her another appletini before we gotta explain to Hector 'Mr. Edge' Chavez why his woman wants to strip."

Everyone started laughing and I did, too.

Hard.

So hard, my sides hurt and I bent forward and wrapped my arms around my middle.

Finally, I found something funny.

The very thought of someone telling Hector I wanted to strip, not to mention Shirleen calling him "Mr. Edge"...

Well...

It was, quite simply, hilarious.

Stevie found a waitress and we all got more drinks.

And I sat with my girls and (some of) my boys and looked around them, something settling safely inside me. That something was me thinking that, finally, I was living a beautiful life and hoping that, wherever she was, my mom could see me and she was happy.

It was on my fourth sip of my new appletini when Roxie said something to me. I looked at her and she looked blurry.

I blinked and lifted my hand to my head, all of a sudden feeling funny.

I couldn't put my finger on it but I wasn't right.

I felt a presence at my back and Lenny leaned into my ear. "Gotta go escort Bonnie to her car. She's got a kid, her shift ends early. I'll be back in ten. Don't move."

I nodded, but it felt like my head was immersed in water, not in a warm, snugly, comfy, safe way, and I was fighting the current.

I took another sip of appletini, hoping to wash the weird feeling away, but it didn't help. In fact, I felt worse. Woozy, fuzzy and not myself.

Boy, those appletinis were serious business!

I leaned in to Roxie and whispered, "I think I've had too much. I'm going to go splash water on my face."

Roxie looked behind me, saw Lenny gone and I heard her say, "Wait," but I got up, shoved my purse strap over my shoulder and tripped. I grabbed onto the back of a chair, righted myself and staggered forward.

I definitely needed to splash water on my face.

Definitely.

"I'm going with Sadie, we'll be back." I heard Roxie say, but I didn't wait for her.

I moved forward. The room seemed to be swaying, the huge crowd of people going in and out of focus.

Something was really wrong, terribly wrong, and because of that I was on a mission, pushing through, sliding by, evading, weaving. It was easy for me, even though I was in pumps. I was small and the men were stationary, eyes on the stage. I nearly made it to the hall where the bathrooms were when I ran headfirst into someone.

I felt arms go around me and I looked up at the man I ran into but I couldn't keep him in focus.

I was almost certain he was smiling at me then the smile faded.

"Hey babe, you okay?"

"I'm sorry," I whispered.

His fuzzy face got closer. "You gonna puke?"

And I knew, somehow, this wasn't drunk. This was something else. Something bad. Really, really, *really* bad.

Something that happened to Veronica Mars!

I shook my head.

"Sadie, hold up!" I heard Roxie call from what seemed like far away. I looked over my shoulder, trying to find her and thinking I saw her fighting the crowds to get to me, Tex close to her back.

I turned to the man whose arms were around me.

"I've been roofied," I said to him.

"What?" he asked.

"Roofied. Someone slipped me a date rape drug."

I felt, vaguely, his body going solid, and I saw, in a fuzzy way, his head whip to the side.

"Jamie, see that big black guy? He's the owner. Get to him, fast. Tell him someone's slippin' date rape shit in his drinks." He started pulling me back out of the crowd to the hall, "You got friends here?" he asked me.

"Yes." I tried to lift my arm but it didn't work. Still I said, "Over there."

I felt my body collapse into him because I couldn't hold myself up anymore.

He took my weight. His arms went tighter around me and he muttered, "Fuck. Hang on." Then something happened. I couldn't tell what, but I heard the man say, his voice sharp, "What the fuck?" Then there was an ugly thud. He was falling, and as his arms were around me, I was falling with him.

I was on the floor, tangled up with him. I heard my name shouted, then screamed, but I was being lifted in the air, arms holding me tight, someone running with me.

I tried to control my head, look to see who had me. I was jostled when the person turned. He shoved a door open with his back and I felt the cold night air.

All of a sudden, I got scared. The cold night air didn't alleviate the weird feeling or the fuzziness and it didn't give me my strength back. Instinctively, I knew it wasn't a member of the Hot Bunch who had me, or Tex, Duke, Buddy, Ralphie, Tod or Stevie.

"Let me go," I mumbled.

"Now, Sadie, darlin', why would I do that?" Jerry replied.

Darn it all to *heck*.

〜

I woke up and I was cuffed to a bed.

I didn't feel great, I didn't feel bad. I didn't feel entirely awake, but whatever drug I'd been given, which made me pass out about two minutes into the ride in Jerry's BMW, had worn off.

I looked around the room and knew I was in a hotel. I could tell the sun was weak, but it was coming in around the curtains and there was a light on. I looked down at myself and saw, thankfully, I still had on my jeans, wide, tan belt and cream cashmere sweater with a deep V and three-quarter sleeves. I even still had on my gold cuff at my wrist. However, my tan, peek-a-boo-toed pumps were gone, my feet bare.

The bathroom door opened and Jerry walked out.

Damn and blast.

"Does my father want to talk to me again?" I asked, my voice snotty.

He stopped at the foot of the bed and grinned. He was in a pair of well-fitting gray suit trousers with a tailored, low-sheen, soft-gray shirt. No tie, sleeves rolled up his forearms. I found myself thinking, stupidly, that he was handsome. Not Hector "Oh my God" Chavez handsome, but someone at whom you'd look twice. For some reason, I thought this was a crying shame.

"No," he answered, then he leaned down and his fingers curled around my ankles.

My body froze.

He pulled my ankles apart.

My body unfroze and I twisted viciously.

He was stronger than me. He kept me where I was with little effort. He put a knee to the bed between my legs and then moved forward, planting himself on me full body, except his hips and legs were between mine.

My breath suddenly coming in sharp gasps, I put my free hand to his shoulder and shoved at the same time I bucked.

He ignored this and buried his face in my neck. I opened my mouth to scream right before he said, "You make a fuckin' sound, I give the order and your dad's breakfast gets Harvey Balducci's special sauce."

The scream died in my throat and my body went still.

I heard him laugh against my neck.

"Nice to see you cooperatin', darlin', showin' some love for your father."

*You swine,* I said in my head, but not out loud. I couldn't speak, mainly because bile had forced its way up my throat and I was worried, if I opened my mouth, I'd throw up.

His mouth was at my neck, it moved along my jaw then to my lips where he kissed me lightly.

I stayed stock-still, and when his eyes caught mine, I glared at him.

"Been waitin' for you to wake up, Sadie. This'll be so much more fun with your participation."

The bile disappeared, but my heart slid up in its place and lodged in my throat.

I decided to try to talk my way out of it.

"Jerry—"

One of his hands slid down my side, the other one went to my free wrist and pulled it over my head.

"I'm thinkin' I want it slow and sweet, first, then I'll do you rough and hard."

I closed my eyes tight.

Somebody, please tell me this wasn't happening.

I turned my head to the side, opened my eyes, my mind spinning from unhappy thought to unhappy thought and I saw my purse sitting on the hotel desk.

The stun gun Hector gave me was in my purse.

My heart slid back down and my breath started to come fast again.

All I had to do was get uncuffed and get to my purse. I was in a hotel, by the looks of it a nice one. There had to be tons of people around. I just had to get out and get to a phone. I'd call the Nightingale offices, tell them, and they'd call the prison and stop my father from having breakfast.

I looked back at Jerry. "So, I'm taking this to mean you're not pansy-assed anymore."

His eyes narrowed and his face started to turn ugly.

I laughed softly at him then I lifted my head and slid my nose along his jaw.

At this, his body went tight.

"You playin' with me?" he growled.

I felt my heart beating in my throat. My stomach clenched with nausea, but I put my lips to his ear and whispered, "You want to know what it was like being Seth Townsend's daughter?"

I dipped my face and used my nose again to flick his earlobe and went on, still whispering.

"Under his thumb? Watched? Protected? Suffocated? His shit-hot gentleman army wandering around, I could look but I couldn't touch? Shit-hot guys like you?"

I felt his body jerk then grow tighter when I put my mouth closer to his ear and talked low in my throat.

"Do you know what that was like? What it was like for a girl like me? Can you imagine how I feel…" I paused for effect, waited then continued, "How I feel, now that I'm free?"

My mouth moved along his cheek to his mouth. He didn't speak and our eyes locked.

"Can I make a request?" I asked against his mouth. He still didn't answer, so I lifted my head, pressed closer and whispered, "Let's start with hard and rough."

He stared at me, hard, trying, I guessed, to see if I was messing with his head.

I blinked slowly, not opening my eyes fully, then let the corners of my lips tip up.

He watched my eyes, then my mouth, then he groaned and kissed me.

I guessed I had a new Sadie in me. I didn't know who she was, but I hoped like hell she could get me out of this latest trauma in one piece.

I kissed him back and hated every second of it. It was nowhere near a hot, hard, urgent, fiery Hector kiss. Jerry might have been handsome, but he wasn't a good kisser. His kiss made my stomach turn unpleasantly, but I ignored it and pressed my body into his, curled a leg around his hip and wrapped my arm around his back.

I pulled at the other arm. The handcuff made a loud clunk and his head came up, his eyes going to my cuffed hand.

"Leave it, it's hot," I breathed and put my mouth to his neck.

His eyes flashed and he kissed me again. One of his hands went into my hair. His other hand was everywhere. I acted like I loved it, wanted more of it, was gagging for it.

But I hated every blooming nanosecond of it.

I grasped his shirt, yanking it out of his trousers. My hand went up his back then I engaged my nails, digging in perhaps an *eensy* bit harder than I needed and I pulled at my cuffed hand again so it made another clunking noise.

His mouth went to my neck and down, he muttered, "Wildcat," to my chest.

My lip curled in disgust, but my hand went to his side, drifting softly there then between our bodies and down his abs to the waistband of his trousers.

I pulled at my cuffed hand again and it made another clunk, then I did it again and the clunk was louder.

His head came up and his hand went to his pocket.

"Fuck it," he snapped.

I felt my lungs fill with anticipatory oxygen.

"Jerry, leave it. I've never done it cuffed to a bed," I fake protested.

His eyes came to mine and his hand came out of his pocket. "I been waitin' years for this, Sadie, and now that I got it, I want you to touch me," he told me, and I felt triumphant elation slide through me.

I hid it and muttered, "Whatever."

He leaned up and uncuffed me. Keeping the other cuff on my wrist, he slid the key back into his pocket and his eyes came back to mine. "You're playin' a game and you think to fuck me over, you're back to bein' cuffed. I'll also gag you and I won't give a fuck if you enjoy it or not."

I was a little surprised he wanted me to enjoy it at all, but I shook this off. Both my arms went around him, my mouth went to his, my eyes open and our gazes were locked again.

I smiled against his mouth and said, "You're a pig, Jerry."

Then I kissed him.

We went at it. There was a lot of rolling, hand action, more rolling, mouth action. I managed to evade him taking off any of my clothes (though I let him unbuckle my belt), but I got his shirt unbuttoned and used my mouth on his chest. Then, when I thought I had him, I rolled on top, straddled his hips and whipped off my sweater, exposing my lace-over-satin, blush-colored demi-bra.

I pressed my hips into him and asked, "Do you have a condom?"

"Jesus," was his whispered answer. His eyes were on my breasts, his hands sliding up the skin of my sides.

When he didn't answer, I lied, "No worries, I do."

I lifted a leg, rolled off him and jumped off the bed.

I was across the room and digging through my purse when his arms came around me from behind, his hands moving across my belly and ribcage, his mouth in my neck.

I tried to stay cool, not to tense and freak out. I kept digging through my purse, trying to find the stun gun, hoping I'd get it out without him seeing it.

I found it, closed my eyes tight, took in a deep breath and relaxed back into him as my fingers curled around the stun gun.

"Never thought you'd be like this, Sadie," he said into my neck. "Thought of this a thousand fuckin' times, never thought it'd be this good."

I felt a shiver flow through me. It wasn't pleasure. It was fear mingled with repulsion mingled with something bizarrely sad. Jerry mistook its meaning and smiled in my neck.

"Jerry?" I called. His head came out of my neck. I turned my own and kissed him, pulled out the stun gun and twisted in his arms, our lips still attached. I went up on tiptoe, pressed myself against him and my arms went around him.

My thumb searched for the on button as I stuck my tongue in his mouth and tried not to gag.

I found the switch.

I flipped it on.

He deepened the kiss.

I heard the crackling.

I positioned it, pressed into his body and touched the prongs to his back.

One...

His mouth tore from mine, he went still and I kept the prongs on him.

Two...

Three.

He went down.

I bent over him and went back in and touched the prongs to him again. His body jerked and I kept it pushed in, counting to three again for good measure.

Then I pulled away, and without delay, I ran to my sweater on the floor. I yanked it on and grabbed my purse, left my shoes, and not looking back, I ran to the door. I threw it open, was two steps away before I was nabbed at the waist and pulled back roughly.

I let out a little surprised scream. I twisted and stilled when I saw, to my shock and horror, Glover, another of my father's henchmen.

"What the...!" he started, but I still had the stun gun in my hand and it was on.

I put it to his shoulder. He tensed and I kept it there, but a hand curled around my wrist, It was pulled back. Glover sagged against the wall, but I didn't watch. I whirled to see who had my wrist.

It was twisted. I cried out as pain shot up my arm and dropped the stun gun. Looking up, I saw Cordell, another of my father's gentleman army, and he looked bizarrely confused.

Really, why, why, *why* was everything so fucking *difficult!*

"Damn and blast!" I shouted in his face.

He bent down, put a shoulder in my belly and lifted me, carrying me back into the room.

I had the sinking feeling that, at this juncture, I was majorly screwed.

# Chapter 28
# I'm Sadie

*Hector*

"Find her," Seth Townsend said in Hector's ear.

Hector's jaw clenched, his eyes on Eddie, his body tight.

"Jerry, Glover and Cordell have been off the radar since we did the raids yesterday. All night, the whole team and half the DPD have been turnin' Denver inside out. No fuckin' sign. You got any fuckin' clue where they'd take her?" Hector, hating his need to make the call, ground out each word.

Hours had gone by since he got the call that Sadie had been nabbed. There was no sign, no word, and now the fear was a constant, bitter ache in his gut.

"You boys are supposed to be the best. How'd this fucking happen?" Seth snapped.

Hector didn't know how to answer him. He'd been asking himself the same fucking question for the last five hours.

"Her cell is tracked. She left it on the table at the club. We planted a device in her lipstick. She must have left it behind. The guy guarding her left his position but warned her he was goin', explained when he'd be back and told her to sit tight. She was with fourteen people, but walked away from the table alone. One of the girls and men tried to follow but they got held up by the crowd. A witness who tried to help her told us she told him that they roofied her. She was dazed and not in control. He got clubbed on the side of the head with a gun butt, went unconscious and Sadie got taken."

"Why weren't *you* with her?" Seth clipped.

"Because I was huntin' down your rogue soldiers," Hector shot back.

"They went rogue because Sadie's with you," Seth returned.

Hector lost his patience and his temper.

"They went rogue because they're assholes, Seth. Don't fuckin' lay this shit on me. This whole trip is yours, from the Balduccis down. You left her alone, unprotected. You knew the Balduccis were out for revenge. You had boys at your disposal and you left her exposed. *You* put her in this position and I've been workin' my ass off for six weeks tryin' to pull her out."

"Chavez—"

"She's been raped, assaulted, kidnapped, now twice. Once by you, I'll remind you. She found out her mother was whacked, had her fuckin' gallery torched and has been drugged against her will. She's been holdin' on, but she's gonna fuckin' break. After all that, anyone would fuckin' break."

"Chavez—"

Hector cut him off, his voice had gone low and it shook with menace, "Seth, I find her and they've broken her, you'll pay."

When he spoke again, Seth's voice had changed too, it had gone soft. "Hector—"

"No joke. You'll pay," Hector repeated.

The door opened to Lee's office and Lee's upper body swung in with it, but he didn't enter and he didn't take his hand off the knob.

"Call came in. Darius spotted Jerry's BMW in the parking lot. Hyatt Place Hotel, DIA."

"Anyone close?" Eddie asked, already moving around the desk.

"Marcus is headin' his way," Lee replied. "Said he'd be there in five."

"Hector, what's happening?" Seth asked in his ear.

"We got a lead," Hector replied to Seth. "Pray she's not broken." Then he flipped his phone shut and moved toward the door. "Let's roll."

⌧

## Sadie

Cordell threw me on the bed.

I rolled off and scrambled. He cut off my exit. I feinted to the left (he followed) then to the right (he followed again!) then stopped and we went into a stare down.

Glover lurched in, closing the door behind him. His eyes went to Jerry, still on the floor, but he was now moving around.

Great.

*Just great!*

Then Glover's eyes came to me and he snapped, "What the fuck's goin' on?"

I looked at him then I put my hands on my hips and said, "Are you kidding me?"

Glover and Cordell stared at me.

I knew them both.

Like Jerry, Cordell had worked for my father for years. I didn't know him very well, but we'd chatted because, well, he was around and not to chat would be rude.

Glover had been a new recruit a few months before my father went down.

Both of them were good-looking, fit, well-dressed and well-groomed.

All of this slid through my mind in a flash.

But mostly all I thought about was the fact that I was done.

Done.

Done!

Did I say *done?*

"Seriously!" I threw my hands out. "Did you think I'd just, I don't know... what did you think I'd do?"

They kept staring at me.

"You roofied me!" I yelled.

Glover's body jerked and his eyes shot to Cordell. I watched as Cordell's brows drew together.

Then Cordell hissed, "Jesus, Sadie, keep your voice down."

"Are you going to poison my father like you did Harvey?" I snapped, and Cordell and Glover looked at each other while Jerry pulled himself up to sitting position. It would dawn on me later that they looked at each other in confusion. Since I was in a full blown hissy fit, I unfortunately didn't notice it at the time.

"Well? Are you?" I pushed.

Everyone stayed silent.

"Whatever," I snapped and put my hands back to my hips. "Let's play let's make a fucking deal. All right?"

Cordell and Glover just kept looking at me like I was some unknown entity as yet undiscovered, not like I was someone who served them coffee on more than one occasion.

"I need clothes, nice ones," I went on. "I'm not going on an international flight without good clothes. We'll call my father. I'll get the Caymans account info. We'll all go on a trip. You can have it. All of it. Every penny. You just promise to let me go at the end of it and promise you won't poison my father or hurt him in any way."

Glover's eyebrows shot up and Jerry pulled himself unsteadily to his feet.

"Sadie—" Jerry started.

"You, shut the fuck up. I'm tired of talking to you," I clipped at Jerry. Then, apparently not tired of talking to him, I went on, "And by the way, you're cute, but you're a crap kisser."

So stuck in my hissy fit, I was on a roll. I looked back at Cordell then at Glover and both of their eyebrows were at their hairlines after my "crap kisser" comment. I ignored this and kept right on talking.

"I call my father, warn him about the poison so you assholes don't kill him anyway, just to be assholes, and he gives me the account numbers."

"What's she talkin' about?" Glover asked Cordell.

Cordell shrugged.

It was my turn to stare.

"What do you mean, what am I talking about? Jerry poisoned Harvey Balducci and told me if I didn't sleep with him, he'd put that same special sauce on my father's breakfast," I informed Glover and Cordell.

They both turned to Jerry.

"Jerry?" Cordell called, and something in the room made me snap right out of the hissy fit and start to pay attention. "I thought we were runnin' an errand for Seth. Gettin' Sadie out of a bad fix, gettin' her free from Chavez. What the fuck is this?" Cordell asked, turning away from me and toward Jerry.

Jerry was looking pale.

Light, luckily, for me, was beginning to dawn.

"He was working with Donny Balducci," I told Glover and Cordell.

Jerry's eyes came to me. "Shut your fuckin' mouth."

Oh my.

I decided, since things seemed to be a bit confused and Cordell and Glover weren't paying much attention to me, that I should start moving slowly toward the door.

So that was what I did.

But I kept talking.

"The Caymans accounts," I said to Jerry as it hit me. "The Balduccis wanted the money in those accounts. Revenge against my father. You were going to get your share, weren't you?"

"Shut the fuck up!" Jerry shouted, starting to come toward me, but Cordell and Glover moved, fencing him in, so he stopped.

"Mickey Balducci killed my mother," I announced to the room. "My father avenged her death. The Balducci Brothers wanted retaliation. Jerry was working with them."

Cordell and Glover didn't move, but Jerry's eyes were locked on me and his face twisted with rage.

"You fuckin' bitch," he hissed.

I kept moving slowly to the door, but, for some bizarre reason, Jerry lost it, totally and completely, and he kept talking.

"I was Seth's boy. *Me*. Then fuckin' Chavez comes along and Seth thinks his shit don't stink. 'Hector this...' and 'Hector that...' like he fuckin' walked on water. Everyone knew, once Bernie left and Seth settled on his new boy, that new boy would get you. Everyone. We all worked on it, we all wanted it. We knew the only one Seth would trust with you, the only one Seth would trust to take care of you, was his boy. The one who'd take his place when he retired. That was *me* until fuckin' Chavez came along."

I couldn't help myself. His words shook me so much, I'd stopped and was staring at him, mouth open.

"Then Chavez fucked us," Jerry snapped, his eyes moving to Cordell and Glover. "He fucked you, too. Made Seth look the fool and he fucked us all."

"Don't know about you but I'm still gettin' paid," Glover returned.

"You dumb fuck. Seth isn't eligible for parole for years. Do you think—?" Jerry started but Cordell interrupted him.

"Yeah, and for those years he put you in charge. He made you his boy again and now *you've* fucked him. So, tell me Jerry, who's the dumb fuck?"

Then Glover remarked, his voice full of disbelief, "Shit, Jerry, you roofied Sadie? Jeez, Seth's gonna be pissed."

"Like I said. Dumb fuck," Cordell put in.

"Fuck you!" Jerry shouted in Cordell' face.

"Blow me," Cordell returned.

Oh my.

This wasn't going well for Jerry, but also (more importantly) I had no idea what it meant for me.

Then everything happened at once.

Jerry charged Cordell. I could tell it was not to fight him, but so he could get by him and get to me.

I came unstuck and ran to the door. I got my hand on the knob, but it flew open when I did. I wheeled backwards, lost balance and landed on my behind.

Marcus and African-American Hottie were in the room, guns up and shouting.

Cordell and Glover twirled, pulled out their guns and started shouting back.

Jerry jumped across the bed, toward *me*.

I got on my feet and twisted. I grabbed the first thing I could find, which was a lamp, and twisted back to see he was nearly on me.

"Stop!" Marcus yelled, but Jerry didn't stop.

I swung the lamp just as a shot was fired. I hit Jerry in the shoulder with the lamp and he went down, but his hands went to his thigh where blood was coming from a bullet wound.

"Stay down," Marcus ordered, advancing, gun on Jerry as African-American Hottie was still in an armed faceoff with Cordell and Glover.

I stood, clutching the lamp and breathing like I'd run a race.

"Sadie, you okay?" Marcus asked.

I slammed the lamp down and then put my hands back to my hips.

"No. I. Am. *Not*. I'm *sick* of being kidnapped. *Hector's probably out of his mind!*" I screeched.

Marcus kept his eyes and gun on Jerry, but I could swear his lips twitched like he was fighting a grin.

Now, really, seriously, by all that was holy, somebody, *please tell me*, what on *earth* was funny about *this?*

I looked at African-American Hottie and he looked like he was amused, too.

"What's fucking funny?" I shouted.

"Maybe you should sit down, love," Marcus suggested.

"I don't want to sit down. I want coffee. And brioche with marmalade," I snapped back, then I looked back at African-American Hottie and realized he was still in an armed faceoff and I should probably do something about that. "Um… African-American Hottie?" I called. "They're good. They're with me."

Cordell, who was also African-American, had his eyes locked on African-American Hottie and he asked, "Is she talkin' to you or me?"

"I've no fuckin' clue," African-American Hottie replied.

"I know *your* name, Cordell. Blooming heck, I've known you for years. I'm talking to the *other* African-American Hottie in the room," I explained.

Marcus (I'm not joking) started laughing.

Laughing!

"My name is Darius," African-American Hottie said.

Without anything else to say (and not wanting to be rude), I replied, "Hi, Darius." Then I waved for good measure.

"Who *are* you?" I heard said from below me, and I looked down to see Jerry staring up at me like he'd never seen me before.

And that was when I knew.

I knew *exactly* who I was.

So, because I knew, I told Jerry, "I'm Sadie."

❦

The police arrived, then the hotel management and security arrived. I redid my belt, put on my shoes and was sitting in the hotel room desk chair, handcuffs finally off, just about to put a cup of coffee to my lips when Hector, Eddie and Lee arrived.

Hector stopped just inside the door. His eyes scanned the room, found me, did a head-to-toe. Then they moved to Jerry, now on the bed with hotel towels wrapped around his leg and a uniformed officer guarding him.

Hector didn't order everyone out and he didn't move. His body was solid and his eyes were scorching and that scorch was directed at Jerry.

Then I saw his jaw clench and a muscle move in his cheek.

Oh my.

I put my coffee cup in its saucer on the desk and moved swiftly across the room toward Hector.

I got within touching distance and Hector's hands came to my hips, but he didn't look at me. His dark, angry eyes were locked on Jerry.

"I'm gonna fuckin'—" he started, but I pressed into him, put my hand over his mouth and muffled the rest.

"The police," I warned, but his hand came from my hip and his fingers curled around my wrist. He pulled it away. Before he could speak, quickly I said, "I'm all right, I'm fine. Everything's okay."

His scorching eyes turned to me.

My free hand went to the side of his face.

"Babe, I'm okay," I whispered.

He looked at me for a second, then two, then three, his eyes scanning my face, reading me.

I got up on my toes and pressed even closer to his heat.

"Hector, baby, I'm okay," I repeated softly.

Suddenly he let go of my wrist. His arms went around me, crushing me to him, and his mouth came down on mine in a long, hard, closed-mouthed kiss.

When his mouth detached from mine, his face went into my neck and his arms got even tighter.

"Fuck," he said against my neck.

My arms wrapped around his shoulders and I held him close, thinking it was best not to tell him, just yet, that I couldn't breathe.

Finally, his arms loosened. His head came up and I pulled in a deep breath.

"Sorry, Chavez, we need to ask Sadie some questions," a uniformed officer said from our side just as the paramedics came in with a gurney.

Hector nodded. We moved away so the paramedics could see to Jerry and I sneaked a peek at the bed while we moved.

Jerry was glaring at Hector, eyes filled with hate. His obvious emotion made me sad, angry and happy. I couldn't process this. It was too complex. So I decided not to think about it until... well, never. I thought it best never to think about it.

Ever.

We moved into the hall (unfortunately, away from my coffee) and I noted the Hot Bunch were amassing there. Darius was, obviously, a part of the rescue effort. Lee and Eddie had come with Hector. Luke was now with them. The elevator pinged and Vance and Matt walked out of it, their eyes coming directly to me as they moved down the hall toward us.

The uniformed officer had to wait while the Hot Bunch did their Sadie assessment. I got hugs, cheek kisses, temple kisses, and there were a lot of set but relieved male faces and firm, clenched, square jaws. I noticed they looked tired. None of them had shaved and none of them were wearing fresh clothes. Mace and Bobby showed up in the meantime, and both of them (even Bobby) engulfed me in bear hugs.

The elevator pinged again and Detective Marker walked out when the uniformed officer asked, exasperated, "Do you guys mind if I talk with Sadie?"

I was feeling weird. A good weird.

No, a *great* weird.

Not that they'd obviously had a tough night looking for me.

But, (I hated to admit it but had to) because they'd spent a tough night looking for me.

And they were relieved they found me alive, well, and none the worse for wear.

They cared and they didn't mind who knew it. Not the hotel staff and customer onlookers, the police or the paramedics.

Tough guys or not, I was one of them.

I wasn't Ms. Townsend anymore.

I was Sadie, Rock Chick.

How great was *that?*

"You get her statement?" Detective Marker asked, coming up to me with a smile.

"Tryin'," the uniformed officer replied.

"Well, fuck boy, get it so she can go home," Detective Marker snapped.

The officer looked at the ceiling.

I pressed into Hector. His arm went around my neck and he pulled me deeper into his side, partially into his front.

The officer asked me questions and I answered, telling my story.

I was, of course, not thinking clearly, considering all that happened. If I was, I might have asked for privacy before I shared in front of Hector how I duped Jerry. The Hot Bunch clearly found my tactic amusing. Hector, I could tell by the electric current whipping around the hall, absolutely did not.

I hurried through the rest. The officer finished with some questions. Detective Marker asked a few more and finally the officer flipped his notepad closed, nodded and took off.

The Hot Bunch and Marcus had been joined by Tom, Hank and Monty by this time. I got a couple more hugs and cheek kisses and we all stood around in the hall with Detective Marker.

"So it goes." Detective Marker looked at me, "The Balduccis are all talkin'. Pointin' fingers at each other. It's confusin' as hell and most of it's lies, but far's I can read it, they been gettin' pressure from outside factions."

Detective Marker's eyes slid to Hector, then to Marcus, and I could tell he was lying when he went on.

"Don't know who. Don't care."

His eyes came back to me.

"Those boys never trusted each other anyway. For weeks they been establishin' and breakin' allegiances to each other and outside the fold. Marty was the smart one, pullin' ahead of the pack, feignin' loyalty to the brothers but makin' outside deals. Donny felt the pressure, allied with Ricky, and he knew where Jerry's head was at regardin' Seth and you. He used it, fed Jerry some of Marty's potions so he would take out Harvey, the weak link, but also so he'd cast suspicion on Marty. Don't know where Glover and Cordell fit into all this, but Cordell has always been loyal to Seth. I'm surprised he was involved."

"I think Jerry lied to him about what he was doing. Neither he nor Glover seemed to know what was happening. They didn't even know Jerry roofied me. They thought they were doing something for me on my father's orders," I told Detective Marker.

Detective Marker nodded.

"At least that makes sense," he said then he got closer. "Ricky, Donny and Jerry obviously are goin' down. But you gotta know, we don't have shit on Marty. Nothin' that'll stick anyway. He's doin' okay and he'll be released without charge."

Well, wasn't that *just great?*

Still, I had to worry about a mean, crazy, fucking Balducci.

I moved closer to Hector and his arm got tighter around my neck.

Detective Marker's eyes took in Marcus and the Hot Bunch, then they came back to me.

"Marty's always been the brains of the bunch. Don't suspect he'll be stupid enough to do anything with the kind of protection thrown down around you. Regardless of this shit, Seth cuts a menacing figure, even in prison. Word on the street isn't just that you got the protection of Chavez, Nightingale and the

Denver Police Department, but Marcus and Vito. Donny and Ricky are crazy motherfuckers, but Marty'll think twice."

Detective Marker glanced at Marcus again then to me.

"He's not in a good position. Part of the pressure the Balducci boys got means that their men and their contacts have been warned off in no uncertain terms or recruited away. He's marked, and not in a good way." He got in even closer and muttered, "Your boy's done good." He nodded to Hector. "It'd be practically impossible for Marty to build up business again."

That made me feel the *eensiest* bit better and made me think perhaps I *should* buy Hector an island.

Detective Marker looked straight at Hector, and I didn't know if he was talking to Hector or me when he finished, "Keep safe anyway."

The elevator pinged and out surged a bevy of Rock Chicks led by Daisy, Shirleen and Kitty Sue (Rock Chick, The First Generation, according to Kitty Sue's stories). The paramedics wheeling Jerry on the gurney had to fight through them as I was surrounded, hugged and kissed. There was relieved laughter, a few teary eyes, then Tex showed up, wild-haired, wild-eyed, obviously having been on the Sadie Hunt.

He boomed, "Outta my way!" shoved in and hugged me so tight both my feet came off the floor.

Ralphie and Buddy were there. Tod and Stevie, Duke and Dolores, Malcolm, Blanca showed up with Gloria, Nancy arrived with Jet's sister Lottie.

Everyone.

All my friends (and Lottie, who I hadn't met yet).

In the hallway of a hotel.

Genuine, honest to goodness friends.

*Mine.*

I was sucked down, deep, deep, deepest, into the warm, clear, comfortable, snugly, safe waters and somewhere, I knew my mom was smiling.

"Christ, can I get to my fuckin' girlfriend?" Hector clipped (loudly and irately).

The crowd stilled, even the hotel onlookers and lingering police, and then parted. He and I had become disengaged, but now he came through, grabbed my hand and tugged me away.

"We got a floor to refinish," he muttered on the way to the elevator, tagging the button when he got there.

I turned to my friends, smiled and waved.

The doors opened and Hector dragged me inside (without, I noted, a smile or a wave at anyone).

The doors closed, and without hesitation, he curled me into his front. His hand went into my hair, his head came to mine, slanted, and he gave me a hot, urgent, fiery kiss.

In the nanosecond before I melted into him and all thoughts flew out of my head, I figured (correctly) we weren't going to get to refinishing the floors.

⚞⚟

"'Night, Double H." I heard Ralphie whisper.

"Later, Hector," Buddy whispered soon after.

Hector's body moved slightly under me and I could visualize him jutting his chin.

I kept my eyes closed and feigned sleep, liking being tucked into Hector's heat on the couch.

After my latest trauma was finally over, Hector took me to his house and not, as I reckoned, to refinish the floors. He took me straight to his bedroom and we had the best sex *ever* in the *history* of *man* (in my personal opinion).

Then, there was no other way to describe it, he pretty much passed out.

I stayed with him for hours as he slept. Sometimes, I'd doze. Sometimes, I'd daydream. Sometimes, I'd kiss his chest or neck while he slept. But mostly, I just got used to feeling warm and safe and happy.

He woke up when Buddy called, inviting us to dinner.

We showered (yes, together!). Hector "did" me in the shower again and then we laid in bed, him wearing his cutoff sweats, me wearing one of his flannels and my panties, and him holding me while I called the prison to talk to my father.

Cordell had already reported that I was all right. The conversation was short and uncomfortable. I didn't know what to say; neither did my father. After, even though I tried not to, I cried again, quietly into Hector's neck. He held me while I did that then held me after I was done.

We got dressed and went to Ralphie and Buddy's. Hector and I took YoYo for a long walk, we had an early dinner, then we crashed in front of the TV to watch *Veronica Mars*.

This time, I burrowed into Hector's side without prompting and put my feet into Ralphie's lap for a massage. Neither man disappointed. Hector's arm curled around my shoulders, Ralphie's hands were pure heaven.

After a while, I fell asleep.

Now, as I laid tucked into his hard body, my head on his chest, I was deciding that this was my third best day *ever*.

"*Mamita*, I know you're awake." Hector's voice rumbled over my head at the same time it rumbled in my ear that was pressed to his chest.

I pushed up and twisted to look at him, my hand pulling my hair out of my face.

He looked rough. He needed a haircut, even though he'd just had one. His stubble was back, even though he'd shaved only ten hours ago. He was wearing a tight, long-sleeved, army-drab t-shirt and faded jeans.

And he never looked better.

"We gotta talk," he said, his voice firm, serious and slightly ominous.

My body froze and I felt a small spiral of fear in my belly.

"About what?"

"About you and me."

Oh no.

No.

Somebody, tell me, no.

Here it was.

I knew it.

I just *knew* it.

I pushed further away, but his arm slid up my back, catching under my shoulder blades. He curled it, at the same time pushing himself to a less lounging position on the couch and twisting me so I was in his lap.

Then he started talking.

"I got a few things to say. I know you've had a rough time, but it's better this shit is out and you understand."

I stared at him, mentally girding, preparing for the worst. Namely, it being over. Namely, me being too much trouble. Namely, him losing interest and moving on to the next Sadie or Natalie or whatever.

With these dire thoughts in my head, mentally girded, I nodded.

Might as well get it over with and then revisit my opportunities in Crete.

I wasn't going to pack beach towels. I was going to fill my luggage with Kleenex.

"First off, I want you movin' in. Not in a few months, now. I want you in my bed. I want you in my house. I wanna come home to you."

I blinked in shock, mainly because what he said was shocking and not at all what I expected.

"What?" I breathed.

"You heard me."

I blinked again then, for some fool reason, I asked, "Don't you think we should, I don't know… date? At least for a while. You know, like normal people."

His mouth started moving like he was fighting a grin and I felt my blood pressure rise. "*Mi amor*, you are definitely not normal people, and this is definitely not a normal relationship."

I decided to ignore that and went on, again foolishly, "It's too soon."

"I've known you over a year," he returned.

"We've only been together two weeks!"

His voice got low and his mouth stopped moving like he was fighting a grin. Clearly Mr. Mood Swing's mood was swinging. "*Mujer*, we been together a lot longer than that and you know it."

I had to admit, he had a point.

And he wanted me to move in with him!

Yay!

I smiled, mentally ungirding. I snuggled closer and said softly, "Okay."

His body, which I hadn't realized was tense, relaxed under mine and his hand sifted into the hair at the side of my head, his fingers curling around my skull.

"Now that's decided, we gotta talk about your money."

I should have regirded.

Instead, in Innocent and Happy About to Move in with Hector World, I asked, "My money?"

He nodded.

"What about it?"

"You just agreed to move in. That means you just agreed to officially becoming my woman. I take care of my woman. I pay the mortgage. I pay the bills. I fix up the house. We go out, I pay. Your money is for you. I take care of us."

Now hang on a ding darn minute.

My body went straight.

"Excuse me, but—"

His fingers tightened on my scalp. "You're not gettin' this, Sadie. I'm tellin' you the way it is. I'm not opening it up for discussion."

I felt my eyes narrow.

"Hector Chavez, don't you—"

He cut in again, "You agree to try life out with me, you get what you see. I don't do that designer shit. I don't have any fuckin' desire to live in a house that's bigger than what I need. Life for me is simple. My car's gotta work for my lifestyle and get me from point A to point B. My house has gotta be as I like it because I made it that way. My job's gotta be somethin' that presents challenges and doesn't make me lose sleep. And my woman's gotta be in my bed when I get home at night. You don't fit in with that, this isn't gonna work."

I was finding it hard to breathe. This was good because if I'd been able to breathe, I might have been a lot louder when I answered.

"You think I want the designer clothes and the mansion," I accused.

"I know what you want *now*. I also know that can wear thin when you're used to havin' a lot more. You think you'll start wantin' that, you think you can use your money to push me into it, then we should stop right here."

I tried to shove away, jump off his lap, but his hand left my hair and both his arms went around me tight, holding me in place.

"Let me go," I hissed.

"Sadie, you gotta answer this now."

"Oh? Did you ask a question?" I shot back.

"*Mamita*—"

I kept pushing at him, so angry I was mumbling to myself, "I need to call Jet. Is it too late to call Jet?"

"Jet can't help you with this one," Hector told me. "It's gotta be all you."

I glared at him.

Then I shared.

"You can't know this so I'll explain it to you. And, Hector Chavez, you better listen good. I like clothes so I'll buy what I want. I like pretty things too, so I'll surround myself with them if I want to. I like to do nice things for people, and since you're people that means I might do nice things for you. If I do, you're gonna have to deal. But I don't want ivory towers and fancy cars. I want people in my life who care about me and who'll let me care about them in return. I want to use the gift my mom gave me and use it right. She didn't die for me to live large. She died for me to live happy. Happiness is not money. I've had money my whole life and it *never* made me happy. These last few weeks, I've been happy and I've barely stepped foot in my fancy car and I certainly haven't been living in an ivory tower. So, you can just—"

I didn't finish because Hector moved. One second I was struggling and ranting while sitting in his lap. The next second I was on my back on the couch and he was on top of me.

This knocked the breath out of me so all I could do was stare at his face, which had gone that soft, hard possessive; the look in his eyes was uber-warm.

Softly he announced, "All right, *mamita*, we got that out of the way. One more thing."

I expelled the breath caught in my lungs and snapped, "What?"

This, for some bizarre reason, made him smile. It also made him touch his lips to mine for a quick kiss.

When he was done kissing me, he said, "*Tu padre, mi cielo*, it's unlikely he's ever gonna welcome me with open arms. What you and I got plays out like I think it will, you gotta know that and be able to deal."

"You're wrong," I told him and watched his eyes narrow. "Totally wrong," I whispered, the fight and anger left me and I wrapped my arms around him. "He wants me to be happy. It'll take time, but he'll come around."

Hector shook his head. I nodded mine.

Then his whole face went warm. "Sadie, you're settin' yourself up for disappointment if you think that way."

"Hector," I returned quietly, "trust me."

He bit his lip, looked over my head for a second then back at me. "Just guard your heart, *mi amor*, that's all I'm sayin'."

I lifted my head, touched my mouth to his and then, keeping my mouth against his, I whispered, "Okay."

His body relaxed into mine.

My hand slid up his back and into his hair while I dropped my head back to the couch and asked, "Now, are you spending the night or what?"

At that, he granted me a glamorous, white smile.

Then he spent the night.

# Chapter 29

# Gardenias

---

*Sadie*

Hector and I stood together in the little, gray room.

My body was tense and ramrod straight. I was staring out the bars on the window but seeing nothing.

Hector was standing behind me close, his extraordinary heat beating into my back, his arm around my waist, his chin brushing the hair on the top of my head.

For some bizarre reason, I was worried about what I was wearing.

Daisy, Ralphie, Roxie, Tod and Stevie and I spent five exhausting hours at the mall trying to find the exact right First Visit to Your Incarcerated Father Outfit. Even though they assured me it was absolutely perfect, I was uncertain.

I needed my father to know who I was. The Real Sadie. The one who owned her own gallery. Who moved in with Hector "Oh my God" Chavez the Sunday before last, the day after my ordeal was officially over. Who spent her days hanging at Fortnum's with the girls and Ralphie, redesigning her burnt out gallery. Who, thanks to Blanca, now knew how to cook tamales from scratch— and they were tasty. Who begged her boyfriend to take her out on his motorcycle after dinner—which he did, but only after making her get creative, earning the ride in a variety of delicious ways. And, who, last weekend, by his side, refinished his living room floor.

But even so, I didn't want to be too in your face about it.

That would be rude.

I was wearing a new pair of Lucky jeans, a camel-colored, tailored cotton blouse that fit snug up my sides and midriff and showed a hint of cleavage at the opened buttons (this made Hector's mouth go tight, which was good, since it kept it shut), a chocolate-brown suede belt with a heavy silver buckle, a pair of kickass (Daisy's words) dark brown boots that were both stylish but also rock 'n' roll, and a chocolate brown suede, two button, blazer. My hair was down

Kristen Ashley

and wild, falling on my shoulders, down my back and sometimes in my face (my father hated my hair down; said a lady wore her hair back or up, anything else was common). I was wearing long, wide, gold hoop earrings (a surprise present from Hector that he gave me the night I moved in with him; how he managed to shop, I don't know, but he did) and my mother's initial necklace was at my throat.

The outfit looked casual, but cost a blooming fortune.

I loved it, it was me. But I knew my father would hate it.

"I'm scared to death," I whispered to the window.

Hector's arm got tight. His chin left my hair and I felt his mouth go to my neck. He was kissing me there when the door opened.

I jumped and turned.

Hector didn't jump nor did he drop his arm, but his head came out of my neck and he moved with my turn.

My father stood there, wearing prison blues, but other than that, looking surprisingly just like my father. Face tan, hair well-groomed, body fit, he made prison blues look like the next big thing in men's fashion.

I wanted to say something, but didn't know what. I had practiced a lot of openings, none of which I remembered at the crucial moment, and in my hesitation, I caught the killing look my father was giving Hector.

This, of course, robbed me of speech. Not that I knew what to say anyway, but still.

"You think I could spend some time with my fucking daughter without you standing there with your hands on her?" my father asked Hector.

Oh boy.

This was not a good start.

"Daddy—" I said, but my voice sounded small.

My father didn't even look at me.

Surprisingly, Hector moved.

He got in front of me and grabbed my hand. He gave it a squeeze and I knew he intended to go.

I looked up at him, beginning to panic and blurted, "I don't want you to go."

"I'll be right outside."

"Hector—"

Another hand squeeze, then a repeated, "Right outside," before he touched his lips to mine, and without a glance at my father, he left.

So did the security guard.

My father and I were alone.

Blooming heck.

"You get a kick out of that, Sadie? Bringing him here and shoving him in my face?"

I stared at him.

I felt my heart start to beat faster and waited for it to happen. I waited for who Hector called Stepford Sadie to slip into place. I waited for the automatic dutiful daughter to arrive and be apologetic and hide the fact that Hector was in my life or promise to get rid of him altogether.

Instead, Stepford Sadie, now good and dead, didn't appear.

"I'm sorry if that upset you, but you already know he's in my life," I answered softly.

"He won't be for long," my father returned.

My body went stiff. "Why's that?"

"Been lookin' into Hector Chavez," he replied, his tone cold. "He's got a string of pieces, Sadie. You're just the most recent one."

I let out a breath and shook my head. "I know about the other women."

"Then you aren't as smart as I raised you to be."

"I'm living with him."

"Then you *really* aren't as smart as I raised you to be."

I stared at him.

He stared back.

This went on for a while.

I was not going to give in.

I knew he wouldn't either.

So it went on for a while longer.

To my shock, he finished the stare down by asking, "Are we done?"

And also to my shock, I had the perfect retort, "I don't know, Daddy. Are we?"

It was clear he didn't expect this answer, and also clear he didn't understand it.

I decided to explain.

459

"You have two choices. One, you stay the way you became after Mickey Balducci murdered Mom, and that means we go our separate ways. I won't be a party to that kind of relationship with my father. Or two…"

I stopped and went to the vinyl couch where my bag was. I pulled out a large photograph, a duplicate of the picture I took from Mom's storage locker (the original now residing in some boxes in Hector's spare room, waiting for the downstairs to be finished). I turned back to my father, walked to him, closer this time, the picture turned to face him.

"We can go back to this. A family. Even without Mom with us." I shoved the photo at him and his eyes didn't move from it. "Take it," I said. "I'm allowed to give it to you."

Slowly, his eyes moved from the picture to me.

I took a stunned step back at what I saw.

Pain.

Utter, devastated, unhidden pain.

What was in his face sliced deep through me. So deep I whispered an uncertain, "Daddy?"

"Where'd you find that?" he whispered back.

"One of Hector's friends found Mom's stuff."

He wasn't listening. His eyes were fastened at my neck and I watched in horror as the color drained out of his face.

All of a sudden, he tore his eyes from my throat and walked by me without looking at me to the window where he stopped.

His back to me, he stared out the glass.

Then he said, "Get out."

My body jerked as if he struck me.

"What?"

"I know what you're doing Sadie. It's clear you're here with Chavez, with those things, to get a piece of me. Take it, cherish it, and get the fuck out."

I stood, stunned immobile for a second. Then my heart started beating, my blood started pumping and I stomped to the table in the room, put the photo on it and stomped to the window, right in front of my father.

"I will not get out," I snapped.

His eyes didn't move, but he put his hands in his pants pockets and stared over my head.

"Look at me," I demanded.

He didn't look. It was like I didn't exist.

I shoved his shoulders with both hands and yelled, "Dad! Look at me!"

Only his cold eyes tilted so he could look down his nose at me.

"I know everything. *Everything*," I told him and he just kept looking down his nose at me so I repeated, "I know everything about you."

I watched his lip curl before he said, "You don't know shit."

"I know you loved her," I shot back. "I know your parents weren't nice to you. I know she loved you, too. I know that you were her world. I know you were mine too, once, before she went away. I know you fed me in the night when I was a baby—"

"Shut up, Sadie."

"I know if I hurt myself, I went to you—"

"Sadie, shut up!"

"I know when I got up all sleepy, if you were home, I'd go directly to you—"

His hands shot out of his pockets, grabbed onto my arms and shook me hard as he shouted, "*Shut up!*"

"*I will not shut up and I will not get out!*" I screamed in his face. "Decades ago, I had a father! I want him back!"

He shoved me away. I went back two feet, righted my involuntary retreat and advanced again, grabbing on to his shirt with both fists and shaking.

"You used to kiss my head and tuck me into bed—"

His hands wrapped around my wrists and he pulled, but I held on tight.

"Why'd you leave me? Once she was gone, I needed you!"

His body went still and his chin tipped down so he could look at me.

"You didn't need me," he said.

"I did," I returned.

"No, you didn't."

"*I did!*" I screamed.

"I killed her."

It was my body's turn to go still.

"What?"

"I didn't pull the trigger, but what I did put her in that position so I might as well have been the one to blow her head off."

His words cut through me and I closed my eyes tight.

"That's what he did, Sadie. Mickey blew a hole in her head."

"Quiet," I whispered.

He got close, his mouth came to my ear and he whispered, "Before I did the same to him, I made him take me to her. Bernie and I got her body—"

"Please, don't."

"We paid heavy to have her put in a marble tomb—"

"Don't."

"Pink marble, her favorite color."

"Stop it."

He kept whispering in my ear. "Even now, when I'm in here, I know that gardenias are placed on the steps of that tomb every Sunday afternoon."

I couldn't help it. The fight went out of me. I let go of his shirt and fell into him, my arms wrapping around his waist. The tears were heavy in my throat, sliding down my face. I heard my own choking sobs, but he didn't put his arms around me. He didn't hold me.

"But I wasn't done, was I?" he asked softly.

I tilted my head back and stared at his blurry face.

Only then did he touch me. I blinked and focused, catching his eyes staring at my cheek. Then his hand came to the side of my head, his thumb out and tracing the scar there.

"I got you raped. You. My sweet Sadie. All those years of protecting you so no one could hurt you. No one could get at you like they did Lizzie. Then, when I got sent down, I stepped back, wanting to give you your life, the kind of life your mother wanted for you. A good life, a clean one without me in it. And still it was me who got you violated." His voice got deep and rough before he said, "My sweet baby."

"Daddy—" I whispered, fresh tears sliding down my cheeks.

I watched, fascinated, as his eyes cleared. His head cocked and he asked almost casually, "How can you even look at me?"

I blinked once then again then I said, "Because I was made from love, that's who I am. And Hector says if you love someone, you forgive a lot of shit. So," my voice dropped, "I'm guessing I can look at you because I love you."

He stared at me and I waited, my body still, the tears coming and seconds sliding by slowly, each one of them taking hours.

Then his arms came around me and he pulled me deep into him. I felt his mouth kiss the top of my head and I got up on tiptoe, my arms going tight, my face going into his neck.

We held on to each other for a while, until my tears stopped, until the strength came back into my legs, and then I whispered in his ear, "Will you please take the photo?"

His arms gave me a squeeze. "I'll take the photo, Sadie."

I pushed it.

What could I say?

My father taught me to know when I had the advantage and when to push it.

So I did as my father taught me.

"Do you mind if I wear the necklace?"

That got me another squeeze. He didn't answer, but I took it as a yes.

Then because I had to, because it was important, I took it further. "If he gets up before me, he tucks the covers around me so I won't be cold."

My father's body got tight.

"I don't know why, but I went to him after the rape. He took me to the hospital. When the staff tried to separate him from me, it took two men to pull him away."

He gave me a different kind of squeeze, one that told me to be quiet.

I didn't listen to the nonverbal command. I went on, "He makes me feel safe."

Finally he spoke. "Sadie—"

My voice went so low, I barely heard myself. "I think I love him."

Silence again.

Then a deep sigh.

"It'd be a lot easier to hate the man if he wasn't such a clever bastard."

I blinked into my father's neck. Then I pulled back and looked at him.

"What does that mean?" I breathed.

His hand came back to my cheek. His thumb again traced the scar then his eyes moved to mine.

"Can I just get to know my daughter for a while before I have to put up with her new fucking boyfriend?"

My body sagged into his with relief.

Then I nodded.

Because I knew. It would take a while, but it would happen.

"I won't miss another visiting day," I promised.

"Good," he returned.

"I want to know where she is. I want to take the gardenias there myself."

He sucked in breath, held it, then let it go and nodded. "I'll be sure that's arranged."

"I want you to be good so you can get out soon."

This made him smile. Not huge, but his lips turned up.

So, I smiled back.

Then I whispered, "I'm glad to have you back, Dad."

His hand sifted into the side of my hair, cupped my head and tilted it down.

He kissed the top of my head.

"Thank you for taking me back, Sadie," he said into my hair.

At that, for the first time in eighteen years, I gave my father a hug.

# Epilogue
# Como Quieras

---

### *Sadie*

"Jesus, Trish, I'm payin' for the booze, I should be able to get drunk on it," Herb Logan, Roxie's father, snapped at his wife (loudly).

"Keep your voice down, Herb," Trish Logan, Roxie's mother, hissed back (also loudly). "Do you want your daughter's wedding to be marred by memories of her loud, drunken, hillbilly father?"

I looked at Jules, Vance, Stella and Mace, who were standing with me, Herb and Trish in our little (but loud) group.

"Roxie don't care, she wants everyone to have a good time. Shit, look at Ally, she's three sheets to the wind," Herb returned.

We all turned in unison to look at Ally.

She, like Jules, Stella and I (as well as Annette, Daisy, Indy, Ava, Jet and Roxie's sister, Mimi—being a Rock Chick, by the by, meant having an enormous wedding party) was wearing a glamorous, deep green, long, velvet dress; strapless, form-fitting with a sexy slit up the front and an elegant twist of material at the bodice. We all had perfect, oval rubies (Roxie's bridesmaid's gift—the green and red color combination was because it was Christmas Eve) winking at our throats and matching studs at our ears, both of these displayed beautifully because our hair had been swept up in elaborate up-dos.

Ally and Ren Zano seemed to be having a very intense conversation. Ren's face was set, his jaw tight. Ally's face was red, her eyes flashing.

Then, all of a sudden, she shouted, "Go to hell, Ren Zano!" took a step back and cocked her arm, hand in a fist as if she was going to strike him.

"Oh my God," Jules breathed as Ally let fly. But Ren caught Ally's fist, twisted it down and behind her back so her body slammed into his. His mouth went to her ear and he said something that made her struggle. He turned them both, his and her arm still behind her back, and marched them out of the elegant Donald R. Seawell Grand Ballroom of the Denver Performing Arts Complex.

"What was *that* all about?" Stella breathed as we all kept our eyes locked on the empty space where Ren and Ally used to be.

"Should we help her?" I asked, and Stella and Jules both looked at me and gave me small shakes of the head.

I didn't like seeing Ally so upset, but I figured Jules and Stella had more practice with this Rock Chick business. Not to mention, I knew Ren was a good guy, he'd never hurt anyone. So I let it go.

"If she can shout 'go to hell' in this fancy-ass ballroom then I can have another fuckin' drink that *I'm* fuckin' *payin'* for," Herb announced and stomped to the bar.

Trish's eyes did a scan of Jules, Vance, Stella, Mace and me.

Then she asked, "Which of you girls are married? I forget."

"Just me, Mrs. Logan," Jules answered.

Trish's eyes came to me then went to Stella, "Don't do it."

Then she stormed off toward Kitty Sue, Malcolm and Tom.

Mace and Vance grinned at each other. Stella, Jules and I started giggling.

I felt heat then I felt Hector's hand at the small of my back. It slid along my waist and his mouth came to my neck. I shivered, twisted my head to the side and smiled up at him.

His face got warm when he caught my smile, but his eyes went to Mace and Vance.

"What's up with Zano?" he asked them.

Silence.

But I got the feeling it wasn't because they didn't know. It was because they weren't saying in front of the loose lipped Rock Chicks.

Stella got the same feeling and she turned into Mace. "You know something?"

"Fuck," he muttered.

"Spill," she shot back.

"Kitten," Mace replied (though, you will note, he didn't answer).

I smiled.

I loved it that Mace called Stella "Kitten". It was very cute. There were a lot of things Mace was (he was hot, he was tall, he was handsome, he could be a little scary and moody; he could also be surprisingly sweet), but there was one thing he was not and that was cute.

Except when he was around Stella.

"Kai," Stella returned, and I loved it when Stella called Mace by his given name. No one else did, but she did. And when she did, it was also very sweet (except now, when she did it with narrowed eyes).

My eyes moved to the door as Indy and Lee came through it. She was adjusting her bodice. Lee had her lipstick on his mouth.

I giggled.

Jules leaned in and whispered, "What's funny?"

I tilted my head to Indy and Lee. Lee was now wiping the back of his hand against his mouth.

"I think Indy got some," I whispered back to Jules.

Jules grinned.

"Weddings do that to people," she told me. "Luke carried Ava out in a fireman's hold at my reception. Took her home, gave her the business, brought her back. Her mouth was swollen, her face was flushed and her hair was all over the place."

My eyes got round. "No kidding?"

She shook her head.

I had to admit (privately, to myself), she wasn't wrong. At Jet and Eddie's wedding a few months ago, Hector "gave me the business" in a haystack.

It was *way* better than s'mores.

"What's up?" Indy asked, she and Lee hitting our group.

"Not much. Herb's shitfaced. Trish warned Sadie and me not to get married. Ally nearly punched Ren in the face after shouting 'go to hell', *loud*, and the boys know what's going on and aren't spilling," Stella answered.

Indy turned to Lee. "Ally nearly punched Ren? What's that all about?"

Lee shook his head.

Indy's eyes narrowed.

"Maybe you shouldn't have given him naked gratitude in the cloakroom five minutes ago. Saved it for later," Jules threw out.

Indy's face got red. Her body turned slowly to Jules and Lee started chuckling.

"I don't see what's funny," Indy snapped at Lee.

His mouth went to her ear, his hand went to her midriff and he said something to her that made her eyes go lazy and her body relax.

"Whatever," she whispered and rolled her eyes at me.

I smiled. I had no idea why. I just did.

"What's going on with Ally?" Roxie asked, her hand in Hank's, both of them joining our group.

Roxie and Hank's wedding couldn't have been more different than Eddie and Jet's.

As Jet wanted, she got her hog roast outside a barn/hayride/s'mores reception. It had been a blast. Everyone kicking up their heels on the wooden slats in the barn to rock 'n' roll and country, getting drunk on beer and cocktails, eating roasted hog, toasting marshmallows outside around a massive bonfire with big logs covered in fluffy wool blankets set all around and letting their hair down.

The only thing that slightly marred the festivities was when Ally started a hay fight during the hayride. It got a little rowdy (Tex was on that ride) and we got threatened with hayride-ejection from the irate hayride driver.

But other than that, it was the best.

Jet had looked gorgeous. Incongruous with the surroundings she chose, she'd gone the full-on, wide skirted, tons of tulle, lace and beading, huge wedding dress route, truly looking like a fairy princess.

I wasn't the only one who thought so.

Standing at the front of the church, when Jet was about to hit the aisle, my eyes had moved to Eddie. The minute he saw her, his whole body changed. It went still, then his eyes (no kidding) went liquid and (still no kidding) he broke tradition and walked right down the aisle. Right in front of everyone. Like he couldn't wait for her to walk to him (which, obviously, he couldn't).

Ray, her father, who was escorting her down the aisle, burst out laughing, but Eddie ignored him. She ended up with Eddie on one side, Ray on the other, both her father and her fiancé walking her down the aisle.

Blanca, who I thought would blow the roof off at this display, instead burst into loud, happy tears.

It had been the most romantic thing I'd ever seen in my life.

Until that day.

I looked at Roxie.

She was wearing an ivory satin gown, snug-fitting at chest, midriff, waist and hips, its full skirt cut on the bias. There was a deep V at her cleavage, material coming up and gathering in points into tiny, spaghetti straps at her shoulders which went up and over and draped down her back, I swear, holding up the material of the dress at her bottom by a miracle. Her back, if seen from afar, looked totally exposed. The dress managed to be both refined and uber-sexy. It was, put simply, breathtaking. The most unusual and fantastic wedding gown I'd ever seen in my life. Her hair was in an elaborate up-do of twists and there were diamonds that were her "something borrowed" (from me) at her neck and ears.

It was a night wedding, starting at five thirty, the ceremony held at Cheesman Park Pavilions amidst huge bouquets of bulging cream pom pom chrysanthemums and thousands upon thousands of twinkling, white Christmas lights.

It was freezing so we all had velvet capes, but Roxie walked through the standing crowd toward Hank wearing only her dress, her shoes and my diamonds, carrying her mums, Herb on her arm.

Then she started walking faster, Herb (shorter than his daughter) struggling to keep up.

Then faster.

Then she was (no other way to put it) jogging on her high heels toward Hank, dragging her father with her.

Hank was standing at the front, shaking his head and laughing, and by the time she got to him, she was laughing too, out loud.

She kissed him the minute she got close enough to touch him.

"Jesus. You think I could give you away before you kiss him? Shit," Herb had muttered (loudly). Then he turned to Trish. "Trish, this proves it. She's *your* daughter."

The Rock Chicks all stood to the side giggling our behinds off.

Roxie wasn't embarrassed at all. She just leaned in, kissed her father's cheek, turned and linked arms with Hank.

I watched as she rested all her weight into his side like they were standing waiting in line to get into a movie with no one looking, not standing in front of a crowd of family and friends, waiting to get married.

"The Hot Bunch knows, but they aren't talking," Stella filled in Roxie, taking me out of my trip down Recent Memory Lane.

Roxie turned to Hank. "Do *you* know?"

"No idea," Hank returned.

"You're not lying to me on our wedding day?" Roxie asked, but it was more of a warning.

469

"Sorry, Sunshine. Ally doesn't keep in touch with me about her love life. She's my sister. I don't wanna know. Never did. Never will," Hank replied.

Roxie's eyes went round. "*Love life?* Ren and Ally? Whisky, you *do* know something!"

Hank's eyes slid to Lee then he said, "Shit."

Vance burst out laughing.

Jules hit him in the shoulder.

That was when I burst out laughing.

Hector put pressure at my hip and curled me into his front.

I tilted my head back to look at him, still laughing.

He watched me, his handsome grin in place, until I was done.

Then he bent forward and his mouth touched mine.

"Do *you* know?" I asked softly, my arms sliding around his waist.

He didn't hesitate in answering. "The men talk. I don't listen much. I know Ally's got some business. Zano's involved. They got history. That's all I know."

I looked at the place where Ally and Ren disappeared and mumbled, "She's a dark horse. She makes everyone spill their secrets but keeps her own."

"I've known Ally Nightingale since I was six. She's the second most complicated woman I've ever met," Hector replied. "One thing about Ally that's always been the way, *mamita*: you do *not* get what you see."

I cuddled closer, my elbows cocking, my hands going up his back to his shoulder blades. "Now, I'm intrigued."

He shook his head. "You're just gonna have to watch it play out like the rest of us." Then he added, "And hope to God no one gets hurt."

Before I could say anything, Tex (wearing a tux, and *not* happy about it) boomed from across the room, "Roxanne Giselle Lo... I mean, Nightingale! When are those fuckin' harpists gonna shut the fuck up and so we can get some rock 'n' roll?"

⌖

I rested my head against the window of the Bronco and watched Denver slide by as Hector took us home from the wedding.

I was pleasantly drunk from champagne and totally exhausted from a day of bridesmaids duties (if I never saw another Christmas light again, I would *not* care; until tomorrow, that was) and the last two hours of dancing like a wild woman (mostly with Ava and Daisy) to rock 'n' roll.

My hand was taken from my lap. Hector's fingers linked through mine, and he set the back of my hand high up on his hard thigh.

"Did you have a good day?" he asked quietly.

"It was great. The wedding was beautiful. But I'm tired and my feet are killing me."

"We'll be home soon, *mi corazón*."

"I know."

"I told you after Eddie and Jet's wedding not to wear those fuckin' shoes," he reminded me. "You complained then, I knew you'd complain again."

"I'm not going to wear ugly shoes with a bridesmaid's dress, Hector."

"Isn't there such a thing as not ugly shoes that are comfortable?"

"No," I said shortly (and honestly).

He chuckled.

I rolled my eyes.

Hector, even after months together, still thought I was funny.

I still didn't get it.

"Jet's pregnant," he said suddenly.

My hand tensed in his.

"What?"

"Eddie told me tonight. It's early. They're keepin' it to themselves for a little while. Whatever you do, do not tell *Mamá*."

"Oh my God," I whispered. "Are they happy about it?"

His hand squeezed mine. "Don't know about Jet, but Eddie's over the fuckin' moon."

If that was the case then I knew about Jet. She was sure as certain over the moon, too.

"That's great," I said softly.

"Yeah," he replied, just as softly.

It was my turn to squeeze his hand. "Uncle Hector."

Silence.

Then, "Shit."

Then it was my turn to laugh.

We walked up to the house, hand-in-hand.

Hector let us in.

I flipped the switches and the lights came on.

Then I reached down, slipped off my high heels and tossed them over the back of the couch into the living room. They bounced off the seat of the couch and I heard them hit the floor.

I tossed my purse in the same direction. It bounced on the seat and stayed there.

The renovating the house business wasn't playing out like in my dreams (exactly).

Hector and I fought tooth and nail about everything *house*.

Once we were done with the floor, the mantel and the skirting boards, Hector announced he wanted the living room off the kitchen—better access to beer during games.

I explained (patiently, at first) that the *dining room* had to be off the kitchen.

We hit a stalemate that meant weeks of stacked furniture covered in plastic.

Then one night I got creative with lingerie and talked him into it (about two seconds before he climaxed).

It wasn't fair. In fact, it was really not fair, but this lesson served me well in the coming weeks.

Hector didn't seem to mind.

To the right was an antique, walnut, twelve-seat dining room table I found on Antique Row on Broadway. I had it refinished, the seats of the chairs redone in a dusky gray and dusky gray-blue stripe. It now had a big round vase on it filled with calla lilies. A matching sideboard sat against the wall to the kitchen, displaying my mom's Waterford crystal that I took from her locker, the family photo of Mom, Dad and me and another photo of Hector and his dad taken when Hector was nineteen. There were white Christmas lights weaved in real pine greenery on the mantel.

To the left was Hector's midnight blue twill furniture, but I'd added some toss pillows with blue, gray and chocolate brown designs. The TV from the bedroom was installed in the corner, all the furniture positioned for maximum viewing potential. In another corner was a huge, real fir Christmas tree decorated in blue and white lights, and blue, silver and white ornaments. There was more greenery and lights on the mantel weaving around silver-framed photos of Hector's family and other photos of my mom, grandmother and grandfather. A huge white poinsettia in a shiny blue pot sat dead center on the coffee table.

To the back of the living room through the French doors was the den, complete with big desk, reclining chair and Hector's desktop computer.

The front rooms were all perfect.

The kitchen was now a pit. Everything had been yanked out by Hector, Buddy and Eddie a few weekends ago and carted off in a reclamation truck.

My cooking lessons were on hold. With the kitchen like it was, we were definitely not hosting Christmas dinner (Blanca was).

I walked in, pulled off my cape, draped it on the banister then went up the stairs and straight to the bedroom, where I fell face first on the bed.

I didn't used to be the kind of person who threw her shoes across the room (or her purse) and left my coats on the banister.

I used to be clean and tidy.

Obsessively so.

I also used to be the kind of person who woke up at the barest hint of sound.

I wasn't either of those anymore.

Real Sadie was a lot more relaxed. She slept better and she didn't get wound up about stupid stuff.

I liked Real Sadie. Most of the time, she had it going on.

I felt the bed move when Hector sat on it and the zipper at my back started going down.

"I'm going to sleep right here," I informed him.

"*Como quieras,*" Hector said softly, and hearing those words, I smiled into the bed.

I didn't have to open my eyes to see the room.

Hector had made the bedroom his next project (after the living room and before the kitchen). He'd taken time off and we'd slept on the pull out couch for a week while he refinished the floors, replaced the skirting boards and painted the walls (I wanted to help, but the gallery was being redone and Roxie's wedding plans were heating up so Ralphie and I were kind of busy). The walls were a warm gray-green and there were new, shiny maple skirting boards. Hector had bought a new bed, nightstands and two new dressers, one low with a mirror on top, one tall and wide with six drawers.

We fought about the furniture because I wanted to help pay.

He refused.

I pushed it.

We came to a stalemate.

Days later, in bed, he held off letting me finish until I begged him, then he demanded I shut up about the furniture, and I agreed.

Turnabout, I guessed, was fair play.

I wasn't complaining.

The zipper went all the way down. Hector got off the bed. The dress was pulled off at my ankles and I heard the heavy material land somewhere in the room.

This should have alarmed me. The dress was velvet, it was gorgeous and it was expensive.

I didn't lift my head.

Instead, I laid in nothing but a pair of emerald green, French cut panties on the bed.

I heard Hector's boots then clothing hit the floor, then he came back to me. I was pulled up, rolled into him, the covers yanked out from under me then snapped back over me. I settled with my head on his chest, my arm around his abs.

"Sadie, the pins in your hair are jabbing my skin."

"Blooming heck," I muttered. I rolled with a heavy sigh to my back and started to pull the pins out of my hair.

Hector got up on an elbow and watched me.

Then he asked, "What'd we buy Hank and Roxie for their wedding?"

My hands in my hair stilled and just my eyeballs rolled to look at Hector.

Hector and I had bought Eddie and Jet a brand new kitchen for their wedding. Jet loved to cook. Eddie was fixing up their house, but on a cop's budget and with work and Rock Chick duties taking up most of his time, he'd not gotten around to giving her a new kitchen. I heard her (on several occasions) waxing poetic about how she'd love something "state-of-the-art".

So Hector and I gave it to her.

It cost twenty thousand dollars and it made two hot-blooded Mexican-American men temporarily lose their minds.

Jet, at first, had been shocked.

Then, when I explained myself, she'd been understanding, then appreciative, then gleeful.

Blanca went straight to gleeful and started hinting (broadly) that she needed a new kitchen too (Hector didn't know it yet, but that was her Christmas present).

Jet had talked Eddie around. It took a while but she did it.

"Um…" I answered Hector's question.

He fell to his back, stared at ceiling and muttered, "Fuck."

I got up on my elbow and looked down at him, hair half falling down, half still in pins.

"Hector! I'm loaded! What am I going to do with my money but spend it on friends?"

He got up on his elbow. Mr. Mood Swing fully morphed into anger and faced me.

"I don't know," he clipped. "Save it? Put our kids through college with it? If tonight was anything to go by, we'll need it to pay for their goddamned weddings. Fuck, knowin' you, we'll need every last penny to pay for ours."

My breath went out of me in a whoosh.

Then it came back on a surge.

Then I whispered, "What?"

"You heard me," he shot back.

I sat up and looked down at him. "Are you asking me marry you?"

He sat up and faced me. "Are you shittin' me?"

I blinked.

Then I said, "No."

"What do you think we're doin' here? Playin' house?"

I blinked again.

"Christ, Sadie," he clipped. "Look at my fuckin' arm."

I looked but I didn't have to. He'd had the rose tattooed there months ago, within weeks of me moving in.

It was extraordinary. The stem, leaves, petals all exquisitely drawn and filled in with vibrant colors. It had taken two goes, the outline first, then, weeks later, after that healed, the filling in.

My heart fluttered, then my belly fluttered, then I whispered, "Hector—"

"What'd we get Hank and Roxie?" he ground out, interrupting me.

I decided just to answer and get it over with.

"It didn't cost as much as the kitchen," I told him.

"What'd we get?" he repeated.

"Nowhere *near* as much as the kitchen," I said for good measure.

He gave me The Scorch.

I sighed.

"We bought them a full set of Mikasa china."

Hector just kept giving me The Scorch.

"Twelve place settings," I went on.

He continued The Scorch.

"And... um... serving dishes."

More Scorch.

"And their silver."

Still more Scorch.

"With the hostess set."

More Scorch.

"That's it," I finished.

He dropped to his back, muttering, "*Dios mio.*"

I pulled my lips in then my hands went back to my hair and I yanked out the rest of the pins.

While I did this, Hector laid with the back of his arm over his eyes, the rose tattoo on full display.

I shook my fingers through my hair then leaned in to him. Reaching to the nightstand, I dropped the pins on it and then settled with my chest on his.

"Hector," I called.

Silence and no movement.

"Maybe we should..." I hesitated, not sure if now was the right time, "talk about what I did for Christmas."

All of a sudden, he moved. His arms went around me; I was on my back, he was on top.

"I hope you got your energy back, *mamita*, because you owe me for this," he announced, displaying, again, very bizarre Hector Logic. Then his face disappeared in my neck.

His tongue touched below my ear.

I did a casual back flip in the lovely warm waters where I cavorted now in my life as a happy mermaid. My arms went around him and I smiled at the ceiling.

Early Christmas morning, the doorbell rang.

Since I'd been up for the last hour waiting for it, I was awake and immediately rolled out of bed.

"I got it, *mamita*," Hector muttered, rolling out the other side.

I ignored him and put on my panties.

"Sadie, I got it," Hector repeated, and I looked at him as I shrugged on one of his flannels. He had on a pair of rust-colored, drawstring sweatpants, the hems loose around his ankles.

I pulled on a pair of heathered gray, fleecy shorts with notches at the hips while Hector yanked on a black thermal.

I also, by the way, pulled in my lips.

Hector stopped dressing and stared at me.

Then he put his hands to his hips.

"What have you done?" he asked.

The doorbell rang again.

I dashed out of the bedroom.

Hector followed a lot slower, but since his legs were also longer, he caught up to me at the foot of the stairs and pulled me behind him. I got close as he walked to the door, unlocked it and tugged it open.

I peeked around Hector's body.

Jack stood there.

"Hi, Jack," I said. "Merry Christmas."

Jack's eyes came to me, and then (no kidding!) he winked.

Then his hand came up and he held out a set of keys to Hector.

Hector looked at the keys then at Jack.

Jack jerked his head to the street where a brand new, shiny, black GMC Yukon was parked behind Hector's Bronco.

When Hector didn't take the keys, Jack tossed them in the air. Hector's hand shot out and caught them. Jack grinned at me. He turned, walked across the porch, down the steps and to the car parked behind the Yukon. Jack's girlfriend, Melinda (one of Smithie's strippers; Jack was the only Nightingale man who didn't care if his girlfriend stripped), was sitting in the front seat waving at us, a big, goofy grin on her face.

I waved back.

Jack got into the driver's side and took off.

Hector closed the door.

Then, slowly, he turned to me.

I got one look at his face and started backing up, across the platform then down the steps.

"It's really for me," I told him.

He advanced.

I kept backing up.

"It's selfish, I know, but you never take one of Lee's Explorers. I want to make sure you're safe."

He kept advancing.

The back of my foot hit the stairs.

"Merry Christmas!" I shouted stupidly.

He stopped advancing slowly and launched himself at me.

I whirled and ran up the stairs.

I tripped almost all the way up and he caught me at the waist before I fell. He swung me up in his arms, my limbs flying out-of-control.

"Hector!" I yelled, but he walked with long strides to the bedroom and tossed me on the bed.

I turned, got on all fours and scrambled.

He caught my ankles, yanked my knees out from under me so I was on my belly, and he landed on top of me.

I squirmed.

He slid off the side, but one of his heavy thighs was on mine, his face in my neck. His hand went straight into my shorts and panties, sliding over my bottom to between my legs.

I stilled.

His hand kept going until his fingers curved around and hit the spot.

I whimpered and twisted my head. His mouth was there and he kissed me, hot, deep, wet, urgent and fiery.

We went at it, all hands, mouths, teeth and tongues (then other parts of our anatomy).

It was wild.

It was beautiful.

After, I was on top, still connected to him, my face in his throat, my breath still heavy.

Both his hands were cupping my bottom.

"You just can't stop yourself can you?" he asked, referring to the Yukon.

I shook my head, burrowed closer and gave him a squeeze with my arms (and other parts of me besides). His fingers tensed on my bottom.

"Had my eye on one of those for a long time, *mamita*," he muttered, still referring to the Yukon.

"I know," I replied softly. Then, for some reason, into his throat, uber-quietly, I whispered, "I love you, babe."

His body went still.

Then he rolled so I was on the bottom, he was on top.

His head came up and I saw his face was warm, his eyes, though, were hot. He touched his mouth to mine and muttered, "*Y te amo también, mi cielo.*"

And, from Blanca's lessons, I knew this meant, *And I love you too, my sky.*

My belly fluttered and I smiled at him.

He smiled back.

His mouth was coming toward mine when the doorbell rang again.

Instead of kissing me, his forehead came to rest on mine and he mumbled, "Jesus."

We did the getting up and putting on clothes thing again and walked downstairs, side-by-side, his arm around my shoulders, mine around his waist.

He opened the door.

Buddy and Ralphie were standing there. Ralphie was holding a squirming, panting, blond-faced, black-bodied German Shepherd puppy with a big, red and green striped ribbon around its neck.

"*Oh my God!*" I squealed. The puppy jumped at my squeal, its eyes coming to me. It leaped out of Ralphie's arms into mine. "Buddy, you wonderful man, you got Ralphie a puppy!"

I held the puppy to my chest. I walked into the living room, nuzzling her soft face and puppy floppy ears with my nose, smelling the sweet puppy scent as she licked me all over. I giggled and gave her soft puppy body cuddles.

I looked at Buddy. "You're the greatest. I want one just like her."

"Um… sweets?" Ralphie called and I looked at him.

I saw all three men standing there. Buddy and Ralphie were smiling huge. Hector had his arms crossed on his chest and his mouth was doing that fighting-a-grin thing.

"What?" I asked.

"Buddy didn't give me that dog," Ralphie answered.

My eyebrows drew together. "Did you buy it for yourself?"

Buddy chuckled. Hector lost the fight with his grin and smiled, full and glamorous.

"What's funny?" I asked.

Buddy answered, "She's for you, sweetheart."

I blinked.

"From Double H," Ralphie added.

My eyes flew to Hector.

"It's selfish," he said. "I want to know you're guarded when I'm not home."

I felt tears clog my throat.

Then I shouted, "I am *not* going to cry!" right before I burst into tears.

In a flash, the puppy and I were in Hector's arms.

He held me. I cried, the puppy squirmed and licked, and Ralphie produced a camera and took a photo of the three of us.

It came out beautiful. Hector's arm around my shoulders, his fingers in the ruff of the dog's neck; his head bent to us, my forehead tucked in his throat, the puppy looking like she was smiling at both of us (but, really, she was panting).

I named the dog Gretel (she *was* German).

I put the picture on the mantel in the dining room.

*The Rock Chick ride concludes*
*with* **Rock Chick Revolution**
*the story of Ally and Ren*

37854411R00301

Made in the USA
Lexington, KY
16 December 2014